A Lif

Jan 2015.

To

Mary

Best Wishes

Barry Marchant.

Also by Barry Merchant:

Seeking a New Voice: Autobiographical Perspectives
Memoirs Books, 2013. ISBN-13: 978-1909544543

A Life's Journey

A Working-Class Saga

Barry Merchant

DIADEM BOOKS

A Life's Journey: A Working-Class Saga

For information, please contact:

Diadem Books
16 Lethen View
Tullibody
ALLOA
FK10 2GE
Scotland UK
www.diadembooks.com

ISBN: 978-1-326-06260-6

For Lawrence Darani (1951-2014)

I would like to dedicate this book to my friend and co-walker Lawrence Darani. He and I, along with our friend Tony Green, had wonderful and enjoyable times walking hundreds of miles of the British countryside together. I shall miss his good humour and raucous laugh.

Acknowledgments

Heartfelt thanks to Lis Bird and Anthony Green for reading and correcting my manuscript.

I would also like to thank Lawrence Darani for his kind support and endless patience.

Thank you to the editor of Diadem Books who skilfully knocked my book into shape.

Last, but not least. I would very much like to salute those individuals who gave me a leg up along life's highway. May you be happy—may you be well.

Table of Contents

Prologue

1. My birth, schooling and growing up
2. My first job.
3. Absconding to Scotland
4. My stint in the Merchant Navy
5. Branching out into forestry
6. A new job: Forestry promotion in Devon
7. My parents and family buy Buttercup Farm
8. Moving on: Forestry work with the Woodland Trust
9. Scotland beckons again: Forestry on Arran
10. Living with my parents: My father dies from cancer
11. Selling Buttercup Farm
12. Landscaping in beautiful Sussex
13. The beginning of my long term relationship with Helen
14. A sea change: A new career as a garden representative
15. The tragic suicide of my dear friend Bert Moore
16. Mother dies in Hospital
17. My enjoyable life with Helen, my last years at Alders and I purchase my first home
18. Reflections

PROLOGUE

ALTHOUGH I LEFT YAPTON when I was twenty-one years old, it has nevertheless left an indelible mark on my mind. I lived there, with my hardworking parents, in a most attractive village full of mischievous and gregarious young people, who sometimes behaved unsociably. I assume that kind of annoying behaviour must have happened, and still does, by most young people around Britain. From twenty-one years of age, all my employment, other than one short period, required me to work away from home, although I did irregularly visit my parents and friends in Yapton. As I am now a mature man, or rather of mature in age, I can look back with the pleasure of hindsight, realising I had what could be called a healthy upbringing although some of our antics, unfortunately, clearly crossed the line of moral ambiguity. Not that that really concerns my conscience—not one bit of it. What makes me irritable now, when I try to fully assimilate those hedonistic days after a few strong beers in my local dive of a pub, is that we didn't go far enough. But, of course, as I grew older, I continued my wicked ways, wherever or whenever it was possible. Most of my cohort and I were constrained by our class, or rather our conditioning, from having set the world ablaze starting with little old Yapton. In those far off days the village was full of boundaries: emotional, intellectual and, more importantly, physical, because farmers and the landowning elite were the dominant class. From the 1970s, these subservient relationships started to change somewhat, due to the working classes becoming more educated. Hitherto nearly all the senior positions in Yapton, and the outlying districts, such as magistrate, farm manager and councillor, were held by the same families, generation after generation. Now I am informed that one of my friends, who used to be in our gang all those years ago, has a grandson who is a manager of a large local dairy farm. I hope this young lad is a bit more discreet than his, over-sexed and sometimes, rampant, grandfather was. But the overriding concern for me, even at a young tender age, was to travel, or failing that, to at least experience working in other areas of the country and meet different people. Why? Even as I approach my middle sixties, I'm still not sure what motivated me to work for so many years away from my home of Yapton, other than my mother's regular encouragement throughout my childhood not to follow in the footsteps of my farming forebears.

MY FAMILY

My paternal grandfather, Peter Morris, was born in 1890 in Colchester, Essex. He had moved to Yapton in his early thirties, some six miles from Norwich, when he successfully applied for a labouring job at Meadow Hall, a large dairy farm with several hundred head of cattle, which was owned by the Boswell family for many generations. Along with the poorly paid job came a two-bedroomed tied cottage with enough back garden to grow vegetables for his three children. Grandfather was not conscripted into the 1914-18 War as his employer argued successfully that he was needed to keep production going on the farm to help feed the country. At least he did not have to experience the immense suffering and slaughter that befell many young British soldiers. Prior to moving to Meadow Farm, my grandfather had worked for several different dairy farmers around the county. Farm labouring, with the usual tied cottage, made it easy for farmers to blackmail workers into working long hours, knowing that they had nowhere else to go with their families if threatened with the sack. During the 1920s farming was very hard, and if you were fortunate to find a job, like my grandfather did, then you kept it regardless. However, to his credit, he worked hard for many years and was eventually rewarded with the position of head cowman. When I was growing up in Yapton, I fondly remember my grandfather and grandmother visiting our home on numerous occasions for dinner and tea. At those times grandfather always insisted that my father went for a beer or three with him to the local pub called the Country Squire. When I was old enough, I would have been about six, I used to go with them to the pub and hide away in a corner out of the sight of the governor called Tandy Peters. He was a rather big, tall man with many tattoos all over his muscular body. Most of the time his fierce demeanour used to frighten me, especially when I first met him, but as time went by I got to know him quite well and he nearly always acknowledged my presence, notwithstanding that in those days it was illegal to have children on the premises.

As time passed I became more aware of the physical presence of both my grandfather and father. They were both short, tough and well-built with brown arms and faces which no doubt had come about after years of working in the sun for twelve hours a day. Natural selection at its best! Both had a typical workingman's moustache that was worn in those days to show other workers that you had some rite of passage from having grafted night and day for the privilege.

When I was still very young, about eight, I remember my grandfather died of a heart attack. He was only 67 years old. Very young even for those days and, it was probably brought about by a lifetime of excessive hard work, beer consumption and smoking Capstan cigarettes. On top of that his diet, although healthy, consisted of red meat nearly every day—and lots of it. He had a great send-off; nearly all the village turned up for the funeral, and others from around the district, to pay tribute to a good, decent man who had worked hard all his life for his family so that they could have a better start in life than he had. Even his wealthy pompous employer, Major Boswell, was there to pay his respects to a former employee who, no doubt, he overworked and underpaid. Grandfather was buried at the local church, St Peter's, his gravestone overlooking the farming land that had brought about his premature demise. During one of the many sessions he had with my father in the local pub, he told me, with a wry smile on his old lined face, ' Many times boy, I've 'ad a piss all over the late vicar's grave, 'oping he doesn't remember me at the gates of heaven.' After the funeral, my grandmother (née White) who was born in 1892, moved back to a small Yorkshire village, called Cranbrook, from which she had moved as a young wife, with her then young husband, many years before to seek their fortune. Thereafter we saw her only on rare occasions when Father used to drive to Yorkshire to visit her. I remember visiting her on one occasion only.

Within ten or so years my grandmother died of a stroke, aged around 75 years old, and was buried in her home village next to several generations of her family. She was a good, decent Christian person whose background was steeped in taming the harsh lands around that part of the country so that they could feed their families. Most of them were tenant farmers determined to leave their mark on the land just as their forebears had done from time immemorial. At least grandmother, although getting rather old, watched England beat Germany 4-2 in the 1966 World Cup Final.

My uncle Eric was born in 1923, uncle Jack in 1924 and my father, David, in 1926. They were all born, socialised and educated in Yapton. That is, if you could call it 'educated', as in those days during harvest time farmers could just walk into the classroom, and without saying a word to anyone, including the teacher, walk out with several young boys who would work long hours every day until the harvest crop had been collected. All three of them had participated in football, cricket and athletics, with some distinction, for the school, Yapton Manor. That was not the only physical activity they ventured into, as my father alluded to one evening, when I was about ten years old, after a few beers had loosened his tongue somewhat. Sex has always been a natural temptation since time immemorial, especially in village life when young people would venture off into miles of uninhabited countryside for endless hours of sex, drinking alcohol and smoking. Of course that was a time when the so-called village idiots would also have come into existence through incestuous relationships. I often thought years later that my village friend Richard Arrowsmith, a good footballer and quintessential shagger of females, reminded me of the school caretaker whose large bulbous ears could only be found on one person! When Father was still young, he recalled, several of the young girls had become pregnant but nearly all of the their babies were adopted, and two girls subsequently never returned to the village. Also some babies were looked after by the young mother's parents or grandparents until they were mature enough to care for them themselves. I am so pleased we didn't have that punitive attitude towards young pregnant females when I was growing up, and unlike today, one-parent families have the same legal rights as anyone else. Self-responsibility of course is another matter!

My father and his brothers had worked in Yapton, and surrounding villages, ever since they were young boys helping out different farmers with various tasks from mucking out pig sties, assisting others with lambing and even milking the cows on their own. Their efforts brought in a few shillings to help out their overworked parents buy a few extra things for the household during World War Two when most British families were having a hard time. However, it was not all doom and gloom around Yapton as my father, his brothers and their gang of friends used to roam the village and countryside and to climb large oak, beech, sycamore and horse chestnut trees. 'We were all free as birds,' my father used to explain to me when I was old enough to understand what he did with his decadent younger life. His gang in those days consisted of about six to eight boys and all were determined to enjoy themselves regardless of the interfering farmers who tried to make their lives difficult. Many times, my father emphasized to me, they would run across a farmer's field—it was called trespassing in those days—and into a dense wood where they built tree houses high up out of the gaze of others. The tree house became their own secret world, where all manner of things could be discussed from sex, cigarettes, football to village girls. One activity my father and uncles really enjoyed was to go walking for endless miles in the local countryside, as John Clare the poet had done two centuries before. They were interested in finding various birds' eggs in the hedgerow, listen to the bees singing their melodies, watch the rabbits scurry to their burrows, and most of all, at least for my father, to look at the wild flowers that proliferated in the meadows. In those days my father used to collect birds' eggs and animal skeletons, and their class teacher encouraged them to take in all the marvels that nature had to offer them. During the four yearly seasons, weather permitting, she also used to take the children out of the class and into the countryside for nature study which most working class children really enjoyed. Father explained to me that my two uncles, Eric and Jack, were skilful water colour painters who had won numerous prizes at school for painting wildlife in the local woods. Many times throughout the years Father, rather animated, used to say, 'Your two uncles was bloody good painters and should 'ave gone to art college. They was just as good as Constable or Turner that's for sure. It was all about bloody money that's all. My parents didn't 'ave any bloody money to send 'em there. Only the posh kids went to college in them days.' I used to have deepest sympathy with my father's sentiments. In those times only middle class males, with a few exceptions, went on to study at college and university. That class-based system has been eradicated somewhat due to education, and is now open to all who are willing to make the effort and sacrifice to further their life chances. Education is what transformed the opportunities for those working class people in Yapton.

When the time came to leave school, aged fifteen, it was most unequivocal where my father would earn his living. He followed his two older brothers into farm labouring. Both Eric and Jack had left school a few years earlier, with no qualifications, to work for a local farmer called Benjamin Leader who farmed a mile outside the village. He himself had inherited, as most farmers do, a large dairy farm from his cantankerous, alcoholic father, Major Leader. 'He was a right bloody tyrant he was and treated 'is workers with complete disdain,' my father bitterly recalled when he had too much to drink. In those days all that working class men had to talk about was work, the farm and the farmer. They had very little else to discuss as their lives were stuck in the past. That is why education was so important for the young village people, who for the first time could travel to Norwich and further afield on motorbikes to meet other young men and women not connected to farming.

All three brothers worked for Mr Leader for many years developing important farming skills, knowledge and experience that would hold them in good stead for their future. Lavender Farm, the name of the farm that Mr Leader had inherited, had expanded due to the hard work of the Morris brothers which considerably enhanced their pay and conditions. From those humble labouring positions all three men over time were promoted into positions of due responsibility. Eric was in charge of milking the large herd of cattle, their well-being and taking them to market where they would be sold. Under Jack's hard work and guidance the farm bought a large flock of hardy sheep from a farm in Essex. Within four years the flock had grown four-fold due to the assistance of modern farming methods and long hours of hard, diligent work. As the farmer had bought many acres of extra land, my father had overseen the introduction of the large cereal crop they went on to produce in abundance. To keep up with the enormous challenges that the Common Agricultural Policy brought upon Lavender Farm, and most other farms around the country after the second World War, Mr Leader took on substantial loans so that he could invest in mechanisation to increase production. My father was at the forefront of this development which witnessed the phasing out of the obsolete horse and plough, and the introduction of tractors and other machinery that revolutionised the way British farms did business. I still have in my possession a black and white photograph that I took of my father and two uncles some considerable time ago. There they stood, among a large flock of hungry looking sheep, all of them upright like a three-hundred year old oak tree, wearing overalls, neckerchiefs and Wellington boots. They were all about the same height, about 5' 6", stocky, with short brown hair and tough looking faces that no doubt had been bashed about by exposure, throughout the years, by all kinds of different weather.

The time was right for the three brothers to leave home; Father always maintained they were kicked out, to marry the girlfriends they had known since there teenage days. The three women, Jane Smith, Sarah Mercer and my mother Jennifer Armitage, were all born and educated in Yapton. Their parents too were born in the village and had been associated one way or another with farming. There was immense joy and happiness when in June1946, with the problems of World War II now fading for most village people, all three couples married in St Peter's Church. That was not unusual before the war. As money was so tight after the ravages of war, it was not surprising the three brothers married their childhood sweethearts on the same day to keep expenses to a minimum.

Over the years one of the keen interests my mother had was photography. Many people called her the unofficial photographer for Yapton village. Even as a teenager Jennifer Armitage could be seen walking around the village, looking in different farms and further afield in the woods taking photographs of the varied beautiful, colourful images that attracted her. Her physical presence was not difficult to miss as she was tall for women in those days, and also slim; she had long brown hair and wore bright attractive clothes. My father told me that she had had many male admirers all willing, no doubt, to be her suitor. There was even some talk among the village gossips that my mother had the chance of marrying a young middle class man who stood to inherit a large farm when his father died. Be that as it may, through her own efforts she in time had several photographic exhibitions in the village hall and two in the Civic Centre, Norwich. She had over a number of years collected a large body of work which had been collated into several large photographic albums depicting very skilfully how village life, and its characters, had evolved. I've looked at many, but not all, of the thousands of photographs my mother took of the world she lived in. Not one to miss a creative, artistic opportunity, she asked a childhood friend to take photographs of her wedding day outside the church, and at the village hall reception afterwards.

My mother was born in 1924 to Joe and Margery Armitage, who had themselves been born and lived all their life in Yapton. From working class stock, James Armitage had held various unskilled farm labourer jobs, but finally after many years of sweat and toil he had been promoted to foreman for the last five years of his working life. His wife, Margery, had also held various unskilled jobs around Yapton and surrounding villages, cleaning the large detached houses owned by farmers and landowners. Jennifer Armitage attended the same village school as my father, but being two years older than him they went to different classes most of the time. Jennifer played with school girlfriends in the evenings and weekends, that is if she was not helping her mother cook, clean and generally help socialise her two younger siblings. Her mother encouraged Jennifer's passion for photography, story writing and cooking. The latter two interests fell away not long after, but of course her love of photography continued for years. After leaving with no qualifications, very few working class people did in those days, Jennifer's first job was in a factory, in nearby Gresham, as a semi-skilled worker making lampshades for a London Company. After that job she found employment in Norwich waiting at tables in a small restaurant frequented by local bank and insurance employees. My mother enjoyed so much working at Sherries Restaurant, which she found to be very friendly, that she stayed there for five long happy years and over time made several female friendships. Three of those friends were invited to her wedding. Unlike my father, who was usually on his own working fifteen hours a day in summer, mother found great sustenance from her friendships, due to being on her own a great deal. For whatever reason, my mother said very little about her three close women friends. We knew of course that one of them was Minnie Anderson, our neighbour. She was a kind, supportive person, but the other two, Pat Colley and Susan Denton, who lived in another village, we didn't know at all. Perhaps my mother was afraid that local gossip, it was the early 1950's, would try to besmirch her name by thinking she was having sexual affairs with other women.

Chapter 1

MY BIRTH, EDUCATION, FRIENDSHIPS
AND GROWING UP

I WAS BORN Richard David Morris on 20th January 1950. The birth went well for both mother and child. Although I don't remember a great deal of those earliest two years or so, I was informed that I quickly put on weight, thrived and once given my head you couldn't stop me from running and touching things all over the place. That included my grandparents' house and any other house that had the courage to let me in. The first day that I really remember being a conscious individual, I was about three years old, was when I met another young boy about my age called Terry Anderson. Minnie Anderson was a good friend of my mother—they had first met several years before working as waitresses. As both women had a local part-time job working in the same village stores, but on different days of the week, they babysat for each other so that both women could earn an extra few pounds for the home. Terry used to rush non-stop around his mother's house knocking over chairs, plants and over the years he must have smashed many pieces of decent crockery. He used to try it on in my mother's attractive terraced house, but she certainly didn't allow him to go as far as smashing up the household. In those days mothers in the village were particularly proud, no doubt they still are, of their small well painted terraced houses with flowers growing over the wooden porches. On only one occasion do I remember Terry trying to break something in my house and that was my father's ceramic pots, which he used for growing vegetables. Terry climbed up on a chair to open the shed door, but before he could take the pots out into the garden my mother had intervened by taking them away before any damage could be inflicted on the aforementioned. He started to scream for attention but Mother took no notice of his behaviour, but when his mother walked in from working she told him he must not do that again and smacked his bottom. 'If I find you doing that sort of thing again Terry, you will go straight to bed without any tea. Do you understand?' explained his angry mother who looked pointedly at him not two feet away from his face. That made Terry even more determined.

Over the next eighteen months, before Terry and I started infant school together, we saw each other at least once a week or sometimes twice a week, usually in each other's homes. On warm days one or other of the mothers used to take us down to a pond on the outskirt of the village to feed the ducks, swans and all manner of smaller birds that congregated there waiting to be fed their daily rations. The pond itself has a colourful history, according to legend, dating back at least one hundred years. In Victorian times wealthy men who had made their pile through banking, spices or any other money-making ventures, started to invest in buying land. In Yapton, and around Britain, lots of farmers were offered over the top prices for the sale of their farms and many couldn't resist the temptation. Once the Victorians had moved into their pricey acquisition new draconian bylaws were introduced to keep the wandering working classes off their land. Hitherto, with the consent of the farmer or landowner, one could walk over their land as long as no damage was caused. Thereafter, when a new farmer in Yapton caught someone on his land the offender had a choice of either going to the police station or carry out something useful to the community. Most offenders chose the latter whereby the farmer would be applauded for his noble work in helping the village clear up criminal activity, and bring about something useful that would benefit all concerned. With this in mind, one William James, a local character fond of drinking ten pints of ale every night and poaching on someone else's land, was caught one late November evening by the gamekeeper stealing a sack full of rabbits off his master's estate. Brought up in front of Sir Anthony Stockbridge, the farm owner concerned, William James elected to dig a village pond instead of presenting himself to the local police station. Big of frame and simple of mind, William dug the pond out in two days stopping only for a few pints of beer before the fifteen feet long and six feet deep pond was completed. He was buried at about ninety years of age, some say head first, according to local legend. But at the time we found it was good fun feeding the ducks even though we were confused as to where the flatulent-like noises came from, but assumed it was one of the overweight swans trying to draw attention to something.

On another occasion I remember when my mother took Terry and I to the pond to feed the birds, when he fell in and was saturated from head to feet. Fortunately he fell into the shallow end of the pond, and not the deep end. No doubt Mother would have preferred the latter! My mother immediately took off all his clothes, dried him sufficiently and put her large jumper over him until we reached our home where he then had a bath and change of clothes. Both Terry and I nearly always seemed to be in trouble one way or another, which was perhaps an ominous sign of things to come. The young girl who lived next door to him, Daisy Lattimer, was quite a frail little girl with long pigtails and buck teeth. Given the opportunity, she enjoyed playing with other children of her own age. Her mother invited Terry and I into her house to play with Daisy for a few hours one morning. 'Daisy isn't as strong as you are, so don't hurt her and play together nicely,' remarked Mrs Lattimer, who must have been full of fear at the sight of two young bruisers standing next to her shrinking violet of a daughter. Play in the back garden started well enough with all three of us climbing the large apple tree at the bottom of the garden, until I accidentally on purpose dropped a large oversized apple on Daisy's head. With a large scream she ran from the garden crying into the arms of her waiting mother. 'There, there sweetheart, everything is all right, don't worry,' her mother comforted her wailing daughter. Mrs Lattimer then walked down the garden towards us. 'I think you had better go home, the two of you. I don't know what happened but Daisy is upset. I will speak with your mother later on, Terry,' she said with anger written all over her attractive face. We quickly said our goodbyes and fled the crime scene.

There were many other local boys and girls that Terry and I played with in the village, and in the local woods. Many years ago farmers and landowners did not allow people on to their land, but now that attitude has changed and you can cross their land as long as you keep to designated paths. At weekends, and especially during the summer holidays, a gang of us used to meet outside the local pub, and armed with our sandwiches and orange squash, we were ready for several hours of exciting and mischievous fun. Two friends in particular, Richard and Dennis, were always up for a good laugh, but it was nearly always at the expense of others. Those two friends were always around the village doing something bordering on the illegal or immoral. It was Richard and Dennis that threw the village seat, donated by the former mayor, Councillor Bannister, into the local pond. It was the Richard and Dennis duo that put horse dung through the letter box of the local history teacher Mr Gordon's house. The same intrepid pair went hedgehopping and ruined the greengrocer's much loved yew. It was also the same two villains who on numerous occasions stole empty beer bottles from the Country Squire pub, and afterwards took them to the local off-licence to claim the deposit money. There were many more misdemeanours that they and others, including myself, carried out over those earliest years in and around Yapton. Yes, some of them were minor crimes, but allowing for our age and background they were certainly not included in the annals of criminal history!

It was September 1955, and the time had come for me, and many of my friends, some mentioned above, to attend the local school. All I had known since I was born was the security of being alongside my mother most days and playing carefree with friends in and around Yapton. Now that was about to end; as my mother explained, 'You have to attend school for the next ten years so that you will learn things just like your father.' With that I started bawling my eyes out until Mother put her gentle arms round my body to reassure me that school was a good place. Besides, she would be walking with me to school in the mornings and home again in the afternoon. Furthermore, my friends would also be there which convinced me that school was for me. Wearing a new dark blue blazer, short grey trousers and carrying a case full of school equipment, I left the security of my home and walked the half mile to my new school, Yapton Manor. Life was never the same again. We arrived ten minutes before the 9am bell was rung, by which time all schoolchildren had to be standing in the assembly hall before Mr Coates, the tough looking headmaster. Before I said goodbye to my mother, I noticed the reassuring figures of several of my friends, with their new colourful clothes on, kissing their mothers or fathers goodbye. That was it, as our parents had gone back home, or wherever that morning took them, and we were left attending our first assembly in front of Mr Coates who was dressed, I remember, in a black suit with white shirt and blue tie. He was tall, slim, aged about forty-five, with a military way of talking which meant loud, clear and to the point. That morning, standing before him like underlings waiting to be slaughtered, Mr Coates welcomed us to the school saying, 'Whenever you are at this school or anywhere else, I want you to try your best, boys and girls. I want all of you, during the next four years, to soar to the heights of educational excellence. Learning is all about effort and commitment in your everyday lessons. I wish you all well'—or something like that, but I didn't really understand a word of what he was talking about.

So begun my first day at Yapton Manor School, hoping that I would not meet up very often with the forbidding headmaster. The school itself was built during the early Victorian period and had one large playground, a small apple orchard with a small flower garden and outdoor toilets. On the plastered walls of the assembly hall were black and white photographs, the newer ones coloured, of former teachers and pupils dating back to the late 19th century. There were photographs of various football, cricket and rugby teams. There were also many photographs of former teachers, and one teacher in particular who had won the Victoria Cross for valour during World War II in occupied France. As I became more aware, I realised that there was an old black and white photograph of my Father and his two brothers standing in the back row of a school football team dated 1936, not that long before the outbreak of World War II. Seeing that family photograph made me proud to think they had attended this school, learnt things to the best of their ability, left school, to earn a living during the war, to work on a local farm. I too hoped that I could make a positive contribution to help make the next generation proud of me. What a tall order.

Compared to most town schools, Yapton Manor was a relatively small school which was made up of an infant school and a junior school next door. Although pupils, who lived in other local villages, did attend our school, there were only sufficient numbers for two classes in each year. That meant the first year which I first went into had about fifty pupils, twenty-five being in Form A and the same in Form B. The brighter pupils were put in Form A and those not so bright, like me, were put in Form B. Now, being placed in either A or B was a rather arbitrary affair in those days and was simply based on a very rudimentary pre-school tick box form that all pupils were required to complete. There were several young pupils of my age, whom I realised later on did not attend the pre-school interview, yet were put in Form A. (Mine is not to reason why but only just to do or die!) Working class parents, unless compelled, did not conform to middle class aspirations to send a child along for an education interview, especially if he/she was busy helping Mother with house chores.

My first-year class teacher was truly a decent young woman, called Margaret Smith, whose attractive features resembled a film star from Hollywood. Her tall, slim body, short blonde hair and sexy walk used to turn the head of many a good man including one or two male teachers. She hailed originally from Surrey, but her parents moved when she was about ten years old to a small village, called Oldbury, in Suffolk. From there she went on to a teacher training college in London and found her first job teaching literacy in Wandsworth Prison. One can imagine the old lags in prison giving her a torrid time. Their putrid smelling body odour and incessant farting must have put her off for life from applying for similar vacancies. After that job she worked in a secondary modern school in Colchester for two years and then she found her way into the lives of the geniuses at Yapton Manor. To her credit she emphasized the uniqueness of all individuals to us youngsters—something that she would regularly highlight whenever the opportunity presented itself. Mind you, one had to stretch the imagination when looking at Bert Moore. She would clearly inform us of the inherent importance of any work, whether it be labouring or professional. Ms Smith would always remind us: 'Boys and girls, don't let your past hold back your future.'

Ms Smith took our class for most subjects, excluding history and geography, which were the domains of Mr Hester, a short, balding decent kind of chap, who volunteered at the age of thirty-nine to enlist to fight in the Second World War. After two years of action he was injured by flying shrapnel—that is what he told us—and convalesced in an army hospital in Hampshire for the remainder of the war. Mr Hester was indeed a lovely old chap, ancient to us youngsters, but everyone's ideal of a forgiving uncle. He used to tell us amusing, amazing and adventurous stories about his young life with his parents in a small village on the north coast of Cornwall. Most of his paternal family had been tied up in the fishing industry going back several generations, starting apparently with one Reginald Hester, whoever he was, who used to hunt with aristocracy in the Sussex Weald. Be that as it may, most of the children appeared to enjoy being in his lessons as he was determined to help us make the best of our limited time at school. We didn't realise that at the time of course, but he obviously understood all these things, as he had lived an interesting life. Especially commendable was his personal initiative in volunteering to enlist in the War, when most men at his age would rather be at home with their families, or having a few beers with friends.

But a few boys in our class did give Mr Hester a difficult time during the first year of class teaching. One boy in particular, Billy MacDonald, who had a hard, difficult life because his father, after returning home from the local pub drunk most nights, used to beat in turn his mother, his older sister and then Billy. Most days Billy failed to turn up for assembly. After a short while, Ms Smith had no option but to send Billy to see the headmaster about his continuing lateness and absenteeism. The headmaster of course took a dim view of any child missing out on their education, especially those children who were considered to be falling behind academically as was the case with Billy. The officer concerned, James Trundle, an affable intelligent man then wrote to his parents several times and also visited the home on numerous occasions, but no one ever answered the door. Mr Trundle always left a calling card but communication was not forthcoming. Eventually after all avenues of contact with the parents had failed, Mr Trundle was left with no option, and assisted by a police officer, he visited Mr MacDonald's place of work.

Early one windy April afternoon Mr Trundle, and PC Denman, drove into the drive of Swallow Farm, a small early Victorian sheep farm, owned by a Mr Drew who had farmed there with his father ever since he was a teenager. After a few minutes of discussion with the farmer, explaining the nature of their visit, he and the police officer were given permission to walk about half mile to one of the outlying fields where Mr MacDonald was found cleaning out rubbish from the hooves of young sheep. With a startled look Ted shouted at the two men, 'What are you doing 'ere while I'm trying to make an honest livin? I 'ope the gaffer gave yer permission?' The reply was immediate: 'Calm down Ted, your employer gave us permission to come and talk to you about your son's poor attendance at school. Due to him missing so much schooling over the past months he is falling behind academically.' Mr Trundle's voice was quiet and reassuring voice as he tried to explain his presence to the fierce looking Ted MacDonald. 'Why you people always pickin on the likes of me, ain't yer got anyfink better to do then goes round makin me life difficult?' was the angry accusation that came from the quivering lips of the stocky tough farm labourer Ted MacDonald. The three men walked back to the farm, where Mr Trundle explained to Ted that under education law, his son Billy had to attend school and that it was his responsibility to make sure he did. After some time of explaining the pros and cons to Mr MacDonald, he reassured both officials that he would make sure that his son did not miss any further school lessons. That was nearly always the case through Billy's primary school education, but he always found it very difficult to read and write. Billy suffered from chronic insecurity.

After a month or so, I started to settle down into a new way of life, learning how to get on with other boys and girls, even though I knew, or had seen most of them around Yapton for several years. Far gone were those enjoyable carefree days that I used to spend with my mother, or my carers, playing on the local swings, catching small fish and eating liquorice sweets with my friends. I thought I was a kind, friendly sort of person around the school who got on well with most people including the older generation. The one area of school life that I most enjoyed, as most boys at the time did, not surprisingly, was playing competitive football in the playground during lunchtime and field games with my class during lessons with Ms Smith. The former were rough and tumble times with other boys, where we cemented our friendships, which gave us the confidence to familiarize ourselves with the girls. But some of them stayed away from the village ruffians like Richard Arrowsmith, Dennis Zeal, Bert Moore and myself to name just a few. It did not surprise me to find out later that some parents had told their children not to play with certain boys, who they had assumed, rather prematurely, to be a bad influence on them. To stigmatise young people like that certainly did not help to understand the influences that motivated them to act in certain ways. Later on I thought if we could understand what happens to certain individuals, then surely we might help them change their disruptive behaviour.

As usually happens in schools, boys and girls split up into various groups and sub-groups, which can be very healthy for children to sort out who they feel comfortable with in the various hierarchies that develop. In my gang there were about six to eight boys, all of them pretty tough characters it must be said, who had no qualms, when it came to dishing out punishment to those they thought deserved it, or were deemed weaker than them. We ran round the playground for all we were worth, until confronted by other boys determined to take over our territory. We usually won our brief skirmishes with other boys and then set our sights on making inroads into the world of girls; some of the more confident ones would venture amongst our gang looking to make friends. One girl in particular, Audrey Manning, was a tall confident person who stood out from most of the other girls. She lived with her parents and brother in a nearby village called St David's. Her father owned a small garage in Norwich and her mother taught English in a large secondary modern school in the same town. It was quite obvious that Audrey came from a different background from most of the class pupils by the way she spoke so clearly in classroom lessons. She usually raised her hand, on any subject, when responding to a question by Ms Smith or Mr Hester. In time I came to admire how clever she was, as she stood head and shoulders above me and my thick gang members. Others, understandably, did not see it that way at all, instead being hell bent on giving her a difficult time. During one first year history lesson, Mr Hester, who must have become somewhat exasperated with the inept response from the class, said, 'Now boys and girls, you must try harder to answer some of my questions as there is usually only one person amongst you who really does try.' Of course we all knew who he was referring to. For most of us that was another nail in our education coffin.

However, similar to most other pupils in my class, I was about educationally average. I had basic competence at writing, reading and history to give me sufficient knowledge to be able to communicate my way round the school and village. Mind you, that doesn't say much for other people. During the first academic year I especially enjoyed writing about fictitious football teams and individual footballers heading for stardom. My favourite team, who I named Norwich Wanderers, had been promoted to the senior division in England primarily due to their top goalscorer Andy Simpson. All rather basic boys' stuff which is something most generations of youngsters indulge in to take them away from everyday realities for a while until teacher, parents or something else breaks through their barriers to demand more of their precious time. One dreamy composition comes to mind that I had written for Ms Smith's class during the end of the first year. Briefly it was about a young male football hero—all children love heroes, don't they?—called Danny Osborne, who goes to Wembley Stadium with his team and scores a hat trick of goals thereby winning the cup for his team Yapton United. One morning at the start of an English class, Ms Smith rose to her feet holding a few pages of A4 and waved it in front of her saying to the whole group, 'Boys and girls, I have in my hand a very good composition written by Richard Morris. The composition is about a cup final where one player scores three goals. I think I am correct in saying those goals win the cup for his team. Well done Richard. Let us all give him a big clap!' With pride I ran home alone, as I now went to school on my own, to show my mother what I had achieved. No sooner had my father walked through the door with all his dirty farming clothes on than I thrust my short essay into his bony hard hands. Both my parents congratulated me on my first success at school.

With the first year at Yapton coming to an end, and with our school reports firmly in our hands to show our proud parents, we stood in the Assembly Hall in front of our intrepid headmaster Mr Coates standing there with a beaming smile on his craggy old face. 'Well done, boys and girls,' he boomed at us all, 'you have all done marvellously well this year in school and I am proud of you all. Go from here, enjoy your summer holidays, and when you return to this school I want you all to work even harder next term.' With that we marched out of the hall, our former cohort beaming down at us from the walls, really happy knowing that our headmaster was pleased with the way we had performed.

We had started our six weeks summer holiday, which meant, among other things, meeting up with Dennis, Richard and the gang to play around the village getting up to no good. Why not? There would be exciting days walking into the countryside to climb trees, or if the weather was awful, sit and watch television. 'Allo Mrs Morris, can Richard come out to play?' I overheard Bert say to my mother. 'Yes, come in, Bert, and wait for him to put on his old clothes,' she quietly told him. 'Now don't forget what I told yer, Richard, please stay out of trouble like a good boy, won't yer?' Mother said in a most emphatic way. Mother opened her leather handbag, the bag that Father had bought her for Christmas, and took out a two-shilling piece that she gave to me saying, 'Yes, I know what you have told me, but most of the time you do the opposite. Anyway buy yourself some sweets. And you have not eaten any breakfast, it is not ten o'clock and you will be hungry later on.' With that Bert and I left the house as we walked down the road to our usual meeting place, the village war memorial, to wait for our friends. About fifteen minutes later Terry, Richard and Dennis arrived all wearing their flash new jeans, like real cowboys, recently bought for them by their parents from a market stall in Norwich. 'The other lads 'ave gone out with their mums somewhere so won't be 'ere,' Dennis informed us. 'Let's all go to the woods,' Bert said enthusiastically. We all agreed.

Five scallywags set off to head for Littleworth Woods, about a mile from the village, just behind Farmer Dyson's small pig farm called Hedley Place. The woods, of conifer and native trees, had always been used by local children as a place where they could inhabit their own make believe world away from the prying eyes of those adults intent on giving them a hard time. There my friends and I used to climb the oak trees; one in particular was very tall and said to be three hundred year old. There we gouged out our initials, using a pen knife, on the bark of many trees. In one of the oak trees furthest away from Hedley Place Farm, we had made a weather-proofed small tree house with old rubbish we had found around Yapton. We had also helped ourselves by taking several corrugated metal sheets from an old shed owned by the ageing Farmer Dyson. Given the opportunity I know Mr Dyson would have loved to have set his terrifying Alsatian guard dogs on to us. He was a decent kind of chap even though at times our behaviour pushed him to the edge of insanity.

Nonetheless, once we were in the woods we all decided to make our way to Mr Dyson's orchard as one side of it conveniently backed onto Littleworth Woods. The orchard was full of various fruit just ripe for picking on this warm sunny day. We made our way quietly through the hole in the fence, which we had made six months previously and into the orchard full of luscious fruit ready for eating. Most of the trees were so overladen that it was possible to grab apples, pears and golden coloured plums from the ground and stuff them into our shirts and pockets before running off to hide in our tree house. Once there, with no time to waste, we all started devouring our ill-gotten gains and hoping the farmer had not detected that we had been robbing him of his fruit. As usually happens on those occasions, after stuffing ourselves with pounds of fruit we all had to quickly take down our trousers to relieve ourselves.

Three hours later with boredom setting in we all decided to move on from Littleworth Woods, and try our luck in another large wood. Hill Wood was about a mile from where we had previously been. It was a wood that consisted of deciduous trees of oak, elm, ash and beech. Most of the woods around Yapton were owned by farmers or landowners. Hill Wood was no different, and had been for some considerable time. After stopping many times to look at various things that caught our boyish attention, such as occupied birds' nests in trees, or catch jumping crickets that we put in our match boxes, watching a fox scavenging for food, and picking a few hedgerow blackberries. Eventually we arrived at Hill Wood, where we had made another tree house in a large tall ash tree which was ideal for kids like us who tried their utmost to keep out of the sight and sound of adults in general, but farmers in particular. If they caught us, as they did on rare occasions, most farmers would just tell us to get off their land. But a few would shout and swear and threaten to call the police. Most older people have seen signs that were so commonplace years ago in the countryside: 'Trespassers will be Prosecuted.' Fortunately today we have a more tolerant attitude about ownership of land where the public can use permissive paths, or even legal rights of way to venture over it.

In Hill Wood we set about foraging for small dry pieces of wood and with the aid of old paper we kept in the tree house we prepared a fire for the potatoes we were going to steal from the adjoining Highbrow sheep and cattle farm belonging to Percy Tate. Percy, who was single, and walked with a limp he sustained in an accident when he was young, had been farming at Highbrow for over forty years. He was a local character full of the joys of spring until he had a skinful of beer inside him, which used to send him crazy for a few days. He was a good old sort who cared about the way he treated his animals and land, always insisting that farmers must look after land for future generations. Husbandry, he insisted, was paramount. With delicious hot potatoes in mind, we made our way into Percy's large allotment, when all of sudden a great boom came from his voice: 'You lot get off my fucking land, or I will call the police, do you hear me!' With that we ran for all we were worth out of his allotment, through the woods and down to a stream that bisected two large fields used for pasture. 'The old sod, he must 'ave been on the booze,' Bert insisted. We sat there for some time hiding from Percy knowing he was too old to have chased us. We sat overlooking the stream trying to think of what we could do next to cause some mayhem on an unsuspecting resident of Yapton.

I came up with the idea of stealing potatoes from a landowner's allotment. 'About 'alf mile from here is land owned by the Fry family, who also have large commercial fields full of vegetables. Let's go over there and steal some,' I shouted enthusiastically at my friends. With that in mind we made our way to a hamlet called Panton, two miles west of Yapton. The Fry family were very wealthy, had owned land in Panton for at least two hundred years and also owned land used for training their race horses about three miles away in West

Meon. Even at our young age we realised it would be dangerous trying to steal anything from a family who would not hesitate, if they caught you on their land, to call the police or even set their ferocious dogs on to you. By this time it was nearly four o'clock but, undaunted, we walked down a well-trodden track for a while, then over a large arable field of cereal crops. Being ultra-quiet, we climbed over a wooden fence and into the Fry family allotment which was abundant with many different kinds of vegetables. With my heart thumping so loud, I thought it was going to burst! We soon located the potatoes next to a high hedge. Once there we dug the dry light soil with our hands and revealed many sizeable potatoes which we immediately put in our pockets and scarpered at great speed, dropping a few on the ground as we ran like greyhounds back to Hill Wood. We didn't go back to the fire we had already prepared as it was too near to Percy Tate's property. Instead we made another fire in a nearby clearing, with dry paper and small pieces of dead wood lying on the ground. After about thirty minutes, with the potatoes cooked in the hot embers, I took a stick and pulled them out of the fire. Burning our hands and mouths in the process, we ate three steaming potatoes each until we were all full to the brim. With all our hands and mouths covered black, my friends reminded me of clowns in a circus. As time was getting late we all agreed it was time to head home after another varied, yet enjoyable day around the byways of Yapton. Most of that summer holiday, and other holidays too, were similar to that day, when we sought out our own pleasure; which required a certain amount of energy, an acute sense of adventure and joy of playing with friends, but no need for any adult guidance or money save for a few pennies to buy sweets at the end of a successful day.

During this time, although I was hardly conscious of it, the security that family cohesion brings continued to sustain our everyday lives. Mrs Anderson and my mother continued to work in the village shop, 'a great place to learn about new gossip', according to mother, on different days so they could continue looking after each other's child after school or at weekends. It also gave them the opportunity to earn a few much needed pounds to help out with the household bills. Most of the village women in those days earned meagre amounts of money from cleaning in the larger houses nearby. It supported the inadequate wage their husband brought home from farm labouring. Typically mothers not working outside the home used to look after working mothers' children, thereby giving nearly every mother an extra few shillings at the end of the week. For most of those working class women it meant a eighteen hour working day: Out of bed at 5am to cook their husband's breakfast; next, the children had their breakfast. Usually in the mornings they went out cleaning. Then back home to cleaning their house, wash the clothes by hand and prepare dinner for the family. After dinner they would darn the children's clothes and prepare supper for their husbands, who usually came home drunk from the pub. If Mother was lucky, she had time in between to have a brief rest and eat a few mouthfuls of food.

My father and two uncles were nearly always very busy working for Mr Leader at the ever-growing Lavender Farm. Father said very little about anything other than you must be practical—he just got on with things; except when under the influence of alcohol when he became a little vocal, but on the whole he drank very little, unlike a lot of the farming fraternity who were big drinkers who spent most of their social life in the village pub. He found most of his colleagues, and village blokes, to be terrible bores when under the influence of alcohol. Besides, most of the time, especially in summer, they all worked long hours which gave Father and my uncles extra money and which helped the farm develop into a modern business. Time permitting, Father loved working in our large rear garden tending the succulent vegetables and divine smelling roses he grew. Mother enjoyed nothing more than home grown roses in the dining room. Many working class men from Yapton also found solace in their gardens, which probably enhanced their quality of life. You felt that the garden, along with a sound dry shed, gave those men a kind of retreat away from the demands of work and home. They could take stock of their hard lives and fantasize about a better world. Other than my father and grandfather meeting each other in the local pub for a beer, my father preferred to have a party with his family at home. Throughout the years we had many enjoyable parties at our house for most of the extended family who used to have a good old knees up.

On my father's side of the family, as indicated above, they came round regularly, especially my dear grandparents who were always good fun. I enjoyed playing with the various toys they had bought me. My two uncles, Eric and Jack, always came with their wives, Jane and Sarah, and four children. Both uncles had a girl and a boy each; Eric fathered Mick and Lynda, and Jack fathered Bob and Maria. As they were all older than I was, I didn't have a great deal to do with my nephews and nieces either at school or village life. Occasionally my mother's parents, Joe and Marcia Armitage, used to turn up but did not stay very long as they were religious people who thought that sex before marriage, drinking alcohol and popular culture was the work of the devil himself. They, nonetheless, appeared to be kind genuine people, full of positive goodwill toward their fellow human beings. Their daughters, my two aunts, Bunny and Sarah, were both married to local farm workers Ted Nugent and Harry Gregg and between them had four children. Ted Nugent had three children and Harry Gregg one child. Suffice to say these aforementioned people were an early part of my family life, although for the most part, I did not see much of them, especially on my mother's side of the family. The modern family today, unlike when my parents and grandparents were young, have their own cars, motorbikes and even aeroplanes at their disposal. Instead of having a holiday in Cromer or Yarmouth, as many did when we were children, young people today think nothing of flying to Florida, Mombasa or even Sydney in Australia! Good luck to them.

With the summer holidays over for another year, we were back at school for the second year with great hopes of doing even better than last year. Well, that was what my mother told me time and time again—work hard and do your best. She used to emphasize this point to me repeatedly: 'If you work hard you can get a good job when you grow up, not working on the farms like your father but a clean well paid job with a good pension.' And to be honest, my mother had made a valid point which I used to carry in front of my mind for many years thereafter. It was during my generation that life chances improved considerably for working class people. However, back to school, I was now Jack-the-lad in the classroom and especially in the playground, where big boys played football and girls watched them with avid eyes—or so I thought. At the start of the second year we stood in the assembly hall in front of our formidable headmaster Mr Coates, our role model and inspiration. Once again he invited us back to Yapton Manor for another year, he hoped, of diligent hard work as his austere looking colleagues sat behind him with the likeable Mr Trundle, smiling like a Cheshire cat, in attendance. With the same teachers we basically continued where we left off from the year before being taught English, History (1066 and all that), Geography, Games and Nature Study. When I mentioned to Ms Smith during the last term about how good it would be to have a class outing to visit the countryside, I thought I would hear no more on the subject. But to our surprise she mentioned that she was taking our class out the following week to have nature study around the local woods. Incidentally, Audrey Manning, the intelligent girl who last year was head and shoulders above us all in class, had, perhaps not surprisingly, left our school and had joined a private school in Norwich. By moving on she had now given other people in the class, including me, the opportunity to re-assert themselves by taking over the group dynamics. In other words we could beat up anyone we didn't like very much.

One of the major problems that a lot of pupils had experienced during the first year was the inadequate quality of school dinners. In fact, halfway through that year nearly half of the pupils had either changed by taking a packed lunch to school, or they went home for their midday meal which meant extra work for their mothers. This was brought about by many parents complaining to the school about the unacceptable poor quality of food their children had to eat. Some mothers were more vociferous on the subject. I remember that I was not that impressed by the school dinners either. Nevertheless, when we sat down on the first day of the second year to our first school meal they had been transformed into well cooked, quality food. Mr Coates was there standing just inside the canteen to welcome us and reassure all the children that we could in future expect a hot nourishing dinner!

We carried on with our everyday classroom lessons taught by the kind and friendly Ms Smith. I suppose you could call our learning in those days rote learning. Basically the teacher wrote something on the large blackboard in front of us and we copied it down in our writing books. We would read and reread what the teacher had told us, which we assumed and believed, was factually correct. Not too many years ago I read that educational psychologists had developed something similar using rhesus monkeys. I found that to be most reassuring!! But of course we learnt different interactional skills amongst the class during the various games we played that both challenged us physically and emotionally. This helped us to understand peer pressure and acceptance. In other words if you don't co-operate with others you will lose out. Today I watch with interest when I see children playing games and the complex way they interact and communicate with each other. Interestingly it was around about this time that some of the girls started to assert themselves with a new found confidence, especially now that the former dominant girl had left the school. Two girls in particular were not slow in coming forward; they were Gillian Davies and Maureen Fox, but not so poor old Daisy Lattimer who appeared to be content sitting in the background eating sweets.

Came the day when Ms Smith was going to take the whole class out into the countryside for an extended nature study lesson. Did she realise what she had let herself in for? We were all very excited that morning as we had anticipated a great day out by the time we arrived at school, on a warm sunny day, holding bags full of sandwiches, soft drinks and writing books. My mother, I remember, had made me several tasty salad sandwiches, a cream cake and homemade soda pop. As it happened most of my sandwiches were gulped down by Richard Arrowsmith. For a short while he was affectionately known as the school dustbin as he used to consume anything edible in sight. After assembly we all congregated outside in the playground, holding onto our goody bags for dear life. As

Ms Smith counted how many pupils were present, she reminded us about being good to each other, courteous to the public as we would be carrying the proud name of Yapton Manor with us. Giggling and laughing we walked out of the school holding the hand of someone opposite you. I remember holding the clammy hand of Susan Cummings whose buck teeth and freckled face, I remember at the time, did not encourage further inspection. On the outward journey that day I also held the warm hand of Maureen Fox, a short plump girl with brown hair, who wore a light blue dress and matching shoes. Our young loins were on the move as we travelled to our nature study destination. During that journey I remember the warm sunshine, as fat cows munched the lush green grass, and the occasional village dog barking at the presence of laughing, innocent children! Well that is what Enid Blyton had to say about the countryside in those days as she became the author par excellence in describing, from a sentimental point of view, the lives of country folk.

We walked along the road for about half mile, passing along the way, lots of proud old women outside cleaning their attractive homes. Some of them said hello to us. 'Mornin' boys and gels,' sang one old lady scrubbing her front doorstep, something she had probably done all her life, and generations before her. At the end of the road we walked onto a track, called Woodland Way, used by farmers requiring access to their land. At the end of the track we all climbed over a wooden stile and into a field full of sheep munching the short green, daisy infested, grass, who did not even bother to look up to enquire about the laughing children who were about to invade their territory. Then we made our way over another style on the other side of the field and into a large deciduous wood, called Spankers Hill, our first destination. Over two centuries ago this particular wood supplied Government with endless tons of timber to build ever bigger and stronger naval ships to fight off European invaders. Ms Smith found a clearing in the wood where we were all able to sit down on the various covers or clothes we had brought with us. The teacher referred to the small textbook we had all been given for the day. 'Children, I hope you all remember that this nature book I gave you this morning is about identifying different trees and their names,' she said in her usual quiet reassuring manner. The class divided into four groups of six pupils as Ms Smith gave us instructions as to the different trees we should identify and write down about in our books. We had to be back in the clearing within two hours. Our group just instinctively came together as arch villains: Terry, Richard, Dennis, Bert, Philip and I prepared ourselves for action.

As soon as the teacher, and the other pupils were out of site, our group consensus was to climb a few trees deeper in the wood. We came across a large tall oak tree, but being autumn all the deciduous trees were uninteresting to climb as most were nearly bare having shed their seasonal leaves. Then Richard noticed a rather tall single conifer that had somehow managed to self-seed, probably with the help of bird droppings, in amongst them. Due to the usual dense growth of conifers very few birds nest in them; however, if you look on the ground underneath you will notice it will be bone dry, but life abounds as various insects thrive on conifer needles. After a determined struggle all the way up, Terry eventually heaved his fat frame to the top of the tree, tired, dirty yet triumphant. Once at the top he started shouting to anyone who would listen: 'Yes, I've done it boys and girls, look at me right up the top of this almighty tree!' Some of our class must have heard his exhaustive cries as a little while afterwards we heard loud shouts from two or three of our other classmates. Dennis also wanted to climb the same tree but we dissuaded him, under great protest, saying we had all better move on together as we only had just over an hour to find several different trees to write about. Mind you, both Richard and I were good at identifying trees, as were most local people who had grown up around them, so we knew which to climb. Incidentally one local old chap named Ben had died just two years ago, aged 89 years, and had made a living for many years from these woods, carving ornaments, brooms and other gardening items.

I was in my element when it came to finding, naming and writing about different trees. That skill had originally been nurtured by walking the many local woods with my father and two uncles. 'It's all about keen observation of the bark, its colour, height, colour of the leaves, fruit, flowers,' my father would keep drilling into me. 'Get those right boy and you can't go wrong,' he used to say. Not far from where our class was going to meet, we came across a small wood with a fence around it to keep out the likes of us. Probably owned by a local landowner, but not knowing who, we jumped over and found several trees which were ideal for writing about in our nature study books. I identified oak, beech, hornbeam and sycamore all within a hundred yards of each other. Something else we had identified that day, although not required for classwork, were rabbit, slow worm and pheasant. When my father, and his brothers, were young, their father used to take them in the countryside shooting rabbits, pheasant and anything else that was edible. Apparently grandfather was given permission to shoot on the estate of the late Sir Oswald Tracey, former criminal barrister, and in return he used to keep the estate trees well pruned for him. As we sat under a large hornbeam writing up our notes on tree identity for Ms Smith; Terry got out of his pocket a bent dirty cigarette followed by a book of matches. 'You lot fancy a drag on this ciggy I found in the ashtray this mornin? I fink it was me old mum's cigarette,' Terry told us with a smirk on his dirty face. No one was interested in smoking that old fag; besides, we had all tried smoking before and found the experience smelly and something that left a horrid taste in our mouths. With about ten minutes to spare Richard and I managed to finish writing about tree identification whereas the others just copied mine down into their own books.

When we arrived back in the clearing all of our class had already assembled round Ms Smith who was eager to hear which trees we had identified and our description of them. It was just after midday and the warm sun shone brightly through the trees down onto our faces and clothes as Ms Smith asked the first group to describe what they had seen. Dave Williams, a tough bloke, whose family lived on the outskirts of Yapton, was the first to talk about his team's experiences of identifying oak, elm, horse chestnut, beech, birch and a Victoria plum tree (our group didn't see that one). 'Well done, David and your team,' a smiling Ms Smith said warmly to the attentive class in front of her. I thought the smart Dave Williams was too big for his boots, but I didn't fancy taking him on. Ms Smith then pointed at me to say my bit. 'We looked all over the place for trees, but the one place we found nearly all of 'em was at the end of the wood. We found all the same trees that Dave's team found but also found cherry, walnut and yew,' which I knew was a blatant lie. I looked at Dave and he looked at me with a frightening scowl on his ugly face. The teacher praised my team and the other two teams who gave equally good presentations about their activities. Afterwards we all sat down to consume our sandwiches and drink when Richard and Brian Tripp starting fighting each other in front of everyone. 'Stop that fighting immediately, you two!' said the irritated teacher. I thought, wrongly, that a mass fight would ensue. Sod it!

Around 1-30pm, Ms Smith told us that we were now going to walk to our second destination of the day, Windover Hill Wood. Many years ago before World War Two, this particular wood was the scene of the brutal murder of a young local woman. Linda Douglas was single, 33 years of age and lived with her parents not far from our school. She had worked for at least ten years in a local farm as secretary to the owner Ted Pitchey. The woods, known locally as Lover's Lane, was frequented by courting couples. It is not known what really happened but Linda Douglas was found dead under a tree by a woman walking her dog early one morning. After an intense police investigation a young man from a nearby village was arrested and subsequently imprisoned for her murder. That story was told to me by a local farmer years later over a beer in the local pub. The teacher stopped the class on the outskirts of the wood, where it was short grass, so we could place our personal things on the ground. That was a green light for Dennis to start touching Dorothy Taylor's bottom, but she elbowed him off with her muscular hairy arms. With all of us sitting like angels, Ms Smith went on to talk about what was required of us for the second project. 'Class, you have to find three more different trees if you can; also, you have to identify at least four birds by name. I want you to write about what you have identified. You have two hours,' said Ms Smith.

The same pupil groups as before went their different ways into Windover Hill Woods, a place most local kids knew well. 'Right, what we goin' to do then?' I asked excitedly. The consensus was that we should walk deeper into a particular place of the wood as Richard, who had walked it a few times with his father, knew we would come across a wooden hut used for making tea by local foresters. It was also a place where a tramp called Wild Billy used to sleep. After fifteen minutes we came across this old dilapidated shed with a torn tarpaulin roof, three out of the six windows broken, no lock on the door and it smelt like a pigsty. I looked under an old wooden table and found old smelly clothes probably belonging to the tramp. But there were no tramp or foresters around right now. If nothing else, we all agreed, we could write up our nature watch observations on the old table full of ringworm and tea stains. Afterwards we walked further into the deciduous wood until I saw a large tall oak tree with several crows' nests on the top of it. The crows themselves were making a huge din bickering and fighting amongst each other. 'Now there is a good one for us to write about. We all know,' I said arrogantly, 'that a crow is more strongly built than a rook but smaller than a raven and is usually found in pairs.' Just like identifying trees, I was also good at naming birds and other countryside animals. The countryside in those days was full of nature waiting to be explored by young enthusiastic kids like my friends and I.

We decided against climbing the oak tree, because crows can be very dangerous and territorial especially the higher up the tree one climbs. Instead we spotted a smaller sycamore tree about a hundred yards further on down the track. Full of devilment, three of us, Dennis, Bert and I soon made our way to the top of the bare tree, and once there, we all shouted and bellowed to our schoolmates below. They didn't appear to be interested. We walked further on exploring the wood as we searched for trees, animals or any other thing new that would stir our young excited minds into action, until we came across a clearing where we decided to sit down for a while as a pair of hungry magpies hopped on branches nearby. In the centre of the clearing were a lot of ashes, probably the remnants of fires made by the foresters to keep warm or somewhere to boil water for tea, or even local boys cooking their spuds. Our motley group just sat there day dreaming for some considerable time until Richard alarmed us by saying, 'According to my watch we only have thirty minutes left (or something like that!) to write down names of animals and trees for Ms Smith.' With that prompting we starting writing down the names of the various trees we had seen; we made up a few of them, and used our imagination when it came to identifying several wild animals such as jay, fox, rabbit and frog.

With our writing books full of animals we saw roaming the countryside, or thought we saw, we returned to meet up once again with our class. Similar to the first project, Ms Smith asked each group in turn to read aloud to the class their experiences of what they had seen and where they had seen it. It was interesting to hear what the other groups identified; for example, one saw a stoat, and another a grass snake and the other a pied wagtail. The other groups had similar interesting sightings. With that project successfully completed, we gathered our things together and set off to walk back to our school, passing along the way several farm workers repairing fences, painting large field gates and cleaning various machinery before the winter set in. 'Allo young children, 'ad a nice time 'ave yer?' asked one old worker with deep lines etched all over his dark brown suntanned face. That old face was no doubt a legacy of years of back-breaking hard work exposed to the elements. Incidentally it is not surprising that a lot of the younger generation of farm workers explain enthusiastically to anyone who will listen how mechanisation has transformed the way things are now done in modern farming. We carried on walking fast; no one appeared tired, until we reached our school where we said goodbye to the irreplaceable Ms Smith, thanking her for an enjoyable day. I eventually arrived home to tell Mother of the exciting day we all had, but omitting the naughty things we got up to.

At the end of the third year of school, I was then approaching nine years of age, we had our first family holiday away from home. Hitherto we used to make day visits to various family members, and occasionally to a single female friend of Mother's, who used to live in Norwich. As Father could not afford to buy a car in those hard-up days, we used to travel usually in a Leyland single decker green bus owned by the Norwich Council. I found those bus journeys very exciting as I sat on the back seat watching the green fields, full of smelly farm animals, go by. Sometimes I used to count the number of domestic animals in any one field and then write it down. I also enjoyed waving at other people, usually older people, from the bus. Once one old lady I was waving at took a photograph of me inside the bus. I felt rather proud of myself. When I was young the no. 5 bus passed through our village three times a day so that people were able to go shopping elsewhere. In those days the driver used to manoeuvre the bus slowly round a warren of narrow country lanes stopping at several hamlets and villages to pick up mostly women who used to be destined for Norwich Town, where they could buy better quality food and clothes. As Father had been working for Mr Leader for some time, it gave him the opportunity to save his money, so that he was now in a position to buy our first car, a second-hand Ford Prefect.

It was a gorgeous sunny June morning in 1959, how could I forget such a momentous occasion, as we loaded our things into our green car, and set off for our first seven-day holiday, in Cromer, about twenty miles north east of our village. Father, who was an experienced driver, soon negotiated the country lanes and in no time at all we were on the B1145 heading towards Cromer, a place where my grandparents had enjoyed holidaying years previously. Father drove on to the A140, the first time I had been on such a busy road where lorries, coaches, buses and cars all appeared to fight each other for the limited available space. I remember at the time, as I looked out of the car window, being frightened by the size and roar of large lorries as they drove past our small car with ease, making it shake, rattle and roll.

After about one and half hours we reached our destination: our first, small, self-catering two bedroomed chalet some five minutes from the golden sandy beaches of Cromer. Excitedly I quickly jumped out of our comfortable car, and ran into the small front garden full of delightful, different coloured roses surrounded by a tidy green lawn. With that inspection over, I hurriedly made my way round to the back garden to see what else was available over the next seven days for me to explore. I noticed several small house sparrows feeding on a seed container hanging from an apple tree. There was small wooden garden shed; the lawn was slightly bigger than the front garden, and the borders full of red Valerian, Kidney Vetch and Ox Eye Daisy. What a wonderful delight it all was. Then Father and I walked down to the bottom of the garden to where the shed was, and as we looked through the small, dirty, cracked window it revealed an electric lawn mower, various gardening tools, a few old clothes and a black pair of Wellington boots. Father turned the handle of the shed door and in he marched to inspect the implements therein. 'There you are me son,' Father smiled at me, 'you can do some gardening while you are 'ere to keep yer out of trouble.' As we walked out of the old shed we were joined by Mother standing on the lawn with a broad smile all over her face. 'Well I 'ope the weather stays good for us during the next few days so that we can sunbathe on this pretty lawn,' said Mother, looking forward at the prospect of doing very little work for once. With Mother's intentions firmly implanted in our minds, we walked back to the car to collect our bags and took them inside our abode for next few days.

There were two bedrooms, one double for my parents and a single for me, both colourfully decorated with white ceilings and floral pink wallpaper. There were light blue covers on the beds, and next to them was a small ceramic table lamp ideal for reading my books in bed. My single bedroom had a clean light brown carpet, and there was a dark brown one in the other bedroom. I was so excited that I jumped onto my bed and pulled back the lemon coloured curtains that revealed several Daniel Defoe, Billy Bunter and gardening books. It was at this stage that I decided to take my two heavy bags into my bedroom and carefully put away my clothes, two pairs of shoes, toiletries and bucket and spade into the tallboy standing there, rigid and upright, like a soldier, behind the bedroom door.

As we looked further round the chalet, we found a toilet and bathroom in the same room decorated with light blue walls and ceilings. In the kitchen stood a smallish wooden table with four chairs neatly tucked underneath. This place, I thought, is where we would eat our meals and plan each day's activities together. The white metal sink had a worktop next to it, two wall mounted units, clean black and white lino on the floor, like our kitchen at school, and plenty of cutlery and crockery. All very posh. After my parents had finished putting their personal items away in their bedroom we sat down in the kitchen for our first family meal together. Super-efficient Mother had brought a cooked delicious hotpot with her from home. With my parents at my side, I felt so secure being in a strange place miles from my home but determined to enjoy myself for the next few days on the beach, and although I couldn't swim, I would still venture into the cold sea to get my feet wet.

The next morning we washed, though the water had a funny smell. We had breakfast together, Mother made sandwiches for us and we made our way out of the chalet into a bright sunny day ideal for walking on the beach and playing sandcastles. With our colourful car locked outside the chalet, we walked down the road passing many attractive chalets with neat tidy gardens catching the eye. When we arrived at the beach, I realised that at nine years of age it was my first venture onto a sandy beach. It was quite full with other families, children playing with the sand next to their parents as they sat ensconced, minus socks and shoes, in deckchairs. Father went to hire two deckchairs himself so that he and Mother could sit comfortably for a few hours dreaming of anything except work. With a metal bucket and spade in hand, I moved ten feet or so away from my parents, and started digging into the pale yellow sand for all I was worth, until a scrawny looking boy, aged about ten years, wearing only trunks came up to ask me where I came from. 'From Yapton,' I replied. 'Never 'eard of it, where is it—near Clapton?' the thin looking boy asked. 'No I am from Yapton, it's near Norwich,' I said once again. 'I've never 'eard of Morwich before, where is it then?' 'No, it's Norwich,' I nearly shouted at the boy who had a funny accent that I had never heard before. 'I must get on me bike cos I'm going to catch sea monsters wi' me Dad. See yer'—with that the boy ran off to join his family; I assume they were his family, some hundred feet along the beach. I rejoined my parents who were half dozing and still sitting comfortably in their deckchairs no doubt enjoying a relaxing time away from the everyday rigours of earning money. When my mother noticed that I was once again digging in the sand, with the intention of making sandcastles, she asked me and Father if we would both like one of the sandwiches she had made earlier on in the chalet. 'Here is your favourite meat, Richard, it's the delicious home reared lamb from the farm where your dad works,' Mother said smiling at me. 'Yes we 'ave been rearing these young lambs since last year and they are so sweet to eat it's like butter melting in your mouth,' Father explained with a proud voice, highlighting the good work he and his brothers were doing at Leader's Farm. Work it seemed was never far from their imagination.

In the afternoon we left the sandy beach, and made our way to a small brightly painted fish and chips restaurant, called Ted's Place, just across the road from where we had been sitting among the many other working class families also on holiday for a few days respite from their difficult mundane lives. A sharp looking lady of about fifty, with a dimple on her left cheek, welcomed us in and showed us to a vacant table with a brightly coloured tablecloth. She, the waitress, I remember had large breasts, although I was still very innocent in those days knowing nothing about the female body, except perhaps, of the three or four times I saw my mother's leg above the knee when she was taking her stockings off. Also around this time of sexual awakening, some of my male classmates and I used to snigger at the sexy sight of Ms Smith. We thought we knew something about sex but at that stage we didn't even have hair round our ever-growing penises. One or two of the lads would make great gain amongst the sniggering all-boys group about how they had seen their older sisters with miniskirts and deep red lipstick before going out with their long haired boyfriends dressed in modern clothes.

All the walls in the fish restaurant, I remember, were adorned with various sea shells, an old oar, rope, a large paddle and black and white photographs of old fishermen with white beards holding aloft a large fish they had presumably caught. 'What you having madam?' the same lady politely asked my mother. 'Well, I will 'ave cod and chips. What about you Dave, what you 'aving?' 'Plaice and chips for me, please.' 'And 'ow about you Richard?' Mother asked, at the time probably

45

thinking she didn't have to cook it like she did at home. I thought to myself that I had eaten fish, sausages and pies before but not Cornish pasty. 'Cornish pasty and chips for me mum,' I enthusiastically replied. It was with great relief when the large pasty and chips was served to me on a round yellow plate, and I ate the tasty meat and vegetables with great relish. That was the first of many pasties that I would wolf down over the years to come—although due to high levels of saturated fat, I recommend you eat them only occasionally.

The holiday in Cromer with my loving parents was great fun. My parents also appeared to be enjoying themselves. We visited the beach most mornings so that the three of us could go in the sea, or just sit in a deckchair, and let the world go by. My parents were aware, no doubt, that in no time at all they would be back working in Yapton to earn enough money to pay their way in the world. The one afternoon I really enjoyed most of all was when we visited a small family owned zoo a few miles south of Cromer. Father paid our entry fee into the zoo that specialised, so they advertised, in retraining young monkeys that had been abandoned by their mothers at London Zoo. This was the first time that my parents and I had seen live wild animals roaming around in pens, but I know that I felt sorry for them being locked up with very little space to exercise. There was an absolute din, as the young monkeys fought each other, as they chased the peanuts I threw into their cage for them. Most retrieved the peanuts but three or four of them were content biting lumps out of each other. The mature monkeys that were in the cage managed to bring about some sort of peace amongst them, except for one youngster, who raced non-stop round the bars of his prison shouting at those ogling him outside. Altogether we spent about four hours in the Zoo visiting mature monkeys, elephants, zebras, who stank abominably, and many other animals I had only hitherto seen on television or in books.

On the day we left Cromer, with our interesting holiday finished, I remember how much we had all enjoyed ourselves on our first holiday to the sea. It was this holiday that would stay in my mind, as I reminisced to others at school about the thrill of running on the sand, and listening to the sound of waves crashing on the beach. My friends were interested when I explained how I had looked up many times at the mysterious deep blue/black/grey sky surrounded by large white clouds. I was also fascinated by the old men, with various tattoos on their big brown muscular arms, who used to sit outside a little beach hut repairing fishing nets. Several times during our visit to the beach, I had walked off to where they were sitting just to watch them working together. Sometimes they stopped to speak to one another, light a cigarette, or on one occasion while I was there they made tea. One morning, as I sat watching them, one of the men looked up at me with a smile on his brown leathery face and said softly, ''Allo me boy, you on 'oliday with yer mum and dad?' 'Yes I am,' I replied, pointing with my finger to where my parents sat on the beach. 'Well, I tell yer what young feller, would yer like this large shell I found out at sea?' asked the same man. 'Yes please,' I said rather excitedly. He put the shell in a large plastic bag for me and I wandered off to rejoin my parents. 'No, you could not 'ave done all that on one 'oliday Morris,' said indignant Bert later.

One naughty incident that Richard, Dennis, Terry, Bert, Philip Maynard and I carried out was printed in the local newspaper, *Clarion News*, about a week later citing the local angry farmer. The farmer in question, pompous David Summerfield, was opposed to any new plans to develop the village especially if it entailed improving the lives of working class people whom he called 'unofficially, riff raff'. On this occasion he vehemently opposed the council plans to build a new community centre which would benefit all the local people, not just the working classes or young children. The existing village hall, the place where my parents had their wedding reception, was very old, decrepit and close to falling down. 'This is an ideal opportunity,' according to local councillor Ted Harper, 'for the council to invest in a new community centre so that villagers can enjoy various services and activities under one roof.' 'The money is available now, so let's go forward and build it,' he enthusiastically told the *Clarion News*. Ted Harper, and many others, it must be said, wanted Yapton to succeed, although there were those people who had nothing better to do than undermine the good work being carried out in the name of progress. The killjoys reside, of course, wherever you find groups of people living together, but Yapton village was nonetheless a decent sort of place to live.

Now two days before the council were due to meet to discuss the new building proposals, my five partners in crime and I made arrangements to meet early one evening to try and put David Summerfield in his place, as he had been a thorn in the side of village life for some considerable time. Knowing that he would be away at a particular time, we made our way up to his farm, called Ivy House, to set our plan in motion. We went quietly into his large barn where cattle were housed, and scraped up onto a shovel some fresh cow dung. Then we made our way to the front of his large Victorian detached house, with three cars in the driveway, and walked up to the front door. With my heart thumping away like a ship's engine, I held the shovel with a rich mix of dung on it, and Richard, with the aid of a flat piece of wood, pushed all the steaming dung through his letterbox onto a polished parquet flooring. We hoped that the rich cow offering would sort out his arrogant behaviour towards local people. The consequence of our morally reprehensible behaviour was that the following week in the local paper, referred to above, was the most vitriolic attack on those 'local savages who took upon themselves to carry out their summary justice without allowing democracy to take its natural course'—in the words of the pompous David Summerfield. After listening to the various arguments put forward by local people, it was decided that plans should go ahead and build the community centre which was completed within a year thereby benefiting all concerned. For several weeks after, farmer Summerfield continued ranting on about the decadent working classes and how they will bring down society, until he finally put his farm up for sale, and eventually moved to a smallholding in Stornoway, Scotland. The new farmer was an entirely different man who had progressive ideas, in particular about farming, but also wanted the village people to visit his farm.

I remember the opening day of our community centre very well indeed. It was a warm sunny day in the first week of July, with coloured streamers and banners on nearly all the buildings, and the mayor himself, Councillor Peter Enright, was there to cut the ribbon and declare it open. Local people had set up stalls consisting of various things to sell, with lots of goodies such as fried burgers, sausages, chips, toffee apples, clothes, tombola, to name but a few. I remember Bert, Richard and Philip gorging themselves on numerous burgers and chips. One old chap from the village, named Cockerel, who used to walk round impersonating his free range chickens, had walked off with several burgers and sausages in his jacket pocket. There was a large marquee that was playing loud rock and roll music, as the adults inside relaxed with a beer and a cigarette.

Next door was another marquee full of local people drinking tea or coffee and talking amongst themselves. Those I recognised were my parents, my uncles and aunts, the Andersons and the Reverend Lionel Barrett who was wearing his large colourful hat. And many others were all sitting down relaxing in the warm summer sun knowing that all their hard work had paid dividends for little old Yapton.

In the evening there was dancing and singing on the village green. Most of the children, including myself, stuffed ourselves with burger rolls and washed them down with gallons of locally made lemonade. Whilst all the adults were thoroughly enjoyed themselves, several friends and I had sneaked away from all the activity to hide under a large lorry about a hundred yards from our parents. Richard put his hand into his pocket and pulled out several dirty looking cigarettes. 'Give us a light Den,' asked Richard who, like the Flying Scotsman, started puffing for all he was worth. Seconds later he was coughing and spluttering and gestured to the others to take a puff. I tried it, as did Dennis, but Philip refused saying his uncle coughed all the time due to years of smoking cigarettes called Senior Service. As the four of us were frightened that our parents might find us smoking, we quickly put the cigarette out and ran back to rejoin them all.

Not long after the Summerfield incident, the same gang carried out another similar raid on the local magistrate's house. Brigadier David Supple had been a magistrate for a number of years based in Norwich, which took in the areas of Yapton and surrounding districts. He lived in a large detached house called Atwood's Farm. Early on in his life, but after military retirement, he had also been a commercial smallholder owning and rearing many rare old English pigs. It was his ilk that had ruled the English countryside way of life for centuries, but things were changing slowly! He had over the years handed down severe prison sentences and heavy fines to Yapton men, who were caught only trying to poach a pigeon, hare or grouse to feed their hungry families. One summer evening around 9pm, with dusk fast approaching, we walked the long way round to his house hoping that we would not be recognised. Knowing that he would be out for the evening, we entered his premises from the rear garden and walked fifty yards to the front of the house. Bert had carried from the village a large sack full of pig manure, a kindly present for the good Brigadier. Very quietly Bert and I walked up to the large green wooden door and placed two large shovels of dung through the large metal letterbox, allowing it to drop onto the wood tiled floor on the other side. There was the almighty roar of a dog barking somewhere inside the house, which told us to get out of the garden immediately as the Brigadier's notorious Alsatian was about. Nothing was ever heard of our anti-social behaviour again.

It was September 1961. My class friends and I had done our best at Yapton School. We had grown both physically and mentally during the last six years from studying under the careful guidance of Ms Smith. None of us could ever be described as intelligent, or articulate, but now that we were eleven years old we knew enough to meet the needs of the situation we would encounter at our new senior school. Rawlinson Comprehensive School, named after a local 16th century monk, was a five-mile bus journey from my village to the outskirts of Norwich Town. Several of my friends and I congregated at the village bus stop at 7am early one cold September morning waiting for the number 9 bus, a single decker, to drive us to our new school. We sat there on the old Bedford bus, wearing our new green blazers and caps, not saying a word to each other but thinking of the challenges and responsibilities that lay ahead for us at Rawlinson School. The weather had brightened up somewhat, as we new pupils were led by a young teacher, called Mr Hinton, who was tall, slim and wearing a dark suit, through the playground of the attractive Edwardian school. Once inside the large assembly hall, we were told to sit at the front directly opposite the stage where several stern looking teachers sat. After waiting for eternity, but really only minutes, an elderly looking man walked onto the stage holding some papers in his hand. 'Good morning boys,' he almost sang, with a smile on his round red face, to the assembled boys of Rawlinson School. 'Good morning Sir,' was the loud enthusiastic response of the boys. 'For the benefit of those new pupils here in front of me, my name is Mr Bayfield and I am the headmaster of this school. I hope your stay here for the next five years will be most productive and enjoyable. Diligent hard work is what we subscribe to here at Rawlinson School.' And so he went on, like the last headmaster at Yapton. Mr Bayfield, who was far friendlier than Mr Coates, was a short stocky man with a bald head, except for a few strands of hair that hung precariously at the back of his head. He wore round plastic framed spectacles, walked with a limp yet enjoyed walking around the school so that he could talk to as many pupils as possible. He also had a wicked sense of humour, especially when he recognised pupils that had been at the school for some time. On one occasion he saw me walking out of the changing rooms having just changed from playing a soccer match. He came up to me and remarked, smiling, 'If you get any slower on the football pitch Morris, my grandmother will have to take your place in the team!'

Rawlinson Comprehensive School started life as a medical college way back in the Edwardian era. Many years later it became an approved school for young delinquent boys. After the Second World War the Local Government acquired it, then extensively enlarged it to cater for the ever-growing number of people living in Norfolk. When I was a pupil at the school there were approximately 500 boys and girls aged 11-16 years. It was the largest school in Norwich although there were several other smaller schools. Apart from providing comprehensive schools, the local Council also provided three grammar schools for the brighter boys and girls, but these places were not for the likes of the Yapton riff raff. Rawlinson also provided two football pitches, a cricket pitch, running track, netball and basketball courts and a large playground area. The school had also won a prize, before we arrived, for producing the most attractive and varied gardens in the area.

Along with nearly all my old mates from Yapton, I was selected to attend Class Two of the first year. Each year had three classes with about thirty pupils in each class. Our first year form teacher was Mr Diamond—of course we nicknamed him Boozy from the Double Diamond advert—who taught history and physical education, and was a bit of a colourful character. He was middle aged, tall with a stooped walk, single and loved the great outdoors, having been an ardent walker from his early days living in Devon. From when we first went to his class, Mr Diamond encouraged all of us to keep fit by walking not only the flat plains of East Anglia but further afield in Britain. 'The mind and body,' he fervently explained to us, 'both need to be kept healthy if you are to do well in life.' He was a good laugh especially when he took us for physical education. One autumn afternoon, with most of the leaves having fallen off the school trees, we were playing six a side football when Mr Diamond was knocked senseless by a football that was innocently kicked at his head by one of the girls. Having recovered after several minutes, he picked himself off the ground like a military general and preceded to run, with most of the class following him like clapped out tortoises, round the outside of the football pitches. After completing two laps we all stopped, but Mr Diamond continued for another two more—and when he stopped to talk to us his breathing was normal. Suffice to say he was very fit, and practised what he preached, so we were left in no doubt about his physical competence when it came to looking after himself. After nearly every game of class football or rugby was over—by this time the girls had their own female teacher for physical education—Mr Diamond used to join us with his mud-splattered boys in the showers, which, of course, caused hoots of laughter. Now we knew why a Double Diamond works wonders!

Even during history lessons with Mr Diamond things were great fun where he encouraged both boys and girls to enjoy themselves. He used to stand in front of the class and sing various patriotic songs of the kind that were sung by British soldiers going to or coming home from war. Or he sang songs that were familiar to country folk many years ago, or the passionate songs, as he put it, one overhears coming from a church. He certainly didn't glorify war but he did try to instil in us a love of learning by encouraging us to learn about various cultures around the world. 'History is among other things a branch of knowledge that records an interesting past,' Mr Diamond used to regularly remind us. He thought that learning was a process that should be enjoyed, not just tolerated.

Other subjects in the first year such as Geography, English and Religious Instruction were taught to us by Mr Sands and Mrs Knight. Geography and Religious Instruction were the domains belonging to the ever faithful Mrs Knight who tried to expel the heathen out of us and convert us without success to Christianity. Looking very much like the late Margery Proops, Mrs Knight unfailingly saw the good in all things, even in Billy

MacDonald when he tried to glue soiled underpants to her chair. She also forgave Richard Arrowsmith for urinating in the class store when he explained he had an infection and was unable to reach the toilet. Her faith was surely stretched when she caught Bert Moore and Terry Anderson stealing pencils from her desk to use at home for a forthcoming essay, but forgave them because all they had in mind was their lessons. Sandra Harris was surely stretched to ask for forgiveness from the almighty when Mrs Knight found out that her charge had dug up a few plants from the school garden. When Mrs Knight asked Sandra why she had dug up the plants, her reply was that she was going to donate them to the local charity shop in Yapton. I'm afraid to say that I was not immune from giving Mrs Knight a tough time even though I enjoyed listening to what she had to say about Religious Instruction. My mischievous behaviour is really unforgivable, in the eyes of some, when you consider the following: Religious Instruction textbooks were handed out to the class so we could follow a paragraph that the teacher was about to read out aloud to us. During this time I was busy beavering away drawing Hitler-like moustaches on several pictures of Jesus Christ that were in the textbook. Mrs Knight, still reading to us, started to walk slowly round the classroom and noticed that I had, like a fool, left the defaced pages open. She at once stopped reading, took my textbook to the front of the class and held it aloft for all to see. 'Boys and girls, this is a terrible thing that Richard has done to our saviour Jesus Christ. He has defaced him on several pages of this book by scribbling all over his face. The next person I find doing this sort of thing will be sent immediately to the headmaster.' Mrs Knight made me, quite rightly, remove all the offending scribble. I'm afraid I could not be saved!

English lessons with Mr Sands were completely different to Religious Instruction, whereby from the first lesson he asserted his authority on the class. He was around forty years of age, short, slim with grey thinning hair, and he nearly always wore red colourful bow ties which made us all laugh behind his back. At the time English was the most spoken language in the world; indeed, Mr Sands went to great lengths to make us aware of that fact. 'English spoken correctly, for example in great works of English literature written by Shakespeare, Dickens or D.H. Lawrence, is the finest there is,' he would frequently comment. However, most of the time we spent learning how to use grammar and syntax, how to put words together to form sentences, phrases or clauses. After a while I became interested in the subject and I tried to understand how I could communicate effectively by writing to another person. Somehow Mr Sands had opened up for me, and others in my class, a new world of creativity that appealed to my thoughts and feelings. During the first year he encouraged us to read aloud, in front of our peers, a written piece of our own choice. The piece I chose to read was an excerpt taken from *Angel Pavement* by J.B. Priestley.

With the first academic year over at Rawlinson School, I had done quite well with exams and course work, finishing in a reasonable middle position in my class. It gave my friends and I the opportunity to spend more time together in and around Yapton. But due to the increasing demands placed on us by our various teachers to produce more written work at home, it gave us less time to indulge in our own world of playing games, climbing trees or making a nuisance of ourselves around the village. With the summer holidays in full flow, Richard, Bert and Terry called on me early one morning, around 9am, loaded with fishing tackle for our pre-arranged visit to fish in the River Yare, about three miles from our village. As the buses in those days were infrequent in the countryside we decided to walk there through local farmers' fields. Once we arrived at the river we immediately assembled our fishing lines, fixed bait on the hooks, about twenty feet apart of each other and sat down in earnest to catch fish. The River Yare was well known by local anglers for being stocked with fish such as dace, roach and even the occasional pike. Pike was the one fish none of us had caught before but would dearly love to. That was until there was an almighty shout from Bert who had fallen into the river, but fortunately he was able to swim a hundred feet down the river to safety. 'Sod this, I'm bloody well fucking soaked! I'm 'orf home to get changed into dry clothes.' With that Bert collected his fishing equipment and ran off back to the village. Poor Bert, he did look an awful sight as he walked off down the road soaked from head to toe! We left our fishing lines tied to the river bank as Richard had brought three stolen cigarettes he had taken from his brother Tom. After Richard had lit his cigarette, we once again tried to inhale the smoke, but the strong smell, which resembled horse manure, overwhelmed us. Only Richard managed to keep inhaling the smoke. 'What's the matter with you fairies, can't yer take it!' Richard roared at us. Cigarette smoking was the activity that I never indulged in throughout my life. In fact I thought it anti-social to smoke in front of people within a confined space.

Another time during this summer holiday, Richard, Bert, Terry and I took the bus from Yapton to Norwich Town to watch a cowboy film starring John Wayne at the Loader Cinema. The cinema in essence was a large block of unattractive concrete, known at the time as Brutalist architecture, that provided over 1,100 seats. Having paid our entrance fees, we decided to sit behind three girls, about our age, not far from the back of the cinema. After the film had been showing for about twenty minutes, with most people engrossed by the action, all of a sudden all chaos ensued. Someone to our left had thrown a tub of ice cream which hit a young girl on the head at the front of the cinema. Another ice cream was thrown where we were sitting and this time it splashed all over the coat of a young boy. There was a spontaneous eruption as various objects began to fly all over the cinema and land on innocent people. I retaliated by throwing the ice lolly I was sucking in amongst a large group of young people not far in front of me. Richard, Bert and Terry all followed by throwing anything they had, sweets, chocolates and cigarettes at young boys who were by this stage standing up shouting at the top of their voices for others to stop. Then the film was turned off and the lights came on, quickly followed by cinema staff who were physically restraining people from throwing objects at others. One worker was hit on the head with a tub of ice cream. He clipped the culprit round the head. Minutes later several police officers ran into the cinema shouting at people to refrain from throwing missiles at them. After the police had brought the mayhem under control, we were all ordered to leave the cinema without our names being taken. When we walked outside the cinema we were all hugely relieved that we had not been arrested and our parents would not be informed of our behaviour.

With that unruly incident behind us, we attended assembly for the start of the second academic year at Rawlinson School. My friends in crime and I were very relieved indeed that Mr Bayfield, our headmaster, had not known about our anti-social behaviour (as it is called today). During his annual motivation speech at the beginning of a new academic year to the assembled boys and girls, Mr Bayfield spoke about hard work and success. With that over we filed into a single line, as directed by our form teacher Mr Diamond, and marched out of the large Assembly Hall, past a large shield holding names of all the previous head teachers. We continued marching down a long corridor, like workhouse kids eager for their food, and into the classroom. 'It is good to see all you boys and girls standing here before me, ready for another year of hard academic work in front of you,' said Mr Diamond with a large grin all over his lean face. He then went on to explain the 2nd year syllabus, how we could proceed to find out the relevant textbooks, and then he handed out a sheet of paper to all pupils with dates when homework must be submitted. During most of that academic year we focused on notable dates when England won various wars around the world, led by our so-called great leaders from the front, but not a whisper of those countless individuals who were slaughtered making history for their mother country. And that was something the good Mr Diamond never mentioned, not once, even though he himself was against violence on principle.

The one area where my class friends and I were after seeking some respect was out in the playground, especially during lunch time. We used to race to the school canteen for a quick lunch of usually poorly cooked meat and two vegetables, but I must say the puddings were something else. Fifteen minutes later we were back roaming around the playground looking for a first year boy to punch, or maybe, with a bit of luck, chat up one of the second year girls. During one of these lunch time escapades we had a real set to with boys from the third year. It was all rather fuzzy how the fight actually started, but an innocent onlooker explained later, that six or seven boys crept up behind and began hitting us without any provocation from my friends and I. With the initial attack over we fought back as Richard knocked one of their boys to the ground. We stood toe to toe punching and kicking one another for all we were worth, until all of a sudden, I was grabbed by the collar by a male teacher I had known only by sight. 'Stop fighting you damn fool boy! Where do you think you are, in some sort of cowboy film?' the young teacher shouted angrily at me. 'What is your name boy?' he asked in the same breath. 'Richard Morris, Sir.' By this time boys from both sides had been restrained from fighting by three other teachers including Mr Sands. 'What happened, Morris, why were you all fighting?' asked the young teacher who still appeared to be angry. 'That other lot from the third year just attacked us for no reason,' I blurted out to him. 'We were standing there talking amongst ourselves when that mob came up and punched me on the side of the head,' I continued protesting to the teacher. 'That's enough from all of you. I want all eight of you to walk at once to the headmaster's office and stand outside until I arrive,' said a sullen Mr Sands, renowned for his authoritarian attitude. Suffice to say, all of us were given a good ticking off by the headmaster for fighting, yet we did not receive the cane or any other punishment deemed worthy of such behaviour.

Several weeks later Mr Diamond, also the school football trainer, informed the boys in my class that the forthcoming soccer trials for the school junior team would be held on the football pitch later that week. He went on to explain that the junior team trials were for the first and second year pupils, and the senior team for the third and fourth year pupils. Thank God, I thought to myself, we wouldn't have to do battle with those third year guys we had a fight with four weeks ago, in the school football trials. Before the commencement of the football trials, Mr Diamond had gathered all the boys from our class together to inform us all, that he was aware of the fight we had with the other boys and under no circumstances must it happen again. 'If there is a repeat of your appalling behaviour then none of you will play for the football team,' he said, stating his case most clearly.

On a very warm late afternoon, with school finished for the day, about thirty boys wearing an array of colourful football outfits turned up for the trials. For the first ten minutes we just ran up and down the long pitch spurred on by the many vocal second year girls who were sitting down watching us strut our stuff. After an hour of continually playing football, where I was kicked in the shins at least three times, he made a few positional changes. Due to Bert's crunching tackles on at least three players, Mr Diamond, frightened that most of the team would be unfit for the first match, replaced him with another boy. Mr Diamond called us into a group to explain the trials were now over and we would hear who was in the team within ten days.

Religious Instruction under Mrs Knight was going to take us to loftier heights, as she was taking the class out on a visit to a Norman Church near Dersingham, some thirty miles from the school. We were waiting outside Rawlinson at 9am, when this most attractive blue Leyland coach turned up to drive us to visit St Dunstan Church, a church that could have been built by one of my ancestors. The ninety-minute journey gave us sufficient time to snog our girlfriends, occasionally sometimes a little more daring, at the back of the coach. On the whole, in those sexually innocent days, physical contact with girls meant a kiss and occasional horseplay. My girlfriend for a while was Barbara Tufnell, who was short, thin, always wore lots of make-up and lived in a small village east of Norwich. She was not particularly bright at academic subjects, but was interested in riding horses and looking after animals (not sure if that included humans). I did meet her parents at least three times, but I still wasn't convinced that her father was as intelligent as the family pig.

About thirty giggling noisy children jumped down off the coach some fifty yards from the old Norman Church. 'Now listen to me, boys and girls, to what I am about to say,' Mrs Knight half bellowed across the heads of children who were doing everything but paying attention to our beleaguered teacher. She explained that the history of the old church dated back to not long after the Norman Conquest of England. Dennis quipped that he had had a conquest only last night with Jacky Wilson in a local barn. We all walked into the church led by our Christian teacher. She told us of the local materials, including flint, timber and lime, that were used to build the now ageing church. 'We are now going to climb the many stone steps that will take us to the top of the church. Walk up the stairs in single file and do take your time,' Mrs Knight said, at pains to emphasise this important point. 'When we reach the top we will see why the Normans built here and the strategy they used to empower themselves. For example they were near to a fresh water supply, and a large wood supplied the timber for them to build their homes and pastures to feed their animals,' she said, although no one was listening to her. On top of the church we could see for miles around. All this was rather boring to Bert who took it upon himself to throw a small plastic pot of jam over the side which landed below on someone's grave. 'Sod off Bert, you'll get us all into trouble,' I said to my friend who appeared to be looking for another missile to launch over the side. After an uneventful time at the top of the church, Mrs Knight led the way down the rickety steps to where we congregated outside the church for her to take a group photograph of the assembled brutes.

Back at school, Mr Diamond had pinned up on the notice board the football team to take on Rexley Comprehensive the following week. Three boys from my class had been selected— Richard, Terry and myself. Well, I thought to myself, I hope some of the boys and girls will be impressed by my successful inclusion in the school football team, after fights with various pupils had done my street credibility no favours. Later that day in class Mr Diamond congratulated the three of us for working hard at the trials and we now had the honour of representing Rawlinson School at football. After class that day we ribbed Bert mercilessly about how he should join the girls' netball team. He took it all in good fun.

Later that day, feeling excited at the prospect of informing my parents of my minor success, my friends and I ran for the last bus that took us back to Yapton village green. Bursting with pride, I ran all the way from the bus stop to my house where I gave the great news to my mother who put her arms round me and gave me a big hug. 'Well done Richard, we will have to buy you a new pair of football boots from that new sports shop in Norwich,' said a delighted mother who was full of praise. That evening my father arrived home around 7pm to be greeted by my good news. During the pandemonium you would have thought that I had won something extraordinary, but nonetheless being chosen to play for the school team was a bit special at the tender age of twelve.

Nonetheless, after a long hard day working out in the fields under intense heat with his two brothers, Father was very tired indeed and in need of his dinner. At this stage in his life Father was about thirty-six years of age and was still full of energy and motivation. Farmer Leader had grand plans for the development of his growing farm, whereby Father and my two uncles would be an integral part of that vision. My mother still earned a few welcome pounds in the village shop. Our extended family enjoyed meeting for dinner or small parties especially now that my late paternal grandparents were no longer around as head of the family. Infrequent as it was, I was always pleased to see my two uncles, Eric and Jack, and their two wives, Jane and Sarah, but as the years went by I saw them and their children even less. In my case, that is not surprising, as I worked away from home most of my adult life. Also it is not surprising that social contact became infrequent when you think that all three brothers, working with each other every day, would not want to meet again at night. However, I can remember that on several different occasions Eric jokingly saying to my father, 'Give Richard a drop of cider, Dave, it'll put 'airs round his willy!' My uncles had an extensive range of musical records of the early Rock and Roll artists such as Elvis Presley, Chuck Berry, Gene Vincent and Bill Haley to name but a few. As the year went by, I too collected records by the Beatles, Rolling Stones and Moody Blues but nothing to the extent that my uncles did. Around the same time I also bought a new Philips record player which gave the music I possessed a different and clearer sound. My maternal grandparents used to visit our family infrequently as their interests were elsewhere. It was only by chance, in the village shop for example, that I met my two maternal aunts, Bunny and Sarah. Their husbands, Ted Nugent and Harry Gregg, who were farm workers, saw my father regularly, but visited my parents at our home only on rare occasions. Because their fathers were Catholics, their children attended a religious school in Norwich.

The day of our first football match came round to play Hudson Comprehensive School, a relatively newly built school ten miles from Norwich. The pitch had been reseeded during the summer and looked ideal to play on. After a pre-match discussion with Mr Diamond about playing good clean football, we walked out onto the pitch to cheers, whistles and hoorays coming from our supporters. The main culprits were Bert and Philip who were blasting out noises from their newly acquired trumpets, but personally I loved that kind of loud behaviour, especially from friends. The only one notable incident during the first half was when our captain, Dave Bent, a first year pupil, badly missed a penalty when his kick went at least ten yards wide of the right-hand post, nearly hitting a cat lazing in the sun. 'Never mind that penalty miss,' insisted the animated Mr Diamond, 'go back onto the pitch and play the way we have been practising the last few days.' In the second half we certainly tried our best to follow the instructions of our trainer, but we would have been better off, according to some of our supporters, acting as old donkeys in a knacker's yard. Late in the second half the opposition scored the winning goal to the delight of their few supporters. Back to the drawing board!

'Never mind boys, you will get better in time, don't fret. The first thing you have got to learn is discipline. Training is next Wednesday at 4pm, don't be late.' Mr Diamond's words were reassuring even though some of us doubted we were competitive enough to compete in the inter-schools league. In the following practise match Mr Diamond suggested we do *that* with the ball, do *this* with the ball, run *here* and over *there*. Was this instruction called rocket science or bullshit? More instructions followed that were more relevant to Olympic Athletes than tenth grade footballers as we then were. Football matches both at home and away followed, but we got no more competent at playing football than we did at our first match débâcle. The only match where we demonstrated some sort of credible performance was against a school that only had about one hundred mixed pupils. Even on that occasion we just scraped through by the odd goal. By the end of the playing season we languished at the bottom of the league having only made two points. We were all disappointed by our pathetic football performances, although according to the effervescent Mr Diamond, 'You can only improve boys.' Holding up all the other teams with only two points—I thought that to be an understatement by our soccer guru.

With the second year coming to an end, we had our last English lesson with the resolute Mr Sands. The last term was, for me, the most interesting and enjoyable so far under his teaching. Up until February of the same year I did not look forward that much to attending his lessons due to the dry manner of his teaching even though I found English sharpened and motivated my mind into action. But during the last few months things had changed in that he became more open, friendlier and encouraged feedback from pupils during class time. With that in mind we approached the last piece of work that would conclude the end of term: Write a 1,000 word essay about Winston Churchill.

Summer holidays had come round again for the village lads like my friends and I. No doubt for the next six weeks there would be many good times ahead climbing trees, walking in the countryside, collecting birds' eggs and scrumping fruit from local farmers' orchards. But first of all I had the growing excitement of going on holiday once again with my parents, this time to Great Yarmouth. Father informed us that we were going to live for a week in a chalet, similar to last year, the only difference being that on this occasion we would have to share the large garden with three other families. Having loaded two large brown cases, borrowed from Uncle Jack, containing our holiday equipment into the back of our new Ford Cortina car, we set off for a week away from Yapton. Father sped us along the A47, passing many sleepy villages I had not heard of before, all the way into Great Yarmouth, eventually finding our home for the next week in a quiet cul-de-sac several minutes' walk from the promenade. The chalet had two bedrooms, one living room with dining table, small kitchen and toilet, which were all painted magnolia. My bedroom had a single bed, white small chest of drawers with mirror and red curtains overlooking the small communal garden.

Before breakfast early next day, I was playing in the colourful garden full of summer bedding plants, when I was joined by a young boy about my age whose name was Anthony. ''Allo, want to play do yer?' I asked him. 'I don't mind. I am on 'oliday for another week with me uncle Bob. We 'ad a 'oliday last week, me uncle and me,' came the reply from the rather thin boy with a mop of curly brown hair. 'Anyway what's your name mate?' 'My name is called Richard Morris.' 'That's a funny name init?' he enquired. 'No it ain't a funny name, yours is a funny name.' Mother spoke from the open kitchen window to inform me that breakfast was ready: 'Come along Richard, your breakfast is on the table.' I said goodbye to Anthony and rushed indoors to tell my parents of the boy I had just met in the garden, who, I thought, was a bit odd. 'Where are we going today Dad?' I asked my father, hoping we were going somewhere exciting. 'Down to the beach first of all, and then 'ave somethin' to eat in a cafe somewhere. Will that do young Dicky?' Dad asked me. We eagerly finished our breakfast, collected our beach things together and walked down to the beach passing on the way attractive bungalows and small houses in a quiet residential estate.

When we were on the clean, nearly empty, beach Mother and Father sat down on the two rented deckchairs and I walked along the beach picking up shells, small sized crabs, seaweed and kelp to show my parents. I sat down on the sandy beach and watched the cold sea wash over my skinny white legs. I played around for some time digging holes in the sand with my small spade and making sandcastles that in time would be knocked down by the ferocious sea. There were other boys and girls on the beach running, shouting and jumping as the wind blew soft sand into our faces. For some time I held a small crab that I had caught earlier, in front of me as it anxiously moved its claws trying to seek freedom. After a while Mother called me over to say that I had to dry myself, put my clean clothes on as we were going to a cafe for a meal.

For several days thereafter we visited the beach for a few hours in the morning so that I could play with the sand and run in the sea even though I still couldn't swim. But I was unable to find any old fishermen sitting outside small sheds smoking and repairing their nets, as I had in Cromer. On the last day, when having our breakfast together, Father mentioned that he had been talking to Anthony's uncle who informed him that his mother had committed suicide two years ago after suffering for a long time from drug addiction. The uncle had adopted Anthony and he was doing well after the trauma of finding his mother dead in bed. Father packed our belongings into the car, as I knocked on Anthony's front door to say goodbye to him and his uncle. I was sad to be leaving Yarmouth after another very enjoyable holiday with my parents.

Back home in Yapton, after a truly enjoyable time in Great Yarmouth, I was looking forward to meeting with my friends for another day of adventure in the local woods and fields. The consensus outside the stores was that we should walk east out of the village, over farmer Dutton's field, and then walk about two miles to Goring chalk pits. We eventually arrived some two hours later after taking a detour that took us into an orchard where we took pockets full of ripe Victoria plums. We had no idea who owned the orchard. Goring chalk pits constituted an old landmark for village people all round this part of the world. It's used by mischievous children like us, discreet lovers meeting away from prying eyes, people dumping rubbish, those who require a convenient place for a toilet, and local workers who park here for a cigarette or whatever. It has also been known for police cars to wait there to catch unsuspecting drivers without road fund license or insurance or carrying stolen goods etc. The five of us sat down on the rim of the pit looking down into the centre full of murky water. Over the past few years we had thrown old bikes in there, supermarket trolleys, wood ripped from trees and empty bottles of lemonade. Goring chalk pits has had a most unceremonious past. We all sat there without a worry in the world, unlike years to come later, trying once again to smoke Bert's Old Holborn rolled cigarettes which tasted very much like rope or horse dung. 'Why don't you blokes learn 'ow ter smoke? You 'ave been trying fer ages and still can't do it, can yer?' a stern looking Bert murmured to himself then directly at us. Richard jumped up, 'Fuck this, let's go climbing or scrumping in old Mr Power's orchard or allotment. Me mum needs some fresh veg anyway.' With that we all agreed to go scrumping in Mr Power's well stocked orchard, a place that our gang, and many other local kids, had raided in the past. The old chap himself was a decent God fearing former farmer who at one stage was the tenant of Craggy Farm. He owned several hundred sheep, bred prized Norfolk pigs and was a staunch financial supporter of St Peter's Church.

We all sat quietly devouring Mr Power's blackberries and blackcurrants, when all of a sudden a deafening yell broke the intense silence. 'You fucking kids, get 'orf my land before I send for the police to get you 'orf!" a very angry Mr Power shouted at us some twenty-five yards away at the bottom of his attractive garden. With that we jumped up and ran as fast as frightened rabbits into the nearby Chaley Woods, (owned by a local nature reserve), to hide until it was safe to emerge once again. We walked through the woods down to Spring Bottom, a large clearing in the wood, so that we could climb a few mature oak and elm trees that had been planted over one hundred years ago (by the then owner Colonel Beaumont). After an exciting day we all agreed that tomorrow we were going to walk round the world, but of course we never did.

In no time at all, it seemed, we were back in school for the third academic year. I was now nearly 14 years old. We still had the same teachers, but with an additional teacher, Mr Greaves, who taught us science. He was a kind thoughtful man who emphasized the importance of personal responsibility in all things we attempted. After welcoming back pupils for another year at Rawlinson, with a special message to the new pupils, the headmaster wished us all well as we marched past him in single file out of the assembly hall. During the academic year our history classes with Mr Diamond were interesting as we read a lot about the power of the British Empire, and how it transformed many countries, especially India, where Britain introduced the railways. Under Mrs Knight we were taught how Christian missionaries had taken their religion to various parts of the world to educate non-believers, who they thought were in need of the hand of God. But she failed to inform us that the Christian church supported slavery! With Mrs Knight we also discussed the importance of the Reformation and how it changed the religious culture of Britain. With Mr Sands we developed our oral and written communication skills. I remember the emphasis he placed on being competent enough to write your personal address details on an envelope. When writing a letter, especially a formal letter, 'all the words must be joined up and sit on the line of the page', he constantly reminded us. Science was a subject I found very difficult to understand. After Mr Greaves had demonstrated how to heat a glass tube to a certain temperature using a Bunsen Burner, a gas burner designed by Robert Bunsen in 1899, he expected us to be competent enough to do the same. I'm afraid I was utterly useless at experimenting with most scientific gadgets in the laboratory. Similarly I had the same mentality when it came to metalwork. I just couldn't get the hang of using various implements such as a hammer, chisel or grips, but as I became older, I went on to use many tools and power saws as a forester.

The school senior football team trials had come round for another season. As we changed into our boots for training with Mr Diamond, I was hoping, especially if I was selected for the team, that we would make more of an effort than we did last year when we finished bottom of the league. Well, it transpired that we did better this season than last season, finishing halfway in the league. Two of my classmates and I were chosen to play in most of the football matches, but I was omitted from the team for a while due to fighting in the playground with a pupil from year four. The pupil in question, Terry Butcher, had bumped into me on purpose while we were walking along the school corridor. He aggressively grabbed by the arm saying to me, 'I've 'ad 'nuff of you Morris, who in the fuck do you fink you are, eh! Be out in the playground after lunch for a fight?' With many male pupils making a circle around us, so that no teacher could see us fighting, we laid into each other with fists flying all over the place when the deputy headmistress, Ms Nicholson, shouted at us to stop at once. 'You two boys go immediately and stand outside my office. I will deal with you later!' The consequence of fighting was that two days later, when the headmaster had returned to the school after a minor illness, he gave us both six wallops on our hands with the cane. Similar to most school fights, afterwards we became firm friends.

Now passed my fifteenth birthday, I got a part-time job farm labouring for Mr Heaver at West Ashford Farm, who had a large pig farm next door to where my father worked. Father put in a good word for me. I worked all day Saturdays, and some evenings, as long as it didn't interfere with my schoolwork, as Mother was adamant that learning came first. She didn't want me, nor did Father, working endless hours for small wages with little or no prospects of promotion or security. My job with Mr Heaver also entailed working some days during my school summer holidays, which I did not mind, as I welcomed the money so that I could buy the latest teenage jeans and shoes to attract the girls.

It was while I was working at West Ashford Farm, mucking out the sow and her ten piglets, that I first caught site of the attractive Maria Jackman, a sixteen-year-old old teenager from the nearby village of Denby. She was tallish, slim, had short brown hair and piercing blue eyes and spoke with a slight lisp which was probably brought about by wearing a temporary dental teeth straightener. Her father had a good job working for the RAF as a civilian instructor in nearby Cambridge. As she was a student at Hater College, Maria was working on a three months placement at the farm as one of her four practical placements while studying for a three-year farm management course. She wasn't afraid to use a shovel, get her hands dirty and put her back into loading the barrows with pig dung. I must say, although I fancied her from the outset, I was most reluctant at first to get involved thinking that women should not work alongside men on farms. That attitude of course was a part of my early conditioning. After a few weeks things settled down between us, as we became more confident in each other's company. The inevitable happened one afternoon just as we were finishing our tea break; when I looked at her, she smiled, and I kissed her for what must have for more than a minute, with the stench of pig muck stifling the air. Thereafter we became inseparable for about a year until she successfully passed all her exams and moved away from Norfolk to start her first job as an assistant to the manager on a sheep farm somewhere in Devon. We wrote and phoned each other for about six months until she met another bloke on the farm where she worked. How that first love tortured me when she met someone else!

Due to working most Saturdays it was difficult to meet with my friends. Most of them had also found part-time work farm labouring in and around Yapton, serving in the village stores or delivering milk. As we all became older there appeared to be less time to romp around the countryside, go scrumping or generally idle our time away. During weekdays we were at school which meant leaving home at around 7.30am to take the bus to Norwich. At the earliest we departed from school about 4.00pm, but that could be later if we had to stay behind for being disruptive or whatever. The earliest time the old bone shaker of a bus arrived at Yapton it was gone 5pm. That left very little time for my friends and I to socialise. We did all manage to meet one Saturday at the local community centre, along with many other local teenage boys and girls, for a loud disco run by Dennis Zeal's father. Most of the teenagers there I had known since they were young children, yet here we all were, beyond recognition, dressed in our modern clothes looking stylish and grown up. Some of the girls looked very attractive dressed in sexy miniskirts, high heeled shoes, with cosmetics on their babyish faces. They looked way beyond their real age. Some of those girls had been in the same classes as me for the past ten years. But soon we would all be back at Rawlinson wearing our plain school clothes once again.

Three weeks later a calamitous event badly affected the people of Yapton: Richard Arrowsmith had been knocked down and killed by a car speeding through our beautiful little village late at night. Most of us thought it an outrage that an irresponsible person could drive a car at high speed through our village killing an innocent pedestrian and not having the human decency to stop and help that person, who must have been suffering badly from multiple injuries. A local woman heard a bang, and then a roar of a car, just feet from her terraced home. She then immediately ran out of the house to attend to Richard. The ambulance arrived some twenty minutes later to take Richard to Norwich Hospital for emergency treatment, but he died several hours later without gaining consciousness. The moving funeral service was held in St Peter's church five days later. The motorist was never found. The church was full of people who had known Richard during his short yet energetic life. All his extended family were there, many school friends, teachers from Rawlinson and Yapton schools, and many other people who had recognised him around Yapton. He was buried in the cemetery, next door to the church, alongside some of his family: Richard was my dear friend; we had some great times together walking, climbing, running around the byways of Yapton. Whenever I'm around the village, I always visit Richard to place flowers on his grave and sit on the bench provided by his decent family and think about the wonderful times we all had together.

With Richard's death still a painful memory in my heart, I started my fourth and final year at Rawlinson school, mindful that I had not done particularly well academically so far. Yet I was equally certain that soon I would have to find a job, hopefully, not in the farming industry. I listened to the final motivation speech by the good headmaster. He praised our academic efforts during the past four years. Later in class we all stood in front of our form teacher, Mr Diamond, to praise and witness Richard Arrowsmith's life. In the final year at school we mainly focused on revising for the exams that I would sit, along with most of the fourth year, sometime in May or June the following year. An overall assessment of an individual's work would also include their yearly written work in class. So the grade achieved from exams, combined with schoolwork, was calculated together for an overall position out of 31 pupils. When we had completed all our exams, I personally found them all difficult. The final year drew to a close as we all celebrated the farewell party that was held for our class. About six weeks later I realised that I had done quite well at exams, passing two O-levels and failing three. My overall class position was 12th which was about halfway.

Chapter 2

MY FIRST JOB

NOW NEARLY SIXTEEN years of age, I attended an interview, supported by Mother, with the Youth Employment officer in Norwich, for guidance on the vacant jobs available for young school leavers. The stern middle-aged employment officer, who only had one eye, kept emphasising to me that as I had only passed two O-levels, my personal choice of jobs would be limited. With a wry smile he said, 'Well, Richard, there are vacancies as postmen with the local sorting office. They pay quite well and in time you could be promoted to a senior sorter or even driver.' I didn't fancy doing that, I thought to myself, which also meant getting out of bed at the ungodly hour of about 4am. 'No thank you Mr Osgood,' I replied. I wanted something a little more challenging. 'Well, what else are you interested in, Richard? There are vacancies locally for trainee mechanics, plumbers, porters in Woolworth, the Co-Op are looking for people to work in their warehouse unloading their large lorries which is hard work,' he said, resigning himself to the fact that my lowly job position was inevitable. 'What about working for Courts in their large store just down the road from here—they are looking for a driver's assistant to help deliver furniture to customers' homes in Norfolk?' Mr Osgood continued with a wry smile on his fat face. 'Yes, that sounds okay. What do you think, Mum?' I asked my mother. 'Well, you never know, Richard, it might turn out to be something you will enjoy doing,' she replied, but Mother didn't sound convincing to me. Besides, I thought, I could always work full-time for Mr Heaver even though Mother didn't want me to work for a farmer. 'Richard,' Mr Osgood continued, 'shall I phone Courts to make an interview for you? I know Mr Potts, who is head of personnel. He is a decent man and will help you with any difficulties you may have.' Well I thought, it was better than nothing. 'Yes please Mr Osgood,' I replied. The employment officer duly phoned the above company and arranged an interview for me later that week.

'Please come in Mrs Morris and Richard and sit down there. Now Richard, you have come along here today for an interview for the driver assistant vacancy. What have you been doing at school?'—and so it went on with Mr Potts, a tall, gangly middle-aged man wearing spectacles, who asked me various questions about my education and whatnot... The interview lasted about an hour, and at the close Mr Potts informed me that he would write within three days to let me know whether I was successful or not.

In the meantime I had made contact with a few of my former school buddies to ascertain whether any of them had found a job or not. Bert had had several unsuccessful interviews at Woolworth's and Sainsbury's. Terry felt disillusioned at being given the elbow by a navvy road gang looking for labourers. Dennis was hopeful of getting a hod carrier position on the nearby new housing estate in Norwich. Only Philip had been successful in finding a job with British Railways as a porter based at Norwich Station.

Good news! Courts wrote informing me that I had been successful in my interview and would I commence work four days later, a Monday, at their warehouse in Norwich. Well, I thought to myself, at least I have a job with a regular income until something more promising came along. With some anxiety, I walked through the impressive main gates, manned by three mean looking security guards wearing black uniforms with the gold letters of Courts emblazoned on them, to report to personnel for my first job. As I sat there thinking about all manner of things unrelated to the task in front of me, a young attractive woman walked into the room holding a light blue handbag. She sat opposite me, presumably waiting, like me, and three others to be attended to by personnel staff. I was thinking about farming work, that it must be better than this crummy place, when all of a sudden I realised that the attractively dressed woman opposite me was no other than Daisy Lattimer, the girl who Terry Anderson and I had been naughty to. I remember that while climbing a tree in her garden, I deliberately dropped an apple on Daisy Lattimer's head which had upset her. In those early days she was considered to be a shrinking violet, but as she sat there she appeared to be a rather solid creature. In time, one by one, we were all called into the personnel office to hand in various pieces of information, including my new prized possession: a National insurance number.

Having met some of my new colleagues, a bit of a ragtag bunch, others were out on the road delivering, my new driver colleague and I discussed what the job entailed over a cup of tea, which tasted like Guinness, in the company canteen. Mark was forty years of age, big, strong and full of energy. He had worked for Courts for nearly fifteen years, first joining as a warehouse porter, then showroom assistant and finally as a driver for the last eight years. He was an ardent Norwich City supporter, having had a season ticket for the past ten years. By the time we drove out of Norwich, in a newish light brown Bedford, it was late morning but not too late to make several deliveries that day in small outlying villages. Although not very far from Yapton, I had not been to most of those villages before. By the time I arrived home, I was very tired after humping a large three-piece suite up three flights of stairs. I soon retired to my bedroom and immediately fell asleep, but I had a disturbing dream that night that I had deliberately dropped an armchair on someone's head. Hopefully, I thought, not a sign of things to come. By the time I jumped on the rickety old bus in the mornings to Norwich, had worked all day and afterwards taken the bus back to Yapton, most days consisted of working for about twelve hours. It was at these times, in the early cold wet mornings, that I often thought of contacting Mr Heaver, to ask for my old job back, but somehow I persisted as a lowly driver's assistant.

Most mornings Mark and I, sometimes assisted by porters, used to load the lorry with items of furniture, bedding and so on, to be delivered that same day. Given the opportunity, Mark and I would stop at a transport cafe, not a hundred yards off the main A11 road, or failing that, another cafe near the A47. After visiting the latter cafe, called Archie's, a pretty rough establishment, for a few times, I got into conversation with a young teenage girl about my age called Lucy, who worked there serving and cleaning tables. Lucy was a bit of a scatterbrain but essentially a decent person. She had grown up in Barking, East London, where generations of her family had worked in the London Docks. She had moved with her parents to Norwich six years before when her father relocated with the building company he had worked for since he was a boy. An only child, Lucy did not get on well with her parents, particularly her father, so had chosen to live on her own in a bedsit, but with her parents' consent as she was under the age of eighteen at the time. Although we were both only sixteen years of age at the time, I started staying with Lucy in her small cosy bedsit most weekdays and occasionally at weekends.

Having sex with Lucy was so exciting, but I was afraid that she might become pregnant. My parents were not happy with me at the time, mindful of my age and inexperience and afraid that I was getting myself into deep waters. When I arrived home one evening from work at about 7pm, my parents wanted to discuss my relationship with Lucy. 'You are far too young son to 'ave such an intense relationship with that young girl. You are only sixteen, Richard, and starting to find yer' way in life. You are too young to get mixed up with such a young girl. Why don't yer take things easy and meet just a couple of times a week?' said my father, who cared about me and was only trying to keep me out of harm's way. After spending time discussing my relationship with my parents, I decided to agree with their suggestions and cut down the number of times I visited her each week. When I put my suggestions to Lucy, she agreed with me that we should spend less time together as we were still very young, too young, to have an intense relationship.

Things were going well for me at Courts Furnishing. Mark and I got on well working together and used to have the occasional beer or three together in his village, called Brenchley, which is at least four miles west of Norwich and not that far from Yapton. During these occasional beers, I got to meet Mark's wife, brother and uncle who were all delightful people. Mark's brother, David, worked as a successful self-employed sign writer for many large multi-national companies around Britain. He also occasionally worked abroad, until he decided to buy a franchise and branch out into the complex world of computer engineering. Mark's wife, Tina, was short, attractive with blonde hair. She was like a second mother to me; whenever I saw her in the village she would give me good fashionable second-hand clothes that her younger brother had discarded. The whole of Mark's family were really kind decent people. But after a beer, or two, there was something else I would have liked from Tina. My awakening sexuality was surely attracted to my colleague's attractive wife, whose suggestive smile acted like a magnet.

Sometime later Mark and I delivered a fine looking veneered mahogany coffee table to a large Edwardian detached house in the country village of Rigston in Norfolk. This village only had a few detached houses, but all the occupants were wealthy. According to the wealthy owner of the coffee table, Mrs Elizabeth Howard, there is a record of Rigston dating back to the Domesday Book, when most of the village was owned by a newly installed countryside owner, Basil de Forget, who had fought for William of Normandy. As well as delivering the superb, expensive, coffee table, Mrs Howard requested we take away some old dilapidated furniture that had seen better days. As a 'special favour', as she delicately put it, would we also take away two boxes of old books that were not wanted anymore? 'Regarding the books, gentlemen, I have asked a local charity shop if they want them on three separate occasions, but they have failed to turn up every time. So please do what you like with them,' the charming lady said. 'As for your troubles, please accept ten shillings each. Would you also like a cup of tea, gentlemen?' Ten minutes later a hot cup of tea and a slice of walnut cake were delivered to the large oak kitchen table where we sat. The size of the kitchen alone was bigger than the two downstairs rooms in my parents' home. Where did these people get their money from? What did this woman and /or her husband do to earn a living? 'Please help yourselves to the tea and cake, gentlemen. Have as much as you like. It's tasty, isn't it? I bought it recently from the local Women's Institute,' Mrs Howard commented.

After consuming nearly all the tea and most of the cake, Mark and I removed all the aforementioned goods to the lorry.

As I was returning to the impressive looking house one more time to get the delivery docket signed, Mrs Howard asked Mark and I if we would be interested in knocking her garden into shape for her, as the regular gardener had to retire due to ill-health. The three of us walked round the large garden, full of various flowers, and a small pond with carp, noting what she wanted done. Mrs Howard understood it would be cash in hand work and Mark promised to phone her within a few days to discuss the details. With the promise of a few pounds under our belts, we hoped, we drove the rubbish from the house in Rigston to a large skip that Courts had at their large depot in Norwich. Yes, I thought, I was growing up, living in a man's world and making extra cash gardening for an elegant woman in her big house. Wow!

Given that Lucy and I had had a relationship for many months, I thought that the decent thing to do was to arrange for her to meet my parents. Lucy agreed wholeheartedly with my suggestion. Driving to Yapton in the bus we both felt apprehensive about what my parents would say about our relationship; mindful that at last they were going to meet my girlfriend for the first time. We walked towards the front door of my home, Lucy holding flowers that she had bought my mother, and I a bottle of white wine to have with our dinner. Mother opened the front door and calmly said, 'Come in both of you and take off your coats.' 'Mum, I would like you to meet Lucy,' I rather nervously said. 'Hallo Lucy, so nice to meet you at last. How are you?' said Mother who suggested we all sit down in the front room. 'These roses are for you, Mrs Morris, and the wine for Mr Morris,' said Lucy. 'Thank you so much, love,' said a smiling, yet, nervous mother, as she took the goods into the kitchen. Mother returned with a vase full of beautiful red roses whose scent filled the small front room. 'What are you two 'aving to drink?' 'Thanks Mum. I'll have coffee and Lucy would like a cup of rosy (tea),' I said, hoping to relax the tense atmosphere. We all became decidedly relaxed as we sat down on Mother's new three-piece suite, and started to talk freely amongst ourselves. 'Your Dad won't be 'ome until about 7pm this evening as they are busy on the farm with something,' Mother said, trying to reassure us. 'What about you Lucy, 'ow is work and what is your bedsit like?' Mother asked. 'My job is fine. I take the money at the counter and clean the tables after all those mucky sods like Richard 'ave left. I 'ave a small bedsit in Norwich and I share a toilet with free, sorry, three other girls,' Lucy explained, no doubt still a little nervous after meeting Mother for the first time. 'As you are under eighteen years of age, did your parents give consent for you to live there?' Mother was at pains to know. She had asked me that same question many times in the past year, or so.

Around 8pm my father arrived after a very tiring day working in the fields; digging up food for the cattle and sheep. Most of the year Father worked a twelve-hour day, which left very little time for anything else, particularly socializing. ''Allo love, how are you? Instead of keeping you all to himself, Richard has at last brought you 'ome ter meet us!' Father insisted. 'Well,' Father continued, ''Ow are things with you Lucy? 'Ow is the job? Do they feed you well at work?' 'Yes they look after me all right. The boss is okay, moans from time to time but he 'as his good points.' 'That's good love,' agreed Father. 'Well, as the chicken and roast spuds are now cooked, shall we go to the dining room for our evening meal, and Lucy 'as bought a bottle of white wine for us,' said Mother. With that the four of us sat down to enjoy a delicious meal in a convivial atmosphere. With Mother and Lucy getting on well together, the rest of the weekend went well, although I didn't know my parents' feelings about Lucy and me sleeping together. From my parents' background, especially my mother, they still found sexual relations between people under eighteen difficult to accept. Besides, sexual relationships amongst young people, away from the gaze of adults, had been going on since time immemorial. My father, indeed, had had lots of sex with underage village girls. But I would be most surprised if my mother had had fleeting sexual encounters before marrying my father.

After the end of a few very busy weeks delivering the autumn sales to customers around Norfolk, Mark and I made our way by car to Mrs Howard's home in Rigston to begin our first, belated, gardening session. Her garden was full of various colourful trees, shrubs and flowers, which must have cost her a small fortune over the years. One feature that I particularly enjoyed were the box hedges she had had pruned and shaped into different animals. Mark and I worked for hard four hours in sweltering heat. Just as we were finishing for the day, Mrs Howard drove into the crazy paving drive in her expensive dark blue Rover. 'Good afternoon gentlemen, what a very hot day it is! Ideal for gardening,' she enthused as she closed the driver's door like some ageing Hollywood film star. She came nearer to us to ask how much gardening we had done, and would we like a cold drink? At that moment I smelt the powerful perfume she was wearing on her ageing, yet well maintained feminine body covered with expensive fashionable clothes and what looked like gold jewellery. After we finished our drinks she gave us cash for the work we had done, and we drove off home, pleased, having made a few extra pounds.

Chapter 3

ABSCONDING TO SCOTLAND
WITH MY GIRLFRIEND

LUCY AND I had for some time been discussing moving, or running, away from Norfolk to live somewhere else in country, anywhere, as long as we were together. We thought about moving to the West Country, Wales, Northern England, but eventually we decided on moving to somewhere in Scotland. We felt we didn't know where we were going. We were really too young and immature to make a life together. Neither of us had very much money and, most importantly, we were both under eighteen years even though we thought we loved each other. Most importantly of all, we realised we needed our parents' consent to be able to move away to another part of the country. With the odds stacked against us we impulsively bought two small cases. We bought two single tickets to Glasgow at the local station and jumped on the train for London. Arriving at Liverpool Street station two hours later, we looked like two lost sheep eagerly trying to find their mother for comfort. Rather stupidly we had absconded from our secure way of life, and, of course, we didn't know what lay ahead for us, but we didn't much care. The station loudspeaker nearly overwhelmed me—I couldn't hear what Lucy had to say in the alien world that surrounded us. 'I think we should go back to Norfolk,' I said to Lucy, as I was feeling frightened. Sitting in a platform waiting room, away from the irritating hissing noise of steam engines, allowed us to relax somewhat until an elderly passenger, in the same room, asked us whether we were lost. We explained we wanted to go to Euston station to take the train to Glasgow. She kindly explained which underground trains to take; but as it was the first time for me, I hated every minute of the cramped claustrophobic journey until we reached our destination. Coming from Barking, Lucy had experience of using the underground trains many times before.

On a cold September day, we boarded the long train bound for Glasgow at around 4pm; and walked through several carriages until we found a vacant table where we could sit down and relax for the first time since we impulsively left Norwich early that morning. I deliberately sat opposite Lucy, not next to her, as I wanted to see how she was: I also had some questions to ask her about our trip to Scotland, realising that it was not too late to turn back for home. 'Lucy, are yer' all right, shall we go back 'ome, it is not too late?' I asked her. She thought about it for a while. 'I want to keep going to Glasgow and see what turns up for us. Besides I don't really like my parents that much, especially my dad who is a right pig sometimes,' she confidentially told me. I was somewhat surprised by what she had to say about her father. 'As we 'ave discussed before Lucy, we are breaking the law especially when our parents find out that we've absconded,' I said pessimistically. What kind of law it was and what it meant we didn't have a clue. At first, when we decided to run away, we didn't even realise we were breaking the law until Mark informed me. According to Mark, in the eyes of the law, we were still classed as minors until we reached the age of eighteen. I must admit Mark did encourage us not to abscond, but to discuss our relationship with both sets of parents who should understand our problem. Furthermore, he told me that if the police were to start asking him questions about the disappearance of Lucy and me, he would have to tell them the truth, which I thought was honest of him. As the train gathered speed, I became ever anxious every time an older person with a suit looked at me, as I thought them to be a police officer, or social worker, or private investigator. But when I managed to relax, I realised that neither parents would have known our intentions at this early stage. Instead of running away like two fugitives on the run from prison, I realised that we only had to wait for a few months, then we would be over eighteen, which meant we could go anywhere. Lucy took out the sandwiches she had made the night before, and I walked through about three carriages to buy tea for us. Walking, or half stumbling, due to the unsteady train, I observed the number of young people on the train who might be going home after an unhappy time. Or they could be, like Lucy and I, running away from their parents to seek their fortune elsewhere. Back at the table, Lucy had lit up a cigarette she occasionally enjoyed when things became tough for her.

The long maroon coloured train was approaching Glasgow. I kept thinking over in my mind, shall I phone my parents to tell them we are safe? Yes, I thought, I'm going to phone them without letting Lucy know of my intentions. No, I thought again, I had better not do that, otherwise she would not trust me in the future. Fuck it, I thought to myself, what shall I do? Passengers started to get up as the train slowly, hissing and puffing, came to a standstill on platform 10 at Glasgow Central station. We let most of the other passengers get off first, when minutes later, we found ourselves the last people left in the carriage. Lucy jumped down onto the platform, quickly followed by the two brown cases that I handed to her. There we both stood on the freezing dark, lonely platform with nowhere in the world to go. Our immediate environment consisted of dirty carriages, litter-strewn platforms and someone announcing the names of places that I had never heard of before. Filthy pigeons pecked at anything that resembled food. Several of them sat on the large station clock as it struck 9pm. From the corner of my left eye I observed two tramps picking up cigarette ends and smoking them. I thought that might be me sometime in the future. As we approached the station concourse we found that the tea stall had closed, porters walked round us sweeping up anything that stood still. What had we done to deserve this Dante-like hell that was unfolding before our eyes? Tentatively I approached one of the porters to ask where we could find somewhere to sleep for the night. 'Where yer cum from Jimmy?' the young porter asked me. 'I'm from Norfolk,' I said half-heartedly. 'Where in the feck is that Jimmy?' he said. I found it difficult to understand him. By this time both Lucy and I felt somewhat depressed at the predicament we found ourselves in.

Having phoned the number on a card advertising B&B accommodation outside the station in Union Street, which perked our spirits up a little; we were told to take a no7 bus to a place called Briarwood, only one mile away. On arrival at the large rambling Victorian house, which had an evil smell of curry coming from downstairs, we knocked on the front door. A middle-aged woman opened the green door holding a young half naked baby. 'Hello young people, did yers phone me fifteen minutes ago? Aye yer did at that. Come in out of the cold and warm yer selves laddie and lassie.' Inside, the hall was dark, dingy and dilapidated. Molly, the landlady, took us up the stairs, covered in threadbare carpet, and showed us to our first floor bedsit. 'Here is your key, what's yer name by the way? Right. The keys open the bedsit door and the front door. Now what is yer names?' she asked us again. 'My name is Richard and this is Lucy,' I said, even though I was reluctant to tell her our real names. 'Now yers young ones, as I told yer earlier over the phone, it is £3 per person, per night for bed and breakfast.

You can pay me tomorrow morning after breakfast. Okay. Just tell me if yer want to stay on here okay, that is no problem.' As Molly handed me the bedsit key, her breath smelt like a brewery; it nearly knocked me sideways back down the stairs.

We opened the bedsit door and walked into the bedroom that even the Salvation Army would have been embarrassed to show one of their prospective customers. At this stage, I felt like jumping out of the window as anger welled up inside me for having put Lucy, as I thought, through this humiliation. Even with the dim light on, one could barely see from one side of the twelve foot square room to the other. It resembled an interrogation room, like the infamous room 101 referred to in Orwell's *Nineteen Eighty Four*. 'Lucy, I blame myself for 'aving put yer through this. I wouldn't be so unkind as to put one of Mr Heaver's pigs in this shit house. Do yer want me to phone our parents to explain what we 'ave done?' I said as tears welled up inside me. 'No, let's continue, Rich. Give it a few days before we do anyfink,' Lucy said. She smiled and put her arms round my neck and placed her warm body against mine. We stayed in that secure, cosy position for several minutes until the silence was broken by the noise above us by two men shouting at each other. The walls and ceiling of our room were a dirty magnolia; the double bed had a dirty bed sheet and the three blankets had various coloured stains on them. There was a three-draw tallboy, plastic curtains that had not been washed since Queen Victoria's state funeral, and a small bathroom with a cracked bath and toilet that was not worthy of its name. The whole bedsit had no redeeming qualities whatsoever: we could easily have started crying about the terrible plight we were in, but instead we held each other and just laughed and laughed and laughed. Things, I thought, cannot get any worse than this!

Due to the filthy state of the sheets we both slept with some of our clothes on. After a good night's sleep of about eight hours, we awoke around 8am to a new day as the early morning light shone through the clapped out curtains. I opened the bedroom window, which had moss growing on the glass inside, to gulp fresh air into my lungs, as the putrid smell of the villainous curry from last night hung in the air, like pig shit in a sty. About ten minutes later the two guys above were at each other's throats again swearing and shouting that lasted a full five minutes. Shakespearean actors they were not. We both managed to have a bit of a wash, but drying ourselves on the foul looking towel would have been dangerous, so we used one of my shirts instead. During the past twenty-four hours I had experienced a roller coaster of emotions—from extreme happiness to deep depression. As Lucy had lived on her own for two years, I got the impression that she was not fazed by what had happened since we first left Norwich.

Feeling a little more human, we plucked up enough courage to walk down into the dining room for our breakfast. 'Good mornin' young ones, did yer sleep well? Good yer did. Well breakfast is egg, bacon, sausage and fried slice okay? Yers both having it? Good.' I'm afraid to say that Molly was even uglier this morning than she was last night. She had no teeth in her evil smelling mouth, and her breasts were sagging near her waist. With that in mind, I thought about the quality of our breakfasts at being manhandled by Molly's filthy hands. However, ten minutes later she returned with our fatty breakfasts, on cracked plates. They were edible even though she had left a Walls sausages sticker on the side of my plate. I had felt somewhat self-conscious when I first entered the dining room, but after I had finished eating, I had the confidence to have a quick look round the grubby room. There were about ten men sitting at one large table, all of them apparently under 30 years of age, most of them smoking. They were discussing building job vacancies on the extension to Glasgow Central. One of them, a Geordie, said, smiling to Lucy and I, 'Good morning youngsters, how's it going?' 'Fine,' I said, without really thinking about it. Just as Lucy and I were leaving the brightly lit, emulsion painted dining room, Molly came in with a cigarette in her hand. 'Come on yers bloody riff-raff get out of this room, I wanna clean the bloody thing,' she said in her deep Glaswegian accent. We told Molly that we would require accommodation at least one more night!

Lucy and I had been informed by Molly that whatever we were looking for, a job, accommodation, theatre tickets or second-hand clothes, one had to buy the local paper called the *Glasgow Herald*. No sooner had we left the B&B, than we came across a small corner shop where we bought the aforementioned paper. Central to our thoughts was to rent a small bedsit, not B&B, so that we could be independent and fend for ourselves; but looking at some of the adverts we thought that an option beyond our current financial means. As both of us had withdrawn all our meagre savings from our post office accounts in Norwich, we knew we had to be mindful about how much we were spending. It was probably the case that at some stage, sooner rather than later, we would have to find a job somewhere in this large city. Needing accommodation first, we thought, we made arrangements to look at a bedsit the other side of town in a place called Paisley. 'Good morning, please come in,' was the kind response we got from a fresh looking young local woman. 'You both look very young to be finding bedsits. Are you both over eighteen? Aye, you don't look it and so far from home by the sound of your accent. Never mind, the bedsit is on the first floor,' the friendly, yet inquisitive woman told us. The modern semi-detached house was like a five-star luxury hotel compared to the hovel where we were currently staying. Inside the bedsit itself, the decoration was bright, there was a double bed, a large set of polished drawers for our clothes and the bathroom was clean. 'We like the room, how much is it?' I asked, anxious that we must get a bedsit sooner rather than later. 'That room is £20 per week which does not include your gas heating and hot water. There is a machine over there next to the wardrobe that takes two shilling pieces,' she explained sympathetically. She had realised that we were unable to afford the rent, as we despondently left the house. We saw two other small, yet comfortable, bedsits that day but both were too expensive. Even though both of us felt rather depressed about the insecure position we found ourselves in, we were reluctant to drown our sorrows by spending our meagre savings in a pub. We cuddled to reassure us both that we were doing the right things for the right reasons. Besides, if being young, energetic and determined was a factor, then we would succeed.

After eating cold fish and chips out of a soggy *News of the World* newspaper, and walking aimlessly round the streets of Glasgow trying to find accommodation, we returned late that night to our B&B. Once in our room, we opened two bottles of pale ale and lit up a cigarette each so that we could forget, if only temporarily, our current crisis. We fell asleep some time later, the two guys above arguing once again, with the noise ringing in our ears. Having left the window open all night, we woke at around 6am fully clothed, minus our shoes, to the sweet smell of fresh air in our nostrils. Washing my face and hands in the bathroom basin with hot water, yes *hot* water, I came to the conclusion that even the bugs had done a runner from this unhealthy place. 'How are yer Lucy?' I enquired, as I thought she was finding things quite difficult. 'Don't keep asking me that for god sake, yer must 'ave asked me that twenty bloody times yesterday,' Lucy angrily replied. 'Sorry

Luce, I was only concerned for yer. Let's not start arguing again. We 'ave each other, don't we?'

An hour later we descended into the smoke-filled dining room for our breakfast as most of the group from yesterday sat talking amongst themselves. 'Good mornin' young ones, how did things go yesterday? Did yers find what you were looking for?' asked Molly, who was in her usual ebullient mood. 'Same cooked breakfast for yers? Good, Aye.' We ate our breakfast, and quickly left the house to buy the local morning paper once again, to try and find cheap suitable accommodation somewhere, anywhere, in this Godforsaken city. We phoned three vacancies, from a phone box full of smelly old chips on the floor, but they were all filled. Full of optimism, we phoned the Mayflower Hotel about residential cleaning jobs but they too were filled. That afternoon, walking along the busy main street in Glasgow, Union Street, on a bright warm sunny day, we noticed a card stuck to the window of a pub, The Highlander, advertising for a cleaner/potman. We walked in, asked for two halves of Youngers beer, and enquired from the young attractive woman who served us if the job was still available. 'Aye it is. Wait there, I get the manager for yers.' Things were looking up I told myself. Ten minutes later the tall, fat, middle-aged manager sat down at our table. 'Yer lookin' for the cleaner vacancy young man? Do yer have experience at this work?' he politely asked. 'No I don't 'ave any experience,' I nervously said to him. 'Well I'm sorry, young man, I'm looking for an experienced person as this pub gets packed evenings and weekends, so you have te know what yer are doing, sorry.' As he got up, he smiled and winked at me. At this stage I became depressed again feeling that everything and everyone was against us as we finished our beer and walked back out into the heaving mass of humanity. At that moment a feeling of freedom, of breaking away came across me not for the first time. Many times, even before I left school, I have had these strong feelings of wanting to move away from Yapton, even though my family and friends lived there. It had nothing to do with Yapton per se, but it was a constant desire to travel, to work in other places, and experience the nature of life, whatever that is.

For the rest of that day, and several days thereafter, we spent our dwindling resources phoning vacant accommodation adverts in and around Glasgow without success. We bought other local newspapers, magazines and phoned accommodation advertised in shop windows, but all to no avail. In desperation we also tried an accommodation agency; they didn't want to help either, because they required a sizeable deposit, and besides their market was aimed at professional people. We also phoned several job vacancies, some of them residential, but they all gave us the same depressing response. As we were not yet eighteen, we were most reluctant to use the employment exchange as they could find out our age by our insurance numbers. Due to our financial predicament there was very little else we could do to find work and/or accommodation. 'I'm sorry to ask again, Lucy, but shall I phone my parents to explain the dire situation we are in? They might not be alarmed if we tell 'em where we are and we are both well. We can also phone your parents, can't we?' I asked, trying to be helpful, and at the same time trying to support Lucy. I could even phone Mark, I thought, and ask him for advice. By now Mark must have told Courts the reason why I was not at work, and my parents must have phoned the police. That must also have been the same for Lucy. Her employer and parents must be worried by her absence; this realisation dug deeper inside me. Several times I thought about contacting the police to explain things. 'Lucy, I'm getting concerned about our parents as they will be worrying themselves about where we are. Don't you think we must now phone the police?' I said. Lucy responded by saying, 'Sod my parents and sod that fat employer of mine! Why should I care?' I realised, as the days went by, that there was another side of Lucy, a much tougher resilient side that I had not been aware of before. Lucy was a lot stronger than I had given her credit for.

A few days later we got a break when a hotel wrote to our B&B to inform us that we had been successful in applying for the residential cleaner and gardener vacancy, although we had to falsify information about ourselves. No sooner had we received the letter, than I ran to the local phone to confirm with the manager of the Victory Hotel that Lucy and I would be starting employment the following Monday. Wow, at last! After several weeks of phoning numerous job and accommodation vacancies, we had been successful after searching a great deal of Glasgow on foot. As Monday morning arrived at last, we put all our clothes and shoes into the two cases, tidied the room, went downstairs to pay our bill. We didn't even bother with breakfast, we just ran out of the house, as fast as our feet could carry us, into the street to begin a new chapter for us. Bus 65 took us the whole way to the Victory Hotel, which was in the area of Carling, three miles east of Glasgow bus station. As we stood on the road outside, we saw that the hotel was a fine looking Victorian red brick building. We couldn't believe that our good luck was turning for the better. There were two large gardens at the front of the hotel, full of various shrubs and flowers, although due to the time of the year, most were past their best except for four attractive evergreen yew trees. Round the back of the hotel was one large well-maintained lawn for customers to use at their leisure. Being well suited and booted for the occasion, I had bought a smart blue suit from a charity shop only last week, we walked into the reception and found the manager, Mr Cameron, who welcomed us. After various formalities had been sorted out in his small yet comfortable office, the manager, a short, stout, balding well-spoken Scot of about fifty, escorted us to our staff accommodation on the top floor of the east wing of the five-story building. We had one large well-furnished room, with a spacious colourful bathroom and toilet, overlooking the back of the garden with fine views of hills beyond. The large room was furnished with a double bed with clean blue blankets, two comfortable armchairs, a set of drawers for our clothes, a polished wardrobe, television, radio, and included attractive yellow pelmets and curtains. The room itself was painted in a brilliant white finish. After Molly's run-down fleapit, we couldn't believe our good fortune that we were now working in a four-star hotel which included our own accommodation, all our meals and a small wage. As the jobs were seasonal for six months, we just hoped that they would not have checked all the information we gave them; if they did, then we would be back out on the streets again, aimlessly walking around Glasgow.

After meeting some of our new colleagues over staff lunch, we were given a conducted tour of the hotel by Jane, who had been working in the hotel for two years as a cleaner. The three of us walked from floor to floor, as Jane pointed out that the third and fourth floors were the bedrooms that Lucy would clean; we tried to act as if we were very impressed by her guidance. Fortunately, there was a sizeable lift that could be used, Lucy pointed out, for heavier and bulkier goods, by staff and customers. With the tour complete, I was taken down to the rear garden briefly to meet David, who was the maintenance person and part-time gardener, before they employed me. With years of practical knowledge of trees, flowers, shrubs and so on behind me, I was confident I could do the job well. When I had first met the manager at the interview, he took me round the garden to ask various questions about the names of flowers.

'When would you prune and feed them?' he asked. Afterwards when we had finished in the garden and were back in his office, he commented, 'I'm very impressed by your gardening knowledge, young man.'

Around 8am next day, Lucy and I stood outside the manager's office where we were introduced to more of our colleagues. 'Dear staff, I would like you to meet Lucy and Richard who start work today,' said the manager. He went on to explain, sounding very much like a regimental sergeant major, what he wanted the staff to accomplish that day in the hotel. We then walked our separate ways—I went to the garden to meet David. 'Hi, morning Dave, we meet again,' I said. 'Good morning Richard, on your first working day?' he said with a cheery smile on his thin, lined face. David had worked at the hotel for many years, he wasn't quite sure how many, first as a kitchen porter and the last five years doing maintenance, but they called in a contractor for the sizeable repairs he was unable to sort out on his own. He was about fifty years of age, short, lean with tattoos all over his arms. Half his teeth were missing, the result of the many street fights he had had when he was young man living in a tough area of Glasgow. 'Aye Richard, we had some fights in those days after a bellyful of booze inside us!' David explained on more than one occasion. He took me to the large painted shed down at the bottom of the garden, to show me the various machines and tools that were available to me now that I was responsible for the upkeep of the attractive communal gardens. Today, like most of my days at the Victoria Hotel, I would first of all walk round the front and back of the gardens picking up all the litter that had accumulated in the previous twelve hours. Afterwards I lightly pruned the plants, did a little weeding and collected fallen leaves; every two days I watered the remainder of the summer plants such as the petunias, and occasionally, I lightly ran the new Mountfield mower over the well-maintained lawn. Now into October, with the growing season nearly over, my gardening job was a bit of a doddle, especially when it was raining, as all I could do was sit in the shed pre-occupied with thoughts of my parents, who by now must have be frantic, worrying about my well-being. And what about Lucy's parents—they too must be worried about the disappearance of their young daughter, wouldn't they? Also, what would my dear friends in Yapton be thinking as they had not seen or heard from me for over two months.

After finishing our work one late afternoon, Lucy and I met to have tea and a sandwich with other colleagues in the employee canteen. The place was good for a chin-wag, listening to the new hotel gossip, and who was going where/when and how. Back in our room later, Lucy explained that, unlike my job, she worked hard most days, hoovering, cleaning, changing sheets and polishing customers' bedrooms. Most days all she looked forward to was to be on her own for a quiet cigarette and a cup of tea, resting her shoeless feet on a stool in our room. 'Gawd, I've never worked so fucking 'ard in all me life! They don't let you stop for a breaver 'ere yer know,' explained Lucy, as she painfully looked at me for reassurance. 'I'm sorry things are tough, Lucy. Look, don't yer think we should now phone our parents, just to let them know we are safe?' I appealed to her once again. 'Okay,' she conceded, and added, 'Look, give it a few days and then we will.' But I wasn't convinced that she wanted to. On that day, like most cold autumn days in Glasgow, it was always raining. We had the luxury of turning the central heating on and taking a shower to soothe our tense and anxious bodies.

Two hours later we walked into the staff canteen for our evening meal with other colleagues, who were resident like

Lucy and I. Amongst others, Jane sat there on her own reading a Mills and Boon romantic novel, which she appeared very engrossed in. 'Hi there Jane, how's it going?' I asked. She looked up from her book somewhat shocked by our presence. 'Aye, hallo Richard and Lucy; sorry, I didn't hear yers come in. How's things going right now, all right I hope?' 'Yep fine,'— what else could I say? Jane was a big strong young woman around twenty-five years, originally from Aberdeen. She looked like an ideal candidate for tossing the caber. Jane had worked at the hotel for several years as a cleaner. On her days off she loved nothing more than sinking a few beers or 'heavy', as it was called in Glasgow. At times, especially when she had been drinking, she reminded me of a sumo wrestler. The cook, Mrs Morrison, who was fat with massive arms, brought in our hot steaming meal from the adjacent room. 'That will put hairs on yer willy Richard,' said the laughing Mrs Morrison. After working all day in the cold wet miserable hotel gardens, there was nothing so good as eating one of Mrs Morrison's substantial plates of stew to put a glow back on your face. Food that would put Molly's pig swill to shame! By this time we had been joined by two other colleagues, John and Helena. 'Hi, good evening everyone,' they said in unison. Both John and Helena had moved from Perth, where they had lived together before successfully applying to the Victory Hotel for vacancies as cleaners. In Perth they had been unemployed for some considerable time, which exacerbated John's long standing bouts of depression. Being employed had helped him recover somewhat. Both of them were in their late 20s, intelligent and attractive.

When we had finished our meals, the five of us got into discussion about the local social life in and around Carling. The consensus was that the area was well served by several decent pubs but if you preferred going to a nightclub, then one had to travel into the centre of Glasgow. A few days later John, Helena, Jane, Lucy and I late one evening took a stroll down to a local pub, recommended by Jane, called The Highlander. It was a typical pub that could be found all over Scotland; which was full of working class people playing loud music on the jukebox, swilling down pint after pint of the local heavy and regular heated arguments, all in an atmosphere of dense smoke. After several pints inside her, I didn't understand one word of what Jane was saying when in conversation with local people. 'Shit yer' fuckin' gob,' was one of her post-drunken eloquent statements! For the first few weeks I assumed that local Scots were looking for someone called Ken, as Jane used to regularly ask me, 'do you ken'! It transpired that the name ken means to have knowledge of, to know. Around closing time many of the locals would start dancing, not just in the bar, but also outside on the pavement to the detriment of some of the local people's sanity. Many times the police were called to break up a fight inside the bar, or outside, depending on the time of the evening, and how much heavy the local tearaways had consumed. The two other pubs in the area, called The Tartan Prince and The Bonnie Prince Charlie, were very similar in nature, but the only discernible difference was that The Highlander used to get more of its windows broken. Whenever we went out for a beer locally it would invariably be in the toughest and roughest pub, The Highlander.

On several occasions when we were on our own, also on occasions with John and Helena, Lucy and I used to take a bus into central Glasgow for a night of disco dancing in one of the many clubs that were around in those days. Most of the clubs were well run without any real trouble but one or two were notorious for fighting, drunkenness or smoking of cannabis. Only once did we witness a nasty fight where about ten men used bottles, chairs and boots to not only beat up each other, but also to smash up the inside of the club. For some unknown reason there was always a sniff of violence in the air during those days in Glasgow. After a while we only took the bus to Glasgow to visit a cinema or restaurant.

About two weeks later, after finishing my well-cooked lunch, I walked out of the canteen and along the corridor as usual and picked up the free weekly paper, *Glasgow Echo*, so that I could read it later on in the garden shed. The trusty old shed had become my second home. They were delivered free of charge to the hotel. To help out pressed colleagues elsewhere in the hotel, I started hoovering the large carpets in the public dining areas. I was pleased to help as sometimes doing nothing can be boring and even counter-productive. Back in the shed later that afternoon, I opened the *Glasgow Herald* to read the sports news, and if extremely bored I would scan the personal advertisements to see if any local women were looking for a young boyfriend. Upon opening the *Herald* at page 5, I saw with great horror a photograph of Lucy and I with the headlines, 'Have you seen underage missing sweethearts! They have been seen in Glasgow, London, Aberdeen and Torquay', splashed all over the page. I was dumbfounded! I did not know what to do, and with Lucy still working, I remained in the shed to try and think things out. Should I walk rapidly to the hotel and discard all the free newspapers everywhere? But what about the national newspapers that customers had brought in with them? And I wasn't to know whether the other local papers had also advertised 'missing sweethearts', article or not. I continued sitting in the shed feeling terrible until 5pm, then with the paper safely inside my shirt, and trying not to make eye contact with other people, I walked casually back to my room where I found Lucy sitting down drinking tea and smoking a cigarette. I thrust the paper article in front of her, blurting out to her: 'Lucy, look at the photograph of you and me, and a long article about us being underage missin' sweet'earts in the local newspaper!' 'Fuck me, I can't believe it!' Lucy stared up at me with a lost look on her face. 'What shall we do Rich? I fink we... let's go to the police and tell them everyfink!' Lucy looked cross as she mumbles these words to me. What we didn't know was whether anyone else where we worked had read the article or seen our photographs. Rather prematurely we started to discuss leaving our work and moving to another part of the country where we might not be recognised. 'What we could do is shave off our 'air or bleach our 'air another colour, or you Rich could grow a beard; but as you only 'ave bum fluff round your chin it would take months.' We discussed our problem like professional gangsters trying to avoid Interpol.

We both agreed to carry on as usual and not draw attention to ourselves. That night we still went along for our evening meal with other colleagues in the staff canteen. Also there dining were three other colleagues, Bill, Bonny and Linda, and although they were resident kitchen assistants, most of the time they ate earlier than us or would eat out somewhere else. They were all in their early 20s, worked part-time and attended college on the government sponsored work-based scheme that gave young people, who didn't have prior qualifications, the opportunity to learn new skills and experience leading to a new qualification recognised by the catering industry. You could tell that all of them were eager to be successful: when I saw them, or sometimes when I thought of them, I had   overwhelming feelings of insecurity as I fantasized that I too was on the same course bound for success!

Encouraged by the manager, one of the elderly customers tracked me down to the rear garden as she wanted her new beige coloured Citroen washed and polished. Mrs Blomstein was a regular at the Victory Hotel; she had been residing there at least four times a year for the last six or seven years as she had to negotiate business dealings with cloth buyers from around the world. She owned many women's clothing shops and boutiques in Glasgow, Aberdeen, Leeds, Manchester, Liverpool and London. She was an influential buyer, known in the fashion industry for having an astute eye for details, which had made her a wealthy woman. 'Hallo young man, I've not seen you around before or have I? I am nearly always so busy that I don't get the opportunity to talk with you all. I must try in future. Mr Cameron told me that you are the ideal person to give my rather dirty car a good wash with hot water and shampoo,' she said, as she smiled provocatively at me in a similar way as Mrs Howard did. Neither of them was ravishingly attractive but they oozed power that lots of men seek out. Mind you, I would not have minded being her toy boy.

Sheltering from another Scottish downpour in my humble abode called the shed—I had by this time repainted the inside—I sat down on my old rickety chair feeling insecure as Christmas was nearly upon us. Although there would be annual festivities in the hotel for staff and customers alike, it would be no substitute for the wonderful Christmas parties I've had with family and friends over the years. Father always cooked a local farm reared turkey for the extended family which nearly always provided enough food for three days. Besides, it is great fun receiving cards and presents from various family and friends even though you saw very little of them for the rest of the year. Amongst other things, Christmas was a time for families to celebrate their good fortune, and to remind them of shared responsibilities. I used to love the various local groups, who used to come round the neighbourhood carol singing; Mother used to give them all hot mince pies. Also, I thought of my colleagues, or rather former colleagues, wondering whether they were going to celebrate Christmas together in the local White Hart pub, just as they had done during the last two years when I was there. Mark, my former colleague, whom I got on with so well, also came to my mind. I wondered if he was still gardening for Mrs Howard, and dare I mention it, had they become lovers? And of course, I also thought of dear Lucy who must be feeling really insecure knowing her family in Norwich must be worrying about her. I'm sure her family all missed her terribly. Lucy and I sometimes felt like freaks, misfits and outcasts just for following, what could be termed, our natural instincts.

Opening the shed door, Dave woke me from my little reverie. 'How's it going? His master, Mr Cameron, wants to see you straight away. He didn't say what for.' 'Okay Dave, thanks,' I said as I jumped up off the chair and made my way along to his office. I knocked twice on the attractive oak stained door. 'Come in!' roared Mr Cameron. As I entered the warm room, I was confronted by two rather large official looking men dressed in suits. Lucy was seated next to the small window crying. 'Sit down Richard,' said a solemn looking Mr Cameron. 'Hallo Richard, my name is Detective Russell, this is my colleague Constable Matthew—we are here because both your parents have reported you missing. And as you are both under the age of eighteen, you are considered under the law to be both minors. Your parents have gone to their local police raising concerns about your well-being, so we have to take you into legal custody until such time as you can both be re-united with your families once again,' the officer explained in a clear and friendly manner. He went on to further explain that we would be taken to Glasgow social services, where we would be looked after by a social worker until tomorrow when an official would escort us by train to London. There our parents would drive us home to Norfolk: I felt great relief that it was all over.

On a wet, cold morning, carrying our two cases, we boarded the London-bound train escorted by a young female social worker, named Hilary Yeats. She was a quietly spoken and friendly person who during the five-hour journey bought us refreshments and a paper to read. During the tense train journey home, I reflected on the time, nearly four months ago, when Lucy and I had made the short sighted trip to Glasgow. Most of the time we had spent there was fraught with anxiety and insecurity. Now we were both looking forward to meeting our parents. As we approached Euston station, Hilary explained that our parents were waiting for us in the station police office, where they had to sign a few legal documents transferring our legal custody from Glasgow social services to our parents. On arrival at the police office both parents rushed forward to hug and put their arms round us. Understandably, both mothers were crying as they were now reassured that their children, that is what we were in the eyes of the law, were now safely back with them. During the car journey back to Yapton very little was actually said; suffice to say, my parents were much relieved that I was back home: I was so sorry for what I had put my parents through.

My parents gave me time to relax and find my feet again, after nearly four interesting months gallivanting around Glasgow. It was so reassuring to meet my old friends Bert, Terry, Dennis and Philip once again. We discussed the two different places where Lucy and I had lived, and how the first one wasn't habitable, even for one of Mr Leader's fat sows to suckle her piglets. We did enjoy working in Victory Hotel, even though we did not get the opportunity to say goodbye to our good humoured, decent colleagues over a pint of heavy. But of course it was very good to be home with my family and friends again in the place of my birth, Yapton. Our conversation changed somewhat, as we went on to discuss our late dear friend, Richard Arrowsmith. 'Now that we are altogether lads, shall we go across to visit Richard's grave and place flowers on it?' I said enthusiastically to the others. 'What a good idea Rich,' Bert said. 'Me too. I'm up for it man,' cried Dennis. 'Come on man, let's go down the village shop and buy a few bunches for our dear friend,' Philip concurred. The five of us sat there looking rather sad at the last resting place of our friend and fellow adventurer, Richard. His gravestone read: 'In loving memory of our dear son and grandson.' No more tree climbing, country walking, stealing fruit from orchards, visiting discos, smoking fags or any other morally reprehensible behaviour together. But who knows that wherever he has gone, there may be similar people determined to enjoy themselves just as he had always done.

Chapter 4

MY STINT IN THE MERCHANT NAVY

IT WAS JANUARY 1968, and I was now eighteen years of age; if only Lucy and I could have stuck it out for a few more weeks in Glasgow all would have ended differently. Never mind! After some serious discussion about my future employment prospects with my father, mother and friends, I had decided to join the merchant navy for one trip of six months to see how things developed. That idea, some said an insane idea, came about during the several weeks whilst I was officially registered as unemployed. I had seen a rather jazzed up advertisement, in the Norwich Job Centre, especially designed to attract young gullible men like me in joining the Merchant Navy to see the world. All I had really thought about was the sand, sun and sex that mariners are meant to enjoy in abundance. That same day I had discussed, with an employment adviser, the opportunity for an interview with the Blue Star shipping line at their head office in Leadenhall Street, London. The enthusiastic adviser promptly arranged an interview for me during the following week. I took the train down to London, via the underground to the head office, mindful of the time I was last in the big metropolis. The interview went well, and I accepted their invitation to join their two week's training course held at offices close to Liverpool Street station. About ten young men, all of them older than me, attended the training course that morning. Except for one bloke living in Manchester, all the others resided in the East End of London. Most of them were unemployed, and two had just completed a term in borstal. They all appeared to be tough resilient lads well equipped for a life at sea. The training was pretty basic, but it taught us various things we needed to know about living in a confined space with other men on board ship. We also covered important issues such as health and safety, payment of wages, alcohol and cigarette consumption, assisting to cook meals, sexual behaviour and many more I have now forgotten. At the end of the training only four of us remained undaunted by the potential life ahead of us sailing the seas in a huge piece of metal called a ship. The nearest that I had been to the deep oceans was when I spoke to several former old fishermen on the beach during my holiday in Cromer. Anyhow I was offered the opportunity of a six-month trip to New York leaving the London Docks in two weeks. I made up my mind that I would be on that ship. Be careful, you landlubbers!

Lucy entered the pub dressed in an attractive light blue dress and matching shoes. During our return from Glasgow I had seen her on only two occasions, one for a disappointing meal, and the other when we held hands watching a sentimental Elvis Presley film. 'Hi Lucy, 'ow are you? Are things workin' out living back at 'ome with your parents?' I asked her. 'Yeah, not too bad. The old man keeps moaning at me to get a job. I've tried six jobs, but no one wants to know. I've got an interview wif a Wimpy in Norwich next week,' said Lucy in an understandably glum frame of mind. 'Yeah, I know what yer mean. As I think I told yer the last time we met, I didn't phone Courts my old employer for a job; instead I've joined the merchant navy and sail in two weeks' time from the London Docks. I've got a six-month trip on a ship to New York,' I said reluctantly. 'What, you ain't Rich, 'ave yer? I can't fucking believe it. You've got a job in the merchant navy 'av yer? You 'avent really 'av yer?' Lucy sounded incredulous. After some time, the reality of me sailing to New York, and further afield, started to sink into her head. It must have been difficult for her to understand, or accept, especially as we had discussed the possibility of living together. She must have felt angry that I had misled her in some way, and now very soon, she would be back on her own again. I tried to explain to Lucy, as we were both very young and immature, it would be best to experience some of life while we had the opportunity. It was very difficult trying to explain my intentions to Lucy as I didn't really understand a great deal myself. All I realised was that the Glasgow experience had had an impact on me that I didn't really understand at the time. I still had this compulsion to break free of the inner constraints that held me back. Perhaps it was just teenage fantasy. It was very difficult saying goodbye to her, as I'm sure at some level, we both knew, it was the end of our relationship.

Two days before I sailed to New York, I met up with my friends for a drink in the local pub in Yapton called the Country Squire, a former 15th century coaching Inn. We were there for several hours drinking, joking and reminiscing. Several times I emphasized that I would only be away for six months, then upon my return, I could make an informed decision about whether I should go back to sea or find something else. For all I knew, I might just adapt to a life on the ocean waves. The new owner of the pub, a middle-aged man called Terry Sharp who had been there for only three months having previously had a pub in Hunstanton, kindly laid on dishes of cooked food for me and all the other drinkers. With rock and roll background music being played on the jukebox, we all had a turn to sing a song or tell a joke in front of the assembled crowd, as others took photographs of the pantomime in front of them. Bert Moore, singing a medley of pop songs, had stripped down to his underpants. Not a pretty sight! What a scream we had, it is something that I shall never forget. The following evening, and all next day, I spent with my parents in our home discussing various things such as farming, village life, Richard Arrowsmith, scrumping and, of course, my trip to New York. My mother, quite rightly, reminded me of the many conversations that we had had over the years about getting a job with prospects and security unlike farming, in which most of the family had worked for generations. It was the discussions with my parents about finding a better job that brought on those feelings of travel, and freedom. She went on to say, 'try the merchant navy and see 'ow it goes. See what the long term prospects are on and off shore. At least you 'ave the opportunity to save most of your wages.' My parents wished me well, and I said that I would send them regular postcards. For personal reasons, I travelled to the Royal Albert Docks on my own to board my ship, *Tangmere*.

All the young blokes I had finished training with, Derek, John, Paul and Kevin were there on board waiting eagerly, as I was, for the ship to set sail. Within hours we were on the deep powerful ocean bound for New York with our cargo of rubber, steel and industrial fertilizer. We sat in the staff mess eating our first on board meal of fish and chips, prepared by Victor, our chef for the whole trip. Apparently Victor had sailed the seven seas cooking for numerous shipping lines, which made him the ideal candidate to serve up good wholesome food day after day for long periods of time. We all congregated round Captain Tidmarsh, the boss, for a briefing about high winds, deep sea swells, fire precautions and sleeping in bunks. I was paired up with Derek, a tall, skinny bloke with spots all over his bony face, and tattoos on both his thin arms. That he was undernourished missed the point. He came from Poplar, had lived with his mother and three brothers in a small council flat. 'You bet I'm fuckin' glad to get out to sea and earn a few bob Dick,' said my cabin mate, who also had most of his front teeth missing. Although not an ideal candidate for Mr Universe, Derek was an interesting conversationalist who informed me that his father, tragically, had been shot by a gang from Hoxton. Also I found it very painful to be told that his mother, to make ends meet, worked as a prostitute in the West End. We kept talking incessantly into the small hours until we both nodded off.

Every day, not surprisingly, was very much the same on board ship as it was on shore, where men had their various jobs to do. The huge green monster, which we all depended on for our security, weighing thousands of tons, sometimes rocked from side to side frightening the living daylights out of me. From the dark of night, I used to look up at the countless billions of stars informing me that we were not alone in this amazing universe. As I sat there on my own out on the deck, I projected my mind onto the deep, lonely powerful sea as it reminded me of the countless ships, and the countless lives that had been lost in both war and peace over the centuries. The captain, or his deputy, would ring the bell at certain times of the day which meant meal times, or cleaning, training or one of the many orders that had to be carried out using a sharp response. Most of the working shifts for the younger staff, like me, were between the hours of 6am and 8pm, all the other shifts being for the experienced staff only. Excluding the captain and his deputy, all the other staff, about fifteen men, ate together three times daily in the staff mess where good, varied, food was the norm. Sometimes one of the younger staff, like me, were called upon to help Victor prepare vegetables, clean fish or wash the huge metal dishes used to feed many hungry mouths every day. Washing of personal clothes was carried out weekly by staff operating three enormous washing machines the size of industrial turbines. Smoking and drinking of alcohol was rigidly confined to the staff mess only, and if anyone,

anyone, was caught in possession elsewhere, dire sanctions would follow. As you can imagine, after long evenings of consuming copious amounts of alcohol, it is inevitable that sometimes sexual liaisons follow. That is not to say that sexual relationships are barred, they are not, but one is encouraged, similar to being on land, to be discreet. By the time I took my first trip with Blue Star Lines, homosexual sex had been decriminalised. On one particular evening, when the alcohol started to flow too much, Victor propositioned Kevin back to his single living quarters. Of course sexual liaisons on board my ship between consenting men happened all the time, even though a sizeable proportion of men were married or had female partners. That is the nature of the beast!

After several days on the high, rough unforgiving seas we were approaching the tall skyline of New York where countless thousands of people, from around the world, would have greeted the sight of the Statue of Liberty with relief at the beginning of a new beginning. Hailing from insignificant places like Yapton and Norwich, I was overwhelmed by all the tall buildings of New York. When I later walked round the human jungle of New York City, I frequently found it difficult to see above those tall buildings that dominated the skyline. We docked in late afternoon, when daylight had fallen, to the loud sound of bells, whistles and horns. I have always marvelled at the great skill that captains possess when manoeuvring their huge ships safely into a crowded harbour. Before going on shore we were briefed by the captain about the pleasures and pitfalls of associating with prostitutes, excessive drinking in bars, especially on your own, and the dangers of taking illegal drugs. In the early evening about ten men, most of them rampant for any kind of hedonistic thrill, made their way to the city lights—into a realm that sucks the spiritual matter out of people as they enter the sensuous gates that constantly draw them into a world of craving. The more experienced in our crowd, those who had been to New York many times before, kept close to the youngsters to make sure we did not go astray into the dens of vice.

For the next five months we sailed to different sea ports up and down the vast USA coastline, each time loading on board various goods, mostly flour, sugar, salt and delivering it to another port. Each time we offloaded, we took on board another load and so it went on until we made our way down to Miami for our final load of steel, cement and timber which we took back to the London Docks, our final destination. During those long six months delivering goods around the east coast of the USA, we had very little opportunity to visit and explore those places where we had docked. The one place outside of USA waters, however, where we did go onshore for a most enjoyable evening was Freedman, a small Panamanian town with a deep natural harbour, and used by many of the heavier USA ships trading with South American countries. Apparently it is during these times when American ships, having off-loaded their goods, take illegally on board young local girls, who are taken for a year's jaunt around the Americas. As we were nearing the end of our six-month trip, all the crew hit the town of Freedman for a night of frivolity amongst the local friendly people as we celebrated a successful trip, culminated by throwing the tipsy captain into the restaurant swimming pool. There was some suggestion that Paul, who I had trained with in London, had spent the night with a local woman, the magistrate's wife, in her nearby apartment. Good luck to him, the dirty stop out! It was from this small town that I sent my last post card to my parents informing them of the date of my arrival in London.

On a wet and windy day in late November 1968, the *Tangmere* docked for the final time at the Royal Albert Dock at the end of a memorable experience—my first trip at sea. Other than the senior staff, we all made our way to the Blue Star Lines harbour office to check in our security details, and most importantly, to receive our pay cheque, which after six months, excluding deductions for beer, and other goods, was a considerable sum of money. It was by far the largest amount of money I had earned during my short working life. I thought to myself, I could buy a new Ford Zephyr car, or take three months holiday just lazing around the Caribbean, or take a sea cruise to Morocco. I could impress the local girls by wearing new mohair suits, or ride a flashy 500cc triumph motorbike, or most important of all, take my good, kind parents on holiday. Mind you, a full driving licence would help! Whatever I decided, the money could give me the various choices that had not been there before. Well, I thought to myself, I could be a 'right-jack-the lad'. All my colleagues wished each other well as we hit the road home, which for me was a three-hour train journey from busy Liverpool Street, via a local Midland Bank in Norwich to deposit my cheque for over £400. Eventually the old bone shaker of a bus arrived at Yapton, where I would meet my parents for the first time in six months.

Chapter 5

A NEW CAREER:
BRANCHING OUT INTO FORESTRY

IT WAS APPROACHING MIDNIGHT before I arrived home, yet my mother and father, although he had to get out of bed for work at 5am, were waiting for me. As I opened the front door, we all put our arms round each other for a warm much needed cuddle. 'Hi Mum and Dad, you both look well. Great to be back home,' I said as I carried on cuddling them. 'It's wonderful to see yer, son. Over the past six months we 'ave often worried about yer on board that huge ship sailing on a vast ocean. Did yer enjoy yerself son?' asked my proud father who had realised that I was bigger, heavier, and hopefully more confident, than I was before I left. 'Look at the size of yer, son, you must 'ave ate well on board!' And so the conversation went on for an hour before the three of us, all rather tried, went to bed.

The next morning, a bright warmish day, I was out of bed around 9am to make my own breakfast for the first time in ages. My parents had already gone to work. With a bundle of letters, and a mug of tea in hand, I sat in my favourite wicker chair out on the coloured stone patio my father had built some two years ago. House sparrows darted around the rear garden, as if they were trying to welcome me home. As I sat there, taking in the fresh enjoyable air, overlooking the garden full of flowers and vegetables, I realised how fortunate I really was to have supportive family and friends. There I was fit and healthy after I had been gallivanting in a ship to the USA and back, not a care in the world, and with money in the bank. Most of the letters were either tax forms from the Government, or brochures from various clothing companies trying to sell their goods, but one in particular, dated from October of the same year, came across more favourably. It was written by W.H. Greenwood, a forestry company, where I had applied for a job as a trainee forester before I started my jaunt in the merchant navy. That was some time ago, but due to my knowledge of trees, they said, they would keep my name on file and if any vacancies became available they would inform me. The letter from Greenwood invited me along to be interviewed for a trainee forester vacancy. However, as that was three weeks ago the vacancy would probably now be filled. Luckily the vacancy was still open. Within a week Greenwood had offered me another interview date. Brilliant, fantastic, there was a good chance that employment was coming my way, I thought as I walked confidently into Greenwood's new offices for an interview with the governor himself. 'Hallo, Richard, I remembered how knowledgeable you were about trees when I first met you. We have a trainee forester vacancy if you are still interested?' said Mr Greenwood. 'You bet I am still interested. When can I start work for you?' I asked him before he changed his mind. Mr Greenwood and I agreed on a date for me to start work. Somebody up there was watching over me!

That information was especially welcome as Christmas was only a few days away. My father was now 44 years old and still working long hours, along with his brothers, for Mr Leader at Lavender Farm. Father had said on many occasions that he had been offered good farming jobs elsewhere in Yapton, and in other areas, but he found Mr Leader to be a fair employer who always gave perks such as free meat and vegetables. Furthermore, Father and his two brothers had always been consulted whenever the farmer introduced new machinery or farming methods. Therefore, throughout the years, Lavender Farm continued to grow and prosper, becoming one of the largest and most productive farms in the area. By this time my mother was still working in the village shop, which had now been taken over by a much bigger company based in Cambridge. Harkins had extended the shop to nearly double its original size, modernised the interior, and had taken on more well trained staff. Mother, now approaching forty-seven years of age, still worked part-time in an environment she enjoyed.

Most of my close friends from schooldays had also found work. Bert had originally worked as a farm labourer for a pig farmer in Sweetcombe, a small village three miles north of Yapton. But as he had passed his driving test, it enabled him to drive his small battered Ford van to work, and also drive the truck for his employer, Mr Cox, at Roebuck Farm. Bert had always lived in the village with his friendly parents and two older sisters, attractive young women who I saw only occasionally. But a few months later Bert had fallen on his feet when he found a driving job with a multi-national company in Ipswich. The work entailed driving the company van to various pubs and clubs in the East Anglia area, and further afield, delivering fruit machines. He told me he enjoyed the work mainly because he was on his own all day and he could also use the new Leyland company van for his own social purposes. At 20 years of age, Dennis found it difficult to settle into any one job. He had tried several short-term different jobs, but all to no avail. His current position of delivering milk to the residents of Yapton he seemed to enjoy, as the early morning starting time gave him the opportunity to go river fishing. Besides Dennis was a bit of a loner, who preferred his own company sitting on a secluded river bank somewhere deep in the countryside. Terry was a grafter—he didn't mind getting his hands dirty if he could earn a few pounds to keep life and limb in healthy order. Unfortunately, he had found building work difficult to find, and had travelled, by public transport, over most of Norfolk, calling ad hoc, at building sites trying to sell his labour. At this stage only Philip was without a job, which surprised me because at school he was a bright self-motivated pupil. He had tried working as a trainee postman, farm labourer, office cleaner and local authority gardener but nothing had worked out for him. Over the past year, according to his mother, he had become introverted and secretive ever since getting involved with a group of hippies from London, where he lived for a while. His mother told my parents that Philip had taken various illegal drugs, and this had contributed to his mental ill health for which he was being treated.

For the next two years or so, just a few weeks short of my 21st birthday, I enjoyed working for Greenwood Forestry, where I learnt new skills on the job. Most of the company contracts were around the East Anglia area, but we did travel further afield to Shropshire, Wiltshire, Somerset and once to the Highlands of Scotland. I found travelling to various places with my colleagues very exciting. Even at the early age of 19 years, I realised that this was work I had always wanted. I felt happy, fulfilled, had a regular job with supportive colleagues and a good wage, which I worked long hours for. Neville Greenwood had first started the company in 1955 after working many years as a tree surgeon for the Forestry Commission in the Forest of Dean. While he was there, Neville had become well known for the many new woods he had planted, deciduous and conifer, around Britain. He was instrumental in leading the forestry team that planted several thousand broad leafed trees on the Duke of Sutherland's estate in Perthshire. That ground breaking initiative paved the way for three different species of animals to be re-introduced for the first time since their demise two hundred years ago. As well as being a friendly person to work with, Neville was knowledgeable and always there to give a helping hand. He never played the big boss. He mucked in as one of the lads, drank tea with the workers round the many fires we had, and, when appropriate, loved a pint of beer. I liked him a great deal.

On one particular contract on a large estate in Somerset, where we were required to prune many old oak, sycamore and ash trees that had been allowed to grow wild, one of our colleagues, Jimmy, saved Neville from potentially serious injury, or even death. Even though Neville was over fifty, he used to climb up trees from bough to bough, like a young Rhesus monkey, refusing to wear a safety harness, which he, of course, required his workers to wear. Neville had walked out on a large bough which had to be pruned. Not realising how far he had walked out on the bough, it suddenly started to break; just as Neville instantly seized the bough above him, the other fell crashing to the ground. Most of the other workers, including myself, were working elsewhere, but fortunately Jimmy, who was some fifty yards away, heard the crash and rushed to the aide of his employer who was left hanging from a bough in desperate need of assistance. 'Quick Jimmy, for fuck sake, I can't hold on for much longer! Quick, quick!' a desperate Neville kept shouting as Jimmy quickly climbed the tree and tied the rope securely around the bough above so that Neville could lower himself down to safety. That incident was no deterrent to Neville as he continued just as before.

'Here you are lads, tea is made. Come and get it!' I shouted to my five colleagues working not more than fifty yards away cutting down conifers to make way for the planting of native trees. At some time the whole estate had been planted with dense conifer, which is not surprising as they are a productive source of income, and unlike native trees, they grow very fast. This huge estate in Shropshire, once in the hands of a tea plantation-owning family called Simpson, was purchased years ago by a pension fund, no doubt to maximise its income. 'Nice one Dicky,' said, Bob, one of my colleagues, who put the mug to his parched lips. 'First of the day, good 'ealth lads!' roared another colleague, big Dave, well known for carrying logs nearly twice his weight on his sturdy muscular shoulders. David Ambrose had worked for Greenwood for over twelve years, and was the longest serving employee: he was tall, big, strong with the heart of a lion. Ask him any question about his two interests in life, real ale and trees, and Dave would give you the correct answer within seconds. He would have been an ideal candidate for Mastermind. The other three colleagues, Bill, Fred and Brian, had all been employed at Greenwood for a number of years which demonstrates, I suppose, their satisfaction of working for a decent bloke. Bill in particular was a real character. His arms and body were full of tattoos; dancing women, a snake charmer and dragons that he had acquired from the many places he had visited in the merchant navy. He informed me that the most exciting and creative place for tattoos was in a small village not ten miles from Bombay, where the elderly female tattooist was literally covered in tattoos from the top of her head to the bottom of her feet.

We were all drinking tea, or eating our food, when out of nowhere a middle-aged bloke walked out of the thick conifer wood to where we were sitting on logs round a large warm fire. 'Good mornin' chaps, how is yer all going? I'm dying fer a cuppa,' he said, taking off his dirty old rucksack and placing it on the ground in front of him. 'Sure on yer feller, of course you can 'ave a tea,' said Bill as he jumped up from where he was sitting to fill up a mug of tea for our bedraggled looking guest. When I first saw this dirty, mud-stained man, he reminded me of the rumours we heard, when we were young back in Yapton, of a tramp living in the woods, but no one ever saw him or her. 'Sit down there feller and rest yer knees,' said Fred, pointing to a conifer stump next to the roaring fire. 'What's yer name me old mate?' asked Brian as he offered him a cigarettes. 'Wonderful hot tea, thanks fellers. No thanks, I don't smoke. Me name is Oswald, bit of a silly name, but me father gave it me after his father, who came from Ireland. But that could be a lot of bollocks,' exclaimed Oswald who was warming his dirty chapped hands in front of the fire. We all sat in silence for a few minutes as Bill refilled our mugs with steaming tea from the large metal pot we had bought three months previously in a Somerset supermarket.

'Where yer from Oswald?' I asked, as he scratched his matted beard. 'That's a long story young feller. Let me see now! I'm about fifty years old and was born in Cocking, a small village in Sussex. My parents lived in the vicarage. My father was the vicar of the village, and several others, for many years. He eventually died of an injury, he 'ad a bad limp he sustained in the First World War fighting in the trenches on the Somme. I 'ad been sent to private schools, and lived a sheltered life, so when Father died in around 1935, aged about 45, I was 'ardly equipped fer the real world. Two uncles gave me employment in their solicitors' office but I couldn't cope and started drifting aimlessly from place to place. I usually sleep rough, but if it's really cold I goes into the Salvation Army hostel for a while. I also been in mental hospitals yer know, but I stay well clear of those fucking places unless I need a bed for a week or two. That's your lot young feller,' said Oswald as he stood up to get several crumpled black and white photographs out of his sturdy rucksack. ''Ere are some photos of me parents and I, taken when I was about ten years old in Cornwall at me aunt's house near Land's End. She was a barrister in London, I believe.' Oswald's sad eyes looked to the ground. The dirty, old photographs, the few cherished remains of Oswald's past, were handed round to my colleagues and I, as we witnessed the sum total of his life. It is so easy and foolish, I thought to myself, to judge any person by their exterior appearance. We never really know what is going on in another person's mind. Most of the time, I thought, we only have, at best, a superficial understanding of ourselves.

'I must get going lads, gota buy some food for a few days. I'm living deep in the woods, it's warm there for a good kip. So might see yer all again lads. Thanks fer the tea.' With that, Oswald put on his rucksack and marched off, out of the clearing, back into the dense wood heading for the village a few miles away, where he could buy his goods. You couldn't but warm to this gentle yet vulnerable gentleman, who lived as a nomad. His appearance was of a slightly built, short, middle-aged man wearing dirty old clothes that had not seen water for a considerable number of months.

After that contract had been finished, we had another much nearer to my home, which meant that I could live at home in relative luxury with my parents instead of living in B&B accommodation elsewhere with my colleagues. Smelly feet and a rancid breath were not Brian's most redeeming attributes! Working locally gave me the opportunity to spend time with my parents, and meet with some of my friends socially. After phoning around I managed to meet two friends, Bert and Philip, in a small pub, The Monkey Box, some fifty yards from my former employer Courts. Bert was happy delivering his machines to pubs and restaurants. Besides he was his own governor, could plan his working day, and stop whenever he wanted a break for tea. Philip had some good news to tell us at last, for he had found a job working as a porter at a small general hospital, called Petersfield, a few miles from Norwich. I was pleased for Philip as it was the first job he had found for some considerable time. Also, he told us that his doctor had discharged him from the out-patients' clinic he had been attending for the past eighteen months. It was tragic to recall that Philip had been a bright pupil at Rawlinson Comprehensive school not so very long ago, having been top of the class in most subjects, including science. It was the science subject of biology that interested him most of all. He was particularly disappointed that he failed his biology A-level exam and, was therefore, unable to go to college, although he had the opportunity to resit the exam. That is the time when he started to drift aimlessly around, got involved with illegal drugs and succumbed to his eventual decline into mental illness. But he had got himself off drugs, straightened himself out, found a job and he had presented himself at the pub as a motivated man. Unfortunately, four or five people in Philip's family had all suffered from mental illness, but there could also have been others. Philip's father had been hospitalized many times for depression during his lifetime. Anyhow the three of us had a few beers and went for a meal in the newly opened Chongs Chinese restaurant for an evening of enjoyment. As we stood outside the restaurant laughing, Philip commented, 'I'm feeling a lot better for the first time in two years, and I am enjoying myself working as a porter. Hope we can all meet up again soon lads. All the best!' That night he walked off to get his bus a much happier man, and I was so pleased for him.

As usual, between the hours of 8-9am, Dave drove our six-ton blue Ford Bedford into the transport cafe lorry park, just off the A11, for our usual breakfast fry up. 'Gotta top up the body's fat stores lads,' said Dave. When we were working locally anywhere in Norfolk, it was usually Bob's cafe that we invariably stopped at before a long, hard day's graft in front of us. Bob's was a typical working class place full of tough, dour looking men topping up their energy levels for the day ahead with a plate full of eggs, bacon, beans, sausage and bubble and squeak all swimming in fat. Sometimes there was enough fat on Bob's plates to run a small car—along with a few beers and endless cigarettes, which were the staple diet in those days for the working bloke, whose monotonous life consisted mainly of unskilled, back-breaking work. These shrines to manliness were nearly always full of men whose muscular arms were covered with tattoos. This was their sort of well-stamped passport to being recognised as a man. Most of the older men used to wear cloth caps, which in a lot of instances hid their toothless mouths. In working class families in those days, there was a clear demarcation line of areas of work for men, out earning the money, and women running the household. The demonstration of emotions and feelings were confined to television, radio, newspapers or romantic novels, and were very rarely expressed in working class families in Yapton.

Chapter 6

A NEW JOB:
FORESTRY PROMOTION IN DEVON

TWO **MONTHS LATER** I was faced with the most difficult decision of my life so far. I had made a successful application to a small family owned forestry business in Cornwall, and they now requested that I make a decision about whether I wanted the job or not. The forester vacancy with Wilkes, a fourth generation business from Ivybridge, Devon, had been advertised extensively in professional magazines; they wanted someone skilled, experienced and committed to moving down to the West Country long term. Our employer, Neville Greenwood, used to buy the monthly magazine, *The Tree Industry*, to inform himself of various professional developments and always handed it on to his workers. As I was only weeks off my 21st birthday, I was eager to move on with my chosen career as soon as possible. Indeed, I was becoming desperate to move on with my life. When I pointed out the Devon vacancy to my employer, I had expected him to explain that I would be wasting my time, as I did not have the required experience. Much to my surprise and relief, however, Neville not only knew John Wilkes, the current owner, quite well, as he had carried out contract work for his company in the past, but was willing to contact him with a good reference for me with regards to the vacancy.

Feeling bold and determined to make a good impression, I stepped down from the London train onto the platform of

Ivybridge Station, where Mr Wilkes was waiting to drive me to his forestry yard in Sandstone two miles away. John Wilkes was tall, slim, with very little hair, and piercing blue eyes. He had a good sense of humour behind his industrious business demeanour. Although an employer, he always insisted on being called John, for whenever possible, he used to enjoy working alongside his fellow workers, though due to business elsewhere, that was not often possible. From the outset, the interview with John was informal and laid back, knowing as he did, that such times could be very difficult for a young anxious person trying to impress. Afterwards he took me round the yard where I met a few of his workers loading timber onto a lorry. 'Hope to see yer soon Richard,' one long haired young guy shouted to me from the back of a lorry. 'How did he know me name, John?' I asked, somewhat confused. 'They knew you were travelling down from London for an interview. Don't worry,' replied a smiling Mr Wilkes. About 50 yards from the yard, John Wilkes showed me the accommodation that came with the job. It consisted of a well decorated self-contained studio flat with bedroom/living area, large kitchen and bathroom/toilet. 'Well, Richard, I would like to offer you the job,' Mr Wilkes enthusiastically said to me as we sat in his small bright office, which had a large map, with coloured pins in it, spread all over one of the green walls. 'I would love to accept your offer of a job. Thank you,' I said with a broad smile.

As I sat on the fast train bound for London, I couldn't believe my luck at the prospect of leaving Yapton for pastures new. It also meant leaving home again, but I was eager to do well. Besides I didn't want to be left behind working as a farm worker for a pittance for the rest of my life. No sooner had I arrived at the hectic Paddington Station, than I dived into a phone box to inform my mother of my great fortune at being offered the position of forester with a start date of one week hence. 'Well done, Richard, your dad will be so proud to know that you are moving on with your life!' was Mother's response. With that I took the train and bus back to Yapton and arrived home about three hours later, where my parents were waiting on the doorstep to congratulate me on finding a better job. My father opened a bottle of white wine and the three of us celebrated my success prematurely. As Mr Greenwood had so kindly given me the final week off with pay, I contacted my friends for us to spend a few days together. During the day we went walking over local fields and woods, places that we had visited many times before, looking for mischief, over the years. We walked the two miles to Windover Hill, as it was here that our late dear friend, Richard Arrowsmith, had on one occasion brought with him an unopened packet of capstan full strength cigarettes and a magazine full of nude women. We nearly choked ourselves to death on the cigarettes that tasted and smelt like the rope I had handled many times at sea during my brief stint in the merchant navy. I also remember two or three of us masturbating over the erotic photographs in the magazine. On the way back from Windover Hill, we made a detour to take in the orchards, where on numerous occasions, we had stolen pocketfuls of fruit and eaten them in the nearby woods, until scampering, not long after, to find a secluded place to let nature take its course. I will never forget those exceptional experiences I had with my dear friends from Yapton. They were all characters and have left an indelible mark that shall remain with me forever. On the final day before my move to the West Country, I walked round the village, just as I had done for the past 20 years, taking in all the different shapes and colours which made Yapton what it was: a charming, decent, solid place to live, yet there was room for improvement. But I did warn my friends not to expect that many letters, or phone calls, from me.

My father drove the three of us to Norwich Station, so that I could take the mid-morning train to London. Outside the station, I hugged my parents for several minutes, reassuring them that I would look after myself, and I would try to contact them whenever possible. With a heavy heart, I boarded the London-bound train on the first leg of my journey, which would in time, hopefully, change my life for the better. Not far from Liverpool Street Station, I looked down at my waistline, realising that over the past two years, or so, I had put on too much weight. That, no doubt, reflected the unhealthy amounts of alcohol and food I had consumed. That alarmed me somewhat, due to the fact that from my background we had all been slim because of the healthy diet we ate and the enormous amounts of exercise we took running, walking and climbing. As I was only 5' 8" tall, I realised that if I wanted to make a good impression on my new colleagues, I would have to shed a few pounds.

As I had arranged with my new employer for someone to collect me from Ivybridge Station, I sat there, on the platform seat, pondering the next stage of my life, just a few weeks before my 21st birthday. It was early 1971, and, as the soft rain became heavier, I sat there deep in thought, until I became aware of someone, to my right, asking me a question. 'Hi there, is it Richard? I'm Dave, I work for Richard Wilkes. He asked me to pick you up and drive you back to the yard,' explained a smiling, short, slim Dave Lee. 'Good to meet yer, Dave.' 'Good to meet you, Richard,' said Dave, shaking my hand. We both jumped up into the cab of a black Leyland. As Dave drove us the short distance to the yard where I met most of my new colleagues, it gave me the opportunity to familiarize myself with the place. Just as Dave went to make tea for us both, two large lorries, full of wood and tools, swept into the yard like a riot squad storming a violent demonstration. Six mean looking blokes, all dressed in heavy boots and coats, who resembled artisans from the Aragon front in the Spanish Civil War, jumped down from the lorries. They were all heading my way into the brightly decorated wooden tea room, when on time, Dave appeared with a huge metal teapot, which reminded me of the one on board my old ship. 'You must be Richard?' asked a burly, bald chap around 50 years old. 'I'm Ted Phillips the foreman. This ugly old guy next to me is Mick. Then there is Gordon, Kevin, Bryan and Tim, who, I believe, spoke briefly to you when you came down for your interview,' explained the confident likeable Ted Phillips. 'We are a decent bunch here, Richard. We work hard and enjoy a beer or two, if you know what I mean.' As he laughed, several others cheered. 'I'm pleased to meet yer all. I 'ope things work out for me down here,' I said to my new colleagues. 'Don't worry son, you will be all right with us around, won't he lads?' said Mick, at 53 the oldest worker there. Mick had worked over 20 years for the Wilkes' family business. He had originally worked for John Wilkes' father who, he said, was a good honest person. Mick was a tall, thick-set man, married with three children who lived in a nearby village, called Tainworth.

I settled into my small but comfortable bedsit. Other than Tim, who lived with his mother a few miles from Sandstone, all the other six workers were either married, or had partners they lived with in or around Ivybridge. At Wilkes there were two teams each made up of four men. My other three colleagues were Mick, Gordon and the Manchester United fanatic, Dave. I got on very well with my three team workers from the outset, as they were all friendly, easy going blokes, who usually enjoyed a good laugh when the time was right. But they took their job seriously, as in that part of the country, good well paid employment is hard to find, as Gordon knew only too well. He had been unemployed for two years prior to starting work at Wilkes. Previously he had existed on cash in hand cleaning or driving jobs. His partner managed to get part-time seasonal work in the catering, or public house, business. When she was working, Gordon had looked after their young daughter at home and as she got older, he took her to a local playschool. Gordon was scathing, with some justification, about the plentiful opportunities that were available to city or town youngsters, yet very few jobs were available to people living in the countryside. This historic problem affected most rural communities, just like Yapton, where unskilled jobs in farming were usually the only source of income. During the desperate times when he could not find any sort of work, Gordon kept his sanity by running miles over Dartmoor and surrounding areas. Yet this tall, lean, young man still found time for others by volunteering at two local charity shops. Personally, I thought Gordon could have made a living as a model, as his attractive looks appeared to be ideally suited for a fine artist, or he could even have applied for photographic work. Besides he could also have advertised himself as a toy boy in some upmarket magazine for wealthy women.

Nearly every weekday morning around 7-30am, Mick, our foreman, Gordon, Dave and I would meet in the yard to collect the new 7-ton lorry, a long wheelbase Ford equipped to carry heavy loads. We also had to collect the various implements we might need for the contract such as chain saws, metal ropes, or the various hand tools we used. The time and venue were just perfect for me as I could get out of bed at 7am, have breakfast and walk a few yards from my front door to meet my colleagues. Ideal also when I had had too many beers to drink, but most of the time I was sufficiently inspired to get out of bed early. Getting out of bed early, some working days and most weekends, was a motivation I enjoyed, because it gave me the opportunity to wander in the nearby woods looking for mushrooms, or wild flowers, or take photographs of the many different birds that inhabited this attractive wood. I found those times to be so inspiring, especially at weekends, when I had the time to wander further afield looking for anything that I found to be interesting or unusual—for example, when I came across a vixen carrying all her youngsters from behind an old shed, where they had all been living, to the comfortable rear leather seat of a deserted Humber car. It was a truly exciting sight. On any working day the other forestry team might well be carrying out similar procedures to us, but they had their own way of doing things. Besides, Ted Phillips was an experienced and skilful worker, who knew how to get the best out of his men without causing any animosity amongst them.

Most of the forestry contracts that we had were for large institutions such as the National Trust, Woodland Trust or the Military. Geographically some of the contracts were within reach on a daily basis, but for others, depending on the number of trees involved, we used to book local accommodation. In the 1970s the quality of B&B accommodation used to be indifferent, but this has improved considerably over the years due to the growing affluence of people who now have so many more choices. During one largish contract on a National Trust property near Tavistock, we came across a most terrible sight indeed. Deep in the woods of a large Victorian house, just off a defined track, was the body of a man hanging from the bough of a large beech tree. Three of us took the wet limp body down from the tree, while Mick ran up to the main house to request police and ambulance assistance. Within ten minutes both emergency services had arrived at the scene. After the doctor had examined the deceased's body, it was taken away by the ambulance to a nearby hospital for further tests to be carried out. Meanwhile the police had taken down information from the four of us as regards the time we saw the body, the time when we lifted the body down from the tree onto the ground and similar, related questions. The senior detective informed us that there had been over the years, due to the wood being somewhat remote from the local road, a number of misdemeanours carried out but nothing to the extent of suicide. I wondered what had driven this tortured human being to walk alone, I assumed, into a large dense lonely wood and commit the ultimate act. It transpired that the deceased was a local scientist aged 67 years. Apparently he had had a successful career in cellular biology, but unfortunately had also been dogged with a history of mental illness. We did not hear from the police again.

On another occasion, about six months after the suicide incident, we had a contract to manage many different trees, both deciduous and conifer, on a large private country estate near Buckfastleigh, Devon. Upon arrival at the main gates, we were met by a man who appeared to be dressed like a butler. Some of the owners of the great country estates, and indeed some of the workers, even in the modern world, relate to people as if they still live in the 19th century. The butler unlocked the huge wrought iron gates, with a heraldic design on it, with a key the size of a shovel and informed us to drive down to the main house, where we should park the lorry out of the site of the master's dining room. The butler proceeded to explain that his master wanted us to prune several large oak trees up in the woods, and while we were there, could we take away three decaying deer carcasses? 'Well, we don't usually take away carcasses, that is the work for the local council,' Mick delicately explained to the Jeeves-like figure in front of us. 'Now look here,' the butler pompously retorted, 'my master is paying your company a lot of money to take down a few trees—surely you can find space on your contraption to take away his master's fallen roe deer?' 'Very well. I will take 'em away for you governor,' said Mick, using all his diplomatic skills to lessen the tension.

With that settled, Mick drove the lorry away from the house and up into the woods, where we found the aforementioned trees. With their equipment in hand, Dave and Gordon shinned up one of the large oak trees, just like Spiderman climbing up the Empire State Building, to inspect the dead and dying branches. This oak tree appeared to be so old that it could possibly have accommodated a Tudor gentleman discreetly urinating. With the safety of the workers paramount, both men wore safety harnesses as they began to chainsaw several old boughs off thereby opening a sort of canopy for the light to penetrate. Having lowered the chainsaw to me on the ground, they both started to descend when one of the lower branches that Dave was standing on broke. As the timber came crashing to the ground, hilariously, Dave was left hanging in mid-air like some fighter pilot who had just ejected from his troubled plane. 'You all right, Dave?' I asked, as I fell to the ground laughing hysterically. 'Stop taking the fucking piss Dick and get me out of this predicament,' Dave said, who himself couldn't stop laughing. 'These tight harness straps are squeezing the life out of my bollocks!' he added. At last Gordon had managed to climb out to the bough, where Dave was hanging, and cut him free. He had fallen about thirty feet to the ground, but fortunately he was unhurt except for a sprained ankle and bruised ego. 'Fuckin' branch. I don't know 'ow that 'appened. I think I'm okay,' he said, as he gingerly got to his feet with the help of Mick and I. It was obvious from his first few steps that he had not seriously injured himself. 'Get in the lorry Dave and I'll drive yer to the Queens Hospital A&E three miles from here,' said Mick. 'Sod off, I'll be fine after a few pints tonight,' smiled Dave. But Mick insisted!

As Mick drove Dave to the local A&E, Gordon and I carried on working in the other oak trees, mindful that we must be very cautious indeed as parts of those oak trees were old, brittle and could potentially collapse at any stage. When we took a break from managing the trees, I became aware of the beautiful dapple shade breaking through the quiet environment of the wood, where only the raucous chatter of the crows and rooks broke the silence. We stood there for a few minutes experiencing what was going on around us. The world seemed sublime—all was still, peaceful yet full of life trying to express itself. Somehow I had arrived at a stage where I felt more self-assured and focused about my way of life down here in Devon. At times, I thought of Yapton as being a vague memory from my past, yet I realised that I missed seeing my dear parents, and extended family, who still lived and worked there. Although still in my early 20s, and even though I missed the company of those I had known all my life, I was pretty sure I had made the right decision to move on with my life by moving to Devon. Besides, what did I have to lose?

It was late afternoon, and as Gordon and I had carried out extensive work on most of the oak and conifer trees, we decided to have tea sitting round a small fire we had made from fallen dry bark and twigs. As we sat there sorting out life's problems, we noticed that Mick had driven in through the main gates, and continued up into the woods where we sat. Out jumped the pair of them smiling; Dave walked with a slight limp which reminded me of a similar accident that had occurred to a former colleague during my time at Greenwood's. 'How's it going, Dave, any bones broken?' I asked him. 'Not really. My right thigh and arm are lightly bruised, but nothing broken except my pride. They gave me strong painkillers and cream to rub on the muscles. X-ray showed no breaks, thank

God. They also gave me a letter to give to Wilkes,' said Dave, as he read the letter that the doctor had given him in A&E. Dave was a friendly chap of about 40 years of age, and had worked for Wilkes about six years. He had originally moved down from Rochdale looking for work, after painful bouts of unemployment. He was short, burly, and had tattoos all over his arms and upper chest. He reminded me of the quintessential teddy boy from the 1950's. He loved music from that era, especially Carl Perkins, Elvis Presley, Buddy Holly and Chubby Checker. He had collected many of their records and used to play them a lot at home, but to the detriment of his two sons. As well as his passion for music and Manchester United, he loved walking the open spaces of Dartmoor. The 1960-70s music of the Beatles, Rolling Stones and similar groups was not for Dave. He found that music to be all rather shallow.

It was around this time that Dave, Gordon and I started walking in and around dangerous, beautiful Dartmoor. When family commitments allowed a day off, or two, my two colleagues and I usually met at Wilkes' yard in Sandstone, a convenient place for Dave to drive us along the A38, down to the B3417, for him to park at Lee Moor. From there, one has the whole of Dartmoor, about 30 miles in length, in front of one to walk wherever one chooses. However, since around 1976 there has been a long distance walk, the Two Moors Way, available to those hardy souls who have the opportunity to walk the 102 miles from Dartmoor to Lynmouth. Most of the time we did daily circular Dartmoor walks, but occasionally we went walking for a tough few days, or more, taking in windswept barren places such as Shall Top, Ugborough Moor, Ryder's Hill and up to Princetown, where we took the irregular bus journey back to our conveniently parked car.

From the first time I walked on Dartmoor, I became emotionally attracted to the history, its loneliness, beauty, physical challenge, which kept drawing me back to its lurking danger time and time again. It was as though I had to keep returning to walk on Dartmoor, and latterly Bodmin Moor and Exmoor, to explore an inner part of me that is only receptive in certain environments. My colleagues and I had some moving and interesting experiences out there on the bleak moors, especially when the mist or fog began to descend. It was then that I had a compulsion to get lost and try to find my way back, but I never had the confidence to embark on such a journey. From haunting Garrow Tor on Bodmin Moor, to the spectacular high level path above the East Lyn River in Lynmouth, we had walked in the same steps as those before us; mariners, monks, escaped prisoners, farm workers and miners who all used these rights of way as they walked through this beautiful, rugged and challenging countryside.

My colleague Dave was always seeking out unique ways of advertising his love for his favourite football team since childhood, Manchester United. When the three of us were out walking on the Dartmoor, it gave Dave the opportunity to bring out a glossy photograph of his soccer idol, George Best, and show as many people as possible. Wherever he had been living throughout the years, Dave would travel many miles to watch his United, even if that meant going without money for a week or so. On this occasion Dave wedged the Best photograph, followed by a red and white scarf of United, between two large rocks hoping walkers would notice his reverence of the king of football. As he usually did, he prostrated himself in front of the photograph, in complete adoration, at the feet of his hero, like a Christian monk praying at the feet of Jesus Christ. On another occasion, when walking on Dartmoor together, near Hexworthy, Dave pulled out a sticker from his jacket with 'I love Man Utd' emblazoned on it. He placed the sticker carefully into a crevice, once again hoping that some lonely walker would not only notice his highway shrine, but add something to it such as a United photograph or mug or anything else. In Dave's eyes that would confirm their loyalty to a great football team. He then once again performed the obligatory prostration ritual. His fanatical commitment to a football team was something I had not seen before.

Chapter 7

MY PARENTS AND FAMILY
BUY BUTTERCUP FARM

AT FIRST I tried writing regularly to my parents, but I'm afraid that lasted for no longer than four months. Due to the constant encouragement from my mother, I eventually got in the habit of phoning my parents fortnightly on Saturday evenings around 7pm, when my father would be at home. Occasionally I also sent my parents photographs of my life in Devon. On one particular Saturday evening, by which time I had been working in Devon for about 18 months, my father informed me that he and his two brothers would be leaving Mr Leader's farm to start up in business on their own. It appeared that my father and two uncles had been in negotiations for some time with the owner to buy his sizeable smallholding near Lewes, East Sussex. As well as having a large four-bedroomed house, workshops and two barns, there was also five acres of prime land to sustain pigs and a small herd of cows. From the good money they had made at Lavender Farm, they were able to buy a third of the smallholding each outright. As it was now 1973, the timing was right to get on, as my father and mother were 47 and 49 years old respectively.

Throughout the past years my father, and his two brothers, had worked hard to make Lavender Farm into a successful thriving business. They had been well supported during that time by Mr Leader to introduce various machines to help the farm become more competitive in food self-sufficiency for their animals, and to rearing and selling well-bred cows and pigs. With the experience and knowledge of animal husbandry that my father, and two uncles, had brought to the farm, Mr Leader had an ongoing business capable of competing against the best of its size.

'Great stuff Dad, yer' really deserve some success after what you and yer' brothers had achieved at Lavender Farm,' I said, full of pride for a father and uncles, who deserved to buy a place of their own. I was aware that most farm labourers never get the opportunity to buy anything in their lives. 'Yes, thank yer' son, yer' mum and me are looking forward to moving to Sussex in about four weeks. Anyhow 'ow are you doing in Devon son? All right I 'ope?' said Father in his usual well balanced, unemotional voice. The conversation with my parents continued for about another ten minutes, thanks to the kindness of Mr Wilkes who let me use the office phone free of charge, as long as I cleaned his new Citroen car fortnightly.

Several months later, in May 1974, two of my colleagues, Bryan and Kevin, decided to leave Wilkes, which had brought relative security for them, to take a chance and branch out to work for themselves at forestry. I very much admired the risk they were both taking when you consider that both of them had young families to provide for, even though both had experienced the depressing downside of unemployment in the past. Bryan was under thirty years of age, had lived all his life around the Sparkwell area and married a local girl. He had been employed by Wilkes for six years and everyone knew him as a grafter and loyal friend. His short muscular body was well adapted to work for long hours grafting as a forester in tough woodland terrain. Kevin, on the other hand, was tall, slim and wiry, yet strong enough to work with the best. Putting aside his one foible, excessive alcohol consumption, he was a good provider, having worked for Wilkes for nearly nine years, for his partner and three children. The final contact I had with my two departing colleagues was at the Eagle Hotel in Ivybridge, where we celebrated their time at Wilkes, and wished them well for the future. John Wilkes delivered a rousing speech on behalf of everyone and personally thanked them for their industrious hard work. From all their colleagues we presented them with two recently published Woodland books, two thick shirts to keep them warm in winter and a large rubber axe each to remind them of their productive days at Wilkes.

Although I had by now been living in Sandstone for some time, my social life during that time had been irregular. That was because, although it was an attractive area for wild life, very few people actually lived there due to poor public services. Other than a small grocery store, landscape business and a few large detached houses, one of them occupied by Mr Wilkes' family, it was impossible in Sandstone to meet someone, anyone, my age. Walking with my colleagues was most enjoyable, but they spent most of their social time with families. I had visited two pubs on my own in Ivybridge but found them most uninspiring. The grooviest activity there appeared to be eating beef burgers in Tom's Place, a hip cafe catering for over-aged groupies, on the one hand, and bisexual dog owners, on the other. Well, that is the impression they gave me!

However, I had on occasions made the ten-mile bus journey to Plymouth, which I found to be full of social life for younger people. I had visited a few packed bars full of young drunken girls, all chain smoking, which I hated, as I didn't smoke. Most of them were wearing sexy miniskirts, had painted faces and excessively high-heel shoes—many men's idea of a very exciting evening! I had ventured into three different discos hoping to find myself a girlfriend, or failing this, meet a few blokes to chat and drink with, yet that also was fruitless. Due to a poor social life, I had been able to save a not insubstantial amount of money. However, the fact remained that I was young, socially isolated and in need of meeting people my own age. I had even thought about advertising in the local newspaper under the lonely hearts column for frustrated housewives seeking fun and debauchery!

Therefore, I was exceedingly pleased to find out that the two replacement foresters to arrive at Wilkes four weeks later were a similar age to myself. Derek and Alan were 25 and 28 years old respectively. Both had been socialised in Cornwall, had had various jobs associated with forestry, were single, and were itching to start work after several months of unemployment. As the other team were depleted by two workers, they joined up with Ted and Tim, for a few days of local hard work clearing timber for the local authority. Apparently they worked well, were team players and friendly to get on with. Meanwhile, due to Gordon and Dave being away for two days on health and safety training, both of the new workers joined up with our team as we had an urgent contract to sort out. Severe high winds had blown down a large conifer onto a busy track used by farmers in the attractive hamlet of St Germans, some fifteen miles west of Ivybridge. Upon arrival we realised how handicapped the farmers had become, as the fallen tree had lodged itself between two upright trees. For the next six hours we cut through the hard conifer wood with a chainsaw which eventually cut the tree in two. Then Mick manoeuvred the lorry into place, placed a large metal chain around the end of the section of tree that was half in a field of growing crops, and pulled it out of the way. The second section of the tree was treated likewise. To complete the job thoroughly, Mick pulled both pieces of timber, chained to his lorry, to the nearby farmer's yard and out of the way. The track was now clear once again for the busy farmers to use, even though they complained bitterly about the excessive fee charged by Wilkes.

'Right,' said Mick in a jubilant sort of way, 'who fancies a cuppa and sarnie with the local farmer?' We needed no convincing as we were truly exhausted and parched by hours of hard graft. ''Ere you are lads, on the table over there. Help yourselves to as much tea and sandwiches as yer can deal with. Don't forget to eat the scones, homemade by the missus, or otherwise, she'll box yer ears for yer,' explained the ruddy faced old farmer Tenby, who had a pronounced limp on his left leg. We really didn't know whether the farmer had an old war injury, or was limping due to the cash in his left pocket. I noticed that the farmer had many rusting pieces of old agricultural machinery in his yard including an old combine harvester that my father would have driven not too long ago at Lavender Farm. After our rest, Mick set sail for the yard at Sandstone; it was after 5pm, and all four of us had had enough graft for one day. It was during the journey back that Alan brought up the subject of wine, women and song. That was manna to my ears as we rolled along old country lanes that were originally made for farm animals over a hundred years ago. 'Yea, me and Del often go into Plymouth at weekends for a beer, and dancing in a disco somewhere. Come along sometime Dick and have some fun, why don't cher?' said Alan, who appeared to know what he was talking about. 'Yes, why not. What about this coming Friday? I can meet yer somewhere in Plymouth,' I suggested to my two potential partners in crime. 'Tell yer what Dick, a train from Ivybridge arrives at Plymouth Station at 8pm. We will see yer outside the station, okay?' said Derek, as he stroked his tousled long brown hair. So we arranged to meet the coming Friday, only three days away, and I was thrilled at the prospect.

The following day I phoned my parents at their smallholding, Buttercup Farm, in Offham, East Sussex. My parents, two uncles and aunts had been living there, I was surprised to be told, for nearly eighteen months, and things were going relatively well. They had bought in three sows to breed. The offspring had been sold on to local farmers they had got to know. Most of the sheep had lambed this year, and the brothers were looking forward to visiting the market in Highbury for the first time in September. All six of my family had all been busy with one job or another. The men focused mainly on the livestock, and the women took on the responsibility of looking after nearly everything inside the large detached house. Time permitting, they all enjoyed developing the garden cottage together, turning the soil over, digging in tons of animal waste, planting seeds and young tubers until they are mature enough to crop. They were never going to make a fortune—that was not their goal; all they wanted to achieve was to become self-sufficient and enjoy their lives in rural Sussex. That was the guiding light for all of them; as the years went by the intention was to work hard, save diligently for another day whereby they could buy more productive animals. I was so pleased for all of them.

As agreed beforehand, I met Alan and Derek outside the busy, newly decorated Plymouth railway station. They were there waiting for me, dressed in their modern clothes, ready to entice the young sexy girls of Plymouth into their waiting arms. 'All right Dicky boy, fit for a few beers and chat up a few ol' birds are we?' asked the tall, gangly Alan. 'You bet Al. I 'ave been looking forward to tonight very much,' I said. As the three of us marched away from the station there was only one thing on our minds: hedonism. The first bar we came across was playing very loud jukebox music, as scantily clad teenage girls smoking swarmed around it, pressing numerous random buttons hoping to play their chosen piece. Even though I was mindful of my dislike for cigarette smoke, I nonetheless, along with my two colleagues, walked up to the long crowded bar and joined the other jack-the-lads waiting to be served. With beer in hand, we eventually found a seat outside the bar, where we got into conversation with three smartly dressed young women, although one resembled a punk rocker. 'Hi there, what is your name, whe're you from?' Derek asked the most attractive one of the three. She had long blonde hair, and wore a pleasant dark green outfit. 'I'm Jenny and all three of us come from a suburb not far from here called Crownhill. My two other friends are Rose and Kathleen,' she said rather assertively. 'I'm Del; my two mates are called Dick to my right and this one is Al,' Derek nervously explained to the women sitting opposite us. And so the formal conversation went on for an hour, and in between time, I had bought another round of lager. 'Right, we are going to another bar, would you like to come with us girls?' I asked them politely, which I thought might persuade them to accompany us. 'No thanks,' said the punk looking one with short green hair, tartan skirt and Dr Martens shoes. I looked at the woman who had just spoken and asked, 'Rose, isn't it? Can we exchange phone numbers?' With that she gave me her home phone number and I gave her the office number at Sandstone, asking her not to phone during the day as it would get me into trouble with my boss. Phone evenings and weekends only, I was at pains to explain to Rose. Anyway, with that settled, we walked into several more loud, packed and smoked-filled bars all promising, no doubt, to fulfil our delusional dreams. Half drunk, I said goodbye to my delinquent partners, and, just in time, I caught the last night bus back to Ivybridge, pleased that I wasn't working the next day.

It was now March 1976. I had by this stage reached the grand old age of 26 years, and had been in gainful, yet uneventful, employment with Wilkes for nearly five years. On the whole I had enjoyed working there, but it was the good camaraderie with my supportive colleagues that I found sustained me through those times when I felt socially isolated from other young people. That particular Saturday morning, as I nursed an awful hangover from the night before, came an office phone call to my flat extension from Rose, whom I had met the night before in Plymouth but never really expected to hear from again. You speak superficially to hundreds of people during your travels, though you realise it means very little, or nothing whatsoever. 'Hi, is that Richard?' a soft voice asked from the other end of the phone. 'Yes speaking,' I said rather tentatively. 'Hallo, I'm Rose, how are you? Did you enjoy yourself in the pub?' she enquired. 'Not really. After we finished up our drinks we left, as you know, and later I took the bus back home,' I said, still rather bleary eyed. 'What about you and your two friends?' I asked half-heartedly. The chitchat went on for some time until I made an excuse about my colleague waiting impatiently for me outside my flat.

I met Rose Daly early the following Saturday for a drink in crowded Plymouth, and afterwards we made our way to a new punk rock club which had the ominous name Iron Fist. So began my four years foray into the loud aggressive obnoxious culture of punk rock, which had started in 1974 by a band called The Sex Pistols, and inhabited by characters such as Johnny Rotten and Sid Vicious. Other similar punk bands soon followed called the The Damned, Sham 69, Stiff Little Fingers, to name but a few of them. If nothing else, some might argue, punk blew away the UK conservative cobwebs by challenging the existing status quo. However, many before and since have tried, but failed, to overturn the powerful political establishment. At the time, punk in Northern Ireland gave Catholic and Protestant kids alike the opportunity to rebel against and something different for a while, instead of each other! But once punk became orthodox in the world it set out to destroy, when it was copied by others, it inevitably lost its power.

By now, Rose and I were dating on a regular basis. When I first met her she was 25 years of age, intelligent, attractive, a decent young woman who worked for a charity in Plymouth, giving aid to people in 3rd world countries. Her short, slim body was ideally suited to the hectic office where the maxim was 'time is money'. On several occasions, I met her friendly parents and two younger siblings for both dinner and lunch in their brightly decorated semi-detached house with neatly trimmed gardens, which epitomised the middle class neighbourhood. But they were honest, open, decent people, who encouraged me, whenever possible, to sleep in their comfortable home, realising that it was difficult for me to travel home. If only they had realised what their daughter and I were up to in Plymouth and further afield! Rose's parents managed their own small successful flower business from a large, wooden, tastefully decorated shed in the rear garden. Mr Tribe also drove the company van round Crownhill, and adjoining areas, delivering the phone ordered flowers.

Both Rose and I enjoyed, if that is the right word, visiting the wild Iron Fist punk club at least once or twice a week to dance, smoke dope and generally be out of our heads. Not very spiritual you may think! There were not only other punk clubs in the area, but also cafes, pubs and parties where one could meet like-minded people with a bent for something different. It was becoming more difficult for me to keep trying to balance my days working as a forester in Sandstone and finding time, and energy, to meet Rose in Plymouth. After trying to meet Rose at various venues during weekdays, I realised after a while that it was physically too much for me, which left weekends for us to enjoy ourselves together. During these times we would bed down with any other punks we had just met, but at this stage I was reluctant to invite even Rose, yet alone anyone else, back to my home. Besides I certainly didn't want Mr Wilkes to find out about my way of life out of working hours. One thing for sure is that Rose and I really launched ourselves into the punk scene, first at the Iron Fist, and, as we became known by others, also at other clubs and parties in other areas.

Punk culture can be best summed up in one word: uninhibited. The Sex Pistols had let lose upon the world spontaneity for a younger generation, who didn't show any constraint, or any regard, for what others might think. When Rose and I stepped onto a punk club dance floor, we totally let ourselves go; anything and everything were allowed to be expressed in the name of dancing. It was as though generations of class repression was now finding an acceptable social place, in some areas of society anyway, but in somewhat distorted human behaviour. At various clubs that Rose and I had visited, we danced among 60 to100 young people in a chaotic environment. This produced the conditions which gave most youngsters the ideal opportunity to jump, shout, scream, punch or even head bang in a frenzied manner which some observers might well have justifiably labelled insane. What is shocking, perhaps, is that I behaved outrageously myself amongst those young people who were head-butting each other. But at the time I knew no differently. Many times I have thought about what my parents, employers, colleagues, and even my friends from Yapton, might have said about my unusual—to put it mildly—social life.

At a party held in someone's house, in a small village called Downgate, there must have been at least 100 punks who attended, at various times, during a weekend of mayhem. I must say that I enjoyed the carefree, uninhibited some would say irresponsible, punk way of life or culture. Rose, however, was losing enthusiasm for it, due mainly to the sustained aggressive way of self-expression that at times frightened her beyond belief. To a certain extent, she did have my sympathy! The party at Downgate was at times so loud, that several times I had to leave the house to take fresh air and solitude in the nearby fields. Other than the quiet times in the house between 5-9am, music and human noise roared unabated. Jake, whose house we were using for the party, was unmistakably well into the punk scene. He had short red peroxide hair, a string vest, leather trousers, and large light blue boots. His muscular body was covered in tattoos showing punks in various carnal positions. A constant number of cannabis roll ups were balanced between Jake's fat rubber lips. As Jake had inherited the semi-detached house from his grandfather, a former convicted robber and seafarer, he, therefore, had very few debts or expenses. Jake was well known, and popular, in the punk fraternity for hosting weekend punk raves where no boundaries existed. He was also fortunate that he had young neighbours who either attended his raves, or were at least sympathetic, to a certain extent, to what he was doing.

It was early Saturday morning, about 3am, when things started to get out of hand. There were about fifty young people all dancing, for the want of a better definition, to loud Sham 69 music. Many of us had taken various drugs such as amphetamine, cannabis, acid and cocaine to name a few, which no doubt fuelled the intense atmosphere. In the large lounge most of the punks had taken off their clothes and were jumping about singing, dancing, shouting, even head-butting the walls and doors. Then someone threw a radio through the lounge glass window smashing it to pieces. Then all anarchy ensued. The radio was followed by a lampstand someone had hurtled through another window, as a young girl, wearing large black steel toe-capped boots, kicked in a third window. In a free for all, people threw bread, fruit, cushions, anything they could lay their hands on at one another. Some ravers poured bottles of alcohol, wine, spirits, even milk, over themselves, and over others, as they lay prostrate, in ecstasy, on the floor. One young lad, no more than 16 years of age, started urinating all over the lounge pot plants. As well as making my own destructive contribution, I was also hit in the face when a young woman hit me with a sink plunger making my nose bleed. I saw a young black chap, the first African/Caribbean punk I had seen, looking absolutely fantastic with his short pink hair, a white cross painted on his muscular chest, light blue jeans and the obligatory large painted boots guaranteed to cause maximum damage. While some of the party goers had gone into the back garden for fresh air to help bring them back to sanity, a few others were having sex on the lawn. By this time some of the neighbours were worried for the safety of their children; minutes later fathers and mothers started remonstrating with those having sex in front of others without any qualms whatsoever. Perhaps they were jealous. Other punks had started pulling up Jake's flowers from the borders of the back garden, and were throwing them at other punks. Four more blokes, wearing multi-coloured hair and boots, were kicking in the wooden fence down the bottom of the garden. Three others, including Rose, were knocking the shit out of a sickly looking young male punk, for whatever reason, I never knew, who had told them to grow up.

Minutes later three police cars pulled up outside Jake's house and quickly brought some air of sanity back to the village. In quiet and calm voices, the six police officers told those without clothes, to dress immediately and assembled us on the lawn, as it was now light, and proceeded to take down our personal details. By this time there was less than half of the original number of people around; when they saw the police arriving, they had scarpered over the fields to safety. It made me roll over in stitches laughing, when I overheard one of the punks, his real name was Fred, being interviewed by the police. 'What's your name, son?' asked the surly young copper with a red coloured moustache under his long nose. 'Steel head governor.' 'Is that your real name, son?' 'Yep,' replied Fred smiling. 'Where do you live, boy?' asked the police officer, as his face reddened in anger. 'I live in a tree,' was Fred's unemotional reply. 'What age are you, boy?' came the next question from the exasperated officer. 'I'm 45.' With that the police officer walked away realising he would be more productive elsewhere. No one was arrested as all the damage was carried out in Jake's house, and he told the police to sling their hooks. Punks used different names due to police interference, so you never got to know their real names, but I never did once change my name.

The demanding, yet at times, enjoyable world of work continued at Wilkes Forestry Ltd. There had been no more changes in personnel since Alan and Derek first started work some two years ago. The two forestry teams continued to function well together. Our work output had increased over the past two years, as my colleagues and I all focused on what we were trying to achieve together. Whatever that was! From time to time, John Wilkes used to assemble all his workers in the yard, weather permitting, and deliver a kind of pep talk, just like a sergeant major addressing his underlings, with the intention of motivating us to become more productive. One year his usual spiel went something like this: 'Brilliant, chaps, we had a good year thanks to your immeasurable efforts, but room for improvement.' 'Only two months to go, and with a little more determination, we can beat last year's output, chaps. I know you have all got it in you to do that.' 'Christmas will soon be upon us, and knowing we have all made a serious contribution to the company's success, we can then enjoy the festivities with our loved ones. That requires we all pull together in the right direction.' So on and so forth. However, very little financial reward was ever forthcoming.

That year I decided to take a ten-day holiday with my family down in sunny Sussex. Alighting from the local train in Lewes, my father was there on the platform, with an unusual smile on his weather-beaten face to greet me. For the first time that I can recall, we embraced with such intensity on the station that, at first, I was taken aback, considering the repressed background he came from. But, nonetheless, I enjoyed being held by my father. We drove the two miles to Offham, a small village consisting of a large cattle farm, another smallholding, smaller than my parents', several houses, a general store and an 18th century pub called The Harvester. As we got out of Father's newish dark blue Ford truck, ideal for transporting small loads, my mother, uncles and aunts were waiting for me. We all warmly and comfortably embraced each other for the first time, as Mother reminded me, in six years. I was dumbfounded that so many years had gone by, and shocked that I was unaware of it. Although I had contacted my parents regularly over the years from Devon, including sending cards to celebrate birthdays and anniversaries, I was quite ashamed I had not visited them in all that time. I felt that I had been somewhat selfish and self-indulgent during that time, and that I had paid little attention to my parents' needs.

Sitting round the large oak dining table in the evening, a piece of furniture that had cost the four of them over two hundred pounds and was their pride and joy, eating fresh roast pork from the smallholding, I brought up the sensitive subject of not visiting my parents for six years. 'I'm flabbergasted Mum and Dad, that I 'aven't seen you both for so long. All I can do is apologise for being so selfish.' 'Don't worry son,' said my father reassuringly, 'we realise you are young, and yer want ter enjoy yerself with other young people. Besides, you are a long way orf down there in Devon. Anyhow son, 'ow's the job?' 'Good Mum and Dad, Eric, Jack, Jane and Sarah. I've now been working for Wilkes for six years and the money is good, although we work 'ard for it. I have a girlfriend called Rose. She works for a charity. I sent you quite a few photos of me and her, didn't I Mum? My self-contained flat in the yard at Sandstone is very comfortable, but even though I am not supposed to, Rose has stayed with me there quite a few times at weekends but not during the week, as the guvnor arrives very early each morning. Someday I hope to get my own place. I would also like to apologise to you, uncles and aunts, for only writing to you a few times over the years. I 'ope you all received the photographs of me and Rose I sent last week?' I said, rather sheepishly in one long breath to all of them. I hoped the sincere apologies to my family had laid the foundation stone for the few enjoyable days ahead, living and working alongside my family on their busy smallholding.

Back in Devon, my social life with Derek and Alan continued for another few boozy outings in Plymouth. As usual, we used to meet outside the railway station early evening, and then proceed into the town for an evening of debauchery, wandering from pub to bar around this famous naval port. It was on one of these aimless jaunts that I came across Pippa, a youthful looking, tallish, attractive, red haired Irish woman who worked in the nearby docks, not as a beer swilling stevedore but as a personal assistant to the harbourmaster, the ugly pugnacious Wilfred Capstone. When his belly was full of whisky, he used to goad men in the pub to a fight with him out on the jetty. The loser would have to buy the winner spirits for the rest of the evening. Apparently, his grandfather was infamous for doing his utmost to get non-believers jailed for a few days if he saw them drinking alcohol on the Sabbath. Anyhow, so began a new relationship with Pippa that didn't last that long. Unfortunately, Rose and I had parted company, mainly due to her falling out of love with me, punk, alcohol and most men, but not necessarily in that order. She was desperate, I surmised, to get married, have a family and live happily ever after.

However, it transpired, to my great delight, that Pippa enjoyed the punk scene. She could down gallons of alcohol in any one session, craved smoking large cannabis joints, and afterwards she loved singing punk songs to the assembled crowd. We did a lot of head-banging together, with many others in clubs and bars around Plymouth docks, which was notorious in those days for prostitutes. Many times, I thought to myself, that I had met my match when trying to keep up with her excessive demands for long drawn-out sex games. Mindful, of course, that most men would have given their right arm, or even both arms, to meet a woman like the voracious Pippa. At punk parties, where outrageous behaviour is re-enforced at any, and every opportunity, Pippa used to wear a black transparent bodice, skin-tight trousers with multi coloured boots, fit only for inflicting severe damage on anyone silly enough to challenge her. On many occasions, she really looked the part, as she jumped up and down trying to head butt the bourgeois looking chandelier in the local Chinese restaurant. However, because of having a normal job, so to speak, she was unable, most of the time, to spike and /or colour her silky, long red hair.

On another occasion, at a party, or a rave really, held by one of our disturbed punk friends called Savage Sid, who incidentally had received private education, Pippa and I had hired two outrageous costumes for a few days. We entered Sid's house around midnight, (his parents having gone away to stay in their other house in the Orkneys), wearing a blue, spiked wig each. Pippa had lipstick, mascara and rouge all over her face; she wore a yellow micro bra, a red micro thong hardly covering her genitals, and pink laced thigh boots emitting various flashing coloured lights. My hair was tinged with green and red stripes, my face had mascara all over it, I wore a full-length, transparent, silk female body stocking, and my boots made an outrageous wailing sound. Not a pretty sight to the untrained eye or ear. When she started head-banging in the centre of the room, she was quickly joined by many others; they all began dancing round the outside of her as they flailed their arms and legs in a frenzy of excitement. Her 33-year-old voluptuous body did not inhibit her as teenagers fought each other to kiss her hot, sweating body. Later on in the evening she kept asking me if I would have group sex with her as the central figure of lust. That was one area of sexuality that I dared not venture into, although I was relatively sober at the time. But I'm afraid to say, given the opportunity now, I wouldn't hesitate to participate in such excessive indulgences.

From about this time, I started to change the prevailing conditions in my life. Pippa and I had moved on from each other, although I had really enjoyed her company. Punk was on the wane, but more importantly, I had come to a stage in my life when I had to take stock of my employment and social situation, even though I had, relatively, enjoyed both. I had noticed that frustration, once again, was creeping into my life at times, especially as I was living on my own in the yard at Sandstone. I was mindful, that eventually, I would have to find new accommodation elsewhere if I were to improve my social life and find a woman friend. In essence, I was in a catch 22 situation. I realised that I was fortunate to be living in a free self-contained flat with modern facilities and in a quiet location. But if I moved away, all I would be able to afford would be, probably, a small bedsit in a multi-occupied house, somewhere in crowded cosmopolitan Plymouth. I started subscribing to a monthly magazine advertising various forestry, and affiliated vacancies in the United Kingdom, hoping that something, anything, would help improve my quality of life. After all, now that I was 29 years old, I had assumed that the evolutionary process within me had, once again, started to move me forward, yet, where to, I did not know.

The one pressing desire that I had managed to suppress for some time, but which now needed my full attention, was to meet up with childhood friends from Yapton for the first time in more than eight years. I had phoned, and sent them post cards and lots of photographs. After various phone calls and negotiations, we made firm arrangements to meet in our old stomping ground, the Country Squire pub. Due to the long journey, I had travelled up by train from Devon to London the night before, stayed in a B&B overnight in Norwich and arrived early next morning in Yapton. Aware that none of my friends had arrived yet, I enjoyed wandering around the place that helped educate and socialise me. The village store, the place where my mother had worked hard for so long, was still in business. Her friend, the late Mrs Anderson, had also enjoyed working there for many years. The village war memorial looked clean and proud, adorned with poppies and fresh flowers, saluting local fallen heroes. I walked past my old house, the place where I had grown up and had had so many good times with the support of my parents. The house had been repainted a beautiful lilac. The front garden was full of pink summer roses, and bees hummed around, pollinating them. A modern extension had been built onto the old primary school, which did not surprise me, as it was small even when I went there. A growing number of people had moved into Yapton over the years, so it was not surprising that more space was needed to accommodate the children. Walking past a row of old, attractive, Victorian terraced houses, with front gardens full of roses, lavender and petunias, I came across an old face I had not seen since my schooldays. 'Hallo, young Richard Morris, how are you keeping? I've not seen you for many years,' came a voice from my early life. I realised it was one of the former primary school teachers, Mrs Hegley, who looked so well, and had a memory as sharp as a pin. 'Hallo Mrs Hegley, how good to see you after so many years!' I responded. 'What are you doing with yourself? Are you working?' she enquired. 'I'm livin' in Devon and workin' as a forester. I've been at that job for over eight years,' I told her.

I walked on to the cemetery to visit my dear old friend, Richard Arrowsmith, who was tragically killed as a young boy. Sitting there in front of Richard's grave conjured up so many thoughts and feelings from our past of when we used to walk, run, and climb trees together. St Peter's Church clock struck midday, which reminded me that I was meeting my friends in the local pub. When I opened the pub door, I was confronted by a sea of friendly faces all staring at me from the bar. 'About time you visited us all 'ere! Where 'ave you bin hiding Dicky after all this time?' several friends appeared to ask in unison. Yes, all those rascals were there: Terry Anderson, Dennis Zeal, Bert Moore, Philip Maynard, and most surprising of all, Billy MacDonald, whose life continued to be tough. Other than Bert, who still lived with family at the house where he was born, all the others had moved away from Yapton. In their own way, all my friends, it appeared, were engaged in something, that if it did not interest them, it at least earned them a living. It was most pleasing to know that Philip had managed to overcome his mental health problems, and was now living in Norwich; he had moved on from the porter job to a regular job at British Telecoms as a technician. We all spoke about and discussed various personal problems, from sex, money, work to relationships. After an enjoyable few beers, eating a tasty homemade pub meal together, and catching up on the local gossip, we agreed to keep in contact. But, of course, that did not last for very long. That night, and the following day, I spent some time with an old school friend, Brian Davies, who I had not seen for many years. I had met him only by chance two days before, when I was alighting from my London train that had just arrived at Norwich station.

Although I continued to work for Wilkes for another year or so, I did managed to find myself a large, decent, smartly decorated bedsit near Plymouth railway station. My furnished bedsit was one of six self-contained rooms in a large Edwardian house, where the toilet facility was the only service we had to share. That pleased me, because I didn't enjoy sharing with other people, especially if they were strangers. Being an only child, I was used to having my own space full of toys, books and games which I played with endlessly in my own time. There was also a large rear garden, full of various shrubs and plants, which residents could use. My employer, Mr Wilkes, appeared to be disappointed by my departure from the Sandstone accommodation, but realised that I needed more independence. It was the 3rd November 1980 and I would be 31 years old the following January.   My two supportive colleagues, Mick and Dave, helped me move my few chattels and goods into 6 Dundonald Road, Plymouth. Reassured by finding a decent rented place of my own, now was the time I should invest all my energy in finding appropriate employment for the future. Those intense feelings of frustration, coupled with a desire to make a success of something, began once again to follow me around.

So that I could get to Sandstone in time for the 7:30am meeting with my colleagues, I would be out of bed early to have my breakfast, take the short walk to Plymouth station to catch the train to Ivybridge, where Mick used to drive me to the yard. Our forestry team—Mick, Tim, Gordon and I—had been working together for some considerable time. We all got on well, and supported each other, but not surprisingly there was the occasional bit of friction, mainly due to one of us being late and not telling Mick. Kids' stuff, really. Other than Christmas, or some other notable occasion, we did not socialise together that often. The one incident we did have during our working years together brought out the best in my colleagues, and hopefully, in me. We had driven to a large private country estate, close to Upton Penny, to remove a large beech tree that had been blown down onto the owner's new greenhouse. We worked hard nonstop all day; we eventually sawed the tree into several small, removable pieces that we threw onto the lorry. The estate manager, a pedantic old fart of the first order, emerged to inspect our work; we anticipated he would sign our contract document. 'Hold on there, chaps, whereabouts are the ten African lilies pots I put there, only yesterday, under that bench?' he asked Mick. 'I 'aven't got a clue governor. We 'aven't seen 'em'. 'Are you sure my dear man? They belong to Sir David Napthorne, the owner of this grand estate. I shall phone Mr Wilkes about this,' said the crusty manager.

When we arrived back at Sandstone, Mr Wilkes, and two police officers, where waiting for us. 'Hi, Mick. We have heard from the estate manager that they are missing ten pots. He also rang for the police to sort it out,' explained the unflappable Mr Wilkes. Suffice to say we were all interviewed, at length, about the missing plants, but, we corroborated each other's evidence. The manager had accused us of stealing the pots, but he had not one shred of evidence against us. We took it all in our stride knowing it was all hot air. Three weeks later it transpired that young local boys, who constantly used the woods for climbing trees, had taken them home.

Sandra Greaves was a 30-year-old, tall, slim, attractive woman who I had met one morning on the way to Plymouth station. She had originally come from Somerset, but moved to Devon when her employer, Pipe Accountants, had relocated. Sandra had worked for them, as a bookkeeper, for ten years, and, at some stage, she had wanted to train as an accountant. When we started dating regularly, she used to stay at my place during the week, but she enjoyed spending the weekend with her divorced mother in her comfortable house in nearby Liskeard. I enjoyed Sandra's company; she was good fun, intelligent and wanted to be successful, which was expected of her, as she came from a family of high achievers. She was very pragmatic in nearly all that she committed herself to, including our ten months' relationship. Sandra certainly didn't use me, not at all, but she kept a certain healthy emotional distance in our relationship. I admired her for that; she was focused, and I learned a lot from our time together. Most of all I enjoyed the stimulating conversations we had in my bedsit, especially after returning from the theatre, or cinema, or talks given by a local historian. Nearly a year on, just before my departure from Ivybridge, Sandra left her employer to start an economics degree in London.

Chapter 8

MOVING ON: FORESTRY WORK
WITH THE WOODLAND TRUST
IN SUSSEX

NEW EMPLOYMENT at last: 'Dear colleagues, Richard came here to work, a decade ago, as a bright eyed, enthusiast 21-year-old full of the joys of spring. Over that time I have seen him grow, develop and become an integral part of our successful forestry business. From a slim young man, he has burgeoned, in more ways than one, into a mature man. With deep regret, we have to say goodbye to Richard; understandably, he has sought pastures new with the Woodland Trust in Sussex, where, I hope he will continue to carry on the high standard of practice he has demonstrated during his productive time here. With the greatest reluctance we have to let Richard go forth, but we wish Richard all the greatest success in the future. I proudly present to Richard, this painting of the Golden Forester, to remember us by when he is shinning up a tree somewhere out there. With all our esteem for him, we wish him our fondest farewell. I would like to give a toast to Richard Morris.' I was quite overcome with emotion by what the effervescent Mr Wilkes had to say about my time working for him as a forester, and my future good prospects working with the Woodland Trust. That last evening, and having an enjoyable meal in the local Hotel with my colleagues, shall remain in my memory, hopefully, forever.

The position that I had successfully applied for was as a senior forester located in the Ashdown Forest, Sussex, with the Woodland Trust. Fortunately the job came with a one-bedroom cottage on the out skirts of the forest in the small village of Newbridge. The accommodation was conveniently situated near a small road, just in case I needed to attend, or phone 999, for emergencies such as forest fires, people needing medical attention, or broken down vehicles. There were roadside telephones all around the forest, so users had the opportunity to phone my cottage direct, or contact the emergency service themselves. Working with three other colleagues, forestry duties included the everyday management of the landscape, inspection of various public buildings such as the information centre, tea room and toilets. Most importantly we had to keep the roads clear of broken down cars, remove tree debris and sort out many other problems that arose ad hoc. The manager, Nick Peters, aged 35, who had overall responsibility for the well-being of the Ashdown Forest, was married with two children, and lived in a trust-owned three-bedroom cottage in the small, but expanding town of Crowborough.

The change that I had desperately sought had at last come to fruition. At 31 years of age, I moved into my small, but comfortable, cottage in Newbridge on a sunny autumn day with a brilliant blue sky above. Was that a positive sign for the future? My accommodation had three rooms, consisting of a bedroom, lounge, and kitchen plus a small combined bathroom/toilet. The whole cottage was furnished, and tastefully decorated, with white ceilings and lemon walls. I did supply my own kitchen utensils and bed coverings. More importantly, for me, was the reassuring sight of the two small gardens. The front garden had a small green lawn, a colour similar to the baize on a snooker table, with a large Lavatera, with white flowers, in the centre of it. In springtime the front garden was full of daffodils and crocuses. The rear garden had a mature cherry tree, several different coloured roses and ground-cover plants, including Forget-me-nots, all over the borders. If there were a place where one felt secure and peaceful, then this was it. Nick Peters had phoned to inform me that I could take the next few days off to orientate myself. With that in mind, I potted about doing this and that, but really not achieving very much except sitting out in the attractive rear garden thinking about the past. In the evening I lit a small fire in the half drum provided for such occasions. The wood crackled and sparks shot up into the night sky, as I thought about my life during the past thirty years. How could billions of individual people living in a world full of strife, I thought, possibly find the right conditions to enjoy their lives? But at this moment in time, I felt that I had arrived!

There was a sharp knock on the front door. There stood my manager ready to welcome me to Ashdown Forest. The last time I had seen Nick was weeks ago, when I attended for the job interview. 'Welcome Richard. I'm Nick Peters as you know. Our three colleagues here are Mark Mills, Roy Short and Colin Denby,' said Nick. Using the large Woodland Trust owned Leyland truck, ideal for tough terrains and carrying heavy loads, Nick drove us the short journey to the information centre at Wych Cross. This was our base, where we met most days, usually in the morning, to discuss what had to be done, write out our reports, eat, and dry our wet clothes. It was also at times a place of sanctuary, where one could reflect, dream, fantasize, meditate, or perform any other personal practice that helped an individual. In the centre there were various pieces of written information available free for people using the forest, whether that be walking, cycling, running or driving. From time to time we also held talks about the diverse flora and fauna to be found in the Ashdown Forest. After being allocated a safe cupboard for my personal items—I called it an inner sanctum—Nick explained, in great detail, what the day's work entailed, who was going to work where and so on. 'The most important piece of equipment, Richard, is our two-way radio. This must be fully charged every day before leaving the base. The reason is that we need to be able to communicate effectively, throughout the day, with each other. That means, every day after finishing our work, we must put them on charge all night so they are ready to use next day for our work,' said Nick emphatically.

Most days we worked in pairs. It was only when a large forestry job materialised, or in emergencies, that we all worked together. On this particular day I was paired up with the likeable Colin Denby. Colin lived with his wife and four children in Crowborough. He was 40 years of age, and had worked as a forester for the Woodland Trust for over ten years. He always wore his dirty old blue cap sideways. Colin had a toothless mouth, and a lined, ugly face, typical of most working class men in those days. He was short, muscular, had little to say about anything, and never spoke about his feelings. When he did speak to me, it was obligatory, 'alwight Richy boy'. During the first week of working together he drove the pair of us to his house to collect a saw, which belonged to his employer; he had been using it to repair his old wooden shed. I gave him a hand to finish fixing the last piece of felt to the roof. Afterwards he invited me into his house. 'Tea wif sugar and milk son. Fancy a biscuit?' asked Colin. 'Me and the missus and kids moved in 'ere about six years ago. Belongs to the council. Cheap rent,' explained my mild mannered colleague. While he went to the toilet, I looked around at the clothes, toys and unwashed crockery and cutlery which were strewn all over the kitchen. I was staggered to know that people could live in such squalor. 'It's in a bit of er two and eight [state] in it, Richy' boy,' said Colin, as he put five heaped teaspoons of sugar into his second large mug of tea.

Not long after I had been working for my current employer, Colin and I were called to an emergency in the High Weald area of the forest, where a woman had driven her car into a shallow ditch, not a hundred yards from the B2188. Somehow she had manoeuvred the car over a small parapet protecting the muddy ditch, and had tried unsuccessfully to get it out. I hooked one end of a heavy chain onto the back of Colin's truck, and the other round the bumper of the new French car. With that in place, I instructed both drivers to hit the accelerator while I pushed the car with all my might. We were nearly over the lip of the ditch to safety, when the unimaginable happened; unable to grip the top of the ditch, the car rolled back pinning my shin and foot underneath the car wheel. By the time Colin had pulled my foot out from under the car wheel, I was in desperate agony; I suspected I had sustained an injury to my lower leg and/or foot. The ambulance arrived in fifteen minutes to drive me to the A&E department in East Grinstead. The X-rays showed that two small bones in my left foot had been broken, which, although not serious, meant I would have to be off work for about two months. Nick arrived about two hours later to drive me back to my retreat. What a sorry sight I must have looked as I gingerly, with the help of Nick, got out of the car wearing a plaster cast round my foot, supporting myself on a Charlie Chaplin lookalike walking stick the hospital had kindly given me.

'Well, Richard, I'm sorry to hear that you will be off work for two months,' said my manager. 'I will have to bring you over a bundle of *Penthouse* magazines to read at your leisure, now that you have plenty of time on your hands.' With that he said goodbye, and promised to phone me the next day to see if

I was still alive! Nick was a good manager, whose kind decent qualities I found, at times, quite moving. Here I was in my warm cottage, with plenty of food and living in a quiet, inspiring place with only the animals around for comfort. But in time I would also need sexual companionship! A head-banging, eighteen-year-old punk, with purple hair and white Dr Martens boots, came to mind!

As long as I supported my foot, the physiotherapist agreed that I could hobble slowly round my cottage to cook food, use the toilet and wash myself, but no wandering off at midnight to saw down a tree, paint the cottage, or run round the forest. The night before I had phoned my parents to explain the predicament I was in. They duly cancelled a three-day trip to visit their friend on the Isle of Wight. Instead they arrived at my cottage a day later carrying a large bunch of roses, chocolates, bird books and two carrier bags full of groceries. 'Come in, Mum and Dad. Are you both well? Thanks a million for all this stuff you've bought me. Thank God I'm off work for about eight weeks,' I said as I put my arms round them. I took them out into the garden, and insisted on making them tea and sandwiches, which was probably the first that that I had ever made either of them in their lives. As I looked out at them from my kitchen window, I realised how well they looked after more than nine years of living and working on their smallholding in Sussex. My mother was now 57 years and my father 55 years of age respectively. 'How is the farm progressing Dad? And how are my uncles and aunts?' I asked them. 'Well, yer uncles and aunts are all fine. Like us, they love working and living at Buttercup Farm,' said Father in his matter of fact manner. 'Last year we bought two more acres of pasture land for our ever growing flock of cattle, and we have been doing well selling our sheep at the market in Uckfield,' said Mother enthusiastically. My parents and I spoke at length for more than four hours. It was good to see them again. It was also re-assuring to know that I lived less than 20 miles from their smallholding, and in time I planned to pass my driving test so that I could visit them more often.

Confined to my cosy accommodation, I had the opportunity to phone various people, especially my childhood friends from Yapton. One of my friends, Bert Moore, I phoned several times trying to encourage him to make the longish journey down from Norfolk. As it transpired, he had to drive to London a week hence to deliver several gaming machines to a customer near London Bridge. I was pleased to know he still had the same job, as I had realised he enjoyed what he did for a living. He booked B&B accommodation in South London, which left him with a drive of under two hours to Newbridge. I was sitting in the garden, fantasizing about the number of fair young maidens I was going to entice into my bachelor pad, when all of a sudden a dark green van drove into my shingle drive. The man himself, Bert Moore, got out of the car wearing a bright jumper and smiling all over his chubby, red face. 'All right Bert, 'ow are yer keeping my dear friend?' I said as we embraced each other. 'I'm fine, Rich. Good ter see yer once again. It looks a fine old gaff you 'ave 'ere,', said my friend who still lived in Yapton with his family. 'Come inside Bert and 'ave a look around,' I said. 'What in the fuck 'appened to your foot?' asked Bert pointing at my damaged foot. Without too much embarrassment, I managed to explain how a silly bitch from France had failed to follow my driving instructions. 'Never mind, Richy boy. You fight to live another day as they say in Yapton. Anyway I really like your place and it went with the job, you lucky bastard. 'Ad any birds 'ere yet?' asked Bert, whose sexuality was unclear, I thought, because I had never seen him with a woman during the thirty years I had known him. Perhaps he was asexual, and preferred the security of living with his family, and if that was the case, then I was in complete sympathy with him. Bert's short stocky frame had put on a considerable amount of weight over the years, which isn't surprising, as his mother was well known for making mouth-watering homemade pies and puddings.

We moved from my small furnished kitchen, out into the garden patio, where I placed the tray of tea, sandwiches and cake on the round timber treated table. 'Help yerself to the food and tea, Bert.' He swiftly grabbed, with his large pinkish fingers that reminded me of pork sausages, two cheese sandwiches and two slices of fruit cake. For the next ten minutes we just sat there drinking and eating; nothing was said by either of us until he broke the silence. Hesitating at first, he managed to start talking. 'Richard, I've got something to tell yer. It's about my family really, if yer know what I mean. It was bit of eh bombshell when me mum told me about two years ago. I would 'ave told you before but I ain't 'ad the opportunity, see. Me mum told me that me dad isn't me real dad see. She said that she 'ad a short affair with a young feller who was workin' on the nearby 'ouses in the village. Me mum said she saw 'im only a few times, and then 'e left to go back to Ireland see, and she never saw 'im agen,' explained the sad looking, dejected Bert as tears began to flow down his chubby cheeks. I put my arms round him to try and comfort and reassure him.

'Blimey Bert, I'm so sorry to 'ear that. Obviously I never knew and I've never heard that in the village before. Does your father, sorry, well, stepfather know?' I falteringly tried to ask Bert. 'Yeah, he knows all right. He's known for a long time according to me mum. And me sisters know and other people in me family also know,' explained Bert. 'What about our friends, do they know?' I asked, thinking to myself that I should not ask Bert any more personal questions as he was becoming rather upset. 'Yeah, all the lads know all right. I've told 'em all. Not surprisin' they were all shocked. None of their parents' knew either. It was a well-kept secret all right. On me birth certificate, I 'ave got the name of me dad at 'ome on it. Anyway Tom is my real dad all right. He has always loved me as his own son and he told me so only recently,' said Bert bursting out crying, as I put my arms round him. I held him for some time to reassure him that he was a good person, friend and son. Not coming from a background where people spoke of their feelings and emotions, I felt a little unnerved, holding my dear friend as he breathed heavily inches from my ear. Intense feelings of sadness for Bert welled up in me. But it was certainly important for me to be able to witness what he was feeling at a time of insecurity.

Having been declared fit for work by my GP, after three long months, not two months as was originally thought, I once again joined my colleagues at the information centre in Wych Cross. 'That's a long doss you've 'ad Richard. 'Ope all is well now?' said my colleague Mark, as he stood there testing the two-way radios. Mark, aged 39, was tall, slim, had worked for the Woodland Trust for about six years and lived with his parents in East Grinstead. His one passion in life was river fishing. At every opportunity Mark would take off for two days, or more, with all his fishing gear and tent, and find himself a quiet spot somewhere in the Sussex or Kent countryside to fish. 'Yes, welcome back Richard,' said Nick Peters. 'So Richard, once again pair up with Colin as you did before your accident. Mark and Roy, you work together,' said Nick, as he explained the day's work ahead of us. Just as Colin and I were leaving, Nick reminded me of two important things that I must keep in mind. The first was to prepare myself for the forthcoming visit of children from Tainton School in

Uckfield. I was to talk to them for about an hour in the visitor centre about the various wild animals that live in the Ashdown Forest. The other reminder was about learning to drive. For many years I had thought about the advantages of being able to drive, but inexplicably I never got round to taking the driving test. Now that I was working here in the forest, it was essential that I had a full driving license, not just for my forestry duties, but also when unforeseen emergencies arose at any time of the day or night. Besides, what more incentive was there to being able to drive competently, than to visit my parents whenever I chose?

Today, with the warm sun above us, was as good as any other to start learning to drive. With the L-plates tied on the front and back of the three-ton Bedford, I anxiously drove out of our base onto a public road for the first in my life, hoping that I would not encounter many vehicles. The lorry jumped and spluttered like a young donkey, as I tried to find the right gears. Colin sat next to me laughing, and trembling like a jelly, not knowing what to say or do. All I hoped for was that he wasn't going to jump out of the cab and leave me on my own to crash into nearby trees. It was at this anxious moment that I thought of taking out an advert in the local paper, warning people to take caution on the roads as Richard Morris was learning to drive! With our nerves torn to ribbons after my erratic driving, we eventually arrived at our first job together since my foot injury three months before. Still in one piece, Colin and I jumped out of the cab rather gingerly. 'Bloody 'ell Richy boy, after that escapade, I need a fucking large whisky to sooth me nerves,' said my colleague as he lit one of his roll-up cigarettes soaked in spittle. 'Sorry about that, Colin. It's called beginner's nerves. Sure you don't wanna take over driving again?' I said as I tried to reassure him that I would get better at driving, though nothing was guaranteed. After collecting our faculties together, we starting sizing up a conifer that badly needed to be pruned back. The lower branches were hanging over a busy track, thereby preventing people from passing safely. We always encouraged the public to report to us immediately any type of problem in the forest.

As the first few weeks went by, Colin, who had not suffered from any noticeable mental breakdown, realised my driving was slowly improving. I even found out how to fill the lorry with the diesel and oil, although the dashboard still reminded me somewhat of being in an airplane. Ever since those days of learning to drive, in what most people would consider a small vehicle, I have had the greatest admiration for those people who drive huge juggernauts hundreds of miles, on packed motorways, across Europe. Ever since I first travelled in a car with my parents, I have always felt frightened by the noise and power of large lorries stacked with heavy loads passing me on busy main roads. In fact when my father first took me for a drive on his tractor, when I was about five years old, I felt petrified by the noise it made, and by the size of the back tyres which towered above me like some black monster. Incidentally, my father still insists that it was those earliest, frightening, experiences of noisy farm vehicles that dissuaded me from making a working life in farming.

The day arrived for my first educational talk to children, aged between 10-12, from Tainton School. The school had been sending their children to learn about the flora and fauna of Ashdown forest for many years. It was originally set in motion by a former headmaster of the school, Daniel Woodruff, who was a keen environmentalist and lifelong supporter of the Woodland Trust. Ably assisted by another colleague, Roy Short, Colin was otherwise preoccupied having his last two rotten teeth extracted, setting up the classroom with specimens, such as wild birds, fox and squirrels for the children to look at. We also placed on desks, paper, pencils and crayons for them to write or draw on to record their experiences during their visit. After about ten minutes, when I was explaining the varied and interesting work of a forester, one eager young boy jumped to his feet to tell us that his grandfather was also a forester somewhere in Scotland. The children were most enthusiastic and knowledgeable when I quizzed them about the names of different wild animals or plants in the Ashdown Forest. Having walked there many times with their parents, teachers and friends, most of the children were familiar with the abundant wild life in the forest.

Nearing the end of an enjoyable few hours of teaching, I explained to the children about my own experiences as a young boy growing up in Yapton: I painted a mental picture of my love for the countryside as a place of fun and excitement, where my friends and I climbed tall trees, such as oak, beech and horse chestnut; how we collected birds' eggs, my favourite bird being a jay, and walked long distances over old dusty paths to steal farmer Jackson's prized Victoria plums. That made them all laugh! Furthermore, I explained that the knowledge and skills I had acquired from those early days had put me in good stead later in life to find employment as a forester. Those early childhood experiences, I emphasised to them, nurtured my wonder of all things wild, like the crow, fox or stoat. Aware of their young ages, I told them we must do all we can to eradicate poisons, such as pesticides and herbicides, that kill wild animals, including fish, but also trees, flowers and all plant life. This understanding, and great enthusiasm, for the love of nature, I emphasized, had been fostered by the influential research of Rachel Carson, a biologist from the USA. She had exposed, along with others, the destruction of wildlife through the widespread use of various poisons in the

USA. I concluded that it was a personal delight to be able to experience the British autumn when leaves turn brown, yellow and then red, and drop to mulch the ground below. The children were really interested in listening to what I told them; encouraged by their female teacher, they also wanted to listen to what Roy had to say about his childhood growing up in Anglesey, North Wales. After Roy had completed his interesting talk about his semi-nomadic life as a young boy, all the children enthusiastically cheered and thanked us for inviting them to the centre. It was a great success.

Roy Short, aged 37, had worked for the Woodland Trust for the best part of eight years, ever since he had moved from his birthplace in North Wales. He lived with his partner, but had no children, in a caravan near Forest Row. A rugged sort of bloke, Roy reminded me somewhat of what a true Celtic warrior might have looked like: he was as wide as he was tall, with a huge chin jutting out from his face like a piece of sculptured marble. His big hands, which were supported by huge muscular arms, made his exploits of throwing heavy pieces of wood many yards look like kids' play. Due to his occasional outbursts at his colleagues, and members of the public, we became rather wary of Roy, although he had a good heart.

At the insistence of Mark, my four colleagues and I decided to meet for a social drink in Crowborough. The Golden Hind was a small, comfortable Victorian pub which was frequented mostly by local people. The decorated white walls, with farming paraphernalia all over them, blended in well with the quiet friendly atmosphere of the place. Living just a few minutes' walk away, both Colin and Nick used the pub for a convenient beer after finishing work at the end of the day, or at weekends, when their young families could cavort in the large garden. As I walked into the pub for the first time, my eyes picked up Colin, who had ensconced himself on a large blue cotton-covered armchair drinking a beer and smoking one of his wretched strong cigarettes that always smelt of horse manure. 'Good evening Lord Tenby, 'ow is it going?' I asked Colin, who was sitting there like the Lord of the Manor. 'Hi, Richard. Good to see yer once again. What you 'aving son?' said my colleague. 'Pint of bitter please, me old mucker,' I said. At that moment, my three other colleagues came in and joined us sitting in the corner of the pub. The five of us sat there talking about the inevitable subject of work. Nick bought the next round. 'How is it going, Richard? Is your foot okay? You don't get any pain do you?' enquired my manager. Nick Peters had originally trained in Garden Design at Hadlow Agricultural College in Kent. From there he had worked ten years for the National Trust, where he learnt, amongst other things, forestry. When I met him he had been employed by the Woodland Trust for three years. He was an articulate, intelligent person, who was always prepared to help his fellow beings when needed. His forestry knowledge was quite remarkable.

As Roy was the only teetotaller, he was always happy to take our colleagues and me for a beer in a local pub. On the return journey he would drive Mark back to East Grinstead, and me to my cottage. He did that many times, yet he would always refuse to accept any recompense for the petrol he had used. It was during one of these enjoyable social evenings when we visited a pub in Hartfield, The Hay Rack, where I first saw Connie Harris working behind the bar. 'Good evening, how are you?' I asked the bar lady. 'I'm well thank you. How are you? Are you local—I've not seen you round here before?' asked the tall, slim, attractive woman in front of me. 'I've been living in Newbridge in a small cottage for about 18 months, and work for the Woodland Trust as a forester,' I said, trying to impress. 'What is your name?' 'Connie,' was her straightforward response. 'Look Connie, would you like to meet me sometime? I've written my phone number down for you. Is that okay?' I asked rather anxiously. Afterwards, I wondered, if I had done the right thing. Is she married, does she have children, and am I taking on something out of my league? She might well have a husband, or partner, who could cause me almighty problems. No sod it, even though she was sexy and someone I would love to get into bed, she would not be worth the hassle, I concluded.

My driving had improved out of all recognition—well, that is what Colin told me, one miserable morning as we sheltered from the rain in Morris's Wood. Colin had been a pillar of strength during the time I had been trying to gain experience of driving the Trust's lorry around the Ashdown Forest. Occasionally I had driven the old beast, my name for the lorry, out to other places in Sussex to collect various pieces of equipment needed for our work. 'Well, Richy boy. You 'ave been sitting at the controls for some time, 'aven't yer? It's been about eighteen months, and Nick thinks yer are long overdue taking your driving test, and I agree with 'im, son,' said my critical colleague. With my mind convinced, not by me, but by others, I made a written application for a driving test to be held in East Grinstead.

'Good evening Connie, 'ow are yer?' I said, falling back to my usual way of speaking. 'I'm well, thanks Richard. How are you? Have you been busy at work?' she asked, apparently interested, as we sat together drinking coffee in her local cafe. Beyond my wildest expectations, Connie had phoned me about three weeks after I first met her working in the pub. Though at first I thought it a bad idea to meet her, I had changed my mind, probably, due to one major factor—sex. She apologised for the delay, explaining that, other than working in The Hay Rack four sessions a week, she was studying to be an archaeologist at Kent University. Understandably, her commitments left very little time for socialising. She explained that at 36 years of age, single and still living with her parents in Hartfield, she had to get a professional qualification for the future. We had an enjoyable two years relationship, until she graduated, and went to work as an assistant archaeologist for a charity in Dorset. I was pleased for her. As an interested amateur, Connie had always enjoyed digging around various archaeological sites in South West England, where she had unearthed many interesting artefacts from the past. Connie used to stay at my beautiful picturesque cottage several times a week, most weeks; her individual qualities added a different dimension to our lives for a while. But just like sex, it doesn't last. My relationships with women never lasted very long. Why that was, I do not know. Connie also enjoyed cooking, and many times she prepared a tasty dinner for the two of us. On three occasions we were joined by her parents, Bill and Margery, whose lives had been spent helping others around the world. However, there was one incident that arose during our enjoyable relationship that was never explained. Connie was seen in East Grinstead, by my colleague Mark Mills, who lived there, walking hand in hand with another guy into a pub. But, I put that down to experience, as my ego was a little bruised.

The dreaded day had come for me to take my driving test in East Grinstead. I had driven up from Newbridge, with supportive Colin ever at my side, with my L-plates clearly displayed on the lorry. But I was hoping that on the return journey to my home, I would have discarded my L-plates forever. As I sat trembling in the cab, an official looking middle-aged bloke wearing a dark coloured suit came up to me. 'Good morning Mr Morris. My name is John Hay and I'm your driving examiner.' With that he jumped into the cab and told me to proceed, explaining the route I should take. After driving for a few minutes, he instructed me to reverse, which I did without knocking anyone, or anything, down. Success so far!! Five minutes later he hit the dashboard with his writing pad, which was the cue for an emergency stop. I slammed on the brakes, hoping he wouldn't fly through the windscreen. As I continued driving, my anxiety had somewhat subsided to the point that I felt in control of the situation. After about thirty minutes he told me to park the lorry outside his office. He sat there silent in the cab for about three minutes writing something on his pad. I felt like a person being charged for some misdemeanour by a police officer. This was followed by the dreaded questions on the Highway Code, which I thought I handled well. 'Well done, Mr Morris, you have passed your driving test, but please continue to update your knowledge on the Highway Code,' said the smiling Mr Hay as he handed me the official document confirming my new status. Minutes later Colin and I were shaking hands to celebrate my success. I then ripped the L-plates from my vehicle, and promptly threw them into a nearby rubbish bin. Now that I had a full driving license, I could not only drive my employer's vehicles, but I could also visit my parents, or anyone else, I chose.

Back on the road, Roy had joined us for a few days. I drove to one of our private contracts that the Woodland Trust occasionally carried out. On this occasion we were on a country estate near Godalming, Surrey. We were contracted to cut down and remove several large deciduous trees that had fungal disease. Depending on their size, and the extent of the fungal damage, other trees had to be either pollarded, or coppiced. As in other country estates I have worked in before, I had to ring the servant bell, situated at the side of the huge wrought iron gates, with its aristocratic coat of arms on the top, to ask for someone to open them. Once inside, we were informed by the estate manager, who had an almighty bulbous nose, where he wanted us to go. Halfway through the afternoon, the bumptious estate manager, Mr Platts-Mills, a rather rotund fellow, presented himself up in the woods where we were busily working. He prattled on about the various changes that he had made. Without first asking our advice, he issued orders about the way he wanted some trees felled or pruned. This abysmal attitude was for Roy like a red rag to a bull. 'Can't you make up your fuckin' mind, governor? We ain't at your beck and call all the fuckin' time!' Roy shouted at the estate manager. 'Who do you think you are young man? I'm the estate manager here and I say what has to be done. Not you. Anyway, I don't wish to waste my time on you. I shall phone Mr Roades, at Woodland Trust head office, about your offensive attitude,' said the crusty estate manager as he hobbled back to his highly polished black Rover.

We continued working on the trees late into the afternoon, which included the changes demanded by Mr Platts-Mills, when a green car approached us. Out jumped a young, tall, slim, white man, whose thin body was sorely in need of a good meal, carrying an envelope in his left hand. 'Good afternoon gentlemen. I'm Justin Todd from the Woodland Trust. I trust you are all well. I've just received an alarming phone call from the estate manager here, who informs me that one of you has been most offensive to him when he required changes to be made to the original contract here in the woods. Is that correct Mr Morris? As you are the senior worker, Mr Morris, I request you have some control over those below you. Have you anything to say, Mr Morris?' said the pedantic Mr Todd. 'Yes there 'as been a bit of problem. My colleague did swear at Mr Platts-Sills, sorry, Platts-Mills, but he didn't mean to. I mean that my colleague, Roy Short, is a good worker, and some of the changes that Mr Ratts-Mills, sorry, Mr Platts-Mills wanted us to do meant goin' back over work we 'ad already completed. I do apologise for my colleague's behaviour. I would like to suggest that Mr Short himself should apologise to Mr Mat-Mills, sorry I'll get it right soon, Mr Platts-Mills,' I said, trying to work out a strategy of damage limitation. 'All right Mr Morris. I will go along with that, but any more offensive behaviour from Mr Short, and his employment contract will be terminated forthwith.' With his tail between his legs, Roy walked up to the massive, 30-roomed, stone-built Georgian house to apologise to the good Mr Platts-Mills. Later I was informed that Roy had also received a dressing down from Nick Peters.

It was while I sat outside on the garden patio drinking my early cup of tea, before driving off to work, that I read with great sadness that my former colleague and friend at Wilkes Forestry, Ted Phillips, had died two weeks previously of lung cancer. Tears came to my eyes as I re-read the letter to make sure I had got it right; I thought that that big burly bloke, who had led the forestry team at Wilkes, was invincible. The letter itself, which had been put through my letterbox two days earlier, was written by John Wilkes, who expressed glowing praise for his former employee and friend. Mr Wilkes apologised for not writing sooner about Ted's death, and his church service, which, of course, I had missed; I would have loved to have paid my last respects to a good honest bloke. Another person had succumbed to the Grim Reaper.

Even though I had had a full driving license for some time, and had been given permission by the manager to use the Trust's small van whenever I needed it, my visits to my parents' farm were still irregular. However, one October morning, as the red and golden leaves were being shed, I decided to visit my parents at their small but productive farm in attractive Offham. Since buying the farm in 1973, my parents, uncles and aunts had worked hard to make Buttercup Farm a success, and they were now in a financial position to take things a little easier. However, when I arrived at the farm my father told me that Uncle Jack had injured his knee trying to push the tractor, along with others, out of a rut. According to his GP, he could be out of action for at least three months, but knowing Jack, as I did, he would find something productive to occupy his time. Mind you, Jack was over 60, and had grafted hard all his life. Sitting on his backside was not an option for him. 'How's it going, son?' 'I'm well, Dad,' was my reply. 'How about you and Mum? Are you both well? The smallholding looks well, Dad,' I said as I looked into his weary eyes which bore the scars of the tough challenges he had faced throughout his life as he tried to make a living. I was so proud to call them my Dad and Mum, and fortunate to know that they had kept me safe during the years when I was growing up. At that moment, Mother walked in from the yard where she had been feeding the pigs, but I realised she had lost weight. My instinct was to put my arms round her body. 'Hello Mum, 'ow are you love? It's so good to see yer once again. Are you well Mum?' I asked as she filled the kettle to make tea. 'I'm well Richard. How are you love? You look well, doesn't he, David, and how's your job with the Woodland Trust?' asked Mother, who was always interested in my life. 'I'm well Mum,' I replied.

We were sitting in the spacious kitchen, twice the size of the one we had in Yapton, with my parents discussing what was going on in our lives, when my uncle Jack came into the room hobbling, supported by a walking stick. He had been having a nap on his bed. ''Allo boy, how you going then?' asked the weary looking Jack, who, just like his youngest brother, had grafted all his life for his family to make ends meet. 'I'm well Uncle Jack. I hear you bin in the wars again injuring your knee this time. When you goin' to slow down?' I asked the old warrior. 'Slow down boy, I'm not 61 yet, besides there's still a lot of fight left in me,' came the typical response from a man whose demise was light years away. Jack sat down to a steaming mug of tea as Father and I walked out of the house to find my uncle Eric, and my aunts, Jane and Sarah, who were working in a far corner of a field repairing a fence which a rampaging virile bull nicknamed Big Nuts, that belonged to one of their neighbours, farmer John Snell, had damaged.

During the past few months, one of my colleagues, Roy Short, had left for pastures new. Now over 40 years of age, he had returned, along with his long-term partner, to his place of birth on Anglesey. He had told me that even though he had enjoyed living locally in a caravan, he now wanted to live a rural way of life, free of traffic jams, people and large buildings, a place where he could grow most of his own fruit and vegetables. Roy had bought a six-berth caravan, and two acres of land, which he estimated should be sufficient for his and his partner's needs. He was grateful that he had had the opportunity to work for many years in such an interesting environment, at the same time managing to save enough money to move on. His partner had also enjoyed living in a caravan, and working as a farm labourer in nearby Parrock Farm. One thing that Roy wasn't, was a hypocrite, so when he departed he said, 'Don't expect any letters from me, because there won't be any.' Lucky sod, I thought—I would willingly have changed places with him so that I could live a way of life that I knew would suit my needs!

His replacement was a Canadian, called John Pinet, aged 50, who came from Nova Scotia. He had been a lumber jack for many years. Formerly married with four children, he had ventured on his own around the USA, and several European countries, finding all kinds of work along the way. Not surprisingly, he found the forestry work at the Woodland Trust a bit of a doddle. What I most admired about John was his pioneering spirit. He loved the wild, untamed places, but, unfortunately, there aren't many of those left in overpopulated Britain. His lumberjack work had taken him many miles into untamed forests, which kept him away from home for weeks at a time. Catching, cooking and eating wild animals, he told us, was a way of life, especially when all the rations had been consumed or suppliers could not drop provisions due to snow and blizzards. I was personally pleased when John joined Colin and I, for what turned out to be a positive learning experience for both of us. Whatever work that had to be carried out, John was usually first to lead the way fearlessly. He found it difficult to believe that so many people, not just in the South of England, but in the UK, could live together with very little space for each other to enjoy a decent quality of life. He thought that humans hadn't evolved to live in such restricted conditions. Not many people would disagree with him!

Several months later there was a fatal accident in the Ashdown Forest. It happened on the A22, only yards from Wych Cross fruit farm; a young couple had been driving north-west towards Horsham when, apparently, they skidded off the wet road and crashed into a large tree killing both. When I was called out by the police at 1am, the ambulance was already at the scene and had removed the bodies to a local hospital. According to police sources, the young couple lived in Winchester and both worked in a local school. Any such incidents that involved the police and ambulance I found emotionally difficult to handle.

The Ashdown Forest had a major problem with Dutch Elm disease which had come to the UK in the 1970s. The disease had spread from healthy trees to diseased trees by elm bark beetles. To control the disease was near impossible as it rampaged through woods and forests in the UK decimating nearly all in its path. The five Woodland Trust workers, plus four temporary foresters, worked solidly for many months to cut down diseased trees or prune affected tree limbs that could undermine the rest of the healthy tree. And all the affected wood, including the bark beetles, had to be burnt immediately. At these times I learnt a lot from experienced and knowledgeable foresters like John and Nick, who reassured the rest of us that we were winning the battle to stop the spread of Dutch Elm disease. Afterwards, and for some time to come, the Ashdown Forest looked a sorry sight. It would take some considerable time for nature to repair itself, but the forest gradually took shape as young trees started to assert themselves and replace the fallen trees. As John used to make a point of saying, 'Mankind means well, but nature is all-powerful. Nature will always show us who is in charge.'

As I was approaching 38 years of age, I was determined to find myself a wife, or at least a regular partner. Failing that, I reckoned, people would start a whispering campaign about my competence to add to the gene pool. With that in mind, I contacted a dating agency in Lewes, which specialised in finding partners for those lonely people living in the countryside. What a comedown, I thought to myself, sending in my personal details to someone I had never met, and, at the same time, giving them money for the privilege of reading it. In return the agency sent me the contact details of the women they thought I would be most compatible with. I had these terrible thoughts about making arrangements to meet one of these women, only to find an eighteen-stone sheep shearer, or some highland cable-tossing bruiser with a moustache, standing on my doorstep. Meanwhile I had contacted Heather, who was 34 years, single, attractive, and intelligent, and she lived and worked on a small farm in Arundel. (That was the spiel I received from the agency.) She originated from Devon, but had moved to Sussex three years previously to take up the live-in position as personal assistant/housekeeper to the owner of the farm, Mrs Matthews. Fortunately, my feared nightmare had not come true. Well not yet, anyway.

With personal security foremost, that was the agency's mantra, Heather and I met in a pub (where else?) close to where she worked at Linfield farm, which was not that far from the Duke of Norfolk's pile at Arundel Castle. The old 19th century pub was full of young farmers and countryside people wearing flat caps, gabardine jackets and green corduroy trousers. 'How many blokes have you met so far, Heather?' I asked, very curious to know if any other fully paid up member had beat me to it. 'You are the first, Richard. Three other men had sent me their details, but you are the first I've responded to,' she said, explaining that she felt relaxed about what I had written about myself. That pleased me somewhat, because at first I had had the intention of writing about my experiences of being in Glasgow years ago with an under-aged girl, but then realised it would not have been a good idea to include this.

Over the months our relationship flourished, until we both realised that we wanted to live together in my cottage at Newbridge. Living together for the next three years wasn't easy by any means when you consider neither of us had lived with anyone else regularly before. To some extent we enjoyed each other's company, sharing the gardening, household chores and expenses, although there never appeared to be a close bond keeping us together. Heather did not particularly enjoy the company of children. When pressed on the subject of family, she never showed any great enthusiasm to have one of her own. For whatever reason, some people are just not interested in families. Both Heather and I were quite immature, and probably not ready, yet if ever, to have children. If I was to be ruthlessly honest, even at this stage in my life, I didn't really want to live with anyone long term. However, we had many enjoyable times during the three years that we did live together. Most notably were the great times when we visited my parents for the weekends down at Buttercup farm. Both Heather and I got involved with all manner of work that befits an everyday working farm. Heather appeared to be in her element: when she milked the few cows, mucked out the pigs, drove the tractor like a formula one racing driver, helped Mother make jam and gave a helping hand with most other chores. I got the impression that all she really wanted, was to work for Mrs Matthews at Linfield Farm, an attractive 19th century stone building, and help out occasionally with farming work. It transpired that she had had a difficult early life. Solely on her own she had looked after her disabled mother, as her father had left home when she was a child. At Linfield Farm, for the first time in her life, she had found relative security, and I think it was with great relief, that she returned there.

During the enjoyable times while Heather and I lived together; forestry work with colleagues Colin and John continued to thrive in the Ashdown Forest. We worked on new challenging projects: planting various saplings, overseeing local environmental volunteer groups remove scrub, thereby allowing wild flowers to grow; we removed old trees, pruned others and cleaned all existing areas of rubbish, scrub and bracken. A significant programme for change is regularly needed to help maintain a huge area of woodland, like the Ashdown Forest, to thrive. I was so fortunate to have been around at the right time, and was, therefore, determined to leave my mark on such a wonderful natural resource. At every opportunity I encouraged John, not that he needed any encouragement, to walk round the forest paths and tracks with me. Along the tracks were small pockets of the forest where wild animals, such as foxes, badgers or rabbits, walked at night looking for food to feed their young. After standing still for a few minutes, observing, smelling and looking at animal faeces or examining broken twigs, John could usually determine the various animals that had been there during the last few days. To say he had developed an acute sense of smell and hearing would be an understatement. When you had spent some invaluable time with John, even a small amount, you got the impression that here was a man who had ventured into wild unseen places and returned to tell the story. He explained to me the processes of how sap rises up a tree, the evolution of the wolf family, and how to catch wild Canadian salmon using a piece of string. John was an endlessly fascinating character, and someone with whom I would have loved to have explored the wild places of Canada, or anywhere else. On occasions, Heather would join John and I as we walked, climbed trees, sat in dark thickets drinking tea, and taking photographs of unsuspecting wild animals foraging. Another love John had was writing poetry, although he had to be in situ, and not sitting down in a room somewhere miles away from his immediate physical surroundings. He told us that his poetry had evolved over the years while he had been waiting, sometimes for several weeks, for tools, food or materials to arrive. With just a few colleagues around, and nothing to do, he would walk off to find a small warm place, usually among fallen conifers, to write his intense poetry.

Photography became a passion of mine to the extent that I would feel undressed if I did not take my new Japanese camera with me to work. The forest being only feet from my cottage, I was conveniently placed to take wild life pictures any time of the day. Over time my photography became a pictorial guide of my work and social life. It was during this time that doubts grew about my future, even though I was fortunate being a forester with wild life all around me. What more could one possibly need to enrich and sustain one's life? Even though I was fast approaching a total of ten years of employment with the Woodland Trust, I knew that eventually I would have to make a life-changing decision. Those years I had found enjoyable, challenging, yet at times a frustrating situation knowing that I was capable of more. There weren't many people around with whom I could discuss the working difficulties that I found myself in. Yet I realised I still had that desire within me to break free from what, or who, I did not know.

As John and I sat round a roaring fire at work drinking tea, I told him of the frustration I was experiencing. 'Yeah John, I'm in a bit of predicament at the moment. I just wondered what you would do about it?' I asked my colleague, hoping he could help me. 'Tell me about it Richard,' was his quick response. 'I've been workin' for nearly ten years at the Woodland Trust and it's been fantastic. Good pay, supportive colleagues and even a lovely cottage to live in. Just think over the years I've 'ad no accommodation problems to sort out, yet I feel frustrated with my life because I would like to move on and do something else. Do yer know what I mean, John?' I blurted out, hardly taking in breaths between sentences. 'I think I understand the situation you are in, Richard. I've been there myself many times over the years, so has most of humanity. There is no easy way of sorting things out. You have got to confront your problems, your demons if you like, yourself. But that is not to say others won't help you. I most certainly will support you. To begin with, it is important to disentangle your thoughts from your feelings. Work on that for a few days and see what comes about,' said John, smiling, with a hand of friendship round my shoulder. Mindful of what John had suggested, we carried on felling trees as flocks of noisy starlings flew overhead in the outer part of the forest called High Weald.

Even though I had continuing access to a Woodland Trust vehicle—by now they had bought us three new trucks—my visits to meet my parents were still irregular, although my phone calls improved somewhat. One evening my mother phoned to inform me that my aunt Bunny Nugent, aged 64, had died of ovarian cancer. Naturally my mother was very upset, as she recounted with great enthusiasm the enjoyable times she and her two sisters had had over the years, especially when they were children. As stated earlier, I had had very little contact with my mother's side of the family, even though they were good, decent people. I spoke to Bunny no more than a dozen times throughout her life. She was an attractive woman, of medium built, well thought of by Yapton people, and had worked for most of her married life as a shorthand typist for the Gas Board in Norwich. Two years younger than my mother, Bunny and her two sisters had attended the local school that I had attended many years later. The funeral service was held in the local St Peter's Church, and was well attended by her family including her husband, three children and many local people. She was buried in the nearby cemetery, where most local people find their final resting place.

After hearing this sad news, I was pleased that I had made arrangements to meet my old pals from Yapton. For obvious reasons, Yapton was still the place, the only place, where we would all meet, from time to time, to keep abreast with each other's lives. Besides, Richard was buried there, and he was, of course, an eternal part of our friendships that went back to those days before infant school, when, wearing our soiled nappies, we played in the local playground, our mothers chatting over a much needed cigarette before returning home to make their husbands' evening meal.

''Ow you goin', Dicky?' yelled a voice from the past. 'Gord blimey, my son! How yer goin Tel?' I said, as I greeted my old mucker, Terry Anderson. 'I'm well Richard. Good ter see yer once again. Sorry to 'ear about the death of yer aunt. Me mum used ter see 'er occasionally in Norwich,' said Terry, as he inhaled more smoke from his capstan full-strength cigarette that smelt very similar to rotten old socks. 'Yea, thanks Tel. I didn't know 'er that well.' We walked down the road together and into our old stomping ground, the village pub. As we entered the Country Squire, our three other friends, Dennis, Bert and Philip were sitting near the open log fire. They reminded me of the three just men who were about to help humanity sort out its problems. 'Great ter see you all once again lads. Our meetins are few and far between, but when we are all 'ere it's fuckin great,' I shouted at my friends. ''Ow yer going Teddy. I 'aven't seen you for ages. What yer doin' with yerself?' I asked Teddy Maybank, who went to Rawlinson School at the same time I did. He also used to live in the village with his parents until they all moved away when his father's company relocated to Ipswich. 'Hi, Richard, how are you? I've not seen you for ages. I'm down here in Yapton visiting my grandmother,' Teddy explained. 'Take care, Ted,' I said, as he left the pub holding roses in one hand, and an attractive young woman in the other.

'Come on you fuckin' lot, drink up. What yer all 'avin to drink?' roared Bert, who was ready to drink his fifth pint of bitter in less than two hours. And so the drinking, swearing, smoking and eating, went on for hours. Terry sang several songs in the pub, but I told him not to give up his day job, while Dennis danced a jig with the manager's fat wife, who had enough surplus flesh to feed a small country. Bert and I tried to sing a medley of Beatle songs, but, unfortunately, we sounded more like two old drunks in desperate need of gallons of black coffee! Philip was far too inhibited to perform in front of the public like that; yet it was great news to hear that Philip was not only working, but had been promoted to senior technician. Notwithstanding his years of unemployment, it was Philip, in 1965, who was the first of us to find a job on leaving school. He had also recently moved into a small rented flat not far from where he worked. He no longer had to make occasional visits to see the psychiatrist, as he had reduced his dependence on medication. I was so pleased to hear that things were at last, it appeared, going well for him after years of mental health problems. It was no surprise to hear that dear old Bert still lived at home with his family, and that his sister had recently got married. All Bert cared about was eating his mother's homemade steak and kidney pies, rabbit stews and tons of bread and butter pudding. Due to gluttony, he was fast approaching Billy Bunter status. He could no longer touch his toes, run more than twenty yards without collapsing, and his bed was fitted, so they say, with re-enforced steel. Poor old Bert, but he was still delivering fruit machines for a living, which must have been rather strenuous for one not so nimble. Both Terry and Dennis had found new jobs, since the last time we all met, working as navvies for the same building contractor in Colchester. After an enjoyable and raucous time, and being in no fit state to drive, we all, except Bert, ascended the old rickety stairs to crash out in the pub B&B accommodation, rated no more than1*, until morning.

When it came to mature committed sexual relationships, I'm afraid to say that none of us had been able to sustain one for any length of time. As far as I could ascertain, Bert had never even kissed anyone resembling the opposite sex, other than at the infant school, where he planted his fat rubbery lips onto the mouth of Joan Houseman, the village female version of Billy Bunter. He was not going to move from the security of home life. In a similar precarious position was Philip, whom I had never seen in a sexual relationship with a woman before. Now passed his 41st birthday, as we nearly all were at this stage, he was destined to live on his own for the rest of his life. Dennis had had several short-term and unproductive sexual relationships with women. After a few weeks, without any apparent provocation, he would just walk out and not return, leaving his belongings behind. For whatever reason, he preferred his own company and would no doubt remain living the solitary life. Terry had fathered one child, a boy called Simon, who lived with his mother somewhere in Suffolk. Terry had not seen either of them for some considerable time, and, as far as I could ascertain, he had no intention of doing so. On several occasions, he had mentioned that he would love a committed relationship, but due to his unsettled life, he had found that to be difficult. Last, but not least, is Richard Morris. On several occasions I had been in a similar situation to my dear friends, when I had tried unsuccessfully to develop several different relationships with women. I do not know why I had failed to find a long lasting productive relationship. Perhaps I was too selfish to adapt to family life, or realised its shortcomings, or, more to the point, was frightened by the responsibility of it all. Whatever it was, I have often wondered why five, basically decent men, from the same village and background, had all failed, hitherto, to develop long-term relationships and secure employment prospects. Mind you, I have had only two jobs in twenty years, which demonstrates to a certain extent, I think, some commitment and responsibility.

Another educational talk to the children of Tainton School was due to be held at our information centre, Wych Cross, and for the first time, an additional guided walk in the Ashdown Forest was included. Having delivered several other talks before, I was in a more confident and informed position to help the children to understand some of the behaviour of the wild life around them; especially as John was going to assist me, or rather, as things unfolded, I would be assisting him. We welcomed the children and teachers into the centre and introduced ourselves as foresters who had a working knowledge of the inhabitants of Ashdown Forest. John and I gave a brief outline of what we did in those woods: we cut down diseased trees, pruned, coppiced, pollarded existing trees and planted saplings. We also encouraged local voluntary environmental groups to participate in clearing scrub, bracken and other unwanted growth to help wild flowers and saplings grow.

Afterwards we took the schoolchildren for a two-hour walk round a small area of the Ashdown Forest so that they could experience living nature for themselves. Of course many of them were regularly exposed to nature through walks with their families. John and I guided them into a small copse so they could touch and smell the bark of the forest trees such as oak, beech and conifer. We encouraged the children to collect a piece of bark, old beech nut shells and fallen gold/brown/red coloured leaves that lay on the ground to remind them of their experience of being in the forest. John went on to explain how he had personally witnessed the killing of birds, mammals, fishes and practically every form of wildlife by chemical insecticides which were indiscriminately sprayed over large areas of land in the USA. 'From the people who develop government policy, to individual people like us here today, we are all responsible for our actions,' I explained to the children. When out walking in the Ashdown forest with family or friends, John emphasised the importance of observation. They could write down, or photograph, any dead animals, and report it to the information centre. By doing that, the Woodland Trust could then log what had been found, where, and other relevant information, to ascertain how the animals had died, if indeed that was possible. In terms that made sense to younger people, John also explained that they could all make a practical and valuable contribution, when it came to looking after wildlife, by taking their own unwanted items home, picking up rubbish and placing it in one of the many bins provided in the forest.

After several helpful discussions with John, Nick and my parents about my future, I had realised that after working for ten years for the Woodland Trust, it was time for me to move on. Easier said than done, however. What was I going to do for a living, what other skills did I need to find alternative employment? Perhaps it would be best, at 41 years of age, and with no other responsibilities except for myself, to retrain at college for something that might serve me well into old age. I constantly asked myself searching questions during severe bouts of anxiety. Although I enjoyed photography, I certainly did not want to take that up for a living. Besides, you needed a lot of money to buy professional photographic equipment if you intended to compete with the best, and I was no budding Lord Snowdon. There were managerial and supervisory employment vacancies available within the forestry community, which I thought I could realistically apply for. With over twenty years' experience, I assumed that I would be favourably placed to compete with the most capable. One activity, if that is the correct term, I had thought of as a means of earning a living was as a toy-boy! During my brief employment in the Merchant Navy, there had been at least two colleagues who had worked on large expensive passenger liners as cabin staff. They had witnessed, they claim, young men visiting cabins rented by ageing wealthy women at different times of the day and night. But that is no more than mere tittle-tattle! Being presentable, although I had put weight on over the years, I still had a thick head of dark brown hair showing no signs of turning grey. I could also contact art colleagues to request live modelling work. Mind you, the thought of lying nude in front of the 'pink hair' brigade filled me with not a little fear. The possibilities in my head were limitless, but in reality were few and far between. Nick encouraged me to take my annual holiday which would give me the time and space to think productively about my future. The next two weeks gave me the opportunity to prepare the ground that I needed to explore my options. They included registering myself with private and public employment agencies, contact adverts in local and national papers, magazines and trade journals. The amount of information to read and assimilate was exhausting. If I did not find another job, it wouldn't have been due to a lack of information available.

Upon my return to work at the Woodland Trust, I was still preoccupied with long standing questions that I somehow had to resolve. Do I continue to work for the Woodland Trust, or shall I leave and seek work elsewhere? If the latter, where and who do I want to work for? Other than forestry and landscaping, what else could I do that would earn me a living? In certain respects I felt obsolete! Like never before, I was being challenged intellectually and emotionally. But with kind and skilful assistance from some agency workers, by no means all of them, I had applied for about ten jobs which were considered relevant to my needs, skills and experience. At the same time, I had remembered to widen my focus to search not just for employment, but also college and university courses. The downside of going to study at further or higher education institutions was the financial consideration. For the past twenty years my accommodation had been provided, at a nominal charge, by my last two employers, for which I was very grateful. But elsewhere, I would have to pay the going rate, which could entail sharing a multi-occupied house, for at least three years, full of noisy, rampaging, untidy students, to obtain a qualification which didn't guarantee me any future employment. Even if I found a part-time job, shortage of money could continue to be a problem when it came to renting, especially if I studied in a city or larger town. Besides, I would find it difficult, after a lifetime of living and working in villages or quiet countryside places, to adapt to coping with town existence, with all its alienation, violence and poverty!

As we all sat shivering in the back of the information centre on another cold early Monday morning at around 8am, Nick Peters stood up to address his assembled four colleagues. On this occasion he spoke of my forthcoming departure: 'Well lads, the time has come for me to deliver some unhappy news, as our much cherished colleague and friend for the past ten years, Richard, is leaving us. I don't think we should let him go, do you?' said Nick. He then pulled out a bottle of champagne from under the table as my colleagues and I sat there in near arctic temperatures. 'Let us congratulate Richard for what he has achieved here at the Woodland Trust, and extend to him our best wishes for success in the future,' Nick said as he, John, Colin and Mark stood up with glasses of champagne to toast my health and happiness. Each colleague in turn said a few words about my strengths, weaknesses and foibles, and all emphasised the point that they hoped future

194

colleagues would not have to contend with my incessant farting in the mornings after a meat madras the night before.

I was particularly moved by what Colin had to say about our time working together in the Ashdown Forest. He had prepared a little speech on a piece of old crumpled paper, but he put that down after less than a minute and spoke from his heart instead. 'Well chaps, I wanna thank dear ol' Richy boy for being a decent bloke to work wif...,' said Colin, when he realised that he was not wearing his false teeth. Everyone burst out laughing when Colin put his dirty hand in his jacket pocket and fetched out his false teeth covered in dirt and paper. After washing then under the tap, he continued with his speech about how he had enjoyed working with me, the good social times he had with colleagues and finished by saying, 'I really do wish my dear friend Richy all joy and success for the future.' With his speech completed, Colin sat down with a grin all over his lean, weather-beaten face.

Chapter 9

SCOTLAND BECKONS AGAIN:
FORESTRY ON ARRAN

AS THE ROOM TEMPERATURE started to warm, my turn had come to say something about my ten years or so working for the Woodland Trust, and to explain my next employment venture: 'Thank you all so much for your support, friendship and camaraderie, which over the years 'as given me the impetus, not only to enjoy the enormously rewarding work, but to keep me goin' when times were tough. I've enjoyed the social life we have 'ad together, notwithstanding Colin still owes me six pints of Sussex Ale. With the support of Nick, I'm finishing work today, but I'm not leaving until next week. That will give me enough time to gather all me chattels and goods together and load it into a large van, I 'ave hired, to take me to my next job, which is as a forester/landscaper on the Isle of Arran. I know it is a long way from 'ere, it must be at least four hundred miles, but I gave the opportunity to work there a lot of thought after discussing it with several people who are close to me. It was a tempting offer I couldn't refuse, and of course, the free accommodation was a major incentive. I 'ad also given serious consideration to study at college or university, but that really wasn't for me. With a heavy heart, I feel sad leaving a place that has been my home for a long time. Most loss is painful, and especially saying goodbye to you who have made it all worthwhile during my time here.' We embraced one another, and then I briskly left the information centre before the tears started to flow.

It was April, 1991. With nearly all my belongings packed, I had the opportunity to spend a few hours with my parents down on their farm before I set forth on the next stage of my life's journey. My parents had now been in Offham for about 18 years. One matter that had been uppermost in my mind recently was the ages of my parents: how they would cope in the foreseeable future running a working farm. They were definitely not old, but they weren't young either. Father was 65 and my mother 67 years old. Both of them were relatively fit after a life time of hard physical graft. As well as giving me the opportunity to spend some time with my parents, before the long drive north, there would also be an opportunity of an emotional farewell, knowing our only contact would be by phone or letter. There were other matters my parents wanted to discuss with me; they didn't say what it was, but it concerned me nonetheless. I was anticipating the worst.

'Good mornin', Mum and Dad, I 'ope you are both well?' I said as I closed the kitchen door behind me, and embraced both of them as they sat at their table drinking tea. I poured myself a stewed cup of tea and joined them. The house was quiet, it reminded me of the days when I was a young boy, alone at home with my parents, playing with my toys upstairs in my comfortable bedroom. Compared to a lot of my childhood friends, who had to share bedrooms with other siblings, I was fortunate that, as an only child, I had a large bedroom all to myself. That meant I could pin posters of people like the Beatles, Rolling Stones or George Best on my brightly coloured walls. Not that I was a soccer supporter, I wasn't, but the latter looked like a rock star dressed in his immaculately designed suits and long black hair. What I now realised was, that, due to the lack of bed space in those days when siblings shared beds, sex was a regular occurrence between them. Often when we played in the school playground, one boy or another, used to whisper that they had 'played with their sister', or 'he rubbed my willy', or 'she took her knickers off'. From my early days in Yapton, and other country places I've learnt about since, there is no doubt where the quintessential village idiot came from!

'We are so pleased for you, Richard 'aving found yourself another good job in Arran, and with accommodation too. Where is it exactly Richard?' Mother asked, also aware that my visits to the farm would cease. 'Yes, sorry Mum and Dad, I've forgotten to explain fully to most people where I'm going, including to my colleagues. Yea, this is it Mum,' I said as I handed her a piece of A5 size paper with my new address on it. It read:

'Highland Lodge, Kilmory Estate, Kilmory, Isle of Arran. The Lodge itself consists of many rooms, including several large bedrooms, three toilets, two dining rooms and lounges, and a library which includes a world renowned set of books on Highland Mining. My small, yet comfortable, self-contained flat is situated in the original servants' quarters, west of the Lodge. The estate is owned by Lord Douglas, who actually lives in a small castle somewhere on Lewis, in the Western Isles. Kilmory Estate comprises a large commercial forest several miles in circumference, which, as a forester, is my main place of work. There are other smaller forests where I shall work occasionally. Apparently, the Douglas family had owned Kilmoray Estate for several centuries, but the ageing Lord Douglas visits only occasionally. Brodick, where I shall eventually disembark after my long journey north, is about twenty miles along the A841, which is the only road that encircles Arran. There is also a secondary road, the B880, that is several miles long and goes from Brodick to Blackwaterfoot, which is on the south-west side of the Island.'

'Well, thank you for writing all that information down for us, Richard. We'll photocopy it for others in the family,' Mother kindly said me. 'Richard,' Mother said to me in one of her deeper voices, which meant something more pressing had to be discussed. ' Yer' dad and me 'ave been thinking in the past months about our farm. As we are getting on a bit, we 'ave decided, Richard, to sign our part of the farm over to you from today. We 'ave been to a solicitor down in Lewes who has written this Will for you, and yer dad and I. 'Ere is your copy son,' said Mother as she handed me the legal document; this meant I owned a third of Buttercup Farm on the deaths of my parents. 'We 'ave of course discussed all this with your uncles and aunts, who 'ave done likewise, leaving their estates to their children. We 'ope everything makes sense Richard,' said Mother. 'Blimey Mum, I'm quite relieved, as I anticipated something more serious. Thank you both so much for thinking of me,' I said once again embracing my kind parents, grateful for all they had done for me during my life.

After we had finished discussing legal issues, my parents and I prepared lunch together, which consisted of one of my favourite dishes, lamb hotpot with dumplings. My mother had cooked this meal many times in the past; it was particularly enjoyable after a hard day's work, or roaming fields and climbing trees in the woods of Yapton. Today, no doubt, families eat food from around the world such as curry, pizza and chow mein for their evening meals. The thought of my father eating such food is absolutely hideous.

During the meal, Mother started to open up about her friendship with Mrs Anderson, and how she had enjoyed looking after her son, Terry, while she, Mrs Anderson, earned a few much needed pounds to compensate for not having a husband to support her. Fondly remembering her, my mother said she missed the cups of tea they used to have together. Mother never did say, and I never asked, what became of Mr Anderson. In common with most of my friends, I never really got to know any of their parents, except Bert's mother, who used to give us homemade apple juice and large chunks of apple pie. That same day, my parents and I walked round the farm, into the barns smelling of hay, and over the fields, to look at their small prized herd of Sussex-bred cows. Returning via a large thicket, my father explained that my uncles and aunts had gone to market to sell two of the cows, and if that was successful, they would spend the money on buying four more sows. While there, they would also buy food for the animals, and groceries for the household. Father also told me that my uncle's foot had now healed, and that he was now back grafting in the place he loved so much. When it came to leaving my parents that day, not surprisingly, emotions were running high as we held onto each other, to reassure all concerned, that love and support was always there whenever it was needed.

At the last moment, I changed my mind about driving all the way to Arran. I realised that most of my furniture I really didn't need as my employer was providing nearly all that I required. Besides, things I would need along the way could be purchased locally. So after reducing all my belongings to about a quarter of the size it originally was, I now had just a few boxes holding my personal clothes, books, music, records and record player. I made arrangements with Nick for British Rail to collect, from my former home, my personal things and send them on to Arran, via Glasgow Central, the local train service and the ferry across to Brodick.

On the 10th April 1991, with only my large rucksack to carry, I took a cab to Crowborough Station, where I took the train to Euston, via London Bridge, to board the fast train to Glasgow Central. Not surprising during that four-hour journey, I thought of the interesting 22 years in the forestry profession—starting with Greenwoods, who gave me my first chance to gain experience to develop much-needed skills, so that I could demonstrate to potential employers that I was competent enough to be employed. From there I moved on to work for Wilkes. They helped sharpen my skills, and all-round ability, by placing me in charge of various forestry contracts. Those years of forestry experience all came together when I successfully applied for the senior forester position at the Woodland Trust. Most of all, I kept thinking to myself as the train hurtled towards my destination, I had to sustain that high level of performance and commitment on Arran, as I had shown elsewhere.

After the hour-long train journey from Glasgow Station, I boarded the small vehicle ferry at parochial Ardrossan, and quickly made my way to the shabby restaurant for a much-needed cup of tea after hours of travelling. The place was full of families, commercial drivers, cyclists and walkers, all heading for the popular, attractive Isle of Arran. The ferry crossing did not take long, so we were soon disembarking on a cold, overcast late Monday afternoon at the busy ferry port of Brodick. Walking down the ferry ramp I could see my contact, Duncan Maclean, wearing a pre-arranged yellow florescent jacket, so that I would have no problem finding him amongst the ensuing melee leaving the ferry. 'Hallo there, Richard. How are you and did you have a good trip?' asked the burly looking estate manager. 'Hallo there Duncan, good to see yer—after several phone calls and letters, at last we meet,' I said to my tall, well-built colleague. 'Aye, at last Richard. It was good of my friend and former colleague, David Scott, to interview you for the job in London. Obviously, no one could attend an interview several hundred miles from their home. Anyway Richard, as you have said, after our correspondence, all is well that ends well, as some old sage once said.' With the formalities over, we climbed into Duncan's mud-splattered green Landover, no doubt ideal for the tough terrain on Arran, and he drove us south-west for about 20 miles, along a quiet A841, to the 19th century Highland Lodge.

As we drove up to the big, foreboding, granite house, with the family coat of arms over the huge wooden front door, my mind immediately took me back to the days when servants would be there waiting to open the car, or coach, door for their master. The Douglas family were rare visitors to Highland Lodge; which meant they kept most of their personal rooms locked, but Duncan gave me a quick tour round the rooms that were accessible. As we walked along the old dark, dank corridors, we passed walls adorned with paintings, photographs and drawings of the Douglas family past and present. Apparently, some of the men in the Douglas lineage had been Highland clan chiefs stretching back over three centuries. There were also paintings of other men sitting on horses and dressed formally in fighting uniforms. One can imagine the power these men had in the past to wield over lowly foot soldiers, estate workers and servants whose lives were proscriptive and short. The last room Duncan took me into was the wood-panelled library, which where full old family books, swords, body armour and photographs of the youngest generation of the Douglas family. In one corner of the room I observed the previously mentioned mining books.

With that interesting tour of the grand house over, Duncan took me to my accommodation so that I could rest after a long day of travelling from one end of the country to another. 'You must be tired, Richard? As it is the weekend tomorrow, you can take things easy and stroll about to take in the Highland Lodge environment. Would you like to have a meal with me and my wife about 8pm tomorrow evening? Good, that's settled,' said my sharp looking manager, who by this time had taken off his florescent jacket to reveal an attractive brown tweed jacket with matching trousers. When he left my accommodation, I realised I was on my own for the first time that day. All the human noise, vehicular smell and brutal modern buildings that I had experienced travelling throughout the long demanding day from London to Arran had gone. I was left with sense impressions. I put my heavy rucksack on the floor to rest my tired shoulders, took off most of my clothes, and lay down on the bed in need of relaxation. After a short while I was eager to inspect my new home. What would I have done, I thought, over the years if my former employers had not provided free, or cheap, accommodation? The flat was small, but big enough for me. It was painted brilliant white and had a double bed—an ideal size to bring back a sexy woman, that's if they existed on Arran, considering that I had been warned about their overweight bodies, notorious drinking habits and violent behaviour. There was also a small bedroom wardrobe and table, and a small modern veneered table with two matching chairs in the kitchen/lounge. I wondered if my flat was haunted by the ghost of an overworked servant from way back in time. If it was, then my only hope was that I wouldn't be woken up in the small hours, when I had a hard day's graft ahead of me.

As I awoke late next morning from much needed sleep, the sweet smell of spring was filtering into my cosy bedroom. I jumped out of bed, washed my face in the invigoratingly cold water, opened all the windows to allow the sunlight to flood the whole place, and made myself a cup of much needed tea. A new chapter in my life had begun: I had arrived to start my new job as forester/landscaper at Kilmory Estate. Welcome Richard Morris. In the afternoon, I walked downstairs and out onto the shingle at the back of the Lodge, which looked over a huge garden of mostly dark green lawn with borders full of pruned roses and several different spring flowers in full bloom. Beyond that, and covering three sides of the Lodge, was the Kilmory Estate conifer forest. The front of the Lodge looked out over the cold, greenish grey of the Firth of Clyde. As I stood there wondering about my future on Arran, I observed an Arctic Tern dive about fifty feet to eat something floating on top of the sea.

As I walked back to my flat, my colleague Gordon was walking towards me. 'Aye Richard, have you been familiarizing yourself with the Lodge? It is a huge place full of interest, intrigue and gossip. By the way there is also another couple resident here, Gordon and Mary Barclay, who clean and tidy mostly inside the house, but Gordon also does some gardening. That's if I can cajole him enough,' said Duncan smiling as he explained some of the working politics. 'Yes, very interesting Duncan.' I walked over the back lawn to where the conifer forest boundary was. I then walked round to the front of the Lodge to look at the small, fine looking lawns and newly planted shrubs, and take in the large trawlers fishing for herring in the Firth of Clyde.

After an invigorating shower, it felt like the first in ages, and all spruced up in my only suit, a blue serge, which I bought years ago in Burton's of Plymouth, I set forth to dine with my colleague and his wife. They lived in what was called the Small Lodge. Many years ago, it was the home of the gamekeeper who in those days supervised grouse shooting so that Douglas and his affluent friends could enjoy their sport in private surroundings. After each session of shooting game, the gamekeeper would see to it that the wild birds were delivered to the head chef, who prepared them for the Highland Lodge dinner table. I walked about a hundred yards up a narrow road eventually reaching the Small Lodge. It was like a small bungalow, well decorated outside with an average size garden full of various flowers. I banged the huge metal ornament attached to the front wooden door hoping it didn't frighten the people within. 'Hello there, Richard, please come in to my home and meet my wife Linda,' said Duncan, who I was looking forward to working with. 'Hallo there, Richard, I'm Linda. It so good to meet you after the phone conversations you had with my husband, right here in the lodge, about the forester vacancy. I'm so pleased you are joining us. I hope your stay is an enjoyable one. Now Richard, what would you like to drink?' asked my not unattractive hostess. 'Nice ter meet you too Linda. I would like a beer, thanks,' I replied, as Duncan directed me to a tartan blue armchair. As Linda brought my beer, called Highland Brew, I noticed all the various paraphernalia associated with highland life hanging on the light blue walls. 'The walls are covered from years of collecting things on my travels here on Arran, and further afield within these Islands,' explained Duncan. 'I've not been up this far before. The furthest I've travelled is to Glasgow for a few weeks with friends years ago,' I said tongue in cheek, mindful that I wasn't going to inform my hosts of the aborted journey I made with under-aged Lucy way back in 1967!

We sat down to a feast of a meal, which consisted of roast beef, baked potatoes, three different vegetables and lashings of gravy. The pudding was a delicious homemade apple pie covered in hot steaming custard and washed down with strong red wine. 'Nearly all that food and wine, Richard, was produced locally, by a friend, Tommy Laing, who lives not far from here on Kintyre,' explained Duncan as he proceeded to fill my glass for the umpteen time with the aforementioned red wine. 'That was a superb meal. Thanks very much. I've not eaten like that for ages,' I explained to Linda, who by this stage, due to the effects of Tommy Laing's wine, had become decidedly more attractive. With the first successful social meeting over, I hastily said goodnight to my interesting colleagues, aware that I had had too much alcohol to drink.

It was on a cold blustery day in April 1991, that I presented myself for the first day's work at Kilmory Estate. Duncan was waiting for me, all clad in warm winter clothes, at the iron gates that led into the forest. Tall, massive looking conifers towed above me; Duncan handed me a brief written history of the success of commercial logging on the estate to read. It cited the following:

'The Douglas family have owned this estate for some considerable time, and have made a fortune out of it. In case you don't know there are several different conifers here. There are Scots Pine, Corsican Pine, this one is susceptible to disease in colder climates. Shore Pine is ideal on Arran due to the windswept, waterlogged soils. At the far end of this forest are two or three species of Spruce. Over the years we have had to use different types of effective insecticides to treat and control the various insects and fungus that infest the trees; otherwise, considerable damage can be caused to them. The spraying is carried out using a helicopter, usually every three years, by a chemical company from Edinburgh. They also have the contract to spray nearly all the other commercial conifer forests here on Arran. Extra spraying is important for the additional conifer trees Lord Douglas has recently purchased; the added work that entails is the main reason why we need extra workers. There are only a few non-coniferous woods on Arran and they belong to private residences. With regards to spraying the Estate: We are mindful not to repeat unethical practises of the past, when increased spraying with insecticides caused various insects, not only to return in greater numbers, but they also, it seemed, thrived on the insecticides. We are hoping those days are long gone.

Nonetheless, we are mindful that the inclement weathers on Arran, which also applies, of course, to most of the Highlands and Islands of Scotland, have the capacity to carry these toxic chemicals into the most out of the way places where they could have detrimental effects on wild life, especially birds. During the past we have found dead birds and mammals throughout Arran, and after laboratory analysis of their blood, it was concluded they had been poisoned by a known insecticide. The dead animals included rabbit, fox, osprey and red grouse. We carry out spraying once every few years, and only then when it is deemed to be necessary. The toxicity of the chemicals we now use per 100 gallons of water has been reduced considerably over the years. The Douglas family now realise that nature has its own inherent way of controlling populations of insects or most other living biological creatures.'

'Well that's about it,' I said to Duncan. 'Please keep that important information safe. Sorry if it was so long winded,' Duncan explained as he put his reassuring hand on my shoulder. We started to walk towards his Jeep when he stopped to say, 'One last important thing that I have to briefly explain to you. Time permitting, we also carry out various maintenance work at hotels and large houses, some sites or places of interest, lead forest walks and occasionally help out when the fells or roads become blocked with debris. In order to make a living on Arran, we have to adopt a positive and flexible attitude,' said Duncan. It was not for the first time—we had discussed it over the phone before I started employment—that I was aware of what was required of me now that I was working for Kilmory Estate. 'Now, important things first, we will drive to Brodick Harbour to collect your clothes,' said the ebullient Duncan.

For the next three months, or so, Duncan and I were very busy cutting down conifers from Meekland Forest, which was on the west coast of Arran. With four hired foresters, flown in from the mainland to support us with the demanding work, we managed to load five large articulated lorries full of prime conifer for the commercial market in Europe, where timber usually reached a good price. The foresters, all of them Scottish, knew Duncan well and had worked in several different forests on Arran during the past years. They were well known for their no-nonsense expertise and approach to tree felling. In Glasgow the men had worked for a large timber company supplying timber for large organisations, which made, packed and sold self-assembly furniture from their warehouses around Britain. Meekland Forest itself used to be owned by a local family, but was bought by an international company, as others were on Arran some 20 years ago, to supply the constant demand of the construction company for building new timber-framed houses.

After the Meekland success we were contracted three times yearly to maintain the huge picturesque grounds of Hotel Newton high up on the northern coast in a village called Lochranza. While we were there we also cleaned and tidied the local nature centre, and when required, repair the roof, replace a broken window or renew a tap washer. It was nothing too major. When I used to drive to the aforementioned places to work on my own, I usually took a flask of hot soup or tea, so that I could sit down to drink it somewhere along the beautiful yet rugged Glen Chalmadale. I had many enjoyable hours sitting there on the lush bracken thinking about how fortunate I was to be sitting in a deserted Glen with only the sparse wild life to keep me company. Occasionally I was fortunate enough to be able to follow a gracious flight of a rare white-tailed eagles hunting for food. It was these enjoyable experiences that provoked me once again to reach for my camera and record glimpses of the natural beauty that was all around me. On two occasions I photographed a white male Hen Harrier carrying a small bird not fifty feet from where I was sitting. But I found nature and the beauty of nature frustratingly difficult, and ultimately exasperating, to understand. Although I had been exposed to nature from a young age, I hadn't realised the deeper meaning of those two concepts until later on when I became more aware of the power of nature, and man's incessant drive to abuse it. The meaning of nature, it dawned on me after many excruciating hours of thought, is unable to be grasped via the senses, but exists only within the inner world of feelings and emotions. It was during these experiences that I sometimes thought I was overreaching myself to understand the inexplicable!

On one occasion, I vividly remember driving to Lochranza, as heavy rain lashed around the Jeep I was driving for all of the 30-mile trip from Kilmoray. It was so ferocious in places, when vision was less than ten feet, that I had to stop to wait until the torrential rain had subsided somewhat before I could continue my journey north. The rain came at me like a huge monsoon. I felt terribly claustrophobic as I sat trapped in my vehicle with nowhere to run. Not an experience I enjoyed, but I got used to the frequent inclement weathers. After working four hours in the Hotel Newton mowing the lawns, pruning various trees and shrubs, and a quick clean of the nature centre, I decided, now that the rain had ceased, to take my lunch with me on a walk through lonely Glen Chalmadale. After walking about two hundred yards, I came across a young woman sitting on a small canvas chair painting something on an easel in front of her. I slowly and quietly approached, as I didn't want to frighten her. 'Good afternoon, I 'ope you are well? I saw you painting and thought I would like to see your work,' I said, as quietly as I could, mindful of the fact that we were the only two people in a large deserted Glen. 'Hallo. I'm well thank you,' was her softly spoken response. 'What are you painting?' I asked, hoping I didn't sound too ignorant of such matters. 'I'm trying to produce an oil painting of this wonderful Glen, with a few things added, such as these birds, from my imagination. I love coming here to paint because it's so quiet and peaceful, unlike the noisy world we live in,' she said. 'Yes I know what you mean. My name is Richard and I work as a forester in Kilmory,' I said. 'How wonderful to be working outside with nature. You must be fit and strong. Oh yes, my name is Abigail,' she said, as she stood up to shake my hand.

When I first met Abigail Hartnall she had the kindest face I had ever witnessed. I thought she had been sent down from heaven. It was the sort of face that made you feel good about yourself, especially after a night of drunkenness, or debauchery. She was 28 years old, short, slim with long brown hair usually tied in a ponytail. For the first years of her life she had lived with her parents in London, until the family moved to Scotland when her father had found work as a history lecturer at Glasgow University. From an early age Abigail had enjoyed drawing, etching and painting, and encouraged by her supportive parents, she went on to study Fine Art at Edinburgh University. She graduated at 24, and within weeks had found a job in Glasgow as assistant painter to the flamboyant figure painter, Jason Jackson, that weird and wacky hedonist, who occasionally did some painting, I was reliably informed. That employment lasted for about three years, when she left to develop her own work, using oils to paint landscapes. For the past year Abigail had not received an income other than working for a meagre salary stacking shelves, so she could enjoy the freedom of wandering around some of the islands of Scotland painting landscapes. When we first met, Abigail had been staying at the 4-star Hotel Newton for four weeks, which gave her sufficient time to walk, even dance sometimes, round the local area drawing and painting various scenes that took her fancy. When she wasn't travelling, she was fortunate enough to live rent free with her parents. She informed me many times that she enjoyed bleak lonely places, uninhabited by humans, so that she was able to express herself on canvas. She, too, was in love with beauty! In many ways she was a kindred spirit who disliked the modern world. We had a tenuous, challenging, unpretentious, yet at times, enjoyable sexual relationship that lasted for some two years, although, occasionally, she did find my inner life difficult to understand. Who doesn't? Abigail thought that I did not express my feelings enough. Perhaps she was right! My most evocative thoughts of her take me back to the exciting times when we went fell and forest walking together on Arran. Abigail will always be a figure you cannot pigeonhole.

On a rare, sunny Arran morning, as Duncan drove us towards Haggy Wood, eight miles north of Brodick for another contract to cut down conifers, a large brown mature male deer ran across the road only just missing our vehicle by inches. 'Do you know, Richard, that there is still wild deer here on Arran? That large buck we just missed has a harem of young females north of here round the Makstar area. Occasionally, with permission of the farmer or landowner, a few people are licensed to kill a deer when the group becomes too large to sustain a healthy balance,' my well-built, tough looking colleague told me. There were no half measures with Duncan; when he explained something, you received the full version. Sometimes I admired his articulateness, but other times he irritated me beyond belief. 'No, I didn't know that about the 'arem of deer,' I said, and at the time I couldn't give a bloody toss if it was a 'arem of Arabs or foresters, such was my annoyance. At Haggy Wood we were joined by the owner, Peter Crawford, one of the few local people left who hadn't sold their land, or soul, to international companies. 'Good morning Peter, I hope all is well? Please meet Richard who is my colleague and occasional drinking partner. Richard has been working on Arran now for well over a year,' he informed the ageing, red-faced landowner with a long bulbous nose covered in veins. 'Aye young Richard,' came the abrupt response. 'Good morning Mr Crawford, nice to meet yer,' was all I could muster to say to the old chap, whose dirty torn clothes had seen better days. 'Duncan, as we have arranged, please take down ten of the mature trees and take them over to Brodick Harbour for inspection by an employee of Barnes & Co, the company buying them off me,' said Mr Crawford as he stood pointing towards the conifers in question like an irate football referee sending off a player for misconduct.

As most of the conifer trees on Arran had been sprayed about two years previously, some of the Kilmory Estate conifers were now healthy and big enough to cut down for the commercial market in Europe. As with all the commercial conifer businesses on Arran, and most others in that part of the world, a large privately owned Scottish ship used to sail 2 or 3 times a year to collect home-grown timber and take it to various European seaports to be bought and distributed throughout Europe. Due to the dangers involved in felling large sized conifers, every precaution had to be taken to spare life and limb. On site health and safety training was given once a year. This would entail using appropriate clothing and safety hats at all times. Trainers would go into detail about how to handle dangerous chainsaws, heavy metal chains and winches. Roddy, an Australian, used to drive the powerful crane that was used to load the timber onto lorries, which in turn took it to a specially built modern port, on the west coast of Arran, to offload.

As briefly mentioned above, at Kilmory Estate we were nothing but flexible when it came to making extra money to make ends meet. Several times a year when we weren't particularly busy, usually during the tourist season, but not exclusively so, Duncan and I led groups on forest walks. The walks usually started just outside Highland Lodge, and snaked round the forest, which at times was so dense it was impossible to see ten feet in front of you, finishing about four hours later after having completed nearly six miles. As the undulating forest walks were physically challenging, they attracted walkers from around the world, especially the young competitive north-western Europeans who focused on walking up Goat Fell, 874 meters high, and other similar fells. However, during the winter months we advised fell walkers, because of the ice and snow, to be very cautious because due to the potential danger involved. There were no fatalities during my time on Arran.

We also took people on shorter walks around the Island, which included Machrie, Merkland and Gortonstone forests: these walks also attracted various scientists who were interested in the biology of conifers or insect life underneath them on the ground. They researched information about the animals that ventured into the forests to eat or collect materials for their habitats: according to scientists, there is more life under conifer trees than deciduous trees. I find that very interesting. Another popular outing for tourists was the minibus trip round the Island, which took in an ancient castle, fort and a modern nature centre in Lochranza. After sightseeing, it was convenient to stop in the nearby hotel, the former home of the Macduff family, for lunch. Incidentally, the Macduffs was a former large land-owning family in the Western Isles. We had an unwritten contract with small businesses: if we took paying customers to their premises, we would be recompensed for our efforts. What made those day outings enjoyable for me personally was that the only road around the Island was nearly always clear of traffic. That meant I could stop virtually anywhere to show tourists things of interest, or stretch their legs, or have a comfort stop. Many people just enjoyed walking in the short coarse heather for a short while as they took photographs of the various birds that inhabit Arran. Other interesting places we visited on those trips were a 10th century fort near Sannox, and an old lodge in Corrie, which was reputedly used by Bonnie Prince Charlie. Another, Fort Arthur, was used for defence many years ago, against neighbouring clans near Dippen Head. There was also a rather large attractive, former hunting lodge next to Loch Tanna, which was used by wealthy American businessmen in the early 20th century—apparently a popular seasonal choice for local women seeking not only an income from cleaning, but additional finance from liaisons with the older affluent residents. Duncan and I developed these tourist attractions over the years so they became an integral part of our summer itinerary, making money not only for ourselves, but also for those family businesses whose only income came from tourists.

The attractive scenery on Arran is all around you; in fact, it pervades your everyday life. In some way I wanted to share those sensual and delightful experiences with my friends and family. The most effective way I achieved that was with my inexpensive camera, a gift incidentally from my former girlfriend, Sandra Greaves, in Plymouth. I sent numerous photographs of Arran through the post to people so that I could demonstrate, or really show off, the beautiful Island that I not only lived on, but worked and played on too. Besides, instead of phoning or writing regularly to England, I could write a brief note on the back of each photograph, if that were needed, explaining the picture in question. I still phoned my parents occasionally, of course, eager to learn about my family, but they were more than happy to have received so many colourful photographs from my place of domicile. With great pride, according to my mother, did she invite various family members and close friends round to the farm for tea so that they could get a glimpse of her son's exciting way of life on faraway Arran. Mindful of my friends back in Norfolk, I nearly always sent the photographs to Bert Moore, who could be relied on, unlike the restless wandering others, to keep them safe. Besides I knew that the house he had always lived in with his parents would be the place where he would die, or so I assumed! On two or three occasions, I did send photographs to my former colleagues at the Woodland Trust, but by this stage, I had ceased all contact with those at Wilkes in Devon. The Woodland Trust gang wrote back to me inquiring if I had become Lord of the Manor, or the local town crier, now that most of my communications had embossed on them, 'Richard Morris Esq'. I kept the local shop owner busy by regularly producing camera film to be developed, and at the same time requesting numerous reprints. 'Aye yer wee rascal,' implored Mrs Speedy, 'are you sending all these photographs to your female fan club around the world?'

However, there is no substitute for having a good chin-wag with those people you love, like I did with my dear parents. One thing I was nearly always on time with was my monthly

215

evening telephone conversations with my mother and father, when all would be revealed about family politics. For the first 10 minutes, when I usually held the phone receiver a foot or two from my ear, Mother would try non-stop to explain, nearly all in one breath, who was doing what, and what could be done about it. Some time ago, according to Mother, it was my cousin, Lynda, who had lived a rather decadent life. Now, apparently, it was Bob's son, my cousin, John, who had taken on that mantle. Good luck to them all! When I was younger, I realised Mother was not a talkative person, as she disliked village gossip, but as the years went by she became increasingly vocal. As I had not been around the home very much for the past 25 years, and with few people to talk with, Mother might well have got lonely due to Father working long hours before they bought their farm. But I always enjoyed my mother's enthusiasm for finding out the whereabouts and well-being of her family members. When she was a child things were so different amongst working class village people when most activities were centred upon the needs of farmers, landowners, church and then her father, who was way down the pecking order. It wasn't that dissimilar, of course, for my own father.

Other than the exciting times I had spent with the unpredictable and talented Abigail, my social life on Arran was intermittent. Sometimes after a hard day grafting in one forest, or another, with my taskmaster Duncan, I would not bother going back to my flat to eat or wash. Instead I used to drive straight to a pub or hotel bar, where I invariably met other local blokes for a beer or six. Most of the Scotsmen I had met over the years were heavy drinkers, and came from three, or more generations of tough Arran families socialised into a life of working with timber. Not that dissimilar to Yapton, or any other working class environment, where discussing work was the only interest they had. With very little police presence at the time, you could drink and drive over the legal limit, but you had to proceed with great caution. If you got caught by the police for illegal driving, due to excess of alcohol (actually very few people did), local drinkers had a tendency to look down on you with scorn, as it made it difficult for them to use their own vehicles. Being mindful of the nature of small communities like Arran, it was important not to fall out with anyone or otherwise it could have made my life difficult. However, the police officers around at the time all enjoyed a few beers even when on duty. Many times I drove illegally, and so did many others I knew, but we were never caught.

My two usual watering holes were the public houses, The Retreat, in Blackwaterfoot and, Bonnie Prince Charlie, near Bennen Head. 'Aye good evening, Richard,' enthused one of my drinking pals, squat George Gale, who on most days could be found leaning on the bar. Years ago he used to work with my colleague, Duncan Maclean, delivering timber, but was nearly always drunk. According to Duncan, he was a liability and a threat to life and limb. George reminded you of a Scottish version of a costermonger, as he was nearly always seen selling numerous stolen articles from the back of his dilapidated, untaxed and uninsured, van. 'Well Richard, it is good to see you once again. Can I interest you in a cheap pair of black stockings, or fifty daffodil bulbs, or a second hand bike?' announced George, smiling from ear to ear. 'All right George. How's it going? 'Ave you got light bulbs instead?' I said, as I winked at the unscrupulous scoundrel.

Minutes later we were joined by another two heavy drinkers, Bob Davey and Steve Duncan, local lads always ready to make a few bob. They ran a small landscaping business together, such as it was, mowing and maintaining a few houses in the area so that they could afford a few beers at the end of the day. Personally, I wouldn't have let them lose to prune a small pot of rosemary that I owned. 'Hi, Richard, how are yer?' asked the gaunt looking Bob. 'All right Bob? And 'ow yer keeping Steve? 'Ad a good day out there in the harsh world of high finance?' I commented, as I tried to rib my two drinking buddies. 'Aye it's tough out there. All we have made today is enough to buy four pints each,' moaned Bob. 'Dennis, can I have two pints of heavy?' asked Steve, the shorter, and brighter of the two colleagues. Dennis, the owner of The Retreat, a former 18th century Inn, had bought and extensively renovated and re-decorated the pub a few years after its turbulent history of regular fights between local groups, drug taking and underage drinking. It was fair to say that even the police were reluctant to get involved with customers using The Forest Row, its previous name. Glaswegian born Dennis, once a Royal Marine, did not stand for any nonsense; if he thought you had contravened the pub's ethos, then out of the pub you went, sometimes head first. Before moving to Arran, I had assumed, incorrectly, that such troubled pubs only existed in the sort of places that you read about in national newspapers, but certainly not in a hamlet like Bennen Head.

It was in the Bonnie Prince Charlie, while having a drink with the Macleans and, on this rare occasion, the Barclays that I first met Doris Stockley, who came originally from London. She had been working behind the bar serving drink and food for several years, a job she had found through an advertisement in a trade magazine. After I had ordered the drinks for my small party from Kilmory, I started a conversation with attractive Doris. Mind you, after a few drinks my judgement of women is somewhat impaired, due, I suspect, to the lack of confidence emanating from my working class roots! 'How long 'ave you worked 'ere for then, Doris?' I asked the short, plumpish well-dressed woman, who had a strong London accent. 'Just over three years. I enjoy it here and the manager, Brian Martin, is a decent bloke to work for,' she said. 'I've seen you 'ere on many occasions Doris but never had the opportunity to chat to you until now because it's been packed with tourists,' I explained to Doris as we looked at each other starry eyed across the bar, until her attention was taken by another customer requiring a beer.

Two weeks later in a small cosy pub not far from noisy Brodick, as we sat in front of a roaring log fire, Doris explained to me why she had made the long journey to work on Arran. 'I had this relationship with a fellow in London you see. We both worked in a busy West End bar just off Oxford Street. He was already working there when I first arrived. We went out together for about two years, but after a year he became abusive to me and then started hitting me. He kept phoning me at my shared flat in Hoxton. In the end it got so bad I had to phone the police, who warned him to stay away from me. Anyway I left and got this job,' said Doris, no doubt looking for some sympathy as she lit another filter-tipped cigarette with her nicotine stained right hand. Look out Richard Morris, another painful relationship is about to come into existence, I thought to myself. ''As he tried to find you up 'ere?' I asked her. 'No he hasn't,' came the timid response. Why, I've have asked myself on many occasions, do I get involved with women? Nearly all the women I have met brought emotional baggage with them, and somehow I manage to get sucked into it. Perhaps they saw me as a sucker, an ideal candidate to be manipulated, or whatever. One of the reasons why I haven't had a long-term relationship with a woman is that they are just too complex. And yet sometimes I feel a complete failure at not having developed a committed loving relationship with a woman. What is it that I project onto women that they find appealing? Perhaps I'm kidding myself! Women, of course, instinctively realise the power of enticing men with sex. Suffice to say, I didn't meet Doris again.

In more productive times on Arran, Duncan and I used to drive round the Island, at least once a year, checking on all the bird boxes. We were very much of the opinion that in the modern age of intensive forestry, all living things, including the rich soil bacteria, are an integral part of a diverse forest, not just the trees. We designed boxes for all types of birds that feed during the day, and in the evening, which gave the forest a biological balance to keep it productive. We kept our information updated on healthy forest biology from the various scientists, and others, who regularly used to join our walks. There were others, of course, who researched on their own. One university scientist, Dr Peter Crawley, had been walking on Arran, and other Islands of Scotland, for many years to study the impact modern forestry had had on ants. An Academic, and delightful chap, Peter used to send many photographs, and indeed three of his research papers, most years to Duncan and I. In fact one year he brought ten undergraduates to Arran, so they could carry out research of their own on ants. The whole group lived for two weeks in the nearby Goatfell Hotel, and what a good time we all had in the evenings drinking, singing and dining on Tommy Laing's— Duncan Maclean's friend—locally caught, probably stolen, pheasants. No doubt a few covert relationships were consummated during that summer of love!

So that we could support the group during their research, we made arrangements with a local boat owner, Jock Wilson, to ferry Dr Crawley, his students and I across to the nearby Mull of Kintyre. Their main intention for going was to carry out further research into the behaviour of the charming little critters: ants. It was assumed, according to one bright student, as Kintyre and Arran had been separated for thousands of years, that various conditions here could have led to different ant adaptations. We all congregated early one morning around 5am, outside Goatfell Hotel, picked up the university group and drove the 10 miles or so to Blackwaterfoot, where we boarded our ferry for Carradale. As the little ferry made her way across Kilbrannan Sound, we were thrown all over the place like pieces of flotsam by the vicious rain and wind that blew head first into our flimsy boat. Several times I thought the boat was going to sink with all of us on board. That frightening ferry crossing reinforced my love of being a landlubber. We arrived two hours later in Carradale soaked to the skin, and in desperate need of heating, hot tea and dry clothes. After the kindly hotel owner had sorted out our creature comforts, for a price, we made our way by local minibus along the B842. We eventually arrived at our intended destination, the conifer forest near Gronport, where the university group successfully carried out their research.

Other than the few times I went fell walking with Abigail, and twice with Duncan, I nearly always enjoyed walking the high, mysterious fells on my own. My favourite fell was Tarsuinn Fell; standing at 825 meters, it is just short of the ever-popular Goatfell. Mind you I usually gave fell walking a miss during the summer due to the ever-growing number of people visiting Arran for their holidays. It is understandable that parents prefer bringing their children on holiday to experience the wild beauty of Arran, and the surrounding Islands, to visiting the West Country or flying to join the masses on the beaches of Spain. Personally, I could never understand the attraction of lying in the intense heat, for many hours, being cooked like a Sunday roast! Besides it is well known that extended exposure to the sun increases the risk of contracting skin cancer. Outside of the summer months, and especially in the winter, was the time I most enjoyed fell walking during the seven years I lived on Arran. On one rare occasion, as I was halfway walking up Tarsuinn Fell, a low flying golden eagle, with a small bird in its mouth, flew not thirty feet above my head. It was an extremely moving experience as the huge brown 35-inch wingspan made a whooshing sound as it passed by. Another time on Tarsuinn Fell, whilst I was sitting all alone eating a sandwich, I saw a scarce Corncrake scavenging for food some twenty feet in front of me. The corncrake is a small black/brown bird, and a summer visitor to the Islands and Highlands of Scotland. There were times on the fells when I felt a peaceful, lonely experience, yet interconnected with all of nature. Alone on the fells gave me a profound sense of wonder and of what life could really be all about. On many occasions I have sat on a fell for hours reading, writing, photographing, and thinking, yet I never heard or saw a living being, other than the irritating midges conspiring to eat my exposed skin.

It was sometime in September 1997, at about 7am on a Monday morning, when I received the most devastating news of my life: my father had been diagnosed with abdominal cancer. My mother, sobbing into the phone, explained that 'Father has been 'aving these pains for some time, especially after meals. He thought it was indigestion, and didn't think much of it, son, until one night it was so painful we called for the ambulance, which took me and your dad to Lewes Hospital, who carried out the tests next day, and the consultant told yer dad that he had cancer'. Holding back the tears, I tried to reassure my mum. 'I'm so sorry, Mum, to 'ear that bad news about Dad. Whatever I can do to 'elp Mum, then please ask me. Shall I come down immediately to visit you both? I can get there in about seven hours. How is Dad, is he in pain? Is he on any medicine?' I asked without taking a breath. 'Your dad is comfortable at the moment, he is sleeping. Our GP has prescribed some medication for 'im to ease the pain, but things don't look good, Richard,' my mother said, sobbing uncontrollably into the phone. Unable to hold onto my feelings any longer, I too started crying into the phone as immense pain welled up inside me. I blurted out to my mother, 'Don't worry Mum, I'm always 'ere for you and Dad as I love you both very much.' 'We know you do Richard. You are a good son to me and yer dad. Look Richard, leave it a few weeks, until yer dad has seen the consultant and then we'll know more about 'is condition. I will look after Dad for the time being, and besides, your uncles and aunts are 'ere to support me. I will phone yer love. Okay love?' Mum explained to me. Afterwards I fell down on my bed and cried for some considerable time thinking of my dear father in pain, and being so far away from me, there was nothing I could do to comfort him. Should I quit my job and move south to look after my parents? It came to my attention a while later, and I realised it for the first time in my life, that as far as I can remember, it had been a long time since I told my mother and father I loved them.

I had by this time been working at Kilmory for over six years; yet I had never met the old buffer, Lord Douglas, who owned the estate. He was about to make one of his rare appearances on Arran, three months hence, to survey, no doubt, all that he had inherited, bought or robbed from those generations of dispossessed highland people whom his forebears had kept under the yoke. Due to his forthcoming visit, the Macleans, the Barclays and I were kept busy making household arrangements for Lord Douglas, and his two daughters, Elizabeth and Nancy. Several rooms in the Grand Highland Lodge had to be cleaned, hoovered, sprayed, polished, curtains replaced and God knows what else, to pander to the old man's whims. As Lord Douglas was now in his late 80's, we at Kilmory Estate assumed he couldn't see a foot in front of him. With a bit of luck, Gordon Barclay hoped, he might just fall down the grand 19th century wooden carved stairs and break his neck. Gordon and Mary Barclay were in their early 60s, and had worked as housekeepers at Highland Lodge for many years when it had been the owner's main residence. In those days Lord Douglas had, not surprisingly, been a tyrant to work for, and ruled the roost like some demented fascist. According to Gordon, he had mellowed somewhat, but was given to outbursts of anger especially when the whisky had got the better of him. It was many years ago, Gordon recalls with some bitterness, that during one of his many alcoholic rantings, Lord Douglas had said, 'I'm bloody well fucking pleased that one of my forebears threw those useless bastards off the land during the Highland clearances!' One of Gordon's uncles had himself been thrown off his own land, and emigrated to Canada for a better life. It was well known, understandably, that Gordon would love to injure, or even kill, old man Douglas himself.

Duncan and I stood upright as we waited for Lord Douglas, on the small private jetty at Blackwaterfoot. Dressed in our smart clothes, and looking like two 18th century lackeys, we physically helped Lord Douglas, and his fat daughters, climb up from his private Yacht, called *Success*, onto the quayside. 'Welcome Lord Douglas, I hope you and your daughters had a calm journey all the way from Harris Sir?' enquired Duncan. 'Lewis, Duncan! I live on Lewis. If I've told you once, I must have told you a dozen times before. I reside on Lewis!' explained the snarling old bastard. 'Sorry Sir, you have told me many times. I'm awfully sorry,' said Duncan as he physically recoiled. 'And it is so good to see you Lady Elizabeth, and you, Lady Nancy. Are you both well?' asked dear Duncan, who by this stage looked nothing like that robust chap I had worked with back at Kilmory. 'Yes, thank you Duncan, we are both well,' said Nancy, the fattest one of the daughters, who spoke with a posh cultivated voice that only money can produce. I had been standing at the back observing the surreal proceedings, when I was introduced to the Douglas family. 'Sir, I would like to introduce you to Richard Morris. He has been working here at Kilmory Estate for over six years,' Duncan explained as I walked a few steps forward to shake hands with my employer. Just two feet or so from his ugly lined face, I observed when he opened his mouth, that nearly all his teeth were either missing or were black stumps.

Fortunately for me, the Douglas family ensconced themselves in their Highland Lodge for most of their short stay on Arran. Their every demand being immediately responded to by the Macleans' innate efficiency and hard work, aware of course, that old man Douglas could at any time remove them from their comfortable home and decent livelihood. During their stay on the Island, Duncan and his wife moved temporarily into Highland Lodge where they waited on the family hand and foot. He drove Lord Douglas to various business and private lunches in a new, hired car. On several occasions, Duncan also drove the Douglas family to visit their close friends for dinner, while Duncan, himself sat in the car drinking scotch and eating his homemade pie, waiting for them to give him more orders. Apparently, Lord Douglas had known most of his friends since he was a young man, dating back to when he was first put in charge of the family fortune. It was with great relief for all concerned, that one morning I noticed Duncan driving the three of them back to Blackwaterfoot, where Captain Pleat was ready to sail them back to Harris. Sorry—Lewis!

My mother had been phoning weekly to inform me of my father's worsening medical condition. He had recently been assessed by his hospital consultant, who feared that my father did not have long to live. He discussed with my parents the treatment options open to my father, but they were free, of course, to find their own preferred choice. Essentially there was little left for my father to choose: he could go into a hospice, stay at home taking medication/or cease taking medication. There were also a few other private hospices, which offered many non-medical therapies, but they were expensive. Besides they were all some distance from Offham, which would make it very difficult for my mother to visit my father. Furthermore, my father would not enjoy being in a large institution full of people he did not know. Other than spending most of his non-working time with his family, my father was a loner who would very quickly become isolated outside of his personal environment.

'All your dad needs, Richard, is a very quiet place to rest, sleep and 'ave the occasional meal with us 'ere at the farm. He loves it down 'ere in Sussex, and I will be there for 'im of course. So will 'is brothers and their wives be 'ere for yer dad. So there is no question of your dad living elsewhere. No question at all. Regards medication, he wasn't that sure at first, but after discussions, he doesn't want to keep taking it due to the side effects. He's bin taking it for some time, and it ain't worked for 'im. So no more medicine,' my mother explained in her kind, yet firm way. Fighting back the tears, I spoke to my mother: 'All that makes practical sense Mum. And all Dad's family will be around. Look Mum, I've been thinking of this for months. I've been on Arran for over seven years and it's been a great experience, but now I think I wanna move back to Sussex, where you and Dad are living. I'm 48 years old in a couple of months, and I need a change. You and Dad bought the farm in 1973, so you 'ave been there in Sussex now for about 24 years, and I think you deserve some support from me, and I would love to move down to Sussex. I will find a job and find accommodation nearby. I want a change,' I strongly emphasised, hoping Mother would agree. 'Are you sure son? That's a good job you 'ave up there on Arran. Me and Dad certainly wouldn't expect you to move down 'ere Richard,' said my mother. 'I've made up my mind, Mum. I'm moving as soon as Duncan can find another worker,' I said convincing myself. Hopefully, by now, I had convinced my mother.

All I had to do now was to convince Duncan that my employment prospects were elsewhere, not that he could hold me back, but he had been a supportive and sincere colleague. It was because of the respect I had for Duncan, that I wanted to explain, in some detail, the personal reasons behind why I wanted to join my ageing parents in Sussex. I wanted to leave Arran with cherished memories of my time there, of the decent people I got to know, mindful of how the wild beauty of Arran has touched me forever, and mindful that my emotional departure from this wonderful place would be difficult.

I explained to Duncan, over a beer or two in a small pub in Lochranza, my powerful personal reasons for making the move, after seven enjoyable years on Arran, down to Southern England where I would be best placed to support my parents. Of course uppermost in my mind was my father's terminal cancer, the short time he had left, and how I desperately wanted to hold and comfort him during those last days. Tears flowed, as I explained to Duncan, that I thought I had not been a good son over the years: other than the letters, photographs and phone calls, I had visited my parents no more than twenty times during the years that I had been working away from home. Furthermore, I had not given my parents any grandchildren, and being an only child, that was not about to change any time soon. My mother in particular must have found it difficult, although she never mentioned the subject, as her two sisters, Bunny and Sarah, had grandchildren, who regularly visited their grandparents. Now that they were ageing—my father was 72 and my mother 74 respectively—they found the physical work at Buttercup Farm increasingly difficult to handle. My uncles and aunts were also in a similar position. Uncle Eric was 75, his wife 75, Uncle Jack 74 and his wife was 73 respectively. Over the 24 years that they had been in Offham, they had all worked hard to develop their smallholding from a rundown farm into a thriving productive farm, but within the foreseeable future it would require younger, stronger more motivated people to take it forward. I also explained to Duncan that on the death of my parents I would legally own a third of Buttercup farm. I was now in a position, having saved some money during the years, to financially support them to some degree.

After spending my final night on Arran, and a quiet meal with the Macleans and Barclays, I said an emotional farewell to everyone. I embarked from Brodick on the nearly empty car ferry for the one-hour trip bound for Ardrossan. I looked back at Arran, tears falling, as I thought about my time there, but conscious that a new chapter—it was February 1998—was tentatively beginning to emerge. From Ardrossan I took the train, packed with local Saturday shoppers on their way to Glasgow. Some of the younger, noisy male passengers were off to a football match. Within twenty minutes of my arrival, I was aboard the clean modern Virgin train; I pulled out of Glasgow bound for London, Euston. (A few miles into my one-way journey, I was reminded of the last time I made this journey, in 1967, when Lucy and I, after absconding, were being escorted by a rather kind social worker, Hilary Yates, to meet our parents in London. I wondered what Lucy was doing with her life now.) I eventually arrived at Lewes Station after an eight-hour journey which had begun early that morning at Brodrick. As I got out of the packed carriage of the Eastbourne-bound train, weary and tired from travelling all day, and holding just my rucksack, I noticed my parents were waiting for me at the other end of the platform. I just spontaneously ran as fast as I could towards my parents and embraced them. We stood there on the near deserted station hugging and kissing each other like a scene from a Hollywood war film. 'Hallo Mum and Dad, 'ow are you both?' I asked, as I dried my eyes. 'It's so good to see you Richard. We are fine, aren't we David?' said Mother asking my father for confirmation. 'I feel so good now that I am with you both, and from now on I can support you more,' I said, as the thought of being around my family made me a lot happier. Even my old drive, to work elsewhere, did not have the power to hold me back any more.

Chapter 10

LIVING WITH MY PARENTS:
MY FATHER DIES OF CANCER

MY **FATHER** drove up the muddy track that led to their farmhouse. I had been so pre-occupied by the many thoughts and feelings circulating in my head, that I had paid little attention to the three-mile journey from Lewes Station. As I sat there trying to engage my brain, I realised I would have to collect my books, clothes and other things that Duncan was sending on to Lewes Station for me. ''Ere we are, Richard,' Mother said as the three of us got out of my parents' Opel car into the pitch-black evening. The only lights that were on came from my parents' detached farmhouse, some fifty feet from where we stood. As we approached the house we were met by my uncles and aunts, who in turn kissed and cuddled me. ''Ow lovely to see yer once again Richard. You look so fit and healthy. ''Aven't you filled out over the years! I 'ope you are 'ere to stay young Richard?' asked my uncle Eric, as he corralled us all into the warm kitchen for a much needed hot cup of tea. We all sat round the large wooden table having a chat about nothing in particular, when my father gestured he wanted to say something to all assembled. 'Other than Jennifer, who 'as already been informed, I want to tell you what my consultant told me the other day. He said, that I only 'ave six months to live,' said Father, bursting out crying and falling into my mother's arms. I also started to cry just as I put my outstretched arms round both my parents.

At my mother's suggestion, we all walked into the softly lit lounge and sat on comfortable seats as we continued discussing my father's awful medical situation. 'Dad, I want to say that I'm with you all the way. I will be sleeping in the small single bedroom above, and I have put employment on hold for the time being. I will be around to support you and generally 'elp out,' I said to try and reassure Father, that although I didn't say so in so many words, I would be with him until the end. 'Thank you Richard,' said my father, 'that is so good of yer, son.' I realised that many months of abdominal cancer had left my father woefully thin. 'Well, that goes without saying Richard, we are all 'ere to support our dear brother David, a man I've loved all my life even though we don't say it out loud very often,' said uncle Eric, who was wiping away tears. 'That's right Eric, we are all behind David no matter what 'appens,' said Jack. 'You bet we are David,' said my aunt Jane. 'In this family we all support each other,' said my aunt Sarah, who was holding my father's hand. What wonderful people, I thought to myself, and yet I knew very little about any of them because of having worked away from home most of my adult life. But blood is certainly thicker than water.

While I was still working on Arran I had contacted all my friends, and some of the extended family, to explain my intended action of supporting my father over the weeks and months to follow. Mother had also written, or phoned, some of the older friends at Yapton, to explain about my father's terminal cancer. She said that many people remembered my parents, especially my father, from when they were young. One person in particular I had phoned, John Remble aged 73, remembered my father from sixty years ago as having played in the same football team as him. John wasn't born in Yapton; he moved into the village aged 11 when his late father found a labouring job with a farmer nearby. John explained to me that about sixteen boys assembled on the village green for a game of football for what turned out to be a ferocious match between two teams hell bent on 'kicking each other to near death'. 'Anyway, most boys really enjoyed, and still do, that kind of stuff. Anyhow, after about an hour of continuous football, or rather battle, your father kicked the ball through Mrs Kettle's front window smashing it. She came out of her 'ouse, and told us all to piss orf, or otherwise she would phone the police. Anyway, to cut a long story short, your dad and I went round to Mrs Kettles 'ome and replaced the window with a new pane of glass ourselves. Ask yer dad about it, and send my sincere wishes to 'im, son. Goodbye.'

Another person I had phoned about my father being diagnosed with cancer was an old school friend called Colin Pates. Colin, now aged 74, was born, educated and socialised in Yapton. His father had moved to Yapton as a young husband, and found a job driving a lorry for a builder somewhere near Norwich. Apparently, Colin and several of his friends, including my father, belonged to a gang of boys that used to hang out together. 'On one occasion Richard, we 'ad all bin stealing farmer Webster's fruit from 'is large productive orchard, which was well known for its large juicy plums and sweet cox apples, when he sneaked up on us holding a lethal looking broom. He tried to hit us, but missed and shouted at us to fuck orf from his land. Ask yer dad if he still remembers stealing fruit from the orchard,' he said, as I listened to Mr Pate's amusing story. So many generations of working class boys, no doubt girls too, could recount numerous stories about their childhood escapades that many children of today would identify with.

With the continuing support of my family, I was determined that Father was going to be as comfortable as possible for the last weeks of his life. Although I was only my father's unofficial carer, the local carers association, nonetheless, invited me to a day's training so that I could learn various practical things about how to support my father in the process of dying. They also explained the various benefits available to me, especially if I wanted to register as an official carer. If I did register, then I would not only receive a weekly payment, but would also qualify to have my own needs assessed. But being a private person, father was not interested in having a counsellor visiting him at home, or having his needs assessed by the local social services. Father had always been independent, and nothing had changed his mind, and thought 'those people' were interfering busybodies, so he always kept his distance. He was a self-reliant man who always did things his own way. 'No, forget that lot in the Council, son. I'm fine. I 'ave most things I want. I've got enough money for me and yer mum. I don't want any means testing done 'ere, son. Do you 'ave enough money?' asked my proud and independent father. Well, that was that. Even though he had an advanced illness, and was in some physical pain, Father knew what he wanted, and that didn't include officialdom looking into his personal affairs. To a certain extent, Father had my sympathy.

Because my father didn't have long to live, I had a compulsion to tell my former colleagues about his medical diagnosis, although not one of them had ever met him. I felt I had a duty, misguided of course, to tell the world about one decent human being who gave his best for Queen and Country. Duncan knew already that my father's days were numbered, but that did not stop him phoning me on numerous occasions, enquiring into how things were. He was most supportive, as were my former colleagues at the Woodland Trust, who sent cards of sympathy. But Father, understandably, wasn't interested in any sort of communication with people except his close family. Several people from Yapton wrote to him, and, although he was grateful for their letters and cards, he felt he did not have the energy to reply. Besides, he just wanted to spend the time he had left with those people he had loved all his life. It was so reassuring for my father to know that he could depend on the support of those close to him as cancer made his life increasingly tough.

Sleeping in the small bedroom next to my parents' room was very convenient on several fronts. If my father needed support during the night to go to the toilet, or when the cancer was really painful, I could get him a strong painkiller, fetch him a cup of tea, or a glass of water. Most mornings I helped him out of bed so that he could wash and dress himself. Being proud he insisted on washing himself. Afterwards we used to have breakfast together, and, while the others worked on the farm, we would chat about things ranging from the price of wheat, the state of British farming, to the moral decline in British society. Most of his waking life had been about farms, those places that had moulded his character, had given him a living, and had sapped the strength from his ageing body. From being a strong working man, having grafted for nearly 60 years, cancer had reduced him to a frail, weak old man. That was the main reason, I assume, why he didn't want to meet anyone from the past. He found the cancer inevitability so terribly painful, yet he hung on to the only life he knew.

'Where shall we go today Dad? Fancy going for a drive up to the South Downs?' I asked him. 'Yeah, I would like that son,' came the barely audible reply. After I had made sandwiches and tea for us, I drove Father's Opel car up to a special place on the Downs which my parents had visited many times over the years for a quiet break away from farming. The drive to Ditchling Beacon took no more than thirty minutes;

once there, I could understand why my parents were so fond of this attractive spot. Being about 100 yards from a nature reserve, this small pocket of peace, where one could also park the car, was just right for Father and I to walk a few yards to put up our seats under the shade of mature beech trees. Dapple green light shone through the beech leaves, as blackbirds hopped around on the ground looking for worms. While I sat with my father taking in the immediate surroundings, I was reminded once again of the sharp differences between the flora and fauna of Sussex and the coniferous forests of Arran—both wonderful in their own unique ways. 'Yer mum and I used to love driving up 'ere, son, especially during the week when there were few people around, so we could 'ave our tea and sandwiches in peace. I will never forget, son,' my father explained with a lovely broad smile all over his old lined face that had been shaped by many years' exposure to the elements.

On another occasion, as we sat peacefully at Ditchling Beacon, I realised I had forgotten to inform my father of the telephone conversations I had had weeks previously with two of his old friends. 'Dad, I 'ope you don't mind, but I contacted two old friends of yours by phone to let 'em know of your cancer,' I said, hoping it wouldn't upset him. 'That's all right son. Who were they?' enquired Father. 'John Remble and Colin Pates,' I responded. 'Gawd blimey. Not those scoundrels. 'Ow are they?' he asked. 'They are both well, Dad. John Remble asked me to remind you of the broken window you smashed with a football playing on the village green when you were kids,' I reminded Father. 'That's right son, I did. I didn't do it on purpose mind yer. The old gel that lived there, what's her name now, Mrs Kettle, that's it, son, she was a good old stick. John and me replaced it for 'er yer know,' said Father, winking at me.

'The other old friend I phoned, Dad, was Colin Pates. He informed me 'ow he, you and other friends 'ad been stealing fruit from farmer Webster's orchard, when 'e nearly hit you all with a large broom, and told you all to get out of his fucking orchard,' I recalled. 'Blimey son, that was ages ago wan it? Colin and me were always stealing from those middle class people's orchards around Yapton. Blimey, dear old Colin, bless 'im. 'Ows 'is missus? She was a good ol' sort she was. I've forgotten 'er name now. Good ol' sort she was. Cos 'is father, Brian Pates, 'ad bin in the nick plenty of times yer know. I liked 'im,' said Father, as he reminisced about the past.

The one thing my father always looked forward to was having a Sunday roast, including all the trimmings, at home with his family. But during the last years, due to farm responsibilities, that meal happened infrequently. Mother insisted that, as Father could no longer work, they should begin having Sunday lunch together once again. Throughout the years I had not been around to have Sunday lunch, or any other lunch, with my parents. But at 48 years of age, I really enjoyed having those meals together with my family, and in some way they reminded me of the Sunday meals I had when I was a young boy. From time to time we were joined by various nephews and nieces, which really pleased my father, as he could find out what they were doing with their respective lives. It was during the last months of his life that Father would share his innermost feelings and experiences of his childhood when fathers ruled the household. 'When Father came 'ome from the pub on Sundays, or if 'e had been working, we 'ad to wash our 'ands straight 'way, and sit at the table. Then, if Father 'ad been to the pub, we would all say prayers, but if he 'ad been workin', he told us to enjoy our meals, as they came from his 'ard work,' Father recalled. 'Are you pleased those days are behind us, Uncle David?' asked Mick, his nephew, who was visiting us at the time. 'I suppose I am in a way, son. You younger generation 'ave far more freedom than we 'ad. It's a different world innit, Eric?' Father asked his older brother. 'Different world completely, Dave, to the one we grew up in. And I'm pleased my son Mick, my other son Bob, and grandchildren, Helen and Douglas, have more opportunities today than we 'ad. I don't see our times as the good ol' days. They were bloody awful if you ask me,' Eric said forthrightly. 'What do you think Jack?' he asked his younger brother. 'I agree with what both of you 'ave said. In our time things were bloody 'ard. On the farms you worked night and bloody day for very little money when farmers were all powerful. Today's generation are educated, they move around, and work outside of the villages where they were born. Their lives are not preoccupied with bloody farms. We didn't 'ave vehicles of our own; today's youngsters do and they can meet girls and boys from other places and discover new ideas. We were confined to Yapton. That about sums up our world in those days,' said Jack, who started removing the empty lunch plates from the table.

My father had good days, when he could walk downstairs for his breakfast, and other days when he was in physical and emotional pain, confined to his bed. He didn't like taking painkillers, but at least they gave him some respite from the relentless ravages of the cancer that had, apparently, spread throughout his abdomen. There was that one particular warm November morning that I will never forget for the rest of my life: I helped my father out of bed to wash, put his clothes on and supported him down stairs so that he could have his usual breakfast of tea and toast. 'I don't feel too good today son. Instead of going out today, I would rather sit in the lounge and watch TV if that's all right with yer, son,' explained my father, who was getting noticeably weaker. 'Of course Dad, whatever you want to do is fine by me,' I reassuringly told Father.

Around mid-morning Father's breathing was becoming laboured, and I noticed he was holding his stomach more than usual. 'Are you in pain Dad? Shall I get yer a couple of painkillers?' I asked my father. 'No I'm okay son,' my father whispered to me. I moved from where I was sitting on the armchair and sat next to Father on the large sofa, so that I could hear what he was saying. 'I've 'ad a good life with yer mum, Richard. She is a wonderful woman. I love 'er so much yer know,' said Father, as he began to cry. I also started to cry as I put my arm round his frail body. 'Thank yer, Richard for lookin' after me for the past months, I've really enjoyed the outings we 'ad, son. I've enjoyed driving to Ditchling Beacon and listening to the crows and rooks squawking over the bread we gave 'em. The Sussex countryside is so lovely isn't it?' Father asked in a barely audible voice. 'It is so beautiful Dad. I'm pleased we 'ave been there together,' I said to Father. As I continued to hold him he lay further back into my body. 'Is this comfortable for you Dad?'—but I was unable to understand what his whispered voice replied. For a while he slept in my arms. About ten minutes later he spoke to me in a slightly raised voice. 'I 'ave 'ad a great life with two marvellous brothers, who I love very much. The three of us 'ave worked together nearly all our lives. Eric and Jack are two great people, and I shall miss them very much yer know,' said Father in a laboured voice, as life ebbed out of his frail body: he died in my arms at 3:30pm on 6th November 1998.

My father's funeral was held at St Peter's church in Yapton a few days later. The whole extended family, many of his friends from the village, including my school friends, and also those who didn't know him, attended to celebrate his life. The Rev Peter Goodfellow spoke of the good work my father had done during his life, and the important contribution he had made to help develop Yapton into what it is today. The church was adorned by numerous bouquets of beautiful flowers. Three people and I gave a brief talk about my father's life: as a father, husband, brother, uncle, employee, and most importantly, him as a person. It was during one of those talks that an overwhelming sadness came over me when I thought of the absurdity of life. I felt that life was not beautiful, but short, painful and full of suffering and decay. After the funeral my father's body was taken to the local cemetery where he was buried next to his father, Peter Morris.

Chapter 11

SELLING BUTTERCUP FARM

UNDERSTANDABLY, the Buttercup Farm household was in mourning for a few days after my father's funeral. After we started to re-emerge from our loss, there was the longstanding problem of what was going to happen to the smallholding. During Father's last few months, my mother and uncles did not want to exacerbate his mental anguish by discussing the inevitable sale of the smallholding. The fact of the matter was that they were now all in their 70's, and were much too old to keep working on a farm that required constant upkeep. They all felt worn out, even though working on Buttercup Farm had been their greatest labour of love. The time had come to sell the smallholding and buy a house to live in for, hopefully, the remainder of their lives. As well as looking after the farm animals, Mother had to visit the solicitor regarding Father's will, which according to Mother, was straightforward, as they had discussed the issue many times. Mother, and my two uncles, had the laborious task of finding a buyer for the small farm they had so lovingly developed during the past 25 years. Although I had saved a not inconsiderable sum of money, I wasn't in the position to purchase the farm myself, even though my heart loved the place with its clear inspiring views of the South Downs not far away.

As I didn't want to move with Mother to her new home, I realised that, if I didn't want to be homeless, I had to decide whether to live somewhere else in Sussex, or move back to

Yapton. 'Look, Richard, we understand you need your own independence, but find a job first. If we sell the farm before you find accommodation, then you can stay with us until you find a suitable place. It makes sense, doesn't it, son?' my mother quite rightly pointed out. 'It does make sense, Mum, thank you for thinking of my well-being,' I said, as I kissed my mother and thanked her for being so thoughtful about my needs. My uncles and aunts, who were sitting round the table, also helped discuss my short-term accommodation problem. They were all in agreement with my mother. I found that consensus mightily reassuring, regardless of what might transpire; yet at the same time I had the money to look after myself.

Mindful of my age and work experience, and in a material position where I could look at alternative ways of earning a living, I first contacted a private employment bureau in Lewes for some guidance. In common with most of these commercial places, they unambiguously stated in their customer profile that they 'will find all their customers suitable employment within three months'. I had read their half page advertisement in the free local paper during the time I had lived with my parents. The fee they required was £2000, but it included your own personal adviser, an up-to-date list of vacancies sent to your home and mock interviews with a specialist. The spiel also included a professionally presented CV to send to potential employers. Well, after all that bunkum, I thought, how could I go wrong? Perhaps I should present myself as a high flyer in need of earning at least a million a year—just for starters. Anyway, with nothing to lose, except my credit card, I ventured down to Lewes High Street to meet my intended careers adviser, Mr Jeremy Thorpbridge, who did not waste any time in giving me the same old hogwash. For a considerable fee, of course, he promised me 'this and that', and within weeks, no doubt, I would find myself being wafted to paradise via Hollywood. The good Mr Thorpbridge probably thought that, after ten minutes of discussing my intended career path with me, I was one of the hoi polloi, who could be fobbed off with anything inferior. 'Yes Mr Morris, what do you have in mind as your intended career move?' he said eloquently. 'Let's see, 'ave you got any jobs as foresters available, or hod carriers, or navvies or toilet cleaners? Those jobs would be most suitable, my dear Mr Thorpbridge,' I said as I gave the most deliberate and awful picture of myself to the moron in front of me. 'Mr Morris, there must be some mistake. We don't cater for those types of jobs here. Forgive me for saying that I think you would be better off walking 200 yards down the road to the Job Centre. Goodbye,' said the flummoxed Mr Thorpbridge as I walked out of the offices at Dace Employment with my objective achieved of bullshitting the bullshitter interviewer. I hope that was not too frivolous, but after the powerful experience of having lost my father, the last thing I wanted was to hear at this time was about making money at the expense of someone else. But, of course, that is the nature of life. Thereafter, I concentrated on vacancies advertised via the computer, both locally and nationally. I also bought local and national newspapers, and also ventured into several different Job Centres.

Although I had applied for a variety of different jobs, I had, so far, been unsuccessful. When I arrived back one evening at Buttercup Farm, very tired from searching for suitable employment, Mother had rather good news to tell the rest of the family assembled around the kitchen table. 'Well, mainly good news,' said Mother, 'I've 'eard from the solicitor, and to cut a long story short, David Morris left very little money in his will. What money he did leave will all go to me. I knew that of course when he was alive, but I couldn't say anythin' out of respect for my husband. Again his share of the farm goes automatically to me. I think we all knew that, didn't we?' said Mother, in a matter of fact way. 'Does that mean, Mum, due to his savings, Dad would 'ave qualified for extra money from the Pension Department?' I said, feeling slightly irritated by Father's attitude. 'Yes, that is right, Richard. Also, due to the nature of 'is illness, he would 'ave qualified for support from the local authority.' 'Bloody 'ell, Dad was so stubborn sometimes,' I said, looking straight at Uncle Eric. 'His 'ard life made him like that, son. His motto was self-reliance. He didn't like the professional classes. None of us did,' was Eric's sharp reply.

'Anyway,' Mother said excitedly as she showed me a letter, 'a couple who came several weeks ago to look at the farm 'ave put in an offer for it.' My uncles and aunts had already seen it. 'That is good news, Jennifer, isn't it?' said Uncle Jack, who looked very pleased. 'The offer is only £5,000 short of our asking price, isn't it Jack?' said Mother. 'That's right, Jennifer. That is good news ain't it, Eric? Just five grand short. Shall we accept the offer?' asked the jubilant Jack. After about an hour of discussing the offer put on the farm, all five in the family made a unanimous decision to accept it. Mother said that she would be contacting the solicitor the next day to make a formal acceptance.

'Some more good news, I 'ope,' said Mother. 'Our offer for the four-bedroom house the five of us looked at in Ringmer the other day, you know the one near the church, has been accepted,' said Mother smiling. She told me the other day that she liked that one in particular. 'That's great news, Jenny. Didn't we make an offer of £7,000 less than the asking price?' asked the smiling Aunt Jane. 'That's right love, we did,' confirmed Eric, her husband. All in all good news for the five of them. They had all grafted for many years to buy Buttercup Farm with their hard earned savings. Throughout the 25 years, they had also worked very hard to develop their acquisition from a smallholding, which was hardly functioning, into a productive farm that a new owner could develop. With the sale of their smallholding substantially more than they paid for it all those years ago, they could now afford to buy a new home, wherever it was. Ringmer is a village in East Sussex, some five miles east of Offham, but still with fine views of the South Downs.

Several months later, without too much hassle, the sale of both properties were completed within days of each other. That meant my mother would not have the added expense of taking out a bridging loan when moving from one property to another. On the cold morning of 6th May 1999, Mother and the rest of the family had all their chattels and goods moved from Buttercup Farm, where they had all been diligently working for the past quarter of a century, to their new home in Ringmer. With great optimism for the future, we all arrived late afternoon at the four-bedroom semi-detached house, which was situated not far off the High Street, and within walking distance from St Paul's Church. The new family house was a fine Victorian acquisition, called appropriately Down's View; it was tucked away in a little pocket of early 19th century houses, and situated down at the end of a narrow road called Maybury Gardens. There was a small front garden, full of colourful Easter flowers. In the largish rear garden, there was a profusion of Daffodils, Forget-me-Nots, Broom, Wood Spurge and Buddleia. It was obvious that the gardens had been looked after by sensitive, creative hands. The outside of the house itself was well decorated in a sharp lilac colour. Internally the whole house was very spacious, much more so than at Buttercup farm. Each room was differently decorated, but sensibly and skilfully done. My small, comfortable single bedroom was at the back of the house overlooking the beautiful garden which attracted many pollinating bees. Mother, my uncles and aunts really loved their new home.

Having been unemployed ever since I moved to Offham in February 1998, about 18 months, I realised that I must intensify my search for a job. Besides, being employed would also give me the impetus, I hoped, to find a small flat of my own. Other than supporting my late father for half of that time, I also visited various places, such as Brighton, Hastings and Eastbourne, looking for a suitable job. These were depressing times. At one stage, I even drove to the outskirts of South London looking for a job, but soon turned back when I thought of working, and even residing, in the large polluted metropolis. During early August 1999, on a regular signing-on day at Lewes Job Centre, a vacancy for a local landscape gardener, pinned to a board, caught my eye. After requesting the job details from a young, sour faced woman working behind the counter, I earnestly made my way by car, the family Opel, to a small on site landscaping business in Kingston, two miles south-west of Lewes. Colin Jelly, the middle-aged owner of Jelly Landscapes, asked me about my work history and explained that most of the time there was enough work to keep three people regularly employed with work mostly situated in Sussex.

Chapter 12

A NEW JOB AT LAST:
LANDSCAPING IN BEAUTIFUL SUSSEX

TWO WEEKS LATER, on 21 August 1999, I started work for Jelly Landscapes. Colin was tall, slim, quietly spoken and born in Sussex in 1947. He was married, had two daughters and lived on the outskirts of Ditchling. The other worker, Barry 'Spud' Edwards, was about 60 years of age, short and solid. He lived in Henfield with his wife and three grown-up children. He had been a landscaper nearly all of his life and had worked for Colin Jelly for over ten years. The first contract that I worked on was in a huge Victorian house, called South Hatch, a mile east of South Chailey in Sussex. There we drove through large metal gates, with the usual cherub ornaments and family coat of arms depicted on a shield, and into the grounds. Whenever I observe huge gates, with all the paraphernalia on them, like the ones at South Hatch, a feeling of inferiority wells up inside me. In my case it probably stems from my early conditioning in Yapton. Colin told us that the owner, Lord Ponsonby, had inherited the country pile, as did a lot of such people, from the late Earl Critchlow of Chailey. What a marvellous time those pampered poltroons must have had, and not too long ago, at the expense of poor countryside yokels!

After we had been working for three hours planting various shrubs and plants in the large, colourful and well maintained gardens, a decrepit looking male figure, holding a large silver tray containing a teapot, cups and sugar, shuffled up to Colin. 'Here you are Mr Jelly, his Lordship expressed the wish that I make you all a hot cup of tea on this rather cold August day,' said the man, who had a rather posh accent. 'Thank you David. That is very kind of his Lordship,' said Colin as he took the tray and placed it on a small garden table. 'That ancient old chap has also worked for Earl Critchlow, the current owner's father. He is a nice old buffer, he must be well into his late seventies,' explained Colin. 'I thought he was some mummified figure from Victorian times,' quipped Spud. We continued working for another two hours or so, still planting and pruning in a peaceful atmosphere, when Lord Ponsonby appeared on the patio holding a tray full of a variety of filled sandwiches. 'Here you are, Colin,' said the dear Lord. 'David has made you all cheese, ham and pate sandwiches. The pate is particularly delicious—I can recommend it as it is made by my niece, Henrietta,' said the smartly dressed Lord Ponsonby, who was in his early 50's, tall, fat and walked with a pronounced limp. His face was red and full of veins, like that of a hardened whisky drinker. 'Thank you Lord Ponsonby. What a kind thought of David,' said Colin, using all his diplomatic skills when talking to a Lord of the realm. 'By the way Colin, I shall be away for the next two days. I'm needed by our leader in the House of Lords,' said Ponsonby as he slowly limped from the patio.

The following day we continued working in Lord Ponsonby's professionally designed landscaped gardens. Apparently, they were designed by one of his Lordship's Victorian nephews, who travelled the world looking for new plant species to develop his large family gardens. It is well known, of course, that many trees, shrubs and plants of today were collected by those wealthy Victorians, who had nothing better to do than to gallivant around the world to discover the next new exciting specimen. With an August sun beating down on our tanned bodies, it was an enjoyable pleasure landscaping in a quiet, creative environment. About midday, while we sat under a parasol to protect us from a particularly ferocious spell of heat, Helen brought out a tray of tea and iced lemon squash to have with our sandwiches. Helen had been a housekeeper at South Hatch for over ten years. She was around 50 years of age, not unattractive, short with piecing blue eyes. For most of her life she had lived in Eastbourne with her former partner and son. She still lived there, but on her own in a small rented housing association flat near the sea.

'Good afternoon Helen. Thank you for the drinks. This is Richard, my new worker,' said Colin as he introduced me. 'Hallo, Richard,' came the formal reply from the well-dressed housekeeper. After finishing our sandwiches, and in need of shade from the sun, Colin took the three of us up into the small deciduous wood near the perimeter of the estate. Colin explained that Maresfield Wood, planted about two hundred years ago, was a part of our yearly pruning contract. As I sat under a tall mature beech tree, I was reminded once again of the difference between the flora and fauna in Southern England and the Highlands and Islands of Scotland. I prefer deciduous trees to conifer trees, but the latter do afford a constant yearly growth. There was a deafening noise coming from a few aggressive carrion crows fighting for the remains of some poor dead rodent. Minutes later I was joined by an attractive secretive jay foraging for food, which was voicing its harsh *kaaa* at an encroaching blackbird. As I wandered around the wood with my two colleagues, we came across several wild attractive pink blooms of foxglove, 'but one has to be careful when handling them, as the whole plant is poisonous,' Spud reminded us.

Just as the long day's productive work was coming to an end at around 5pm, Helen walked past me smiling. 'All right there, Helen. Are you off 'ome after another day's work?' I asked. 'Yes, I'm pleased to be going home. I have about 20 miles to drive back to where I live in Eastbourne. When the weather is very bad, such as deep snow, Lord Ponsonby allows me to sleep here, which is good of him. Without my little old car, I would have to find a job locally, but there are so few around,' explained Helen. 'Would you be interested in meetin' up sometime, Helen, for a meal or something?' I asked her, desperately hoping she was going to say yes. 'Yes all right, Richard, I would like that,' Helen replied. 'Shall we exchange mobile phone numbers, so I can contact you at the weekend?' I asked. With relief, she agreed to my suggestion.

Although I had phoned and sent many photographs to them, I had not seen any of my Yapton friends for some considerable time. It certainly didn't help that none of us owned a computer. I had arranged with Colin to leave work on a Friday lunchtime, so that I would have sufficient daylight time to drive from Sussex to Yapton, as I disliked driving in the dark. Terry and I had made arrangements to stay in Bert's home for two nights in the two empty beds vacated some time ago by his attractive married sisters. Terry was the only other friend we knew for sure who was coming to meet us, as the others had not bothered to even contact me. After what I thought to be a long car journey, it took me five hours, but made possible by driving Father's reliable Opel car, I eventually arrived at the old homestead at 6pm.

Opening the Country Squire pub front door, I saw Bert and Terry in their usual position holding up the bar. 'Hi, Richard, my old son, how yer doin'?' asked both Bert and Philip. 'Yea I'm well lads. Bit tired after me car journey up from Sussex, but good ter see you two scoundrels again,' I said as I expressed my deep feelings for two of my oldest friends. We took our beer and sat at a small oak, stained table at the back of the bar. I had just realised that the inside of the pub had been re-decorated in a deep apple green, which contrasted well with the original brickwork. The log fire hearth had been enlarged, and new tables and chairs added to the pleasantness of the old local pub. 'Got some bad news for yer, Rich,' Bert began, 'me old man died of a 'eart attack a few weeks back. He 'adn't been well at all. One day he came 'ome from the pub and fell to the floor dead. We sent for the ambulance, but he was dead when they arrived.' My dear old friend said this with tears in his eyes. 'Sorry to 'ear that Bert. Can't say I knew your dad, but everyone liked 'im. And he worked 'ard for the family, didn't he?' I asked Bert. 'He certainly did work 'ard 'n all Rich,' said Bert, who had realised as he got older, that his father had given a great deal to make their home a happy one. 'At least I can look after me mum, as I'm still delivering fruit machines around the place,' said Bert, who now lived with just his mother.

'What you doin' with yourself Tell?' I asked my oldest friend. 'Things are goin' all right for me at the moment. I'm finished with being a navvy. For the past two years I've been workin' as a porter at Norwich General Hospital. Got meself a council flat, and I'm seeing my son Simon who is now 20 years old,' said a smiling happy Terry. 'That's great news Tell,' I said, as he took a few photographs of his son out of his coat pocket. 'That's 'im lads. What a size, ain't he? He towers over me. He must be well over six feet tall. He is workin' as a chef for Philips Television Company not far from where he lives,' said the really proud father about his long absent son. ''Ow did he find yer Tell?' I asked, really eager to find out. 'He contacted the Salvation Army, and they found 'im for me,' said Terry.

Chapter 13

THE BEGINNING OF MY LONG TERM RELATIONSHIP WITH HELEN

DUE TO BEING BUSY at work, it wasn't until four weeks later that I eventually met with Helen Dearlove, who at this stage was 51 years old. She had lived with her late parents in Worthing, where she was born, until moving out at the age of 25 to live with her former partner Peter. Their son was born three years later. The relationship lasted for another seven years, until Helen moved out to find her own accommodation. 'Hi, Helen, at last we meet?' I said, on her arrival at the Kings Head, Polegate. 'Hi, Richard. Yes indeed. How are you?' asked Helen. 'I'm well thanks. And how are you?' I asked rather nervously. Those short nervous questions went back and forth a few times, until Helen asked me, 'Would you like a drink, Richard?' to lessen the tension. As usually happens on these occasions, we both went through our life's history: explaining, accusing, listening, detailing and trying to be honest about ourselves. For once I didn't hold back about my own tortuous relationships. I was impressed by the way she expressed the view that one has rights, but responsibilities too. She didn't appear to shirk her own failings, which she thought, had contributed to the break-up of her relationship. In fact, Helen, her former partner, and son, had had several counselling sessions together before she had eventually moved out to live elsewhere. I was so moved by her open forthright attitude, that by March 2000, Helen and I started living together in her small, but, comfortable seaside flat. Whether that move was too impulsive, I don't know. But I was now 50 years old, and with many failed relationships behind me, I was compelled to say to Helen: let's try and enjoy our time together.

My mother, my uncles and aunts, and I, had by this time been living together at Down's View for nearly one year. After a momentous and stressful time—losing her husband, selling the smallholding, and moving into a house shared with her relatives—Mother had managed to settle down into an enjoyable and peaceful life amongst other older people in Ringmer. The same must be said of my uncles and aunts. All of them had during that unforgettable period of transition been supported by family and friends. Helen had also visited Down's View several times, and on each occasion she had given them gifts of flowers, shrubs, pots for the patio and pots for the windowsills. One friend of Aunt Jane's, Maisy Turnball, whom she had been to school with nearly sixty years before, had bought her singing bells which were hung on the rear garden trees. What a din they made when the wind started to exert its authority! The loud noise used to wake me in the early hours of the morning. But I enjoyed living at Down's View with my mother and relations. We supported each other and had interesting times planting various things in the garden; it was also enjoyable meeting various people, who cared to visit on a whim, for tea and Mother's homemade scones. I was even inspired to buy myself an inexpensive computer, not that I used it that often, because it was mainly there to show people I wasn't a Luddite. However, it would be an understatement to say that I was pleased to be moving out from Ringmer to move in with Helen. But, only time would tell if I was going to cross the Rubicon.

I continued at Jelly Landscapes for the next two years; during this time we usually worked on small landscaping contracts around Sussex. It was regular employment, made more enjoyable working with two colleagues with whom I got on well. Even when we couldn't work due to bad weather, Colin still paid Spud and I a day's money. During the summer months, after a long day's graft in the sun, we used to have a beer together to quench our thirst. Occasionally, compelled by hunger, we used to have a bar meal together, such as a ploughman's lunch, or a fry up, when our partners had gone out for the day. Besides it was enjoyable having a brief chat with young women who regularly drank on their own in local country pubs. You never knew what was round the next corner! It was an advantage that Colin knew many farmers and smallholders, because we were able to buy meat and poultry at greatly reduced prices. Several times during those years at Jelly Landscapes, Helen and I enjoyed meeting with my two colleagues and their wives in a local pub, restaurant, or at a village barbecue. It was while the six of us were socialising at the Jolly Farmer, that one village tear-away, Bobby Treacy, had fallen, rather drunkenly, into the village pond. At the disruption to their home, three irate geese had bitten his backside many times, before he could pull himself, rather sheepishly, back onto terra firma. On another occasion my colleagues, and their wives, joined us for a lawn party hosted by the residents where we lived in Eastbourne. The consumption of several large glasses of red wine gave Colin, Spud and I the courage to make spectacles of ourselves when we tried, unsuccessfully, to sing a medley of Frank Sinatra songs, while the residents cheered us on. They were good, pleasant social occasions that Helen and I had with colleagues and their wives.

A particularly hilarious incident happened when we were working on a large contract. We started work in a large detached Edwardian house, modernised by its various owners, in a small village in East Sussex. The owner, a rather eccentric lead guitarist with an English rock band, had commissioned Colin to extend the existing patio, increase the length of the lawn, thereby reducing the size of the mixed apple orchard at the end of the garden. During the first morning, as we started work on the patio, the owner came out holding a tray with a bottle of brandy and four glasses. 'Morning lads, I hope you are all well on this fine English morning. How about a large brandy to get you all going on this fine morning? Hey, what,' slurred Dizzy Bluebeat, the stage name of the owner, one Justin Quency. 'No thank you Mr Quency. It is much too early to start drinking. Besides we have a lot of work to carry out in your interesting garden,' said Colin, using all his diplomatic skills to avoid upsetting the drunken owner. 'Okay Colin, I understand old chap. Anyway, if you change your mind you'll find the brandy bottle just inside the kitchen,' said Mr Quency, slurring rather incoherently. He turned round, walked for about ten strides and then fell over a low lying brick wall next to the back door and ended up in a large lavender bush full of pollinating bees. We immediately picked him out of the bush and helped him to his feet.

The next day, in glorious sunshine, we continued laying slabs on the new patio, when Justin Quency appeared on the patio holding the hand of another man. 'Good morning chaps, I hope you are all well on this fine summer day. I would like you all to meet my latest boyfriend. His name is Toby, and he lives in London with his dear mother whom I know very well. Her brother went to Cambridge at the same time as my father. They both studied engineering, didn't they dear?' asked Dizzy, as he squeezed the hand of his thin boyfriend, whose unconventional appearance, to put it mildly, dressed in pink trousers and bleached hair, reminded me of a prancing catwalk model. 'Toby, why don't you show the boys the new diamond ring I bought you the other day in Piccadilly? This boy you know is costing me a fortune!' exclaimed Justin, as Toby held out his scrawny, shivering white hand displaying the diamond ring. During the rest of our time, while we worked on the garden project, something nearly always happened when the English fair maiden, Justin Dizzy Quency, was around.

Not far from the village where Justin Quency lived, was an equally eccentric person, a scientist, who lived on his own in a thatched farmhouse. Roaming free in his garden were farmyard ducks that squabbled most days with his two ageing tabby cats. What started in the morning as just mere gazing at each other, had by the afternoon developed into an all-out war as the ducks proceeded to chase and bite the unpopular cats. Professor Gavin Graham, whose life's work had been researching into the causes of cancer, took the initiative and rode his bicycle some six miles, to deliver a document, by hand, to Colin Jelly's home. The document detailed the changes he wanted done to his rear garden. According to Colin, they were so detailed that you would have to be a rocket scientist to understand them. In essence, he wanted us to prune the existing trees, roses and hedges. After that he wanted us to plant three new plum trees, one at the top of the garden, one halfway and the other down at the bottom of the garden. He also requested we use his scientific implements, to make sure that all three trees were in a direct straight line. Why he wanted that done, we do not know to this day. Within two days we had finished the work he contracted us to undertake. He was over the moon as he could now make various, accurate measurements, he enthusiastically informed us, by using our work as a true guide!

Early one Sunday evening, when Helen and I were watching television, Mother phoned to invite us both to lunch the following Saturday. 'There is something important I must discuss with yer, son. All I 'ave to say over the phone is yer

Uncle Jack 'as been diagnosed with advanced Alzheimer's,' said Mother in a low sad voice. 'What is Jack's age?' I asked my mother. 'Jack is now 78 years old. 'E was born in May 1924. His memory 'as not been very good for the past year or so. At first 'e forgot where 'e left 'is shoes. Then it got worse. 'E was losing things and didn't know where 'e left 'em. 'E went ter see his GP, who sent him to a hospital consultant, who diagnosed 'im with Alzheimer's,' said Mother as she was at pains to explain dear old Jack's medical condition. 'Okay Mum. We will see you all next Saturday around 1pm,' I said to my mother, not knowing what to expect.

On a wet June day, in 2002, Helen and I arrived at my mother's house early afternoon anticipating to hear the worst about my Uncle Jack. Being my father's older brother, Jack had always been an integral part of my family life. The three Morris brothers had gone to the same schools, had worked for the same employer nearly all their adult lives, and the little socialising they did, was usually in each other's company. All three of them had married local village girls, at the same time, in St Peter's church, Yapton, in1946. In Jack's case it was the short, plump, but bright, Sarah Mercer. Although I loved my Uncle Jack dearly, I must confess I did not know a great deal about him. Neither did I, in reality, know very much about Uncle Eric, or my two aunts, Jane Smith and Sarah Mercer. Working class families have this strong tendency not to delve too closely into the private thoughts and feelings of the individual. Instead, it is my experience that they focus on re-enforcing the group spirit.

'Good afternoon everyone. I 'ope you are all well,' I said, rather insensitively, as we both walked into the kitchen holding several bunches of roses and lilies. 'Hallo Richard and Helen. How are you, sweethearts?' Mother asked as she put the flowers into three attractive light blue vases that Father had bought while we were on holiday in Cromer. As Helen and I walked into the attractive back room lounge, we were greeted by the smiling faces of Eric, Jane and Sarah. 'Jack is asleep upstairs in bed, son. His GP has prescribed 'im medication, very strong it is, so he is asleep in 'is bed most of the time. Fortunately there is the three of us around, so we take it in turn to look after dear Jack. It must be very difficult for one person, without support, to look after someone with Alzheimer's on their own,' said Mother rather anxiously. I had this rather awful mental picture of Jack coming down from his upstairs bed and asking me, who are you?

We all helped lay the table and dish up the food out onto plates. We all sat round the table in almost complete silence eating Mother's well-cooked Sunday lamb roast. From my earliest days at home, I had remembered that Mother had always been a good cook, with a flair for cooking beef stew, which tasted particularly enjoyable at the end of the day after many hours of hard graft. 'I don't know whether Mum 'as told yer about Jack, but we 'ave got to give some serious thought about 'is well-being, Richard,' said Eric, with anguish for his brother written all over his face. 'Mum 'as told me a few things about Jack's advanced Alzheimer's. He is taking medication and those sort of things,' I said, as I tried to explain things, but not very well, to Uncle Eric. 'Well this is the position we are in. Jack 'as advanced Alzheimer's, as you quite rightly said son. We 'ave to find 'im a good nursing 'ome ASAP. As his share of the 'ouse goes automatically to Sarah, there is not, I bloody well 'ope, no question of means testing Jack's personal savings etc. 'E 'as some money, but not enough to be means tested. Do we put 'im in a local authority nursing 'ome or a private one?' Eric explained the situation very clearly to all of us. Very animated, he continued, 'If we place my dear brother into a local 'ome, we might 'ave to pay a few pounds, but a private 'ome can cost at least £400 per week and some are much more like £600 or even £700. What do we do?' he asked all of us seated round the dinner table. Mother was eager to have her say, quite rightly: 'Even if we paid £500 a week for Jack, how could we afford that long term? And if we find a private home at £600, or £700 or more per week, it's going to be impossible. So do we sell this 'ouse Eric, Sarah, Jane? And find a smaller house, and then we would 'ave enough money for Jack to be in a decent home. Or get a loan, but none of us is working to repay it, or, I forgot, they could ask Jack to pay for 'is accommodation by means testing his share of the house,' Mother said, full of rage, understandably, at Government Policy.

So the discussions went back and forth, as they tried to work out the most productive way of finding the money so that Jack could live in a decent, stimulating and well cared for environment for the remainder of his life. Over the years I had saved money for a rainy day, so I was willing to contribute towards supporting my Uncle Jack. Adding all the monies together, from Mother, Uncle Eric, Aunt Sarah, Aunt Jane and myself, we estimated that we would only have enough money to pay for top private nursing home accommodation for about two years, taking into consideration that we all needed money to pay our everyday expenses. After some considerable time we agreed to investigate council run nursing homes, but would have to provide a single room for Jack. We realised that would cost about £300-400 per week, but we were prepared to pay it between us. Helen and I left Down's View after a reflective day, reassured that Mother would do her utmost to find Uncle Jack a decent nursing/residential home. Not one of us wanted to dump Jack into a nursing/residential home just because it was inconvenient to keep him at home. His advanced illness meant we had no choice but to find professional support for him. Very quickly his condition would deteriorate that only 24-hour a day professional care could provide sufficient care for him. Instead of looking after our infirm family members ourselves, as in the past when most people had no choice, we now farm them out to others to look after for a fee. I think that is a tragic move in the wrong direction. From the past in Yapton, I know of at least three families who cared for their disabled loved ones up until they died. They shunned all attempts by the authorities to have them placed in an institution.

Two weeks later, Mother phoned to say she had found Uncle Jack suitable accommodation several miles away in cosmopolitan Brighton. Three days later Eric had driven Jack, Sarah and Mother to the large Victorian, council owned, residential home, called Sunnybank. The three of them had stayed there for a few hours to help Jack settle into his own small, but creatively decorated room with a television, comfortable armchair and toilet. 'But unfortunately son, yer Uncle Jack doesn't know where he is most of the time. As 'is doctor told us only a few weeks ago, his medical problem is very advanced. So he can't remember my name. Yer know what I mean, son?' Mother asked in a deep sad voice. 'Thank you for all yer 'ard work, Mum, in finding dear old Jack a decent 'ome for the rest of 'is days,' I said to Mother, explaining that I would be round soon to sort out the residential fees with her.

Helen and I had been living together for over three years. Both of us were relatively happy and settled, knowing we would support each other if any crisis or problems arose in our co-operative relationship. At the outset we spent a lot of time together socialising in many different, and on the whole, enjoyable places. On a regular basis we used various local restaurants, pubs, bars and cafes. One restaurant in particular, called Tom's Pantry, only a stone's throw from the beach, cooked delicious locally reared beef and lamb from Dartnell's Farm near Polegate. The owner, Tom Hide, had bought the newly decorated modern premises only weeks before I had moved to Eastbourne. Furthermore, Helen and I used to meet Peter, her son now aged 25, and his girlfriend there for a fortnightly evening meal. Peter was tall, slim, shy and intelligent. His mop of blond hair covered not just his head, but also most of his sallow face. Later, Helen informed me that Peter's complexion was due to a blood disorder he had once had. At the time he was taking a part-time computer course at Eastbourne College. On numerous occasions we also visited my mother, usually for lunch or dinner, to savour her good cooking. My family were good company to be with. But visits to see Uncle Jack were not enjoyable as his memory had declined, and he now recognised no one. On one rare occasion Helen and I visited Nick Peters, and his family, in Crowborough. Nick and my former colleagues were all doing well, except for one minor problem—Colin Tenby still couldn't keep his false teeth clean.

I explained to Helen that I was getting itchy feet; that meant, I was looking for a new challenge in my life, a different job, ideally, unconnected with landscaping or forestry. But what could I reasonably do for living? To help me think about this conundrum, I drove my car, one warm afternoon, up to a quiet area, near Birling Gap, on the South Downs to stimulate myself into action. As I sat there on the chalk Downland looking out to the sea, and all I could think about for a while was my good relationship with Helen. With my former relationships in mind, was all this uncertainty about finding a new job really a smokescreen for moving to a home of my own? No, I thought,

I loved Helen, and I wanted to continue with a relationship that I actually enjoyed for the first time in my life. As I looked around me, I noticed several young rabbits nibbling away at the short tough Downland turf, ever vigilant of predators. As I moved to get a pen out of my pocket, the noise I made startled the rabbits, who ran, with the speed of an arrow, for cover into a nearby yellow flowering gorse bush. I became aware of pollinating bees, and three blue Adonis butterflies on top of the scented flowers of a self-seeded Buddleia, just a few feet away from where I was sitting. Incidentally, the Adonis blue, along with many other butterfly species, may not be caught and sold. The reassuring sight in front of my eyes reminded me that pollination is vital for food production. I once read what Albert Einstein had said about pollination, that 'if the bee disappeared off the surface of the globe, man would have only four years to live'. This is difficult to believe, but who am I to argue with the great man!

Chapter 14

A SEA CHANGE: A NEW CAREER AS A
GARDEN REPRESENTATIVE

AFTER DISCUSSING numerous job possibilities over the forthcoming months with several people, including Helen, Mother, Colin Jelly—he was very helpful—and Uncle Eric, I decided to take my chances in another field of work. In October, 2003, at the age of 53 years, I said farewell to Colin Jelly, a gentleman if there ever was one, after four years of productive and interesting work, to start employment as a garden representative for a local company called Alders. Working for Alders, and based in a modern concrete building, was not an environment I had experienced before. Walking through the store on my first day, around 8am, I was confronted by a battery of lights which reminded me of Wembley Stadium fully lit for an evening soccer match. I thought to myself, could you imagine working here full-time under the powerful glow of all these lights, and at the same time serve customers with a smiling face? With that image resembling hell at the forefront of my mind, I somehow reassured myself that I would not have to endure such suffering because I would be out on the road driving to prospective customers. Upon my arrival, the deputy store manager, Bill Bosham, tall and upright like a lamp post, came to collect me for a talk in his office. No sooner was I seated, before Mr Bosham reminded me of the merits of hard work. 'Yes Richard, I started here at Alders as a young immature teenage boy working in the furniture department. From there I worked my way up, eventually reaching the position of deputy store manager. I'm still working my damn hardest so that I can get the top job,' said the astute and knowledgeable Mr Bosham, who reminded me of a public schoolmaster. With the first lesson over, he went on to explain, in great intellectual depth, that my first two days would be training, along with other employees, at the back of the store.

Suffice to say the training was not very informative, although the visiting trainer did give me some invaluable tips on how to sell the unsellable. The next day I collected my company car, a new rented Avenger, from a local garage only 100 yards from the store. The way things were done at Alders was that they had a daily list of customers whom I would visit to try and sell them new, and not so new, garden equipment and sundries. Most of the Alders customers had been with them for a long time, so there was very little cold calling, other than those customers, usually small outlets, who required a one-off sale only. Most of the established companies were large garden centres, but we also had companies, British and European, who required garden furniture for home, car, and food exhibitions held in large cities around Europe. I was forewarned that the commercial transactions connected to these events nearly always presented an incentive to fiddle the buyer before he fiddles the seller. Welcome to the world of ethics.

One of my first sales visits was to a large garden centre near Gatwick Airport. The manager, who was a tall, shockingly thin, well suited young man of about 30 years of age, made no bones about the fact that he expected preferential treatment. 'Hallo Mr Morris, or shall I call you Richard from now on? My name is Clive Dancer, but I suppose you were told that by your head office, weren't you Richard?' said the arrogant manager of Longview Nurseries. 'Yes, they certainly did explain that you were the manager 'ere Mr Dancer...' Before I could finish, he abruptly interrupted me: 'Yes, that's what I thought, Richard. We at Longview are an old and cherished customer of Alders, but I suppose you have been informed of that too, haven't you Richard?' 'That is correct Mr Dancer, or will I call you Clive?' I asked the manager, who looked as though he was bordering on some slimming disease. I reminded myself that I must pronounce my words correctly, or otherwise, the good Mr Dancer would, given the chance, make a meal of it.

'Now Richard, business must come first, don't you agree? We require at least ten sets of your new garden furniture for our new cafe at the back of our offices. Your new brochure, which is always sent to us unfailingly every year from your head office, shown on page 67 what I have in mind. That is the timber table with matching set of four chairs, which I like very much, very modern and very sleek. Now in essence, Richard, that means we would like to buy ten tables and forty chairs of your attractive Ragusa line on page 67. Now what about a sizeable reduction? As we have been one of your long-standing customers, I think a reduction is well in order, Richard, don't you?' said Mr Dancer, who no doubt, I quickly came to the conclusion, was well versed in such transactions. Brochure prices were written in such a way that negotiations over the terms of purchases allowed flexibility. We eventually came to an agreement that satisfied both parties. When it came to selling to experienced commercial employees, I was wet behind the ears. Alders knew that my previous employment was forestry of course. However, I was soon able to detect the many nuances of human behaviour, foibles and downright villainy that some individuals tried in their cunning approach to undermine me when buying various garden furniture. Nothing new there.

264

A few weeks later, Mother phoned me crying to say that Jack had died, aged 79, in his sleep during the early hours of 6 February, 2004. 'I know it's for the best Richard, as 'e didn't recognise anyone anymore. Bless 'im, he didn't even recognise yer Uncle Eric. I've known dear Jack all my adult life. All six of us got married together on the same day in St Peter's Church. Ever such a lovely placid chap, similar to your dad. He worked 'ard all 'is life. He kept all 'is family together and looked after 'em. After saving 'is money for a long time with his dear wife Sarah, they were so proud to be able to buy a share of Buttercup Farm,' said my sad mother, who had lost a true friend and supporter. I have fond memories, as a child, of Uncle Jack visiting our house for lunch, tea or just to have a quick word about work with my father. He was nearly always joking, but just like my father, he also enjoyed his own company. I think that originated from working in the fields day after day on his own. The funeral was held a week later at St Peter's church, Yapton. As all the family sat in the front row during the service, mourning the loss of Uncle Jack, I thought about how thriving living places, like Yapton, need people like him to survive. Not surprisingly, there was a great send off for him from the village people. In common with most local people, he was buried near his family in the local cemetery. As a young boy, Jack used to cut the cemetery grass every two weeks for the church and was rewarded with sixpence, and a promise from the vicar that he would, in time, go to heaven for his good work.

Only two weeks later there was another bereavement in our family. Mother phoned to inform me that her sister Bunny's husband, Ted Nugent, had died two days previously from a heart attack, while he was working on his allotment. Ted Nugent, who had worked as a farm labourer all his life, came from a family of farm labourers. No one really knew his age, but Mother guessed he was around 80 years old. His grandfather, Liam Nugent, was born in County Wexford, and had emigrated to England, at the age of 24, to seek work. After several farming jobs, he eventually found his way to Yapton, where he married Dorothy Masters. Ted Nugent, their grandson, met Bunny Armitage and they got married in St Peter's church, in 1946. Like most working class men in those days, he worked hard all his life to keep his family of three children, although he loved a pint or three of draught Guinness. My only real recollection of Ted Nugent was when I was about 10 years of age, one Christmas when he visited our home with his wife and three young children, for dinner. After that I saw him occasionally outside the pub with his colleagues, or shopping with his family. The funeral service was held in St Peter's church, and he was buried in the local cemetery, which overlooked the land that had made him a living, and had, eventually, sapped the life out of his large frame.

Alders had received their first order from garden furniture for a large garden nursery, called Flower Tops, in Birmingham. Flower Tops had had a large extension recently built onto their existing dining hall. As the latter also included large well-decorated spacious toilets and a play area, they needed to splash out on new comfortable furniture to attract even more young families from the nearby suburbs. Acting as a supervisor, I arrived early in Birmingham, ahead of the Alders lorry carrying the garden equipment, so that I could meet the new nursery manager, Philip Hurst. He and I had to make sure that all the furniture was offloaded, clean and unmarked, and professionally placed into position in their new extension. After that, I had the opportunity to discuss further garden furniture transactions for the future with the affable manager.

With all the furniture in place and white tablecloths adorning the timber tables, the new extension was ready to be opened to the public the next day. As I walked round one more time to inspect that all was in place for public use, I was reminded, for the first time in my adult life, that I did not tread the soil for a living. What a great resource soil is, I thought to myself, delivering, as it does, some fundamental benefits for humans, and yet, often out of sight and mind of most people. Lifting up my eyes from the dark green coloured floor, I saw the tall Mr Hurst approaching me with a broad smile on his round spectacled face. 'Well, the cafe looks set for opening tomorrow, Richard, doesn't it?' said the happy manager. 'It certainly does look very good, Mr Hurst. I hope it is a success. I'm sure it will be with local people flocking here in large numbers to eat from your new delicious menu,' I said as I pointed to the newly painted, pale green wall where the menu hung. I was mindful that my language was appropriate for my job.

It was Christmas time, 2004, when Helen and I prepared ourselves for our first Christmas Day lunch together with my mother, uncle and aunts, even though we had been living together since March 2000. This was one time of the year when Mother enjoyed celebrating the festivities with her family and friends. As I had been working most of my adult life away from home, I was hardly ever there to celebrate Christmas with my family, and I knew my parents found it difficult not having their only child around to enjoy the festivities with them. Looking back, I realised I should have made more of an effort to have visited my parents, especially round that special time of the year when families celebrate together. I must have been very selfish not to have thought about my parents' happiness, but being full of energy and curiosity, I wanted to enjoy myself visiting various places with different people. Although as a child, and a lively teenager, I still cherished the happy times we had at Christmas singing, dancing and cavorting with my nephews and nieces. This Christmas I had realised that most of my former colleagues, and two of my old friends, had not sent cards, letters or phoned me. A part of me found that painful, but not surprising as we had moved on with our lives. Things fade away for all living things as conditions change. Apart from my friends from Yapton, I would not hear from any of my former colleagues again. That's life!

After we had been living together for nearly five enjoyable years, Helen and I moved into a much larger one-bedroomed Housing Association flat not far from the beach in Eastbourne. The flat was a new, purpose built, ground floor flat, with a small garden, among nineteen other flats in a quiet cul-de-sac, just off the main coast road. The flat was superbly decorated with new carpets, and gas central heating. Mostly in summer, but at other times too, it was so convenient to walk down the picturesque road with our own deckchairs, food and flask of tea, and sit on the beach all day long, with all the worries of the world off our shoulders. Some of the time we were joined by Helen's son Peter and his local girlfriend Susanne. Peter had by this stage had all his blond hair cut off, was more outgoing, and had found a job in Hastings working as a computer programmer for a manufacturing company. These were the happy times we all had together. More times than not, when Peter visited us on the beach, or at our home, we invariably used to dine at Tom's Pantry where they cooked good wholesome homemade food. My favourite was Tom's pheasant pie, made from fresh birds shot on Philip Dartnell's farm. On one occasion, Tom drove Helen and I to meet the self-made Philip Dartnell, on his mixed farm, for a bottle of home-brewed beer. But everywhere you walked it was ankle deep in either deep mud or cow dung, which gave me the impression that the Grand National had just been run over it.

It was a welcome bonus that we were able to host small garden parties for other residents, family, and friends. On two occasions Mother, Eric, Sarah and Jane visited our home for a party, and met some of the residents, who in time, became our good friends. On one of those visits Mother met two of my old friends, Bert Moore and Terry Anderson, whom she had not seen for many years. ''Allo you two scallywags, I've not seen yers for ages. My God you 'ave grown up 'aven't yer, specially you, young Bert Moore. The last time I saw yer, you 'ad a beard. 'Ows your dear ol' mum?' asked my smiling mother. 'Me mum is well, thanks Mrs Morris,' said Bert, who once stole some apples from my mother's garden. 'And you, young Terry Anderson? I used to look after yer when yer dear mum when orf to work for a few bob in the local store. I 'aven't forgotten what you two did, you and Richard, to that poor little girl called Daisy who lived next door. Your mum told me,' said Mother, who was still smiling at what the three of us had got up to all those years ago. 'This young good looking chap 'ere, Mrs Morris, is my son Simon who is 25 years old and works as a chef. ''Allo Simon, are yers all right? Where do yer live son?' asked Mother, to an even younger generation which she probably didn't really understand.

Several months later, in the evening, when Helen and I were sitting down to our evening meal, Uncle Eric phoned to inform us that Aunt Sarah had passed away. 'She died of a 'eart attack three hours ago in 'er bed while taking a nap. Your mum is very upset, so she asked me to phone yer, son,' explained Eric, while fighting back tears. On hearing that bad news from my uncle, I just burst out crying over the death of my Aunt Sarah. She was aged 80. I shall remember her with fond memories.

When I was a child she used to send me birthday cards and usually enclosed a five-shilling postal order for me to buy something of my own choice. Mother often spoke of those enjoyable times when all three sisters played on the village green, dancing and knitting, for hours together. Four days later, on the 31st July 2005, Sarah's coffin was taken from a packed St Peter's church, full of a variety of fragrant flowers, to the local cemetery, where she was buried next to Jack, her lifelong husband, friend and confidant.

Once the family had had time to mourn the bereavement of Sarah, Mother contacted all the children to meet at her home in Ringmer to clarify the new family Wills. 'With various deaths in the family, me, Eric and Jane 'ave 'ad to sort out our wills. We 'ad them done by solicitors at the Co-operative; they are a lot cheaper than the rest of 'em, especially that bloke in Lewes High Street,' said Mother in her usual straightforward way of communicating information. In essence the changes to the Wills meant the following: I would still receive a third of the value of the house. Eric and Jane's children, Mick and Bob, would also still be receiving a third of the value of the house. But as Jack and Sarah were both deceased, their children, Lynda and Maria, were eligible now for their third share of the house. However, a clause in the Will gave Mother, Jane and Eric 12 months to find another home suitable for their needs. As neither Lynda nor Maria were desperate for their third of the house, they expressed the wish that their uncle and aunts should continue to live there, with no pressure to sell once the year had passed. The nieces' attitude was very re-assuring for all concerned. Mother had become attached to the beautiful home where she had been living since 1999.

By this time I had developed quite a sizeable number of customers who regularly updated their furniture from Alders garden department. Other than the forward looking nursery called Flower Tops, I managed to enlist two other similar large garden outlets in Kent and Surrey. If you drove through narrow country lanes, full of flowering hedgerows, near Horam, in East Sussex, you would come across the half hidden estate of Apple Orchard garden nursery. It is so-named after a large coxes apple orchard at the front of the building, and in season you are able to buy the most delicious apples on earth! When I first drove to Apple Orchard, it took three attempts to find one of the most attractive, secretive places I have ever experienced. Colourful Tommy Benstead, aged 66 when I first met him, had been the owner for over forty years, ever since he first set his eyes on the place as a young man when driving round the area looking for land to buy. Tommy was unconventional, hardworking and enjoyed nothing more than a few pints of fresh, homemade cider. Not for him the crap made in large vats with added sugar, and other gut-busting poison—this was something he detested. On many a visit to sell my goods, I have driven into the nursery to find Tommy, and several others, swilling down their X-pint of cloudy cider drawn from one of his many wooden barrels, made from home-grown apples and matured in his large garden shed.

On one occasion when I was visiting Apple Orchard, with the intention of hopefully selling garden furniture, Tommy beckoned me into his small office to sample the new cider he had made the year before. 'There you go, Richard, try a pint of me latest cider. It's full of kick and has a hearty taste,' said Tom, whose blotchy red face bore the hallmarks of countless sessions of drinking his own cider. I placed the light green, cloudy looking content of the glass, which resembled a scientific concoction from my schooldays, to my lips. 'Bloody 'ell Tommy, that was a strong sharp powerful taste in that glass!' I said, as I continued to consume the whole glass. At that moment one of his employees of thirty years, locally born Billy Jones, who was short, lean and mean looking, walked into the office to ask Tom about the price of bedding plants. 'Ere you are Billy, try this new cider,' Tom said as he pulled a pint for one of his drinking partners. Within seconds Billy had poured the pint down his throat, which probably never even touched the sides, when his face turned ashen grey. 'That was mighty fine cider governor that was. Even better than the first two pints I drank of that new barrel early this morning,' enthused Billy, who spent his days grafting with four other employees, and in the evenings drinking himself to oblivion with Tommy. I got the impression that Tommy employed Billy, not for his industriousness, but because he was the only person he could find to have a regular booze up with. Besides, Billy had no choice, as he was the first person trusted by Tommy, to try the first few pints out of each new barrel of cider to see if it was ready for drinking. If Billy became ill after drinking from a new barrel, Tommy would usually give him some modern poison, like syrup of figs, to sooth it.

When one-eyed Billy, who had lost an eye due to an injury brought about by a shooting accident when he was young, had gone, Tommy and I drank another two pints of his brain-numbing cider; it was only then that I realised I had actually visited the nursery to sell my garden furniture. ''Ave one more Richard before we do some business for you,' replied Tommy, whose large stomach hung precariously over his belt. 'Good idea,' I said, aware at this stage that I was getting drunk. With alcohol uppermost in my mind, we quickly sorted out the various furniture and sundries that he was going to buy, and in no time at all, it seemed, he and I were ensconced, for the next few hours, drinking in his garden shed away from prying eyes. Because of the amount of alcohol I had already consumed, I would not be able to legally drive home. Relatively sober, or not too pissed, I phoned Helen to explain what had happened: that I had embarked on a drinking session with one of my customers and was, therefore, unfit to drive home. I was always open and honest with Helen about any embarrassing or awkward situations, whether at Tommy's nursery, or anywhere else. All I remember next day was having a terrible hangover, and an awful taste, resembling sweaty socks, in my mouth.

It appeared that my gallivanting years were behind me, as my life with Helen became more regular. I felt more relaxed, optimistic and secure within myself. That hard or uncompromising exterior that I had apparently developed over the years had, according to Helen, softened somewhat. At weekends, for example, we looked forward to driving in the Opel car Mother had given me up to the wide windswept Downs for a three-mile walk to Jevington, a small attractive village at the foot of the South Downs. More often than not, we ate delicious homemade food in a small cosy 19th century inn called The Ploughman. Afterwards, as Helen was not really an ardent walker, we took the small local bus back to the Downs to collect our car. At other times I used to drive to Alfriston, another pretty village near the Downs, for a meal in one of the several fine eateries available to the many people who visit this most charming place. In May of 2007 Helen and I took our first holiday together abroad in sunny Malta. We booked into a small family owned hotel called Sand Dunes, which is in the heart of bustling cosmopolitan Buggiba. As the sea was only a stone's throw away, we spent a lot of our time during the day just swimming and tanning ourselves on the golden coloured beach, full of like-minded Brits, under the intense hot Mediterranean sun. Many times I observed young local dark skinned males eyeing up the tanned British women, no doubt, with lust in mind. These local Latin lovers realised that British women were a passport to a better life elsewhere. Some of the evenings we ate locally sourced fish at our hotel, and other times we ate at three recommended North African restaurants. All three places greeted us with superbly cooked, locally sourced food with flavours unique to their regions, and served by friendly people who made you welcome. Each day of the whole two weeks we holidayed in Malta was enjoyable, and full of cultural experiences which couldn't be found back in Britain.

My dear Uncle Eric was the next family member to die on 10th September 2007, aged 84. In spite of the fact that he had been healthy all of his life, nothing more serious than flu or mild arthritis in his knee, he also died of a heart attack while gardening. Apparently Mother found him lying on the ground still holding a pair of hedge clippers. Eric, Jane and their two children had been an integral part of my early life in Yapton. From the earliest days, Eric and his siblings made the best of what came their way. Having grafted, along with his two brothers, for many years, exposed to various inclement weathers, he worked his way from lowly farmhand to farmer Leader's manager, and eventually to owning a third share in his own smallholding. During the service at St Peter's Church, Jane, his kind softly spoken wife, delivered a talk on her late husband, eulogising about his qualities as a good husband, how he worked so hard for his family, and his kindness to others. In line with family tradition, Eric was buried in a twin grave, waiting for his wife to join him, in the local cemetery next to his two brothers, and his father, Peter Morris.

It was while I was out driving on those small country roads, which reminded me so much of Norfolk, that my mind regularly used to scan memories of those past years and of the numerous people I worked, socialised or had relationships with. My uppermost thoughts were of my friends from Yapton school, the former teachers, and many old people from the village to whom I used to say hello, but who are now long gone. I have treasured my friendships over the years, especially when times were difficult, when one desperately needed a familiar shoulder to lean on. It appears that the importance of the family, who once provided the bedrock for a child's socialisation, and as a means to help steer them through a difficult and demanding world, is now obsolete. I have often thought about my own working life, and the close relationship I continued to have with my parents. That leads me to think that I must have been adequately educated and socialised to have been responsible enough to hold down the various jobs I have had. But, of course, being well socialised and educated is not the only prerequisite for a successful life, as we know all too well, when we look at the great and the good who have fallen by the wayside. Although I have lived a relatively normal life, with very few eventful episodes to ponder on, I am, nonetheless, fortunate, to have had decent supportive parents and friends.

Chapter 15

THE TRAGIC SUICIDE OF
MY DEAR FRIEND BERT MOORE

WITH THAT IN MIND, I was devastated when one rainy November morning I was phoned by a sobbing Terry Anderson, who informed me that our dear friend Bert Moore had been found dead hanging from a tree. To this day I don't remember whereabouts I was driving, but I brought my company car to an abrupt halt, to the annoyance to the drivers behind me, to try and make sense of what Terry was trying to explain to me. 'Hello Richard, just 'ad some terrible news from my son Simon, who 'as bin listening to the Police on Radio Essex. A fully clothed body of a middle-aged man was found near to Brentwood two nights ago, 13th November 2007, by a man walking 'is dog in a wood just off the M25, 'as been recognised as Bert Moore—our dear Bert,' said a distraught Terry Anderson. 'Fuck me Terry, I'm sick as a pig. I'm numb. I can't say a lot more,' I said as I stared at the road thinking about my lifelong friend. Trying to pull myself together somewhat, I continued my phone conversation with Terry. 'What else is known about Bert's death, Tell?' I asked forlornly. 'That is about all me son knew, Richy. Just a mo, he said that 'is mother 'ad identified the body and there would be an autopsy within four days to find out if 'e was killed by somebody, or if 'e killed 'imself, or drugs,' said Terry, as he tried to remember, not without some frustration, what his son had told him.

When I arrived back at Alders late that afternoon, still reeling from the terrible news about Bert Moore, I had to explain to my department manager the few gruesome details known to date, and in the light of possibly subsequent developments, I had to request one week's holiday, which was granted. Even though Helen had met Bert on only a few occasions, she was very upset when I explained what Terry had told me on the phone several hours earlier. 'What I can't understand is that Bert was always the sensible one of us. He 'ad always worked, I think. Always lived with his parents. I've never seen Bert with a bird, but that's 'is affair, isn't it Helen? They reckon he 'as got a right few bob in the bank, yer know. I think he was asexual,' I ranted at Helen unaware of what I was really trying to say. 'When are you going to Yapton, Richard?' asked Helen. 'Well, Alders 'ave given me one week's holiday to be taken off my yearly entitlement of three weeks, and I'm driving to Yapton tomorrow,' I said, confused and upset by Bert Moore's death. Within the next few hours my mobile phone was red hot with various people contacting me over the death of Bert. During that frantic time, I had also phoned Mother to inform her about my dear friend, and the mystery surrounding his death. She was upset, and said that she would in time send her condolences to his mother.

As I approached Yapton village, I stopped my car in a lay-by so that I could get my mind straight, and prepare myself, if indeed that was possible, for the uncertainty that lay ahead during the next few days. Not surprisingly, during the past 24 hours, all I could think about was Bert Moore. At 57 years of age, he was so young to die, I conjectured, and in such nasty circumstances: in a cold, wet, dark wood hanging from a tree on his own, with no one to witness his last painful hours. I cried and cried until I realised it was time to drive into Yapton, to support his family at a time of deep sadness. I had known

Mrs Moore all my life; she was a good, hard working mother, who only thought of the well-being of her family. When we used to play football together outside his home, or conkers on the village green, or climb tall trees nearby, Mrs Moore would nearly always be there to give us sweets. I vaguely knew of Bert's two sisters from our schooldays, but being younger than us boys, they played with girls in their class. They both married a few years ago and moved out of the area. As Bert's dad had died of a heart attack, Mrs Moore was now living on her own after providing years of unconditional love, and hearty meals, for all her family. Always busy with her own family, and a regular volunteer at the community centre, Mrs Moore was now 79 years of age, and would soon be needing support herself. In a place like Yapton, such support would not be long forthcoming from genuine local people who had known her all of their lives.

I had booked myself into B&B accommodation at the local pub. It gave me the space and opportunity over the next few days to contact numerous people that I hadn't seen or heard of for some time. The next few days also gave me the opportunity to walk aimlessly over the local fields, sit on many stiles that I had not seen for years, and walk down some of the old gritty lanes festooned with brown, old leaves. It was in those lanes that I remembered farmers, long dead, driving their cattle into the farm to be milked. On another day, at a leisurely pace, I ambled through Windover Hill woods, where I remembered attractive Ms Smith, our teacher, who took us for a nature study class. I sat down on a fallen Horse Chestnut tree, and as squawking crows hovered above me, I thought of Bert, Richard, Terry, Dennis, Philip and myself climbing these trees during that nature study class. How we had falsified the list of animals we claimed to have seen that day. 'Well done!' I remembered Ms Smith saying to us! What glorious days they were, without a care in the world, as we roamed around the local woods, fields and orchards stealing ripe fruit during the heady summer holidays. Determined on this visit to celebrate the life of Bert Moore, I also wanted to try and understand, as much as I could, about others in Yapton. Walking aimlessly through Windover Hill woods, I received a phone call from Terry Anderson informing me of an important meeting, arranged by Mrs Moore, for the next day in the community centre.

At about midday, the diminutive, ageing figure of Mrs Moore, supported by a woman police officer and holding some papers in her hand, stood in front of the assembled family and friends. 'Please forgive my nerves won't yer? I 'ave asked you all 'ere to explain what 'appened to my dear son Bert....' She started to cry. 'You were all closest to my son Bert. Most of you 'ave known him for all 'is life. The medical report showed he committed suicide. My son's life must 'ave been very difficult for 'im, and also very lonely. If only I 'ad known about 'is gay sexuality, I would 'ave helped 'im,' said a tearful Mrs Moore, who wanted her son's family and friends to know about his life so that things could be better for others in the future. 'By informing you about Bert's life, I'm hoping it will help to dispel the falsehoods that others might try to spread in the future.' The following transpired from a letter read by Mrs Moore, which had been found on Bert's body by the police, although it is *not* produced here in the first person verbatim.

Bert had been homosexual from a very young age. He first started having sexual liaisons with local men, most of them having worked on farms, from the age of 13. As he became older, he ventured into outlying villages and used to meet men, some of them from Yapton, in the local woods. There he smoked cigarettes, drank beer and cider, and sometimes had sex with several men during one visit. Bert wrote that none of those men ever did anything to him that he didn't agree to. As the years went by he met many other men, some of them married, in various locations around the local areas. At one of these locations he met a man from Scotland, who lived in a caravan somewhere in Suffolk. Bert visited him on numerous occasions for sex, until he moved away from the area.

The driving job he had delivering fruit machines around the country gave him the ideal opportunity to meet other gay men in motorway cafes. Having established contact, he would proceed to meet them in numerous locations around the M25 at specific places called 'dogging sites'. Those places were where gay men met for sex, sometimes group sex which included smoking cannabis, drinking strong alcohol, showing pornographic films and participating in the making of pornographic films in situ. Bert became an integral player of this gay scene and was known, by other gay men, far and wide. Covert sexual liaisons became an integral part of Bert Moore's life.

As the intensity grew in gay sex meetings, Bert himself was becoming disenchanted, and sometimes depressed, by a covert culture that he felt was not for him anymore. With his mental health problems growing, and further exacerbated by the many gays contacting him on his mobile phone, he saw his GP to request help and support. During the next three years, Bert saw three different therapists to help him come to terms with his gay sexuality and become an openly gay man. On one occasion he also consulted a private psychiatrist in London to help him with his addictive lifestyle, and support him in his strong desire to live as an open and honest gay person accepted for who is was.

That burden, in the end, became intolerable for him, and with nowhere to go, as he thought, he committed suicide. It was the ultimate action of self-loathing. At the bottom of his letter he apologised to his family and his close friends for taking his life, which for him was the only way out from the constant torment he experienced most days. Personally, I thought that at some level I had failed my lifelong friend. If only he could have confided in one of his friends or family about his suffering. But of course, his life was not that straightforward. We try to understand these traumatic experiences after they have happened; hindsight may be a comfortable emotion, yet is ultimately useless. Suffice to say, we were all dumbfounded to learn of Bert's secret gay life. That old maxim comes to mind—you can see the behaviour, but not the experience.

Most of Yapton came out to pay their last respects to a local son who had lived amongst them all his life. His dear friends, Terry, Philip, Dennis and I, supported by two other pallbearers, carried his coffin into a packed and silent St Peter's Church. As a young boy I vaguely remembered Bert singing, like some heavenly cherub, in the church choir. But like most of us growing up in Yapton, he wasn't religious, unlike most of the older women who attended church every day. We all have to die, of course, but I think that the nature of Bert's death had hit a raw nerve with the local community. The solemn funeral service was read by the Reverend Douglas Taylor, originally from South Africa, who had been living in Yapton for some time. He had, over the years, officiated at many local christenings, marriages and funerals. In fact, he had led the wedding ceremonies of both of Bert's sisters. People called Rev Taylor 'the gentle giant' due to his big, tall 6' 6" frame. Several people in the church delivered brief readings about Bert's life. I also gave a reading about how several friends, including Bert, had climbed trees, collected birds' eggs, stolen fruit and generally recounted how our friendships had grown. After the church service, Bert was laid to rest in the local cemetery not far from his father, and within close proximity to his friend Richard Arrowsmith.

After the burial service, on 20 November, 2007, about 30 people gathered in a large room above the local pub for a few hours to eat, drink and generally chat about their families, lives, problems or whatever else worried them. My friends and I stood in one corner of the colourful room like four silent convicted men waiting to be shot at dawn: no doubt we were reflecting on the enormity of the past few days in Yapton. What compounded my intense thoughts was the experience of losing, not only Bert, but several family members over the past years including my father, even though his death was in 1998. As we continued to stand in silence, and probably looking morose to the outsider, I was aware that I was projecting my feelings onto my friends. Perhaps they were doing something similar? I wondered, not surprisingly, if any other of my friends had had regular or fleeting gay sex. Who knows or really cares, I thought, if all, or some of these men in front of me, whom I had known all my life, were straight, gay or otherwise. At the end of the day, perhaps we are all strangers, not only to others, but also to ourselves: How well do we understand our feelings, drives, motivations, instincts or intuitions?

So that I could pay my way, and keep my head above water, I was back grafting at Alders after my week's holiday, even though I was sorely tempted to take another week so that I could spend more time with friends in Yapton. Later that day the store manager had invited me to his office. One rarely saw, yet alone, had a conversation with the 'big white chief' himself. Was I for the high jump, I thought, or about to get

282

fired or be suspended or even get promotion to the higher echelons of the furniture department? 'Come in, Richard, how nice to see you once again,' said Bill Bryant, who had been working as the store manager for as long as anyone could remember. Perhaps they built the depressing, even brutal, looking store around him! With this ultra-efficient chap around, I thought, not even the aspiring deputy store manager, Mr Bosham, would stand a chance of getting the number-one position. Mr Bryant was a committed Christian, who regularly gave bible readings at the local St Anthony's Church. When I knew him he was about 64 years of age, had short, longish grey hair, wore ultra-thick glasses that reminded me of a small television, and had a pronounced squint in his right eye. 'Yes Richard, I was pleased to hear from Mr Bosham, that since you first joined us in October 2003, you have excelled in most things you have undertaken. Well done,' said the enthusiastic Mr Bryant, whose squint, at times, became rather suggestive! 'I've done my best Mr Bryant,' I said mindful that my language was appropriate for the occasion. 'Yes I can see that, Richard. Well, Alders has received a rather large order for garden furniture, placed by a London store, for a forthcoming Trade Fair in Paris. They plan to sell the furniture direct to the public, but if any remain unsold, they will ship it back to London. I want you to be the co-ordinator; you will supervise the loading of lorries from our warehouse, travel with the lorries and staff across the Channel and through to Paris. And, of course, there is the return trip. Mr Bosham will fill you in with the details. Let us make a success of it. I know you can do it. Well done,' said effervescent Mr Bryant, who at this stage appeared to be squinting in both eyes, as my eyes were drawn towards the harsh yellow pavement lights flashing outside his office window.

Very early one morning in Alders warehouse, near to Hastings Town, I met with Mr Bosham and four staff to load many tables, chairs, parasols and other paraphernalia onto two large juggernauts bound for Folkestone car ferry. From the warehouse, Mr Bosham returned to Eastbourne, we travelled across the calm waters of the Channel, along with many other juggernauts and large lorries, arriving two hours later at the ferry port of Boulogne. After driving on the French motorways for at least two hours, passing mile after mile of arable and pasture fields, our driver Brian pulled into a cafe, which was full of overweight drivers tucking into their mountainous plates of greasy food. Brian, Cyril and I had travelled in one vehicle, John and Joe in another. All four colleagues had worked for Alders for a long time. Their accumulated years of service came to nearly 80 years. 'Alders is a good employer,' said the short jovial Cyril Edwards. With little confidence of being able to communicate in French, I approached the counter to be served. 'Five coffee please, five coffee. Sorry I don't speak very good French,' I said to the bewildered looking man on the other side of the counter. Come to that, I thought to myself, I don't even speak very fluent English. 'No problem guvnor, I speak English. I'm from Dover,' came the reassuring words of the middle-aged man serving me. Smiling to myself, I walked back with the coffees to join my colleagues. 'Ever since I've been using this cafe, that bloke has been working here. It must be at least 15 years,' said the other driver called John, who originally came from Wales but had lived in Horsham for most of his adult life.

Back on the road we took another three hours, passing attractive countryside villages and many small farms, before we arrived early evening at our destination, a large concrete building, on the outskirts of Paris. The large slab of concrete in front of our eyes was used, apparently, not only for most of

Paris's international trade fairs, but also pop concerts, sports and political meetings. After waiting at least three hours, it was now late evening and our turn came to register our lorry, which meant we could now unload our goods. Using all my diplomatic skills, aware the French can be quite volatile at times, I managed to encourage the centre co-ordinator, with the help of £20, to enlist several local porters to help us offload our large consignment. The playful, yet rumbustious French porters, shouted, smiled and sang at my colleagues; we didn't understand one word, but they all worked hard and harmoniously together.

When our two juggernauts were emptied, and all its expensive contents securely locked in the space rented for one week by Maynards of London, the French porters started gesticulating that they needed a drink. French men love nothing more than a glass of red wine, and lots of it. Having already booked all Alders workers into a hotel, the Frenchmen took us, like lambs to the slaughter, to a nearby bar for a frivolous couple of hours of consuming very basic red wine that tasted and smelt like diesel. From the minute we arrived until the time we departed the bar was in complete pandemonium with French blokes singing and dancing in an atmosphere fuelled by excessive consumption of wine. Most of the drinkers lived nearby on a large social housing estate, which was rife with crime, and worked in a large cement factory. The one French drinker, who could speak fluent English, informed us that crime was now so bad on the estate where they lived, that they drank in the bar to avoid trouble with local youngsters. At the end of the evening we all fervently sang the *Internationale*, like some working class anarchist group intent on taking over the state. My colleagues and I, rather tentatively, made our way back, via a few dustbins and overhanging vegetation, to our hotel. What a first night in Paris!

The rest of the time we spent in Paris was rather more sober, as we assisted and supported Maynards' staff, who worked in the main trade fair arena selling direct to the public. Whilst I was there, I tried to make the best of my time talking and discussing business with as many representatives as possible. Not just British companies, but other companies from the European Union, seemed interested in doing business with Alders, when I explained to them what our professional, colourful brochures had to offer at special reduced prices. The German contingent were probably the most energetic, interested and also forceful of all the representatives when it came to negotiating a price. Not for them sitting back, and be read the 'riot act'. They were up front, in your face, and always looking to make or save money. They were also idealistic, focused and always determined, whenever possible, to enjoy a few pints of their strong national beer. Several times when hovering around the exhibition floor trying to sell my employer's goods I was accosted by a German, who with the intention of selling me something, would entice me to have a beer, coffee or a meal. With the wind in their sails, there was nothing they wouldn't do, especially the younger Germans, to get you into conversation about buying 'superior' German made goods. All told, we had a successful week at the Paris International Fair: We delivered all the goods to Maynards on time, and in good saleable order. They had a lucrative time selling nearly all the goods they had purchased from Alders. The twenty or so tables that were not sold, they, instead of incurring the expense of shipping them back to London, donated to a local charity as a goodwill gesture between two friendly nations. As far as I was concerned, I had at least three firm orders, with another two probable, enabling me to demonstrate to Mr Bryant, that I had worked very diligently. One early Monday morning, as light snow began to fall, we departed from Paris knowing that we had done our best for our employer. When we got onto the motorway the weather turned to sunshine, and we made our way back to the same ferry port. Once we had landed on the wet muddy English soil, we drove to Hastings, where I collected my car and sped off home to see Helen.

There was much merriment in the household, because while I was away working in France, Helen's son, Peter, had announced that he was going to marry Susanne, a local young woman he had been courting for some time. For the next four weeks we were all rushed off our feet supporting Peter to arrange the church ceremony, order a wedding ring and finalise various details to do with the wedding reception and catering, which was being prepared by James Collins, a personal friend of Peter's from college days. The wedding reception was held in a large attractive ornate room, one of many similar rooms, inside the Grand Victorian Town Hall. Everything was ready, thanks to all those decent people who had given their best for the wedding of Peter and Susanne.

Only minutes before the wedding car arrived, Peter, being rather nervous about the ceremony, was still fiddling with his shirt. 'How is that Mum, is the tie central enough?' he anxiously asked his mother seeking reassurance. 'You look great, sweetheart. I'm proud of you,' said Helen as she put her arms round her son and kissed him. There was a loud knock on the front door. Ben, Peter's colleague and best man, was standing on the step dressed in a dapper three-piece suit, and looking like the perfect master of ceremonies. 'Richard, how is the groom, is he up to it? Not getting last minutes nerves I hope?' said the tall handsome Ben who was sporting a deep red rose on his lapel. 'Coming, Ben,' the equally handsome Peter said as he rushed downstairs, out of the front door, where the large black hired Daimler, with a yellow ribbon tied to the bonnet, was waiting. Several neighbours wished him well.

We arrived in good time at St Francis of Assisi, the Roman Catholic Church in Pevensey where Susanne had lived with her adoptive parents ever since she was a young baby. Susanne had for several years worked as archivist for a national charity in Brighton but was eager to move to another job. As we all waited in near silence inside the church, decorated with colourful lilies and roses, expectant and anticipating, the organist started playing 'Here comes the Bride', the music we had all been waiting for. Susanne walked down the aisle, escorted by her loving father and confidante, dressed in a long white silk dress touching the floor and followed by two train bearers. Then in front of the Father Marshall, the three of them went through the marriage vows, the placing of the rings on the bride and groom's fingers, and out of sight of the congregation, but witnessed by their immediate families, the signing of the register; finally the couple walked along the aisle as man and wife. The wedding reception went well and was enjoyed by everyone. Afterwards we saw Peter and Susanne drive off to Gatwick Airport for a two weeks honeymoon in Spain.

For the past two years or so, Helen and I had been visiting my mother and Aunt Jane fortnightly, or thereabouts, for Sunday lunches. On one particular Sunday, Mother had invited the cousins, Mick, Bob, Lynda, and Maria, plus Helen and I, round for lunch to sort out the existing Wills. All assembled in the dining room, Mother spoke for her and Jane, 'Jane and I 'ave decided to sell this house. I think it is called downsizing these days. The 'ouse is far too big for us to look after. And besides, we are unable to keep the garden tidy, and also it is becoming too difficult to even walk upstairs. So Jane and I would like to buy a small local two-bed bungalow to 'opefully last us for the rest of our days,' said Mother, with a tinge of sadness in her voice. 'Have you looked at any bungalows yet, Aunty?' asked Lynda. 'The estate agent 'as given us a few to look at next week love,' replied mother. 'How are the Wills going to change, Mum?' I asked Mother, knowing it was a question to be broached sooner rather than later. 'Well, this is how things currently stand. When we 'ave sold this house a third of the sale will go to Lynda and Maria. That's from their parents, Jack and Sarah, who 'ave died. Jane's two children, Mick and Bob, are also entitled to a third share of the house but Jane is still alive,' said Mother, so they will have to wait, the same as me, until our parents were deceased.

After I had chauffeured Mum and Aunt Jane round Sussex for several days looking at various bungalows, some tatty, others overpriced, they decided to make an offer for a decent looking bungalow in Hailsham. After straightforward negotiations with the owner, Mum and Jane moved into their new home on 12 September 2008. As it was only about ten miles from Eastbourne, it was close enough for me to visit Mother at any time if the need arose. They had bought the small two-bedroom bungalow, requiring some modernising, in a quiet tree-lined road. It was well decorated, both internally and externally, with a paved front garden used as a car stand. The small rear garden consisted of mostly lawn, but it also had four colourful Viburnum shrubs, borders full of roses, and a small dilapidated shed at the bottom of the garden. For added support, and security, there were six other bungalows in the road all occupied by elderly people. Mother was now 84, and aunt Jane 85 years of age. At their age, understandably, they found the upheaval of moving home rather stressful. But after a few weeks they felt settled, somewhat, in their new home in the town of Hailsham.

'Now that you have been working here for over five years, and have done well in that time, I have asked you in for a sort of "rain check" Richard,' said Mr Bosham. 'Well, I'm fine with my job. I enjoy the challenge of meeting different customers and trying to encourage them to buy our latest designs. I really enjoyed that challenge in Paris,' I emphasized. 'The main reason that I have asked you to meet me today is because soon the deputy manager post in the soft furniture department will become vacant. Mr Turnball, after 20 years in the post, will be retiring. Would you be interested in applying for the job, Richard? It will mean a higher salary than you are receiving now, and less stress, now that you are 58 years of age. The soft furnishing department, I think, would suit you. What do you think?' 'To be honest with you Mr Bosham, I enjoy being on the road, that's the gypsy in my blood. I've always worked outside. When I think of the powerful glare of the store ceiling lights on you every day, all day, piped music blaring away, and the intense heat in the store, I wouldn't last one day,' I openly explained my feelings. 'I understand, Richard. You are doing a good job for Alders,' he said, as he escorted me out of his office.

The good medical treatment provided by the National Health Service plus various state benefits meant that people lived longer and had a better quality of life, so I did not myself feel that working for another ten years was a burden, although I was 58 years old. But there were, of course, many people who because of illness, disability or sheer exhaustion after a lifetime of hard graft, were unable to work past the state retirement age. There were many old men from my father's time, and generations before, who had worked on the land, under blazing heat and driving rain, for 50/60 years, and longer, who would have loved the opportunity to retire earlier. That is the main reason why I was so pleased when farming became mechanized: Less labour was then needed to work the land and it freed the following generation and gave them the opportunity to do something more worthwhile with their lives.

However, practicalities must come first, as my father reminded me like a continually recited mantra. Aware that I must buy a new car soon, I drove the clapped out Opel car the mile or so to Alders Store to prepare myself for the visit to a new customer in Essex. This time, like all the other times, I didn't enjoy driving round the manic M25, because it seemed that most car drivers, whatever for, were hell bent on reaching the maximum speed their cars were capable of. While I was driving a comfortable 50 mph, even large juggernauts were roaring past me so fast that it seemed I was riding a bicycle. I was eternally grateful when I had to drive off the motorway, and take a B-road, then a minor road to my destination, Pine Trees Garden Centre, Thatcham, Essex.

'Good morning, Mr Morris. I hope you are well. I hope the journey went well?' said Mr Rees, the manager of Pine Trees, a tall, middle-aged, balding man with an educated air about him. 'Good morning, Mr Rees. The journey was a nightmare to be honest with you. I feel like drinking a large brandy to get over it,' I said to the manager, who had probably heard it all before. 'As no doubt you have observed, Thatcham is a wonderful little village with only a handful of houses. I've lived here for about ten years and I love it here,' said Mr Rees rising from his office chair to give me a brief tour of the nursery. It transpired that the nursery was owned by a family called Price, who apparently owned several others in Essex. I must say the nursery was well stocked, not just with British or European plants, but plants from around the world. A real feast for the eyes of the connoisseur. In the garden furniture section there were all kinds of tables, chairs, parasols, swing beds and a lot more than my brain could take in the first time of seeing it all. 'This is the section we would like to develop, Richard,' enthused Mr Rees. 'Well, I have the new Alders' brochure with me. Incidentally did you receive the brochure I sent you a few days ago?' I asked. As we continued to walk round, I noticed, just ahead of us, were several ageing nuns, wearing habits and looking with intense curiosity at the lawnmowers. I couldn't hear what they were saying, but as they continued looking they chatted very quietly amongst themselves, as one nun wrote down something on a small piece of white paper. We continued looking at garden accessories, but my mind was focused on the nuns. They looked so happy and contented, yet they probably owned very little. Their religious lives were one of giving, seeking the divine and prayer, unlike the modern world full of strife and unhappiness. Was I truly happy? Of course not, how could I be, when my waking everyday life was all about making money.

Back in Mr Rees' small wood panelled office, with a fan fixed to the ceiling, we discussed business. 'What we need Richard is more comfortable colourful garden chairs and tables. Something which will stimulate the senses.' He explained that a lot of families loved this sort of thing in their garden. After discussing the various items he required, he changed his mind many times, his prerogative, of course. We eventually came to the haggling over prices. This is the eternal walnut! Crack this one and bliss should follow. However, reality kicked in. Mr Rees was well versed in negotiating hard about price: this focus on money and price could sometimes be destructive to trusting working relationships. We haggled for some time, like two gold dealers on the stock exchange, until we agreed on a price for all the new garden furniture that should be delivered to him within ten days. When it came to haggling, unlike the early days at Alders when I allowed the bullshit to get the better of me, I was more aware of the psychology going on. Besides, damn it, commission was a sizeable part of my salary: I had to play a hard game with some of my astute customers.

I had bought a computer some time ago, but even though I continued to pay for the monthly line rental, I didn't use it very much. The package included email address, phone calls and television usage. None of that technology really interested me accept for the occasional email I received from various people I had met throughout the years. After working for the good Lord Ponsonby for several years as a housekeeper, a job she did enjoy, Helen had left that employment so that she could work mainly from home. That meant we had to update our computer. Helen, who was slightly older than I, could have semi-retired, though such fantasies did not enter her head. She had found a job as a phone representative for a large clothing manufacturing company based in Manchester. The new computer package enabled her to contact colleagues and potential customers at any time of the day or night without using the keyboard herself. Amazing technology, although I didn't really understand what is was all about. For all I knew it could have made early morning tea for Helen and me, or made doctor or dentist's appointments for us. The only time I did indulge was when I had to contact certain customers about ordering/receiving goods. At least one day, sometimes two days a week, Helen had to visit established customers, not only to try and flog them new things, just like me, but also to collect new goods they didn't require. She received a decent wage, plus commission, and it was all made possible by obtaining a small loan to purchase a good second-hand Ford car and installing an operating system called Windows on the computer. What did I say earlier on about not being a Luddite!

On the subject of loans: I had finally realised that the old Opel car my late dear father had given to me was ripe for the scrapyard. My sentimental attachment to it had been on the wane for some considerable time, although Mother did mention to me several times that I should buy another up-to-date car. It would have been different if I didn't have enough money, but I did. It troubled me to think that Father had probably worked night and day for ages to save enough money to purchase the Opel. At some stage I had even wrestled with the idea, that if I was to buy another car, I was going to keep Dad's old car preserved somewhere in a garage for his nephews to visit. What complete sentimental nonsense! With Dad's former Opel car recycled to help make another car, or possibly many baked bean tins, I pushed out the boats on my 59th birthday and bought a nearly new BMW, a car I've fancied for years. Besides, at my advancing age, I fancied being a bit of a heartthrob with the local over-age groupies!

Also in recognition of my birthday, something I didn't really enjoy, we had arranged a small party at my mother's home in Hailsham. Jane and Mother were far too old to travel, especially in the freezing winter we were experiencing at the time. I was pleased that several of the younger family members visited Mother and Jane to bring with them some added warmth and good cheer. It was so cold during most of January 2009, that I was unable to visit any customers for three days because of treacherous icy roads. We were later joined by Jane's two children, Mick and Bob, and her grandson, Douglas. Unfortunately, as most of my working career was spent away from Yapton, I had been unable to visit Douglas and his young family. 'Hi, Douglas, how are you keeping? How's your young wife and son?' I said apologetically. 'They are all well. My wife, Sheila, is now teaching in London, and our son, Ben, who is eleven, goes to a Grammar school in Otford, Kent. You know we moved from Norfolk some five years ago when Sheila started work in Bromley?' said the tall, handsome, balding Douglas. It was an enjoyable few hours at Mother's home, until she discreetly asked me into her bedroom to explain that the local hospital had diagnosed her with a congenital heart disease. As the damage had not been diagnosed when she was a baby, her heart had had to work extra hard over the years to function properly. Consequently, the heart was now irreparably damaged. Anxious that I must support my mother, I drove her to the next hospital appointment to see the cardiologist and try to find out the nature of her medical problem for myself.

'Good morning, Mrs Morris. You may recall that the last time we spoke about your heart problem, I said that the heart is so damaged, after a lifetime of untreated damage, that we are unable to repair it. I'm sorry to say that further tests have confirmed that,' said the short, slim, middle-aged Indian male cardiologist. 'Is there anything else you can do for me?' said Mother, who sounded resigned to what the consultant had just told her. 'Yes, there are several different medicines which I can give you. It appears that some of them have shown encouraging results. I have made a prescription out for you. Just follow the instructions on how to take the pills,' explained the doctor. 'I won't 'ave to go inter 'ospital or nursing home, will I?' asked Mother, who was by this stage, understandably, distraught. 'No, not at all,' said the doctor reassuringly. On the way out of Eastbourne Hospital, I made an excuse to Mother that I had to use the toilet. Once in there I sat in one of the cubicles to wipe my eyes because I was upset at what I had just witnessed. Of course death is inevitable, I kept telling myself, but when it's your mother, it's a bitter pill to swallow. All I could do at this stage, and through to her death, was to support my mother, hoping she wouldn't suffer too much. At this stage no one, especially the consultant, had mentioned how long she had left to live. But he didn't have a crystal ball. Besides, at nearly 85 years of age, I wanted Mother to be as comfortable as possible, and not to be unduly preoccupied with her demise.

While I was sufficiently motivated to visit my two dear friends in Yapton cemetery; I was unprepared, as usual, for the depressing drive round the manic M25. I had even given some thought of travelling by train. The journey took me through many back roads until I had to use the M11, then along the A140 into Norwich, and eventually Yapton. Not a very enjoyable journey I can assure you! It nearly always took me a long time to drive to Yapton, because I deliberately tried to drive on smaller, less busy roads. Besides, if given the opportunity, I loved to stop on country roads so that I could sit in a field, especially in spring or summer, to eat a sandwich and take a photograph of whatever was around at the time. Or just think of those days long gone, gallivanting with friends in our local woods. That evoked thoughts of the terrific times I had with those two dear exuberant friends, Bert and Richard, who I was on my way to visit. I also felt rather joyously happy when I was looking into hedgerows trying to find birds' nests, or picking large juicy blackberries that stained my hands, or ate red hawthorn berries, nicknamed by Yapton kids as 'bread and cheese'. I also enjoyed counting how many different species of plants I could find at any one time. All these wonderful sentimental thoughts and feelings were usually of the past. To dwell in the here and now is something I don't practise enough of. Another activity I enjoyed was when Helen and I looked round old deserted farms, sadly an ever-growing problem in the British countryside. If you looked into those old barns you would notice numerous birds' nests. Due to the abundance of food and shelter, especially on the dilapidated farms, you would also find wild cats, rats, field mice, squirrels, foxes and many other animals including homeless people living there.

The country pub had also changed out of all recognition, and not for the best, since the days when I used to sit outside our local waiting for my father to come out. Most country pubs, in common with town or city pubs, are owned by large companies that require pubs to maximise their profits (of course). That meant managed countryside pubs had become, or were in the process of becoming, overblown, tacky, themed establishments playing loud popular music, selling Italian coffee, ciabatta rolls filled with pastrami, or chicken curry served with nan bread, and washed down with Texan lager.

Sitting in my flashy BMW car outside Yapton cemetery, waiting a few minutes before visiting Bert and Richard, I looked rather surprised when I noticed a shabbily dressed figure, from the past, Billy MacDonald, not twenty feet from my car. Over 50 years ago I well remember poor old Billy turning up for school, usually late, with a bruised face and torn clothes, the result of a regular beating from his father, Ted MacDonald. Billy missed a lot of schooling, in part as a result of his father's beatings, and in part because he would run away to hide in the local woods frightened of authority. Billy's father worked locally as a farm labourer. Most nights he drank heavily, and after returning home drunk, used to beat his wife, daughter and Billy mercilessly. Many times the police took Ted away, only for him to return home two days later drunk. 'Hallo there Billy, how yer doing? I 'aven't seen you for ages,' I said to my former classmate, who was limping like an old man. 'Gor blimey, Richard Morris. How's it going?' he said. I could tell that life had treated him badly. 'How's the family going Billy?' I said, fearing the response. 'Me dad died twenty years ago of 'eart attack. Me mum died in a psychiatric 'ospital not long after. Me sister 'as three kids, six grandchildren, and I fink she 'as six great grandchildren, but I'm not sure,' Billy said, who avoided eye contact. 'Do you 'ave a family Billy?' I asked, as I noticed a large bottle of wine in his coat pocket. 'No, I was no good at that. 'Ad one girlfriend but she died of an overdose of drugs I fink. I 'aven't had a job for years. I earn money doing odd jobs for people in the village. Most of the time I sleep in the woods over the way, where we all used to go for a smoke,' my former schoolmate said, as he shuffled a few feet to pick up a cigarette end in the curb. 'Would you like to come with me to visit Bert and Richard in the cemetery Bill?' I asked the tragic, gaunt figure in front of me. 'No thanks. I go in there most days though,' he said. Holding three bunches of flowers intended for my two friends and my father, I handed Billy a £20 note. With that he shuffled off, and sadly, I never saw or heard of him again.

It was May 2009. Spring had arrived, and all was in colourful bloom around Sussex. The hedgerow blossoms shone like shining jewels. The woodland thrush sang its country melodies, as the primrose flowers bobbed their tiny heads in tune to the fluty warble of the blackbirds. All life appeared to come to life in an instant. The communal front and rear gardens, where Helen and I lived, were full of tall yellow flowering daffodils displaying large trumpet heads. We had planted a large sack of daffodils, over two hundred, that we had bought from a local shop some two years before. Other tenants had also bought bulbs and plants that they had planted around the gardens which gave a delightful array of colour for most of the year. From the very outset Helen and I had struck up a good relationship with our fellow tenants. On this warm day, with an optimistic spring in my step, I made my way by car to visit that old reprobate, my dear friend, Tommy Benstead, in Horam. Driving down narrow country lanes full of flowering hedgerows, I was reminded that it was just like that when I last visited in 2006. I was also mindful, that on this occasion, unlike last time, I would not get into a session drinking

Tommy's lethal homemade cider. 'Well I'll be damned, if it ain't my dear friend Richard,' said the brown, lined-faced owner of Apple Orchard. 'How's it going Tommy? I hope all is well? After our last session, my partner Helen warned me not to drink any more of your gut rot,' I said as I looked at smiling Tommy, who didn't take it all too seriously. 'Just one pint of my new batch of homemade cider. Just one pint,' implored the incorrigible old chap. We had the one pint of cider, which was really very good. But Tommy knew that, of course, as Billy Jones had been legless on it the night before. On my insistence, we focused on what I originally came here for, namely so that Tommy could order garden furniture from my new brochure to help modernise Apple Orchard Nursery.

Chapter 16

MY MOTHER DIES IN HOSPITAL

THE VEHICULAR TRAFFIC was particularly bad as I tried to make my way through Uckfield town to visit the manager of a High Street shop, who had phoned me, interested in buying garden furniture. As the vehicles had come to a halt due to road repairs, one of many during that frustrating morning, I sat twiddling my thumbs thinking of nothing in particular, when Eastbourne Hospital phoned to say Mother had been taken to A&E. After about two hours, it felt like a lifetime, I drove myself free of the traffic, and instantly made my way to the hospital. When I arrived Mother was asleep on a bed in a curtained off cubicle. Wherever you walked there was a strong smell of disinfectant. The A&E young woman doctor explained to me that Mother was brought to the hospital by ambulance not feeling very well. Further tests were being carried out to ascertain the extent of Mother's heart problem. She had been given medication to help with the pain and would, sometime today, be taken to a ward for further observation. 'It is important to remember Mr Morris,' emphasized the doctor, 'your mother is very ill due to her advanced heart condition, and she is very weak.' Not encouraged by the latest up-to-date medical information, I stayed with Mother for about three hours until she was taken up to a first floor ward. The nursing sister gave me ward contact details, and asked me to phone back later when they hoped to have the test results.

With Mother safe in the secure hands of the professionals, I drove back to my home to tell Helen about my mother's medical condition: I did not feel optimistic about her chances, this time, of pulling through. Mother was in her 85th year, she had had a long reasonably healthy life with very few medical problems, unlike those unfortunate people who have had to endure years of debilitating illness often confined to four walls. But she was my mother, and the thought of losing her was very painful as it had been when losing my father. I fell into deep reflective thoughts thinking about my mother and tried to envisage life without her. Around 9pm that evening I received a phone call from the ward sister who informed me that Mother was weak, and as they did not expect her to live very much longer, we should make our way to the hospital immediately. When Helen and I arrived in the ward, a nurse explained that Mother was very weak, her breathing very shallow, her injured heart unable to pump blood round her failing body, Just after midnight she died peacefully in her sleep. She lay there like a sleeping angel preparing herself for her final long journey. I kissed Mother on the cheek as tears fell down my face onto her bed, and I thanked her for everything she had done for me, especially giving me the wonderful gift of life.

My mother's funeral was held five days later, on the 17 November 2009, at St Peter's Church, Yapton: she wanted to be returned to the place that gave her life, where she married her husband and gave birth to her son. It was her wish to be buried amongst those people whom she loved. A large black shiny hearse, full of a wide variety of flowers, carried my mother's body from her sister's house to the beautiful old Church of St Peter's, a witness to many burials over the years. The ageing Reverend Douglas Taylor once again presided over the very moving funeral service, which was attended by many people who had known my mother, Jennifer Armitage, throughout her life. Sarah Gregg, Mother's sister, Michael Morris, Mother's nephew and I, each read a piece from the Bible exploring the theme of motherhood, to a congregation bound by the bonds of family, trust and love. Mother's body was driven the short journey to the local cemetery, where the pallbearers took her coffin, made of oak, with a large bouquet of roses on top, to be buried in the same grave as my father, and only feet away from her parents. As I looked anxiously at Mother's coffin being lowered down into the grave, my overwhelming thoughts were that I hoped she hadn't been disappointed in me as a son. Many times when I was young, Mother had kept reminding me of the importance of seeking new experiences, acquiring different skills and trying to be successful. When I was searching for various jobs, I was mindful of what Mother had kept reminding me: I most certainly aspired to fulfil all three of her wishes, but I was aware that it probably had had an adverse effect on lasting relationships and close family life.

There was a brief, but enjoyable, wake in my mother's sister Aunt Sarah's attractive house, where Aunt Jane and I met her husband, my uncle Harry Gregg and my cousin David, for the first time in many years. Short, slim, now 81 years of age, friendly Sarah had worked for the last ten years, before retiring, as a telephonist at Simpson & Son, Solicitors, in Norwich. She had fond memories of the time she had spent with her sisters Jennifer and Bunny. In their own unique ways, the three sisters had made various tree houses in the local woods, enjoyed cycling for endless miles around the local lanes, and over the years had developed books full of pressed woodland and meadow flowers which were still in Sarah's possession. Harry had been a farm worker in Yapton, and surrounding districts, for nearly all his working life. A short, burly, friendly man and, like many men from his working background, he had very little to say. Harry, now about 80 years old, told me that over the years, and especially since his retirement, he had enjoyed shooting rabbits with several former colleagues on land owned by a local farmer. That would have been impossible when I was young! Also over the years he had built a small brick extension onto the dining room, and had decorated the terraced house. I must say their house, what I saw of it, was very well decorated and homely. The dining room where we all gathered had light maroon emulsion walls, a small ceiling chandelier made of transparent glass and new modern furniture. My cousin David, who was around 50 years of age, was tall, slim with short brown coarse hair. He had always been single—'Something I enjoy to be honest with you, Richard,' he had said, with relief in his voice. David had worked for the BBC for over 12 years as a computer programmer in London, where he lived on his own.

As I had a long drive ahead of me, and mindful that Aunt Jane was now 87 years of age, I started the journey back to Sussex as soon as I was able. It had been a sad, intense day of loss for me and many others. So many of my family had died in the last few years, that I was trying to prepare myself for the demise of Jane. But who knows, she could outlive all of us. I had become, for a time, somewhat preoccupied with the ages of family members and how long they could possibly live. The immediate problem awaiting me, however, was to ascertain whether Jane was to continue living on her own in Hailsham. If so, she would, of course, need to have a day carer, or even perhaps a live-in carer, now that Mother was no longer living there to help out. As I was the only beneficiary, there was also the question of Mother's will to sort out. I was aware that I would receive half the value of Mother's bungalow, if I decided to act on the will and claim my legal entitlement. It all depended on Jane being unable to go on living in the bungalow. But, of course, I had to consider that Jane had two living sons,

Bob and Mick, who I assume, would take over the responsibility for their ageing mother. Perhaps they had already discussed whether Jane was going to live elsewhere or not.

Back in Hailsham, after a fairly easy journey from Yapton, I realised that my dear old aunt was now too vulnerable to be living on her own. I had no option but to stay and support her for a few nights, until I could contact her children. I was surprised that her children had not envisaged their mother's plight. Unfortunately they were both unable to attend my mother's funeral due to unforeseen circumstances because they had problems to resolve in London. Early next morning Bob and Mick arrived, very apologetic, for the serious oversight of their mother's living arrangements. 'What do you think we should do for our mum, Richard?' said Mick, who was naturally concerned about his mother. 'Well, what do you think, Jane? You are the important one here,' I said to my aunt. 'I'm fine living 'ere on my own for the time being. I'm 87 but I feel well,' she said, obviously confident enough to live on her own with the support of daily help. We put the details of the Will on hold, and arranged, via the council, for home help to visit Jane for two hours every day. And we also arranged to phone Jane, between us, on a regular basis. Apart from the carer, two or three neighbours would phone, or pop in, to see if Jane was coping all right. For the time being we were all reassured that the right conditions were in place to support Jane, but eventually we would have to find a long-term permanent solution for her well-being. That might well be a small self-contained flat within a secure managed environment. Being a friendly person, she might adapt very well to living with other older men and women in close proximity to each other. With such arrangements, Jane would have the security of others around her, and she would also have the choice of either eating in her room or dining with others in the communal restaurant. We would see!

Having a long weekend to myself for the first time in ages in early February 2010, gave me the opportunity to take stock of my life. First and foremost I had to make sure that Aunt Jane was as well as could be expected, and that her daily help was providing at least an adequate service. From the time my mother had died, which left Jane on her own, I felt I had a moral duty to support her even though she had children of her own. Mick and Bob, of course, loved their mother as they continued to share responsibilities between them providing for her. During those four days off from work, I phoned Jane at least ten times which provoked her to say rather indignantly, 'I'm all right yer know son. I'm not that old that I can't look after myself!' Recently, even more so than before, whenever I thought of Jane I was moved by the hard work she had put in to her life from an early age. All those sacrifices she and her husband had made paid dividends when they were able to buy a third of a small farm. Now years later it was the turn of the younger generation to help those who had gone before us to provide what was needed.

As the years had gone by, even my cherished friendships, not surprisingly, had waned. We saw or phoned each other infrequently. Of course we were all over 60, lived in different parts of the country and led somewhat different lives. I wondered what impact, if any, Bert's death had had on any of us. Perhaps his covert homosexual life, leading to his untimely death, opened a large can of worms that individuals were not prepared to accept or discuss or whatever. That was/still is one's prerogative.

During that long weekend respite from work, I had this surge of energy and desire to phone my friends to try to gather some genuine feedback from them. It doesn't matter who you are, but when you hit on a sensitive issue, even a loyal and trusted friend could become defensive. That was my experience after phoning my three good friends, Terry, Philip and Dennis and enquiring into certain information about the past. Nothing was forthcoming. That was as far as I got to prising open so-called secrets from men I would have thought were mature enough to open up about their past. But these were very personal and painful experiences involving sexual abuse which happened to one of my friends when he was a schoolchild. He shall remain nameless as he briefly mentioned the abuse to me many years ago but refused to name anyone. We suppress childhood trauma at what cost: to the subsequent development of our relationships, friendships, employment prospects and even our sanity. For example, throughout the years when I had been visiting my parents for a few days, I was informed unexpectedly, by two unrelated individuals, that Billy MacDonald had been sexually abused when he was still a schoolchild. Look at the wretched state he was in now. But it was only hearsay; the information had not been independently verified.

On a practical level all my three friends were doing as well as could be expected, although none of them were destined to be rocket scientists: Terry was still a porter in Norwich General Hospital. More encouraging, he was spending a lot more time with his married son, who, himself, now had a son. Philip was working for BT in their engineering section. He was well and had not been on psychiatric medication for years. Good luck to him! Finally Dennis had moved back to Yapton, where he had rented a small one-bedroom flat, and was driving a lorry for a paint company in Norwich. Many years ago Dennis had confided in me he had this aspiration to study Fine Art at the local college. That dream, unfortunately, did not materialise. But at least he was now handling paint all day. From this day forth, any type of communication with family, other than Mick or Bob, was extremely rare. That is the nature of the modern family. It didn't surprise me, as we were all getting older, and personally speaking, I channelled my diminishing energy into my secure and rewarding place of work and enjoyable relationship with Helen. But, as for crossing the Rubicon...!

Chapter 17

LASY YEARS AT ALDERS: MY ENJOYABLE LIFE
WITH HELEN AND PURCHASING MY FIRST HOME

I WAS NOW into my seventh productive year at Alders. Things had gone well for me during that time, as I had developed a large customer base. My ugly face certainly did fit in with some new customers. I put that down to a growing maturity, self-belief and determination to succeed. There had been job opportunities within Alders I could have taken, and I was offered jobs elsewhere, which were tempting indeed. For example, one new nursery owner offered me the position of nursery manager. Another wanted to start up in the furniture business with me as his new partner. But I had established myself as the senior garden representative, so I did not fancy the prospect of starting all over again. I was reflecting on this and feeling confident driving down to greenest Dorset to meet the area manager of the National Trust. Waverley House had been bequeathed to the National Trust by the Gibson family on the death of the former owner, Sir Stanley Gibson. The large detached house had stood in many thousands of acres in the lush Dorset countryside since it was built by one Sir Godfrey Gibson in the early 19th century. Apparently he had made his pile from tea and coffee plantations in the West Indies. As the result of rising costs, the current Gibson family were unable to keep living in Waverley House. Hence they had contacted the National Trust several years before to successfully offer them the opportunity of becoming the legal owners with a proviso that the Gibson family retain a few first floor rooms to install themselves in. The National Trust had completed extensive and expensive renovations to bring it back to its former 19th century glory. All that was left, before the paying public were allowed in, was to buy furniture for the new cafe and gardens.

'Good morning Mr Morris, I'm David Stern, area manager of the National Trust. I hope you didn't have too much difficulty finding us here tucked away in the extraordinarily beautiful Dorset countryside?' asked the tall, thin, middle-aged Mr Stern who had a puce face and spoke with a slight stammer. 'No problem at all Mr Stern. I rather enjoy visiting places somewhat hidden from the rest of humanity,' I replied, mindful that my language was appropriate to the occasion. Before we settled down to business, Mr Stern gave me a brief conducted tour of some of the restored downstairs rooms which looked, according to the new house brochure, 'just like they did way back in time when a large army of servants dutifully looked after the Gibson family'. I was so impressed with the skilfully restored ceilings, walls and original fireplaces, just to mention a few of the original features which caught my attention. Not for the first time, I felt reassured and relieved, that we had well-managed British institutions like the National Trust that kept these large estates well maintained for public enjoyment. These lasting monuments, to a bygone era, were important national legacies that reminded us of our sometimes unpalatable forebears who ruled Britain, and the Empire, without scruples and an iron fist in their own interest. The large gardens too were bursting full of spring flowers. After lengthy negotiations with the astute Mr Stern, he was after all spending members' money, we came to an agreement whereby they would hire tables, chairs, parasols, indoor and outdoor plants for two years. After that, if the cafe furniture got their members' seal of approval, we would negotiate a permanent deal. The contract was unusual, but it was, nonetheless, a good deal for my employer. If eventually they accepted a permanent furniture contract with Alders, it could be possible to tender for other contracts within their huge national operation.

On the way back from Dorset, thinking I was the cat's whiskers, after securing what I thought was a good deal at Waverley House, I pulled into a country pub called The Lamb, near Horsham, for some much needed dinner. As I tucked into my steak and kidney pie, (Bert's mum would have been outraged by such a claim on the part of the restaurant), I received a phone call from Mick Morris, Jane's son. 'Richard, Mum has fallen over in her home and broken her right leg. She has been taken to Eastbourne Hospital, where they have put her leg in plaster and she is now in a hospital ward,' said Mick who was understandably concerned about his mother who had been living, with support, on her own now for over a year. During our mobile phone conversation outside of the pub, Mick and I agreed that the time had come to find Jane a comfortable small flat within a managed environment, as she was now too vulnerable to be living on her own. When I returned to the table to continue eating my meal, I found the plate and coffee had been removed. It was only after minutes of trying to explain to the barman that I had left my meal unattended to take a personal phone call outside the pub that he relented, and with the support of another customer, the chap gave me another meal, not steak and kidney, but fish and chips!

Early next morning I was on the phone to Mick Morris to sort out, with some urgency, accommodation for his mother. Our first step was to visit Aunt Jane in Oak Tree Ward, Eastbourne Hospital, to see how she was coping and to discuss her future living arrangements. 'Good morning dear Aunt Jane, how are you?' I asked the frail old lady lying so helpless in bed. ''Allo Mick and Richard, so lovely to see you both. Look what I've been and done to myself,' she said, pointing to her raised plastered leg on the end of a pulley. We both smiled at Jane and commiserated with her about her misfortune. 'Mum, we are both concerned that you are living on your own with no one to help you if there is another fall or accident. You are on your own for about 18 hours until the helper pops in to help you with food and washing. Don't you think the time has come to find you sheltered accommodation where there is a worker on call for 24 hours a day?' said Mick, as he spoke softly and clearly trying to explain to his mother his concern for her well-being. 'Yes son, you are right, I am gettin' old and frail. I need support now, don't I,' said Jane, realising that she was unable to look after herself any longer. Following discussion, Mick and I met with the hospital social worker to explain Jane's living situation. While Jane was convalescing in hospital, Mick and I eagerly phoned round various places offering sheltered accommodation in Sussex from a list given to us by the social worker.

After making numerous phone calls, and visiting five sheltered houses, we eventually found a place we thought Jane would like to live in. But as she was temporarily incapacitated it would be another three weeks before she could inspect the accommodation: a small self-contained flat, newly decorated, comfortable, and with gas central heating. She could have her own letters, papers and whatever else delivered through her own letterbox. She could dine on her own or with other tenants in the spacious communal restaurant. In the time leading up to Jane's discharge from hospital, we showed her photographs we had taken of the accommodation, and gave her the brochure that Manston, the name of the residential home in Polegate, gave to all prospective tenants.

With the support of a frame, Jane was now able to walk, and, having returned home earlier than was anticipated by her physiotherapist, she was eager to sort out the Will my mother had left. The Will was straightforward: I would receive half of the value of the house that Mother had shared with Aunt Jane in Hailsham. The monies that remained from the sale of the house were sufficient for Jane to purchase her accommodation, which was expensive, but included all the heating bills, maintenance and costs of 24-hours a day security. Suffice to say, Jane was so pleased with her small comfortable home that she moved in on the 20th July 2011, aged 88. It was not surprising that Jane went on to make many friends at Manston, and she went on yearly holidays with them to Dorset, Devon and Cornwall. Over time all her children, grandchildren, great grandchildren and friends would visit her on a regular basis. Helen and I also enjoyed visiting Jane when she would take us out into the attractive colourful communal garden for tea and laughter.

Three weeks after Jane had moved into Manston, I had a phone call from her son Bob. 'Hi, Richard. When I gave you your late mother's goods and things a few weeks ago, I missed something. I've just found amongst my mum's pile of stuff in the garage, a box belonging to your mum. It contains a few old cameras and photographs. I'll drop them off at your place,' explained Bob. When I arrived home after working all day, and in desperate need of food, I saw the smallish brown box in the hall half hidden under the telephone table. It was only some hours later, after I had partaken of my much needed evening meal, that I made a few tentative steps towards it. On closer inspection I saw that the sealed box had stamped on it 'Butter packed for the Co-operative Society, Manchester, United Kingdom'. I cut the tape that sealed the box and looked inside. Years of dust escaped from the box. When I looked inside, I found three old Brownie cameras and a sizeable number of black and white photographs. On closer inspection none of the cameras had films inside them, but they all appeared to work when I clicked the on/off buttons. I took the photographs with me into the lounge, and sat down on a comfortable armchair to have a closer look of them. All the photographs were of teenage white boys and girls whom I did not recognise. By the style of their haircuts, and the way they were dressed, I deduced that the photographs had been taken many years before I was born. I realised that Mother had been a keen photographer from an early age, but I wondered if she had taken the photographs in front of me. There were no dates or other distinguishing marks on either the front or back of the photographs to identify the people, or to tell where they came from. As Mother's interest in photography had started at a young age, perhaps she had herself developed the photographs at home. I wondered whether Mother had known all these attractive young people. If not, then how had she acquired the photographs? I wondered if any of them were her former lover or, even lovers? Were any of them still alive? If not, had any of them produced children who might still be living? Had Mother known any of their children? Many questions were left unanswered, and probably always will be. I decided not to look for answers. The photographs should remain as I found them in the box—anonymous photographs of teenage boys and girls who once lived, who may have known my mother, even my father, but as far as I was concerned, their beauty shall remain intact, yet unknown forever.

Incidentally having looked at all the above-mentioned photographs, I suddenly wondered what had become of all the photographs that Mother had taken around Yapton, and surrounding areas, when she was still a young enthusiastic artistic woman. Although I had been bequeathed several albums on the death of my mother, there were still others that cannot be accounted for. Perhaps she had donated them to other members of the family or to friends, or who knows, perhaps she had given them to a former young lover, as a gift, from way back before she met my father. She could even have donated them to one, or all, of her former Sherries colleagues to keep forever.

Having inherited a lot of money from Mother which represented years of diligent hard work of both my parents, it gave me the opportunity to purchase the Housing Association flat Helen and I were currently renting. At 61 years of age, I was in a position to buy my first home after a lifetime of renting. On a scorching hot morning, with all the necessary legal documentation completed, I carried Helen over the threshold of our own first home to the sound of good wishes from neighbours ringing in our ears. The rest of the day was near pandemonium as tenants, and many others, partied to the sounds of a small jazz band playing in the rear garden. Party attenders, the worse for alcohol consumption, were still dancing at around midnight celebrating my good fortune, being able to buy my first home thanks to the hard earned money left to me by my parents. Purchasing the flat will provide the security Helen and I would need during the coming years as we grow old, gracefully I hope, into old age, after trying for years to break free and make something of myself.

Be that as it may, but for the next two and half years, until December 2013, I continued working for Alders as their enthusiastic Head Garden Representative. Most of my regular customers stayed with me through thick and thin as Alders continually updated the style, pattern, colour and price of their garden furniture. In the latter stages of my work most of my orders came from word of mouth. I was so proud and pleased that my regular customers of years standing had communicated to others the merit of my goods. Suffice to say that during my ten years of selling garden furniture, I had become quite well known, I hoped for all the right reasons, within the garden nursery fraternity. One sad, yet inevitable fact of life is death: I celebrated, along with many others, the death of my dear friend, and sometime customer, Tommy Benstead. I had been offered further job opportunities of working in Alders Store but had declined them all. Further employment opportunities came from the nursery profession, but I resisted. I had even been offered early retirement when Alders dangled a financial apple encouraging me to retire. Not for me, thank you. Even those stalwarts of the Alders empire, Mr Bryant and Mr Bosham, had both retired, no doubt, to propagate their daffodils and tulips, as they pondered, alone, on their respective careers down in the garden shed. Their successors were of a different class, education and mind-set, not that I personally disliked my two former colleagues. I did at times, however, find their company rather stultifying. Both new men were young, classless, gregarious and educated at two of the newer universities. Within a short period of time, so I was reliably informed, the new blood helped change the working environment at the Eastbourne Alders Store. Filtering down from the managerial class, attitudes became less rigid; there was more openness, and workers appeared to be more confident in the presence of others. But allowing for existing conditions: most people, including those decent folk at Alders, wanted to leave their mark with whatever they had embarked on. Change is an incontrovertible fact of life.

Chapter 18

REFLECTIONS

WHEN I THINK OF CHANGE, and it's inevitability in my own short insignificant life, it all seems, at various times, rather confused, nonsensical yet nonetheless worthwhile. The reassuring word I am looking for to excuse my young inexcusable behaviour is relativism—a theory that knowledge and moral principles are relative and have no absolute standard. Well, there I go; what a cop out from all that mayhem I caused many innocent people all those years ago in Yapton! Yet a part of me, a larger part of me, is still gloating over the misdeeds I carried out mainly on those middle class/upper class buffoons who had it coming to them for their bumptious, heavy handed attitude towards working class kids in those times. That we weren't caught more is in itself a small wonder, because if we had been it would have meant, in those days anyway, time spent in an approved school or some other custodial establishment. Let us not forget the people who in those days dominated the magistrate courts: local landowners, farmers, retired military personnel. Woe betides, if as a working class urchin, you came up in court for sentencing in front of the pampered poltroons. In those pre-1970's days, they showed no mercy, were not interested in mitigating circumstances; all they knew was that state institutions should look after its young children, instead of incompetent parents. But, of course, from time immemorial we know that most offenders are: uneducated, unemployed and/or unemployable. Today many still have mental health problems, and are, therefore, released into a life of recidivism. That is the main reason why I mentioned at the beginning of this book that education was important to help working class children move away from traditional farm labouring, and into more productive skilled work. Any success, at any age, in educational achievement is vital for self-esteem; in order that a young vulnerable working class person can apply for a job with confidence. Before, he would undermine himself by choosing the easy way out into unskilled work, unemployment, crime and prison.

So we were very fortunate, my friends and I, that we didn't get caught shoving freshly delivered dung through the local farmer's front door. Or any other of the many misdemeanours we carried out in those days of innocence when growing up in a decent village called Yapton. That we didn't get caught was a miracle, when so many other village kids did get caught and were sent to various institutions. Many of those young boys never recovered from those painful experiences of being incarcerated. From a good home, basic education that they fed us with in those days, I at least had the physical strength, initiative and common-sense to venture out into the world to find work and look after myself. You can have supportive caring parents, which I did, but from a working class culture many never get that vital internal map to guide them in the right direction. Unlike most middle class children who are trained from the time they start wearing nappies to think for themselves. It has always baffled me why educators don't try and find a different way of helping deprived young children to avoid the self-fulfilling prophecy that leads a lot of them into a life of drudgery. I have read that researchers can pick out, even at two years of age, those children in play school who will achieve more than their cohorts.

My six months' stint in the Merchant Navy certainly opened my eyes to a wider world where you had to have eyes up your backside to protect yourself from adversity! Most of the young men, and nearly all the older ones, were from difficult backgrounds. The Merchant Navy gave them an opportunity, not only to get away from their home, or other institutions, but also helped to build their confidence to make a living and see the world. Two of the younger men, and most of the older ones, whom I broached the subject with, had been beaten and abused at home, children's homes, borstals or prisons. Therefore, some of them were tough and mean, so you had to be careful how you approached some of them. Some of my former colleagues found that working in a regimented environment allowed them to form a sort of hierarchy, similar to that found in most institutions, in an atmosphere based on sexual identity, age, rank and veiled threats. Regards gay sex on board the ship I sailed on; from the outset you had to nail your colours firmly to the mast, or otherwise, a wink, a nod, a smile or a prolonged look was all it took for a homosexual to start sizing you up. One had to be very careful at all times when on your own with a gay man or you could find yourself in a compromising situation. On first boarding the ship, even though I explained I was straight, I was proposition several times until it was realised where my sexual interests were.

The next two years I lived at home and worked for Greenwood as a trainee forester; after that I spent 28 years of my life working around the country in forestry, until 2003 when I joined Alders. Greenwood was a very good grounding for me—it helped me to grow in a world of tough uncompromising men. I learnt invaluable transferable skills that I could apply wherever I worked. As my confidence grew so did my job prospects, which culminated in successfully applying for the challenging job on Arran. During the 28 years in forestry, I only had three employers which I think is a pretty good work record. I did my conscious best for each and every outfit I worked for, knowing that when I moved on I had left the business more productive than when I first arrived. I met many good decent working blokes; some of them taught me various things, not just about forestry, but about the wider world of nature of which I had hitherto been ignorant. Quite a few of my former colleagues were so knowledgeable that they could have worked in education, or plant nurseries, or been self-employed. Instead they searched for spiritual nourishment from inhabiting the shaded forests. Their lives, I gradually began to realise, were about understanding the language of various trees, spending time with wild animals, and encouraging wanderers, tramps or the dispossessed to have tea or a cigarette or just a good chat. Eccentric perhaps, but life enhancing! I've realised that it takes an unusual, yet thoughtful, self-effacing kind of person to inhabit the world of trees. Because of all those years I spent working away from home, I know I truly miss the valuable times I could have spent with my parents. More so as I was their only child! Furthermore, working in various places around the country for 28 years must have had a detrimental effect on the limited opportunities I had to find a long term partner, but find one, I did.